The Horse Master's Daughter

Nordun's Way Book One

Also By Elles Lohuis

A Pilgrim's Heart (*Nordun's Way* Book Two)

Echoes of Home (*Nordun's Way* Book Three)

Download your copy of the hand-drawn map of Nordun's
travels, specially commissioned for the *Nordun's Way* series
Books One, Two & Three at
www.elleslohuis.com or scan the QR Code.

The Horse Master's Daughter

Nordun's Way Book One

ELLES LOHUIS

Black Peony Press

First published by Black Peony Press in 2022
ISBN   9789083240848 (Paperback)
ISBN   9789083240862 (Hardback)
ISBN   9789083240824 (E-book)

This book is for my dear nieces
Nordun, Jomo, and Tenzin Tso

Contents

Prologue

There comes a time in your life when what's calling from deep inside of you becomes inevitable, and you have to make a choice.

You either listen and take up the courage to say yes to what lies in the open space of uncertainty, or you ignore it and spend the rest of your life in its silent void, trying to piece things back together as they continue to fall apart.

This time has come for me.

One

The smoldering incense breathes a welcoming warmth in my hands as I walk up to the prayer hall. My toes spread in my sandals and I relish the chill of dewdrops wetting my feet. The first shreds of daylight have barely broken through, and dense mist still shrouds most of our mountain. With the faint hum of morning prayers finished, my time has arrived.

"Come on, she's expecting you." I spur myself on. My fingers slide along the soaked hem of my robe. "It's not that difficult." A deep sigh slips from my lips. *Except it is.*

No, it's not difficult to walk up to the prayer hall in the early morning—it's the conversation I'm about to have.

The path ahead of me has been flattened long ago—finely crushed stones pave the way. As always, I take the road less travelled, this time cutting through the tall grass between the kitchen and the elevated hall. The perfect shortcut really, a hide-away and a lookout at the same time.

From here I can see almost the entire monastery—its wooden gate leading straight to the central prayer hall, the communal kitchen to the right, and the fifty tiny houses of my sisters, timber and clay, stacked upon the slope behind the hall.

The sheds, animal dwellings, and vegetable gardens still hide under a blanket of down and white, with the fog stretching itself over the far side. Even the magnificent mountains with their green pastures and snowcapped peaks lay dormant—their dim silhouettes surrounding us in a patient wait for the day to come through.

None of that matters to me though, for I know this place, my beloved monastery on the mountain, so well. It's been my home for the last twelve years, ever since my father left me here. I was young—about five or six—but the dreadful thought of that day stays with me, buried in the abyss of my mind.

The air was heavy with the smell of blooming mountain meadows—one of those days that was bound to end in either thunder or hail. Father said, "We're going to see your grandmother Dechen today, it's going to be a long ride."

And a long ride it had been, from our home at the stables all the way through the valley, up the mountain pass with the leaping deer and their young, and even farther until the flattened trail had run out. But Father had led the way, his stallion dashing over the high pastures where the nomads had pitched their tents for their yaks to graze.

The nomads. I'd seen their black tents dotting the planes from a distance, but I'd never dared this far out to where they lived.

My pony had booted through the waving fields of golden and green. Scores of bluebells chimed their tunes underneath prancing hooves and turned up their petals to salute us on the ride of our life.

Our last ride. For sure, he must have felt it, that little pony. With his coat of patchy brown, matching bristly mane, and a stubby tail that never seemed to grow, it was the ugliest little thing. Ugly and stubborn—and perfect for me.

With the many graceful and gallant horses at the stables, I'd chosen this pony to be my companion. Or rather, I have to admit, it had chosen me—for as soon as I'd set my first steps as a toddler in the paddock, he had been there waiting for me. He bumped his velvety nose into my bony chest and made it clear—I was his in this life. We'd been inseparable ever since, or for at least the first years of my life.

Everywhere I went, the little pony carried me. Except in the house, that's where Mother had drawn the line.

"Out with the two of you!" She'd scurried the little pony out of the kitchen at my first attempt to sneak it in. "Being the wife of the royal horse master, I delight in the horses. I even delight in having a daughter that stinks like one. But that doesn't mean I'm tolerating even the tiniest one in our living quarters."

Mother had succeeded—the pony never dared into the house again, not even after Mother's passing, when the house was empty, and nobody would have noticed it wandering around.

My pony... His short legs struggled to keep up with father's slender stallion as we flew through the meadows on a ride that never seemed to end. How I'd wished it hadn't, later on, when the purpose of our ride became painfully clear. Especially in the first year, when everything was unfamiliar, and even my grandmother's kindness seemed too much to bear.

Dechen had stood at the gate of the monastery to welcome us that summer's afternoon with the customary white khata draped along her arms.

The first thing I noticed about my grandmother was the reddish color on her cheeks—fierce blushing hearts, just like mine. And like Mother's before hers had paled.

"Palden-la, it's good to see you." Dechen had touched the top of Father's head and draped the white silken around his neck. Still on my pony, I hid behind Father's horse. I wanted to see, but time away from Mother had made me shy.

Grandmother's hands felt cool on my cheeks and she spoke with a voice that was almost too soft to hear. Of how beautiful I was, and how happy she was that I was finally here.

Finally? I'd not understood anything about that day. Why had Father brought me to a grandmother whom I had never met?

I sat in the kitchen, next to the stove, and fed on butter tea and tsampa balls while Father and Grandmother went away to talk. That's where I first met Pema and Tsomo, the nosy twin sisters who'd made fun of my boyish clothes and my unkept hair—a messy bun to keep the unruly strands out of my face.

At the time, I thought they were the oddest girls I'd ever encountered. Actually, they still are. Nobody has ever seen twins so different, yet so alike. They made fun of me the moment we met, and I hadn't minded, for I was just waiting for Father to return and take me home. Too tired from the hot weather, the long ride, and the comforting food. Tea left in my cup, fried breadcrumbs sticking in the corners of my mouth, a tsampa-ball half-eaten, I dozed off.

Dusk peeped her tranquil rays through the tiny kitchen window when the starling snorting of my pony awoke me from a dreamless sleep. Like an arrow shot from a bow too high-strung, I ran outside, and met my deepest fear.

Father stood ready to ride off on his stallion, with my little pony tied to his saddle and balking on all fours. *He was leaving.*

"This is your home now, my daughter. You be good." Father's voice had cracked at his words. He spurred on his horse and rode off in a frenzy without looking back. My little pony struggled as it was forced in his track. *And I was left behind.*

"Apa, apa!" That's all I could call out, as the thing I dreaded most had just become real. Father was leaving me behind.

As small as I was, I couldn't bear the immense truth that came crashing down on me. My insides shattered, my legs gave way, and my body caved in.

Dechen had caught me, and I struggled to break free, my immediate and natural reaction to something I couldn't control. She carried me in her arms, restraining and comforting at the same time.

I howled and wished for the moon, and for my grandmother to leave, to go away. The thunder came, and hail lashed down on the desolate mountain. I cried all night, as there was no mercy left to spare.

When morning came, Dechen took me to the stream, and she dressed me in a maroon robe that slouched around my bony body. I grew into it fast though, for the life she gave me was good. Surrounded by a tight community of devoted nuns, strong female practitioners of the Buddha's teachings, I grew up feeling cared for, and steeped in love that knew no boundaries.

The odd twins had decided we were best friends from that day on. I resisted, of course, for I don't take to people that easily. The sisters didn't care. They kept pulling their pranks to get my attention. It wasn't long before I gave in.

A smile stretches across my heart as I think of all the trouble we got into. Oh, it couldn't have been easy on Dechen, guiding us boisterous threesome through our childhood years. Many times she brought us before our teacher to receive another instruction on appropriate nuns' behavior, and even more often she lectured us herself. Dechen's patience and endurance we tested, for sure. But always—always—she stayed calm and collected, acting from a place of love and compassion, as true Dharma practitioners do.

Not once did she raise her voice at us.

Not once did she lash out.

A saint she is, that's for sure.

My fingers squish the hem of my robe, and dew drops return to the grass. With a heavy heart I walk on up to the prayer hall, to Dechen to make my request. Today I'll ask her what's been weighing me down for so long.

Today I'll ask for her permission to go home.

Two

The wooden door won't budge under the push of my shoulder. Morning dew has lodged itself between the swollen timber and rusted latches. A dull creak, it gives in, and I stumble into the dark to set my sandals beside my grandmother's. A few blades of green tickle my toes. With a quick swipe I straighten my robe and the loose strands of my ever-unruly hair. A tiny shiver runs up my spine as my courage fleets. *This is it, no turning back.*

The incense flares a daring red, beckoning my way into the room. Faint orange rays fall through the tall windows. Slivers of bluish gray release their herbal scent, billowing on the chilly draft up to the wooden beamed ceiling. The butter lamps spread their golden glow with a fiery devotion all over the shrine; they try hard, but they can't cast out the bleakest morning chill.

On tiptoes, I move over and lower myself three times to the statue of our great teacher, the Buddha. Seated on his high throne, his gilded face never diminishes to shine the most radiant compassion, lifting my sorrows time and time again. My hands clasped, I pay my respects to the images that flank our great teacher, Chenrezik, the bodhisattva embodying the compassion of all buddhas, and Green Tara, the mother of liberation. The smoldering sticks find their way between the

offerings. Cups of crystal clear water, a cauldron holding fresh
tea, heaps of creamy butter, molded tsampa, fried breadsticks,
and a stack of shiny apples are all piled up in front of the shrine.
Colorful paintings of deities in their wrathful or peaceful
manifestations hide the crumbling stucco of the white-washed
walls, and intricate mandalas on thin cloth cover the window
cracks. Spiral patterns on vibrant yellow, red, and blue banners
cascade down on the polished rafters and crimson lacquered
pillars. The rustle of silken whispers comes from high up and
from afar. Though not as grand as the shrine room of the
monks' monasteries, this is a shrine of intended beauty and
profound devotion. This is a room curated with care and
treasured by all of us nuns.

Green Tara's generous grace descends upon me, and my
racing heart slows. The deity's hallowed words flow from my
lips—*Oṃ Tāre Tu Tāre Ture Soha*—and I request the mother
of liberation to protect me from fear and obscuration, for I
need it today. To us nuns, Tara is the mother of all Buddhas,
our savioress who hears the cries of all beings and swiftly
helps all being in this worldly existence. With her left leg in
meditative contemplation and her right leg extended, she's
ready to leap into action, relieving all suffering of the world.
Tara embodies the heart of the Buddhist teachings—wisdom
and compassionate action—and she's everything I ever aspire
to be.

Like all Tibetan mothers, my mother taught me the Tara
mantra. "If you ever need help, put your full trust in Tara; call
upon her from the bottom of your heart and she will guide
you," she said.

I could barely talk, and I'd just repeated the words, but
somehow, deep down, my tender heart knew these words to be
important. Turns out it was right. Now that I've studied under
the supervision of excellent practitioners like my grandmother,
I've experienced the powerful effect of the Buddhist teachings.
Even though I'm only a beginner on the path, my dearest

sisters show me the way to live a good, virtuous life in service of all sentient beings. My spirited body and restless mind, always wandering, always wondering, have calmed with prayer, meditation, and studying the texts. I'm grateful for it, every day again.

Keeping my face turned to the images of our teachers, I shuffle to the back of the room. My eyes glance over at the endless rows of books, covered in maroon linen, lined up on both sides of the shrine. *All that knowledge.* Still so much to learn and practice before I can ever be of real benefit to all sentient beings. Hope surges in my heart, for all I aspire is to advance my Buddhist practice here.

Seated in the furthest corner of the room, Dechen rests in mediation as she does every morning for long periods of time. In silence, I kneel before her. The low table between us holds her brass bell and dorje, representing emptiness and form in the Buddhist practice, concepts that are still far from my grasp.

A thick woolen shawl protects Dechen's willowy frame from the morning chill. Her slender hands rest on her lap, a string of yellowed bone beads intertwines between them. The shadows soften the fine lines on her face, but can't diminish the serenity of her being—peaceful and content. How I strive to be.

As my eyes cast to the ground, deep admiration and boundless love rise within me. Admiration for my grandmother's devotion to all sentient beings, and an infinite love for the heartbreak we share—the heartbreak of being denied by our own blood.

She's a dedicated Buddhist practitioner now, my grandmother, spending her days in study and meditation, and it seems she was always destined to be. It must have been over thirty years ago, when she took her full vows as a nun in this monastery, only six weeks after her arrival. This is unusual—anyone entering the monastery, young girl or adult woman, lives at least one full year as a novice. Even I haven't taken my full vows after being here for over ten years. But then again, there's nothing usual about my grandmother's life.

Born into a royal family, Dechen lived a sheltered, privileged life as a girl. Her father, and especially her three older brothers, were fiercely protective of her, never letting her out of their sight. She was precious to them, as a younger woman is a great asset to forge alliances to the other prominent families. Yes, Dechen would have been a great pawn in the game of political marriages had it not been for that fatal summer she fell in love with Rapten, the heir to a nomadic tribe in the high mountain range.

I've heard the story, as my sisters told me, for they know all. How true love had brought shame to the family, how Dechen, daughter of a royal clan, had eloped to live with a lowly nomad.

Her father and brothers had acted as soon as they discovered Dechen gone. They schemed and called on their allies, with patience being their greatest strength. They waited until the moon had gone to renew herself, and in the darkest of the night, they charged to the nomad camp high in the mountains. Rapten and his clan never stood a chance. Swift. Bloody. A single swipe of a blade. My heart hides whenever I think about it. My grandfather, murdered with the most malicious intent.

Dechen was taken home and the spring after that dreadful summer, she gave birth to a girl, Lhamo—my mother, so I have heard. The family had been delighted. A new daughter, a new precious asset. Now they could rid themselves of their shame. So only three days after giving birth, Dechen was brought to the monastery, forced, abandoned by her own blood. She never saw her daughter again.

Given no choice, Dechen immersed herself in the ascetic monastic life and thrived. She's become a respected Buddhist practitioner, known for her skillful means and practical wisdom. Many women—and even men—come to seek her guidance in matters. It is no wonder the nuns chose her as their abbess a few years ago.

Dechen never told me about her life before the monastery. I would sure like to know her side of the story, but I respect her too much to pry. The one thing she told me about her past ordeal is that putting her full trust in the Buddha and his teachings has been her salvation. With my grandmother's serenity enveloping me, I realize again what a remarkable woman she is and how lucky I am to be here. Never again will I let her down, for she's everything I aim to be.

Dechen's eyes open, and with a nod she acknowledges me. Her gaze rests on my heated face as I lean in, my prayer beads a muted rattle around my wrist.

"Ani-la." I lower my eyes down to the floor. "You know why I'm here." My fingernails press into the soft flesh of my palms and force the words from my unwilling mouth. "May I humbly request your permission to visit my father?"

I swallow the dry lump in the back of my throat. No reaction, as I could have guessed. My eyes go up, and there she sits, her lips pressed together. I hold my breath in the bleak silence between us, for I know that unmoving look on her face.

"My child, as I told you before, it is unnecessary for you to go out." Dechen's voice is gentle as ever, yet an edge of impatience rings through. "Your father already gave permission for you to take your full vows when he brought you to me all those years ago." She shifts on her cushion and a faint clicking fills the air as her beads slide between her moving fingers.

A done deal. I clear my throat, but it's no use. My mind searches in all corners for something to say, but there's nothing, nothing to say. Tears well under my eyelids and the heat in my cheeks spreads down my neck. How I hate being here, asking my grandmother this. I don't want to go either, for I don't want to risk losing her. I don't want to, but I have to. I need to hear it, those words from Father's mouth—that he wants me to be a nun too.

"Nordun, my child." Dechen's voice pierces my mind. "There is no need to go out and put yourself in a position like that. Your father, like me, knew early on that a nun's life is best for you." She pauses and even the beads halt to support the weight of her words. "Surely by now you have trained your mind well enough not to give into disturbing emotions that cloud your view, not to give into silly attachments like approval from others?"

Oh, she's right, as always. My lip hurts as I chew it, and my mind's feverish from mulling over Dechen's truth. So right, I don't need to seek Father's permission, but there's this strange, yet profound yearning seated within the core of me, and it's urging me to go home. How I wish I could explain what I don't understand myself. My fists release and my shoulders drop with a sigh. How I wish I wasn't so weak.

"Ani-la, I thank you for your wise words." My voice sounds small now, and it's all I have. "I know them to be true, but I request you one last time, as I have never done before." My eyes meet hers in a burning plea. "Please grant me permission to go home, for I need to hear my father's words."

My desperation is almost palpable now, my cheeks surely fire with the brightest of red. I bow my head as defeat loads me down. This one request might be too much for her, even though I haven't asked anything from Dechen—ever.

Sure, when I'd first arrived, that was a different story, for loneliness and longing for home had taken possession of me, plaguing me without end. I'd been a wild natured, high-spirited child, always on the lookout for the chance to run off home. It took all of Dechen's patience and endurance to first keep me in and later to teach me to obey. She still reminds me of my troubled start many times—with a quip, as is her way. How I've settled down in body and mind. I've even developed the passion and persistence to study—especially the most sacred texts. The monastery has become my true home, and my sisters are my family now. Here I found my purpose, a life to serve the benefit of all sentient beings, and Dechen's unconditional love shows me the way.

The clicking of the beads has resumed again, ringing in their victory over my pathetic request.

"Please Ani-la." My voice pitches in one last attempt. "Under your excellent guidance, I'm ready to devote myself fully to the dharma." A sob escapes from my chest. "I just need this, this one request." An intense heat rims a scorching ring around my eyes. I blink to stop the tears from falling, and this time I succeed.

"You may think your intention is pure, thus sufficient, my child." Dechen lowers her chin, and an ominous frown draws over her face. "But only a steady, well-trained mind will be capable of warding off the obstacles you will meet out there." Her hands clasp around her beads. "Still..." Her last word trickles a little hope in my heart.

The string of beads slide around in the palm of her hands. Once, twice, three times... This time not to pray, but to ask for direction, I know.

My breath stalls, my eyes fix on the bones. Around and around, casting the prediction... what will it be? I lean back to release the nauseating tension weaving through my stomach.

Dechen counts the last bead, and her eyes flash in a moment of fear. Only one moment, and then it's done. Her hands stretch out to me in comfort.

"You may go, my child." Her words release the stalled breath from my lips. "You may go in the companion of Ghedun-la and your trusted friends."

And the ground underneath me falls away.

Incredible. My heart makes a leap, for my grandmother has given her permission.

"Oh ani-la, thank you." My fingers scrape the rough timber boards. A splinter lodges in my thumb. It's an unusual sweet sting, and I don't care. "Thank you so much." I stumble to get up, for she might change her mind, but there's no need. She's already closed her eyes.

My face pressed to the floor, I give thanks to my precious teacher, and sneak out the hall just as I came—but now with a heart full of hope.

Three

The fatty smell of fresh fried bread lingers in the kitchen. A pile of dirty dishes is stacked, left haphazard at the doorstep. The bell for class tolls. It's way past breakfast. Still, my sisters choose to stay and wait for me.

My body breathes a sigh of relief as I plop onto a worn-out pillow. The sweet comfort of the earth rises to meet me as Pema pours me a cup of tea.

"Good morning!" Pema adds a sneaky smile as she serves me. Her big brown eyes hold a long-awaited expectation that she doesn't try to hide.

I bite my lip to suppress my own smile, for I'm going to let her simmer a while. My hands wrap around the cup, seeking the warmth that will settle my mind and soothe my shaky insides. Incredible. *Permission to go home.*

"So...?" Pema's eyes are ready to burst their brown. She can't take it anymore. "When are we leaving?"

My eyebrow raises, but it's no surprise to me. Pema already knows.

I blow the fatty froth aside and take a slow sip from my cup. "You're right," I say. "She wouldn't let me go without you two at my side."

Pema sniggers and hauls the kettle over. Tea spills, and creamy foam hisses a scorched protest on the stove.

"Careful!" I slide aside as Pema relishes in her excitement. "You think Tsomo will come?" A bite of buttered bread spreads its briny taste along my palate.

"Come where?" Tsomo shuffles in the doorway. A basket of dried cow dung swings around her hips.

"Oh, stop pretending." I release the smile on my face and glance from sister to sister. They are twins, but not alike, and certainly not in appearance. Pema is small—tiny, like she stopped growing at the age of six—but she has the biggest brown eyes I've ever seen, set in a gleaming, jolly face. Tsomo on the other hand is tall, slender, almost wiry, with a perpetual frown on her forehead so it looks like she's sort of cross all the time.

Their appearance might be different, yet they seem to share one mind. It's uncanny how they finish each other's sentences, and always know where the other is, even if they're far apart.

Not that they'd ever been far apart. At their birth, the divination was cast; the twins are the reincarnation of an exceptional Buddhist master. And since prophecy has to be followed to avoid a wrath from the gods, the twins were raised at the monastery to start their instruction early. Dolma, the abbess at that time, had taken a personal interest in the sisters, making sure they would fulfill the destiny that's foretold.

Their presence touches me with a kindness that knows no end, as they have been my saviors from the moment we met. That fateful day my father left me on this mountain to carry my immense grief all alone, the twins stepped in and shared my burden, for they had been there too. Home-sick, heart-sick, and most of all feeling forlorn, my sisters in seclusion were the ones that understood. Their friendship means the world to me, and I don't ever want to be without it.

"So, we're leaving tomorrow." Tsomo's frown lightens, and she sits beside me, wiggling the basket between her knees. Sure, all nuns savor the solitude our mountain gives us, but the rare opportunity to go down to the valley—that is something none of us will pass up.

I nod. "Tomorrow." And my little heart makes another leap while the sisters fill the kitchen with their chatter.

Pema babbles about the scenic route into the lower valley, and Tsomo sums up all the precautions that we sure need to take. My family home is at least a day's ride, providing the weather is good. It's not a journey to be taken lightly. Yes, the trail down the mountain sure is gorgeous, but tricky this time of year with the slippery remains of last winter's slush and the abundance of overgrown and budding wildflowers announcing the arrival of spring.

"We'll bring momos and have a picnic." Pema claps her hands, beaming a grin. She's got the day planned. "We might even visit our cousins."

I pour myself another cup of tea and shake my head. There's no way we'll have time to sit around. It will be a stretch to make it in a day, but I will not mention it to Pema. She won't hear.

"Yes, let's all have a party, shall we?" Tsomo rolls her eyes. "Honestly, sis, you're the eldest of us. Why don't you behave like it?" Sparks fly as she throws a few slabs of dried dung in the stove. Pema doesn't budge.

"We have to eat, so I'm making momos." She rumbles through the heap of greens in the corner. Tsomo pokes the smoldering ashes with a stick.

Flames flare and I shift aside. "Gen Ghedun's coming with us." I slurp another chunk of soaked bread from between my fingers. "He'll have none of it."

Tsomo grabs a rag. "Nordun's right." She dusts herself off. "We'll travel straight to the stables. No detours or picnics allowed." With those words she whacks the rag around one more time as if to say "discussion closed."

"Gen Ghedun." Pema hums and turns to me. "Well, then you'll reach the stables for sure." Mischief ignites among the burnished brown in her eyes. "Can't guarantee anything from there on though."

Whack. A rag whooshes by, hitting her head.

"You stop talking, right now." Tsomo's warning soars at her sister. "Nordun's heart is pure—don't you dare think about that." Her frown's back with a vengeance, underlining the weight of her words.

My hands wring around my cup, and my mind spins in a circle. We all know what Pema is hinting about, as it happened before. A novice sister going down for a visit, and never coming back. Families force marriage bonds, and even strong sisters' minds become feeble. It's not something to joke about, but to be honest, it hadn't even entered my mind.

The air stifles and folds a dense layer over the kitchen. Cold sweat breaks on my face. The sisters steal a glance at one another, and their eyes seethe a veiled intensity I've only ever seen in theirs.

I know that look, as swift and black as the flare of a raven's wings taking flight. The twins are having a premonition again. About our trip? About me?

I crane my neck in a reflex to read their faces, but it's useless, I already know. They'll laugh it away, as they always do. And it's exactly what they do now. Pema wrinkles her nose at Tsomo's frown, and Tsomo hits Pema over the head again with that dirty cloth.

My tongue tastes the silty residue at the bottom of my cup—a touch of tsampa, salt and butter, a satisfying end to a great cup of tea. No use asking what's on my sisters' mind; they'll tell me in their own time, or not.

And just like that, the twins are their usual chatty self again, deliberating the best route taken and, most importantly, the food we will bring. My hands gather the empty cups, and I stack them in the basket.

"My turn today," I say. It's not, but they won't mind.

Pema sifts through the cabbages in the darkest corner of the kitchen. "And while you're down the stream, cut me a few sprigs of green, will you?" She winks, and I walk away.

A vibrant orange red waves through a dusty gray, crowning the morning with a golden glow. The remaining drops of dew shine like melting crystals on the grass. The early morning chill has made way for the balmy heat of early spring, but the last of a vague cold latches itself onto my bones.

I haul the basket closer. The old wicker creaks and pricks my hip.

Going home.

I got what I desired. Right?

Then how come that strange sense of unease has sprung itself on me?

Four

Hollow scrapes of hooves herald the arrival of Ghedun, climbing the rocky trail. Dawn's silver rays reveal the sole silhouette of our chaperone on his horse ascending through an opal mist. All nuns are still in the temple, but I've finished my prayers. I was up way before the call of morning, as the night would not grant me my rest.

"Tashi delek, gen-la." I bow my head in respect for the elderly man. "Please have some breakfast before we go." Ghedun only smiles. As always, he is a man—or rather a monk—of few words.

Ghedun lowers himself from his horse—his back hunched, his hands clasped into claws—as I hold the reins. The monk's body has succumbed to bone-disease lately. Old age is one of the most challenging parts of our human existence, as I've seen with our elderly sisters. The body deteriorates, becoming a painful burden while the mind often maintains most of its sharpness. I wonder if I could keep working away with disease as this faithful monk does, serving our monastery whenever he can with the right intention, while carrying his crippling sickness with such grace.

"Gen-la, happy to see you." Pema sprints out of the kitchen, the kettle swinging in her hands. "So sorry, we're almost ready." With a flustered face she pulls a cup from her sleeve.

"Please have some tea." The milky brew slushes over the cup, sharing her enthusiasm. I look away to hide my vicarious shame. Pema's late, as always. How disrespectful to make our trustful companion wait.

Gen Ghedun came to the monastery as a lay warden, in service of Dechen's family. He had been in their service for years as Dechen's personal guard. His orders were to protect the family's daughter, to keep their precious asset from harm. He had failed—failed to keep Dechen and the family from their miserable disgrace.

So when Dechen was sent to the monastery, Ghedun took on the blame. He offered to make amends with the family by serving their sister for life. He ordained as a monk and—since no men are allowed in the monastery after sundown—moved to a small dwelling outside our monastic grounds. He has remained there ever since, working for Dechen, and all of us nuns.

Ghedun has proved himself to be of tremendous value as a representative for the nuns' monastery. As a man, and a monk, it is so much easier for him to go out and forge the necessary bonds with prominent families and bordering tribes. We never see much of him, for he always occupies himself with these worldly matters, making sure our community stays safe and undisturbed. Well, at least Pema brought tea to show our appreciation. If only she would hurry.

My heels churn in the sand. My hands swing the horse's reins back and forth. Patience has never been one of my virtues, and it shows. I crane my neck—again. No Dechen to be seen. Ghedun catches my gaze and shakes his head. My heart sinks down into my chest.

"You know your grandmother's very diligent about her practice." His gentle voice can't comfort me. My hopes are up too high—once again.

"Everything checked." Pema bobs around her mule, a satisfied grin rounds her cheeks. I can't help but smile, as I know—with everything, she means the food.

The gale force batters the prayer flags without mercy as Ghedun leads us out through the gate. The thick fog reduces us to nothing but shades of silver gray, drifting away under a cream-clotted sky. My mind runs ahead, for the trail is tricky, but my heart stalls at the gate. My mind wrestles, and I wring the reins as I turn around once more.

No use.

No Dechen, and no other nuns either to send us off this early morning. All are inside—most likely with Dechen's orders. My heart settles its heavy weight in my stomach. A sigh slips from my lips and gets lost in the wind. I force my eyes and my mind onto the path ahead. My mule hops in a slow trot. Onwards we go.

Loose gravel grinds around the hooves. Tufts of hardy grass and dry succulents scatter around. A few dozen mani-stones, stacked on the right side, signal our way down. This part of the trail I know well; it's steep but easy to follow, as vegetation is scarce at this height. In a few moments a sharp turn will reveal the whitened chortens in which the relics of revered sisters rest. There they are, standing with pride, ominous beacons on our path. Three times we go around with the sun and remember. *May the merit accumulated relieve the suffering of all sentient beings.*

With Ghedun's mare setting a steady pace, our mules have it easy to follow. The sharp gale force lays down, and the sky lightens up—good, we have conquered the steepest part. I lean back in the saddle, as the track widens in soggy, narrow grasslands. An acrid odor lingers in the dampened air. Thin strands of singed, sorrel wood smoke dwindle in the distance. There, on the far end of this secluded mead, a single row of boxed shapes is hiding in plain sight. We have reached the retreat homes of our sisters in total seclusion, the place most nuns aspire to live.

Going into retreat means a total dedication to the Dharma to truly realize the Buddha Nature that's innate to us. We all have the wish to do so—me too—but few of us are called. Only the most advanced practitioners can stay for long periods of time, even live their whole lives in meditation practice here. Needless to say, I hope I will be called too—I'm looking forward to that day.

"Dolma—la!" The twins' cry out in one voice. I veer up.

A tiny figure emerges from the middle hut—Dolma, our former abbess, who chose to spend her last days in solitude here. The twins are already throwing themselves at her feet.

Dolma and the twins are close. I've never seen the sisters as distraught as when Dolma announced she would go into retreat, the day before Losar, five years ago. I remember it well—the only time the twins skipped New Year's celebrations. Tsomo fell sick with ailing fever for ten days, and Pema was caught sneaking out—several times—determined to join Dolma in retreat. Only after Dolma allowed the twins to visit her in private did they settle down, much to my relief.

"I guess we'll pause for a moment." Ghedun's resigned tone says it all; the twins have decided for us.

Pema's already pouring the tea as we enter Dolma's hut. Tsomo fluffs up the cushions for Ghedun to sit near the smoldering stove.

"Ani-la, thank you for receiving us." I lower myself to the former abbess. Her deep gaze settles on me, and my knees buckle. For some reason—and shame comes to me, as I admit this—I've never felt close to the elderly nun. Dolma's presence used to fill me with fear. Like an overly stern grandmother, she had her eye on me, looking to chastise me whenever she could. At least, that's how it felt to me at the time.

"Why don't you take after your grandmother?" she used to sneer at me. I never understood her bitter reprimands, but Dechen explained.

"Dolma wants the best for us," she said, as she dried my tears with the tip of her scarf. "Her formal manner and rigorous corrections are her way to help us become a dedicated practitioner of the path." Then she'd peeled a fresh apple for me.

Well, Dolma's gone, and Dechen replaced the harsh scolding with a compassionate approach, and from what I've experienced, genuine care and honest connection are much more effective in creating discipline than instilling dread and fear.

Dolma leans forward and rests her hands on my head for a blessing. Her thumb scrapes my chin, and I cringe at the thought of her chastising me again.

"It's not the best of places to go to." A shadow shifts over the former abbess' face as her beady eyes pry into mine. I quiver at her words. "Whatever you think you might find there, it's not the best of places." Her lips pinch. What is she talking about?

"Ani-la, we'll be fine." Pema swings the kettle around. "Gen Ghedun's with us." But the cheer in her voice doesn't hold, and a solid silence descends upon us.

"I'm sorry, Ani-la, I don't understand." My mouth dry, I try to swallow.

"Of course, you don't understand." Dolma leans back, but not before throwing me her familiar sneer. "How can you understand something that has not been revealed to you?" She tugs a string from her frayed sleeve and rolls the beads between her fingers.

"Ani-la, please," Ghedun interrupts, gentle but determined. "Now's not the time."

What's going on here? My eyes dart from sister to sister, and a tightness hinges over my ribs. Pema inspects the handle of the kettle. Tsomo's frown has reached an all-time low. What are they talking about?

"It's never the time, Gen-la." Dolma's beads halt with her breath. "But surely the girl's a woman now, and she ought to know."

A rush of blood gushes from my cheeks down to my neck. My mind spins in circles, trying to grasp what Dolma has just said.

"Ought to know what, Ani-la?" I waiver. Dolma's eyes flare up with contempt and stall my question in the tense space between us.

"Well, the prophecy, of course." The spiteful glare in her eyes matches the victory in her voice. "What else?"

A prophecy! I gasp and the moment freezes. My eyes haze as I stare at the old woman's face. She's there, but fades from my vision as her words ring their faint echo around in my ears, and tell a tale of another place, another time. About a divination completed before I was born. About a prophecy that claimed my mother's first child as the successor to my father's stables, the heir, the horse master to-be. And about a high, renowned lama who had been adamant about the divination, even when my mother's first born was a girl—me.

"Now who could ever imagine you, a girl, becoming a horse master?" Dolma's taunting tone shakes me out of my temporary blur. "Impossible." Her scorn slices right through my core, and I flinch. "Your father did right, bringing you to the monastery." Dolma's thin lips twist in disdain.

A horse master. The heir to the stables.

Pearls of sweat drift down my temples. I try to focus. A horse master—me? A woman? Impossible. My mind latches itself on Dolma's words and sprints away.

I've never heard of women being horse masters. There *are* no women ruling over stables. Just the thought of it... me, training horses, reigning over my childhood home. Surely... this divination must be a mistake. The very moment I try to reign in my frantic thoughts, my mind unfolds into a vast open space, and the clearest of a cerulean sky surges from within.

My dreams! My eyes widen and the ground waves beneath me. My lungs collapse and my mind takes a dive, filling itself with the visions I've been trying hard to hide. Those haunted dreams from my childhood, the ones that terrified me in my younger years between sleep and awake. *The dreams—is this what they've been trying to tell me?* Dreams of horses flying through the sky into the midnight, dreams of dancing dakinis on billowing clouds, and a strange, intense longing, calling me home to a place, to a time I've never known. For years, the immense, illusive yearning wrecked havoc within me. For years I fought the battle and never won. *It must be.* It must be this prophecy that Dolma's speaking of—it must be this, my predicted fate, calling me home.

Dizziness grips my being as the terrible realization settles in. My body sways and my fingers find their hold at the coarse weave of the carpet. I turn to face my sisters. *They knew!* A bitter bile lashes at the back of my throat.

"Why?" I blurt out, a cry of desperate disbelief. "Why didn't you tell me?" All those times I woke up screaming in the dark of night, the twins had always been there. Consoling me, squishing next to me, making sure I would be fine. Telling me the terrible dreams would go away again, brushing them off as "silly nightmares," and pretending not to know. *But they knew.* They knew of the dreams that came to haunt me, but they decided not to tell. *How could they?* My stomach clenches and I'm gutted by their betrayal.

"Oh, sis." Pema waves her hand at me. "If we told you everything we know..." She tries on a weak smile, but my heavy heart won't rise from its pit. "Besides, it means nothing. Tell her, tell her, Ani-la." She turns to Dolma, sitting smug in her seat.

"That's right, my child." Dolma snorts ever-so-slightly. "That lama was a fool, delivering a false insight. His heart must not have been pure." Her eyes flutter over me in a hasty flight. "His vision must have been obscured, for a female horse master, that cannot be." Her hands claw her beads. "That's for sure."

False? I jump at the possibility. My hands relax in my lap. False, of course!

"But it all leads to something good." Dolma's content glare meets me half-way. "For now, you've experienced the benefits of monastic life for yourself—and all sentient beings." Her hand wraps the beads around her wrist, and her gaze darts in the distance again.

"We all know that lay life keeps us stuck in this cyclic existence. Especially for women, lay life is suffering." Her lips pinch again. "The pain of childbirth, the heartbreak of fickle worldly love that never lasts, the burden of betrayal or death of our loved ones..." She sighs and turns to Pema. "No, it's better to dedicate ourselves to the dharma, and gain clear insight into the mind." She squeezes Pema's shoulder with a determination that doesn't allow any rebuttal. "Being a nun is better for all."

Dolma's truth soars right through my heart and I heave. The divination, Dolma's disdain, and even my sisters' silence fade compared to the suffering of all beings alike. Dechen's sorrow over the violent murder of her lover and the brutal loss of her baby girl, ripped away by the very hands of those who were supposed to protect her. My father's devastating grief over the death of his wife, leaving him desperate enough to believe he has no more love left to give. How my heart goes out to her, and to him, and all the beings in this life. Yes, human life is suffering, and it's all around. How precious the chance to relieve some of this suffering, how lucky I am to be a nun in this life.

"So true, ani Dolma-la, so true." Pema reaches out to me and a sob escapes me. Her stocky arms wrap around me, and we call it a truce.

Maybe it is all for the best, prophecy or not. Somehow, it led me to be with my sisters in solitude, fulfilling my calling in my monastic family—to serve all sentient beings the best I can. My mind surrenders and Pema hugs me tight. All is well. All is as it's meant to be.

"You'll be fine." Her whisper confirms it. "We're with you—and we'll never leave."

"I know." My lips move, and my heart soars with the gratitude for my sisters, and for my life as a nun.

"We should go now." Ghedun breaks the silence and urges us on in his ever gentle way. "We still have a long day ahead."

With the same flurry as they hurried in, the twins are now the first out on the trail.

The mellow morning sun scatters its bisque beams over the dewy earth. A brisk breeze chases the thinning remains of the mist. With our mules trotting along the widened trail, all looks favorable for our journey.

Yet something's stirring in the hollows of my being. Something I didn't recognize before, but now understand—for at the time of my birth, the dice have been cast, and words of truth and destiny have been spoken. The prophecy that once brought me to the monastery is the same one that's calling me home.

Five

Our animals pick up speed, as if they want to make up for time lost. I slide my scarf down as we descend onto the greener slopes. The sun has awakened in full strength, seducing the sweet earth by caressing it with her warming rays. Banishing the looming prophecy from my mind, I turn my unruly thoughts to the beauty surrounding me.

Patches of brilliant white peep between the rocks, the snow lotus with its soft wooly hairs stands in full bloom. A few more days of good sunshine and Chozem will track down to these budding meadows to fill her baskets with fresh supplies for our monastery's apothecary.

Every year around at the turn of spring and summer, our amchi stocks the storerooms with fresh herbs, berries, flowers, and green, hanging them down the beams to dry. Bundles of bright yellow rose root, deep pink and purple primrose, and shiny orange sea buckthorn mixed with garlands of viridian greens. I love the dazzling array of colors and relish the rich, almost intoxicating aromas—intensifying as the chubby berries release their juices to shrivel dry.

After Chozem processes the preserved vegetation into powders, pills and tinctures, she lays out the thick, fleshy mushrooms to dry. These are my favorite, giving a simple stew in winter a creamy, hearty taste. I always keep an eye out for them. Not on this ride, though, for the windy road demands all my attention.

A vast heap of yak bones, wrapped with a string of faded prayer flags, marks the entrance into the nomad summer pastures. The stacked bones, bleached by sun and wind, serve as a poignant reminder that no being escapes the impermanence of this cyclic existence. Soon the nomad tents will be visible—small black dots scattered over these luscious slopes.

In the summer, the nomads rule these grasslands with their herds of yaks and sheep. Every year, at the beginning of the season, the elders of the tribes appear at the gates of our monastery, paying their respects with offerings of fresh yogurt, dried cheese, and spun wool. Dechen always invites them in for a meal after they receive their blessings—but they hardly ever accept.

There they are, the first yaks on the mountains. Their rough grunt echoes from afar. Curved horns crown their broad foreheads, long strands of wiry hair sway along their bulky frames. These robust animals are revered by the nomads as these magnificent animals provide for their entire livelihood.

"Careful now." Ghedun turns around. "Don't come too close to the herd." Yaks are not usually a bother, but in this season they're fiercely protective of their newborn calves.

"Om mani." Pema's voice squeaks. "Can't we just go around them?" She shifts on her mule.

"We'll be fine. There's a camp already." Ghedun's clawed hand reaches out into the distance. Ahead of us, in the distant valley, the nomads have pitched their tents near a small spring. It's still a good ride away, but I can see there's a bustle around the tents.

"Looks like they are preparing for something." Pema steers her mule to the edge of the path and leans in for a better view.

"We won't be heading that way, will we?" I halt beside Pema.

Then I see them—a party of three dark riders galloping through the pastures.

"Gen-la, there're horsemen coming," I call out to Ghedun, whose mare has picked up speed on the trail again. "Looks like they're coming our way."

Ghedun keeps on riding.

"Gen-la." Tsomo steers her mule beside him. "Gen-la, there're horsemen coming our way." Ghedun's mare halts, and he turns around.

"I know." The old monk straightens himself on his horse. "They are your kinsmen, Nordun." He offers a gentle smile. "Word has spread you're going home. Now they're here to welcome you."

My kinsmen?

I clasp the reins, forcing my mule to a sudden halt. Blood rushes to my head, my mind staggers. *My kinsmen.* The tribe of my grandfather, of Dechen's love, slain in cold blood. Surely, this family has never shown any interest in me, and now they come to welcome me. Why?

"But Gen-la." I open my mouth and the words stall on my breath. *My kinsmen.* They knew where I was all along. They could have come up to the monastery as the other nomads do, but they never did. Nobody ever visits me or Dechen. Other nuns receive family, inquiring about their needs, offering food and goods to the monastery, and paying their respects. Not my family members—they never did. Dull pain wraps itself around my ribcage and seeps its ache all the way to my heart.

"It's good," Ghedun says. He shakes his head at my confusion. "Let the family welcome you."

"But Gen-la..." My voice cracks and shame floods me as I recognize my feelings—I don't want to be welcomed. Not by this family. Not here, not now. "We don't have time."

"It is not fitting to refuse." Ghedun's stern look meets my eyes, and my cheeks are on fire. *He knows.*

Heat spreads to my neck, down my chest, and my body sags in the saddle. From the corner of my eye, I see the sisters glance at each other. Their chatter has died and my stomach knots—yet again, I am the only one who has no clue what's going on.

Ribbons of yellow and red flap in the wind, and clumps of earth trail their horses' hooves. Fast and agile, the riders approach us at the speed of the wind. Ghedun gestures for us to follow him down the slope. I spur on my mule, and it balks as if it feels my hesitation.

"Tashi delek Gen-la, tashi delek." The riders greet Ghedun, draping the scarves of welcome around his neck. Pleasantries are exchanged without introductions. These men know each other well.

The sisters have already hopped off their mules, receiving the welcome with open arms.

"Thank you, brother." Tsomo folds the khata around her neck and tucks it in the sleeve of her robe. "So good to see you all again."

Brother? Again? Stuck on my mule, I bend forward, trying not to frown.

The party of three turn their attention to me. "Sister, please let us welcome you."

My feet hit the ground and my hands brush the dust of my robe, but my eyes are still on the men in front of me. *Brothers?* As I regain my posture and my thoughts, the first man slides a flowing scarf around my neck, the silken soft to the touch.

"Thank you." I whisper and straighten my thoughts. Ghedun is right. We must meet any welcome with respect. I glance up at the man before me. My jaw drops as I stare into his face. Dark eyes glister above a sharp hooked, somewhat crooked nose, long black hair braided, tassels woven through. *This man.* I've seen him before. My eyes widen. This is one of the elders visiting our monastery with bountiful offerings at the beginning of every new year.

He gives me a lopsided smile, a clumsy acknowledgment of my recollection. Yes, it's him. This is the man I poured tea in the prayer hall for at Dechen's request just a few weeks ago. I remember, although he was in a big company, he was the only one who touched my arm—a slight brush—as I handed him a cup. I shrugged it off then, assuming it was accidental—men are not supposed to touch a nun, everybody knows. Now he is here—and Tsomo calls him brother?

"The family has been waiting for you." He speaks in a respectful yet resolute tone. "Let us escort you all to our humble home."

I draw a sharp breath—I don't dare to speak. Thankfully, I don't have to.

"We accept your generous invitation with delight."

Ghedun's adamant reply makes it clear: we all are going to the nomad's camp—and I am going home.

Six

The bones rattle in my body. My mule hobbles down in a pitiful attempt to keep up with the riders. Within no time we've arrived at their camp. The huge main tent stands out like a colossal sky spider, perching itself on the vast plain. A myriad of vibrant prayer flags flutters from the eight wooden poles that hold up the black yak-hair pavilion, crowning the massive construction with a majestic look.

The air is laden, buzzing with anticipation. A bunch of bright-eyed children storm out to meet us, wrapping their shiny satin ribbons around our mules. Women haul water, scrub pots, and stir cauldrons, while men line up in front of the main tent for the official welcome. My initial reluctance fades away with the bright smiles and greetings that meet me. What a fantastic reception. How rude, how judgmental the thoughts I harbored towards these people. My family. I cringe at my selfish behavior.

Ghedun pulls the bearskin aside and I step in. A poignant fume of smoldering yak dung and juniper branches drifts from the humongous stove in the middle of the tent. My eyes water, and I pause. Charcoal shadows surface in the rising smoke.

People rush aside from me, but I need a moment to take it all in. Sacks of barley and other grains line the walls, and slabs of yak cheese hang to dry above a pile of heavy blankets. In the far left corner, a single butter lamp lights a gilded Buddha statue. A few clothed scriptures and the offerings of butter, tea, and tsampa are piled up in front. My eyes dart to the right of the tent where thick woolen carpets line the floor, and fluffy brown and white sheepskins cover the chunky mats arranged in a square.

Then I see him, seated on one of the mats, raised a little above all the others. He has the same striking features as the man who collected me, only his hair is bright silver, a brilliance gracing the serenity on his face. My heart skips a beat, as it understands the soul of this man. *It's him.* It must be.

"Nordun, come and meet your grandfather's brother." Ghedun's already seated beside the man my heart longs to meet.

The old man's hands stretch out, and my mind fevers. I kneel in front of him, my shoulders hunched, my eyes to the floor. How can I face the man whose brother was slain by my grandmother's kin? How can I ever thank him for not seeking revenge, and for leaving them all in peace?

Ghedun places the old man's hands on my head, tender and warm.

"Welcome," he whispers, and my heart is ready to burst.

His hands slide down my heated cheeks. Strong hands, despite his old age. He tilts my face towards him and it's only when our eyes meet I see—the opaque mist that obscures his vision. Yet, this man's soul shines through the milky clouds in his eyes, radiating an incredible kindness for all to meet. Relief washes over me and releases a sob from within. There's not a trace of resentment in these loving eyes. There's only an abundance of mercy, and my heart overflows.

"Thank you, pola." My hands find his, and tears of gratitude spill. Even in this touch, there's only compassion.

"Come sit with us." Grandfather's brother slides his hands in mine. I look at Ghedun, who nods in approval. The twins have already made themselves comfortable, as they always know how.

Tea is served, accompanied by vast amounts of food. The stench of scorched yak dung is smothered by the most delicious smells of spices, cures, and herb. Strips of dried yak meat cubed, cured cheese with tsampa, boiled meat in broth, fresh yogurt, sliced fruit, and dried nuts, combs of honey—it's a proper feast. The women keep the dishes coming while the men eat and talk. And the twins eat and talk too, completely at ease with all that's around.

I sit in silence beside Grandfather's brother. Sipping my tea, I gather my thoughts. No resentment, no grudges, and no revenge, either. There's only grace. A sigh of relief slips away as grandfather's brother still holds my hand.

The conversation picks up, as everybody seems to know each other. And everybody seems to know what they're talking about. I pick at my food, my insides too upset to eat. The harsh winter, the horse—trade, the changes in taxes, the rumors of more foreign raids near the borders. Worldly talk I've never engaged in. I shift in my seat as awkwardness settles upon me. Here I am, amongst friends and family, and I've never felt more out-of-place.

By now chang has replaced tea and the air in the tent has gone stale. A sanguine sun stretches long shadows into the entrance, and the boisterous laughter of children dies down to a single cry here and there. The journey to the stables will take at least another half day's ride, but nobody's in a hurry. The men are drinking, the women are talking, and my sisters are eating and enjoying themselves.

A thin strip of dry meat crumbles under my fingers. I shift again. Restlessness is seeking its way in my seat. This is my family, these are my friends, and yet I feel like a stranger. A pang of loneliness stretches across the void in my chest.

As if he senses my unease, Grandfather's brother puts his hand on my arm.

"She'll be here soon and she's so happy to meet you," he says, and his hand holds mine tight.

I lean in, my hand in his. "Who?"

"Sangmo, my other granddaughter." His eyes keep their distance, but I feel his attention on me. "She had to go out to the herd early this morning, but she should be finished by now."

And just as the old man has spoken, the bear skin at the entrance flings aside. Light streams in on a breath of fresh air. Sangmo has arrived.

"You're here." A flurry of arms envelopes me, and the scent of luscious, zesty green wraps around me. Taken aback by the girl's excitement, I freeze—but she doesn't seem to notice, or care. "I've been waiting for you a long time." Sharp blades of cut grass prick my cheeks, sticking all over her hair.

She finally lets go and drops herself at my feet. An audacious grin comes my way. She's family, without a doubt—she holds the strong facial features that come with our kin. Her long black hair flows over her shoulders, her tanned skin and ruddy cheeks glow with a touch of yak butter, and her burnished brown eyes hold that intense, innate wildness only true nomads possess. *Those eyes.* A small twinge tugs at my heart strings. They shine a frenzied freedom—like my mother's eyes once upon a time.

"Sangmo will come with you on your journey," Grandfather's brother says, before my mind gets the chance to wander back to the past. "She knows the way well. She's one of our best riders, and a skilled hunter too." His eyes still stare into nothingness, but his chin points at Sangmo. "Besides, you'll need time to get to know each other."

No way. Did Grandfather's brother just tell me Sangmo is an expert hunter and that she's coming with us? I frown, and he puts his hand on each of us.

"We're your kinsfolk, my child." His voice lowers. "You may not know us, but we have always been there, looking out for you, keeping you safe." He pauses, and the white mist in his eyes turns into a swirl of hazy gray.

"What happened to our families is a tragedy played out in the past, and for too long we dwelled in anger, obsessing over revenge." His voice trembles yet sounds crystal clear. "But now you have come, and we can put it to rest."

I swallow. *Revenge.* My fingernails dig into my palm. The family didn't seek revenge. How I wish to understand why, but don't dare to ask.

"Dechen distanced herself from our family, and we've always respected her wish." He sighs, and his eyes close for a moment. "But that does not mean you have to, for we are truly your family—in every way." His voice steady now, his hand searches mine.

"You are on the threshold of a new life, for the life you experienced is ending." He raises our hands to his heart and opens his eyes. "Life as you're meant to live seems near, but it's vulnerable, as challenging times are ahead. In these times we will watch over you, your every step." He bends his head, his face close to mine. He whispers on. "But good times will come, that's for sure, and in these times, we will rejoice with you."

The ashen-gray ebbs from his eyes like a dove's wings turning away on the wind, and the most brilliant of bluish white breaks through. Both his hands cradle mine in a blessing and time halts. *Challenging times.* My mind empties itself. I can't speak, I can't move.

A slap on my knee whacks me back to the now. I veer up as Sangmo grins.

"You take my mare tomorrow. She's tame," she says. "I'll take one of the new stallions, a perfect occasion to break him in."

And with that remark, the deal's sealed. Night has fallen and we'll spend it here, at the camp. And tomorrow my family—*my family!*—will accompany me to my father.

It's like I'm waking up to a dream that's not mine, and all I can do is surrender. Yet it is my doing, all that is happening now. Dechen's painful absence at the gate, Dolma's revelation of the ominous prophecy that was kept from me for so long, the unexpected welcome from my kinsmen—because I ventured out to get my father's approval. *What did I set in motion with my selfish desire?*

Weariness cloaks me, pressing my body to rest. My eyes search for Ghedun, for my sisters, for anybody to understand, but find no reprieve. All have retreated, gone their own way.

"Time to rest." Sangmo jumps to her feet. "We've got a great day ahead of us." She pinches my cheek.

Dazed, I slip off my seat and pray for sleep will come with ease.

Tomorrow this will all make sense. Or not.

Seven

They're back. I shoot up. Sweat pours down my back. My heart rattles in its cage like a wild animal captured. Panic has seized me. The dreams from my childhood, the haunting nightmares, they've returned with a frightening vengeance—more vivid than ever before.

Dreams of wild horses flying in full gallop, trampling through narrow gorges and coiling creeks, rolling valleys and staggering heights. Fierce treading hooves conquering the bedazzled snowcapped mountain ranges, and dancing dakinis drifting on billowing clouds. Hands, laughing and shrieking, twirling rainbow hued scarves all around, and urging me up, up, soaring free and fearless over the three realms to the mighty peak, the eternal mount of Meeru.

It's an endless repeat of the same vision in bright golden and green, and red and blue, always ending with me riding a magnificent white mare into a terrifying depth, swallowed by the night that holds no moon. I've been there before. They'll haunt me, shred me to pieces with a nameless sadness and suffocating despair.

Outside. If I don't act now, the dream won't leave until the morning. My hands stumble, my toes catch on my scarf. There it is. I jerk the musky bearskin aside and my feet find the wet green with nobody noticing.

Focus. Gulps of the frosty night air sting my lungs. Good. My hands fold over my belly. Slow down. My breath swells in my abdomen, rising up, slowing down. I close my eyes and focus on all senses—like Dechen taught me when the dreams first appeared.

The prickly stings of the spiky succulents at the soles of my feet, the gentle rush of the stream in my ears, the damp smell of the soggy grass tingling my nostrils. *Focus.* The bitter, raw cold rasping along my palate, rushing into my lungs, the nippy breeze stroking my heated cheeks. Slow and sure, slow and sure. The haunting visions will fade. Another sharp breath in. I will return. I will return to me.

My knees weak, I drop at the fleeting stream. Icy water freezes my face. My teeth clatter as the fever flees from my body. I don't mind though, for I've made it. The dreams have no hold over me, not anymore.

My eyes sprawl into the endless sky and I wait a few more breaths to secure my victory. The last remains of tension trickle away, and a sigh settles within me. How strange, how quiet, this starless night.

The waxing moon dances her silvery light over the rippling water. I haul myself on a bolder and press my toes in its glistering surface, my entire body alive again. My fingers untangle my unruly hair and pick out the speckles of grass, remnants of my cousin's heartfelt hug. I twist my locks secure into a bun, and my thoughts rearrange themselves, back to a logical pattern.

Galloping horses, dancing dakinis, and a sky that holds no moon. I hug my knees and rub the tingling soles of my feet. Traces of the intense sadness fleet by, and the midnight chill gnaws at the tips of my ears and my nose. Soon I'll be freezing out here, but the thought of the suffocating tent halts me and I wonder: *Why do these visions still fill me with harrowing misery after all these years?* Horses, dakinis, a vast moonless sky, innocent images, a meaningless mess.

The prophecy. The hem of my robe weaves in the wind. I pull my scarf tight as Dolma's reminder rings through. Could it be because of a false insight? The horses because I'm meant to be a horse master according to the divination at my birth? And the dakinis—the sacred female sprits—because I've chosen total dedication to the Buddhist path? My mind bounces, and my limbs go numb. *Better stop this silly thinking.*

Whatever dreams look like, they are just illusions. I pinch my toes. For sure, even Dechen said so. Nothing to be afraid of, only imaginary creations of a feeble, untrained mind. Nothing that can't be overcome by prayer and meditation, by a solid Buddhist practice. I plant my feet on the slippery stone and straighten my back. Dechen's right.

"Can't sleep?" A shadow moves in the darkness from behind.

For a moment, I freeze, then I veer up. *Who can it be?*

"Sorry, didn't mean to scare you." The voice steps into the frosted light of the moon, and brings with it a tall man, his long hair hanging loose.

"You didn't." My feet slip. My arms cross over my chest—and again I'm annoyed by my defensive reaction.

"Good to know." A cheeky edge rims his voice. Who is this man?

I take a small step forward. Is he family? My eyes meet him and my heart skips a beat—literally. Broad shoulders, chiseled cheekbones, a fine nose, and only a hint of a tan. This man, I haven't seen him before. For if so, I'd have remembered. He's gorgeous—simply gorgeous. I bite my lip.

"We didn't meet." I hesitate. I'm not supposed to be here alone, unaccompanied.

"Sorry, I wasn't here to welcome you." He moves towards me with an unmistaken, comforting calm. "I'm Karma." A khata comes out of his sleeve.

"That's fine." I clear my throat. "The welcome was a lot, anyway." Feigning a smile, I lean back against the rock.

"Still." He bends his head, and the scarf flows from his hands.

I bow my head and our fingers brush, the slightest of touch. A quiver shoots through my palms and with a jolt, I look up. Our eyes lock and I feel mine widen. *Green!* His eyes sparkle a rich and bedazzling green, like precious cut emeralds, polished at the pearly light of the moon.

"Thank you." I mutter as the silk skims the tingling tips of my fingers. A swift flutter touches my stomach. A sudden heat flares in my cheeks. *What's this?* I cast my eyes down and thank the darkness for being my ally right now.

"The family's been waiting a long time to meet you," he says. "But then I hear you're leaving us tomorrow, so soon." He tilts his head, waiting for me to react. That tone—he knows he's caught me off guard.

"Um, yes." Still flustered, I scoop the scarf in my sleeve. "My father awaits me." My trembling hand tucks a loose strand of hair behind my ears.

"He'll be happy to see you," he says, and there's that tranquil reassurance again. "Just as we are." I shift upright.

"I hope so." My voice sounds thin. My chest tightens. His arms swing loosely behind his back, but he's trying to catch my gaze. Can this situation get any more awkward? My mind's throwing a tantrum. What does he want? To make me uneasy? Well, that worked.

My feet shuffle. I should go before I'll make an even bigger fool of myself. Still, I don't know the family connection. Stay or go?

Get yourself together. As ever, my curiosity gets the better of me. For sure, I want to know.

"So, we're family." I square my shoulders and force myself to face him. He stands so at ease with himself. That quiet confidence of him, how I envy it. If only I had some of that.

"We are," he says. "I'm Sangmo's brother." The ends of his mouth curl up, and he lowers his head to meet my gaze.

"Oh, I see," I say in my most casual tone.

So this is Sangmo's brother—and my cousin. A twinge of disappointment weaves itself through my chest.

"Sangmo didn't mention a brother to me." I shift my weight from one foot to the other. *You fool, stop it.* What are you thinking?

"Well, I haven't been around much." He shrugs. "Family matters, you know." His hand moves to the long knife on his hip and rests it there with a daring smile.

I can't help myself. The sheen of those emerald eyes scatter my thoughts all around. No way I'm supposed to feel, let alone act this immature. My toes curl in the sand. I scold my foolish thoughts, and myself for being here alone with him. *Deep breath in.*

"It's late," I state with reluctance. "I'll better go." I'm not going at all.

"I'll walk you back." His heels crunch, but he's not moving either. And all the while those eyes remain on me.

"No need." I blink at the haste of my reply. That's impolite. "I'm fine." He's family, after all.

"Maybe." He pauses, and the green of his eyes softens into an alluring shade of viridian. "I like to make sure." His posture as relaxed as ever. "Can't guarantee you'll get a good night's sleep, though. That's up to you."

I shrink back. "Sorry?" My voice pitches. No sleep?

"Well." He pauses again. His voice drops. "If you had a good night's sleep, you wouldn't be out here, all by yourself, in the midst of the night." A dim shadow draws over his face. "I guess you're not used to sleeping in a tent?" His eyes narrow, and an inquisitive glimmer peeps through.

"Oh, no, that's fine." I waver. "It's not the tent." For sure, I'm used to sharing with my sisters. "It's..." For a moment my words stall, but then they gush out on the breath of my mind, and I tell him all as he stands with me in the incoherent flood of my words.

I hear myself talk, and want it to stop, but I can't. For the words they keep coming, cascading down from my lips. Of the dreams haunting me, the crushing anxiety they bring, and the intense yearning they leave me with, an inexplicable illusion that seems all too real.

"I'm sorry," I say, as the flow dribbles dry. My mind is empty, my heart shoved deep within my chest. "I shouldn't be talking about all this nonsense." I swallow my foolishness and stare at my bare feet. What must he think of me babbling on like a child? "It's nothing, really." My voice trails off.

"It's fine." He steps towards me, and his voice reaches out. "It's because they make no sense. They shake us to our very core."

I look up and there it is, in the moonlight between us—the unspoken understanding I've been waiting for. *He knows of dreams.* I shiver as the brutal midnight freeze sucks the marrow from my bones. He has them too!

"It's been a long day." He hastens his words. *He doesn't want me to know.* I hesitate, but won't ask.

"Now that you've shared your dreams with me, I'll keep them far from you." His smile is earnest, almost shy. "I promise, you'll have a good rest."

Our gazes lock again, and a vast space cracks wide open in my being, here, right under the flat bone of my chest. I blink, but it's gone, the anxiety of all that remained. There's only lightness left.

We stroll back in silence, with Karma leading the way. The night allows me only the solid outline of him, and we reach the main tent far too soon. How I wish to be in his solid presence a little longer, for as it unnerved me first, now it comforts me, and I want it to stay. *You fool!* My pulse quickens. *Stop thinking like that!*

He pulls the bearskin aside and I slip through, mumbling a hasty goodbye. I stumble to the women's side of the tent, giving him no chance to react.

Out of breath and out of mind, I toss the blanket over my head. Please let sleep come fast. I shut my eyes and pray.

Why do I have to be this awkward all the time?

Eight

Hooves stomp, dogs bark, high-pitched voices spur on cattle—a new morning at the camp is ushered in with a cacophony of noise. The dung-fueled stoves roar, ready to bring the fresh milk to a boil and sizzle the left-over momos into fatty fritters. Sharp smoke fills the air in and around the tents, and if the sounds of the new day won't wake me up, the smell of it sure will.

I don't have to open my eyes, for I know—the twins are gone. My fingers feel the knotted string tied around my wrist. They left me with a blessing and a reminder. A blessing for an auspicious journey, one without obstacles, and a reminder to keep the path of boundless compassion and discerning wisdom.

A mix of emotions waves through me as I rub the knot. There's a twinge of disappointment—my sisters have gone, and I will miss them. And there's gratitude for the reminder they left me with, for I surely need it. I've only been outside the monastery for one day, and look at me now.

The haze of midnight still lingers on in my head. I've found little rest after the embarrassing encounter with my cousin—well, embarrassing on my side anyway. *Only a steady, well-trained mind will be capable of warding off the obstacles you will meet out there.* Dechen's words ring to mind. How indispensable my grandmother's advice turns out to be.

I scramble on my knees and make three hasty prostrations on the mat. *Om Mani Padme Hung.* The steady stream of hallowed words always grounds me in times of dismay. This time's no different. The warmth of my breath on my folded hands, the pressure of my knees sinking in the blanket—my mind appreciates the soothing routine and rewards me by accepting the present moment as it is.

"Come and eat," a familiar voice calls from behind.

"Good morning to you too." I turn to see Sangmo's head peeping around the entrance and laugh. Sticky greens seem to accompany that girl wherever she goes.

My hands grab the hem of my robe and I glide over to the main tent. The grass is drenched from last night's rain. Apparently, it poured out of the heavens. Strange, I didn't hear any of it, not at all.

"Good morning, pola." I kneel before the old man at the stove and tuck his shawl tight to keep him warm. His prayer beads click with content and ease. He raises his head at the sound of my voice and my heart delights in the grace shining through his shrouded eyes.

"Today's a big day for you, my child." His stiff fingers give mine a gentle squeeze.

"It is, pola." I relish the warmth of his company and sit next to him. "And I'm ready." A little morning draft creeps up my spine.

"Of course you are." Sangmo hands me a cup of steaming tea. A chunk of crispy fried bread balances on top. She frowns. "But not before we tidy you up. Come here." She bounces behind me. "A braid will look good on you." In one go she frees my messy bun and starts rearranging my loose strands.

A cozy hush surrounds the three of us, as the morning bustle of the camp dies down. While the stove crackles away, Sangmo's fingers work their way through my hair. Mine dip the fatty dough in the tea. Grandfather's brother continues his mani-prayer. I tip my head back, my eyes close, and my jaws open in a comfortable yawn. For the first time since I've left the monastery, I'm at ease. Entirely relaxed. That being doesn't last long, though.

"I hear you met Karma." *Boom!* Grandfather's brother's words go straight to my chest.

"Good." He nods. "He's a real blessing to the family."

Karma. My stomach flutters at the near mention of his name.

"I miss Karma." Sangmo says, finishing up my hair. "He's never around anymore." She ties a bright green string at the end of my braid. "There you are, looking good." Sangmo clicks her tongue in appreciation of her own work.

"You know he's busy looking after our interests." The old man's hand stretches out to Sangmo's cheek. "With the raids at the borders, the demand for horses is greater than ever."

Raids at the borders. I have a vague idea of what they're talking about. The men mentioned it too, yesterday. Those savage foreigners on fierce horses, the Mongols, they came over the mountains and conquered our lands a long time ago. We've been at peace with them, but their insatiable hunger for power is driving them further, plundering and killing everything on their way. *Gruesome.* Hearsay has reached the monastery, but Dechen keeps us away from worldly rumors. No need to engage our minds in mundane affairs, she says.

Well, my mind isn't busy with strangers on the borders. It's the stranger I met last night that occupies mine. *Karma.* My ribs tighten. It's not only those incredible green eyes that have taken me in. It's his calm demeanor, the way he carries himself with that quiet determination. And even though he didn't tell me, he knows dreams too.

"Yeah, yeah." Sangmo hugs her knees. "I miss him, though." She sniffs and wrinkles her nose.

"Where's he gone to, anyway?" I think I sound nonchalant and distract myself by finishing up my tea.

"He's escorting your sisters." Sangmo wipes her nose with her sleeve. "Back to your monastery."

What? Karma's with my sisters? The tart taste of envy touches my tongue. My lips tighten in reflex. This is not me. *Stop it.* Focus on something else.

I raise my hands and my fingertips follow the intricate pattern of the braid down to my back. Smooth and tidy, unlike my wayward thoughts. *Envy has no hold over me.* I scold myself once again. Look what this whole venture of going out to seek my father is doing to me. Maybe Dechen's right—I don't need approval. Not from Father, not from anybody. The tension in my jaws creeps up to my throbbing temples and a dull headache sets in.

"It's time." As if he senses my doubts, Grandfather's brother puts his hand on my arm. Sangmo hurries out to gather the horses.

"Your father will be waiting in anticipation, just like we did," he adds with a firm voice. His hands reach out, and his opaque eyes search for mine. As his hands cradle my face, a surge of love lifts my heart.

"I'm glad we had the chance to meet." A slight timbre in his tone wavers. "Time is fleeting, and we never know when we meet again." His fingers run along my cheeks. My vision blurs. "Always remember, my child, this family is your sanctuary now."

A serene shadow passes between us and I close my eyes as gratitude streaks my face, wet and burning hot. *My family, my sanctuary.* The taste of those words is new to me, and I savor them with my whole being. Grandfather's grace flushes my mind, driving away whatever doubts I've hidden, and for a moment I float, steeped in genuine love.

A brisk breeze blows through, and Sangmo bursts in with her usual whirlwind of enthusiasm. "Let's go," she yells from the entrance. "No need to keep the horses waiting now."

Nine

I stroke the horse's flank, supple and sturdy. Her lean muscles show through, giving away the mare's actual strength. My fingers fumble. I haven't been on a horse for ages. A mule, yes, but a horse like this? My body stiffens as the cream-colored mare shakes herself and snorts, a brisk encouragement to hurry.

"Come on." Sangmo folds her hands to form a stirrup. "I'll give you a leg up." Both hands on the withers. I pull myself up. "There you are." She hands me the reins and I hold on tight.

"Good morning, Gen-la." I bow my flushed face to the monk next to me. I should have acknowledged him sooner. "Sorry to keep you waiting."

Having switched his old mare for a fierce stallion, Ghedun's horse prances with fervor. The fact he's also coming has slipped my mind. For sure, we could never ride alone. Two women, a nun and a maiden—that would be unheard of.

Sangmo's stallion bucks and neighs, throwing all fours in the air. Sangmo doesn't give in to the blackish devil though—on the contrary. With that audacious grin of hers, she's bouncing back and forth on the horse, enjoying the struggle, giving it not any lead way at all.

"Let's go!" Sangmo's voice gets lost in the wind as her horse flies off. Clods of churned earth and mulled grass trail high behind its hooves. I gulp as my mare jumps in its trail, bolting through the alpine pasture to keep up with the dashing stride. My fingers twist in the coarse manes, and a prayer slips from my lips. *Om Tare.* As long as I'm not the one slipping off.

A swollen yellow sun chases the last drops of dew, and the bountiful meadow releases the sweet scent of summer on its way. Colorful scrubs border a fleeting stream, making its way through the narrow gorge. Surprised by the speed of the sprinting horses, a slender chiru runs off, his long, ridged black horns disappear between the sway of the dragon pines. A pair of fluffy gray heads pop out of the hardy grass, and a bundle of young snowcocks protest our intrusion with a loud call. I can't blame them—I'm still dazed by the breathtaking pace myself.

Mind you, it doesn't take my body long to get used to the rhythm of the swift canter. It's more my thoughts that are rigid, focused on all the potential—and the most painful—ways I could fall off my horse. My hands relax, and my tight grip loosens a little as we come into the lower grounds. I even sit up straight now, instead of being draped in dread around the neck of my mare.

Feeling confident enough to sit back, I enjoy my surroundings some more. A black-necked crane slides lazy-like over the winding creek. A pair of small pikas skirts away, their round ears peeping from under a giant boulder. I can name them all, birds and mammals alike; my mother taught me, like many other things, in the days she was still with us.

Mother. The memory of our parting resides like a heavy stone in my stomach, always there, her blue-veined face, cold and white, her dull eyes far away. How I've tried to ban that ghostly memory out of my mind, for it holds far more memories of Mother, beautiful ones I'd rather recall.

Happy memories of braiding bird shoes from young twigs, and skipping round pebbles across the pond. Of jumping puddles after the summer rain, and rolling snowballs from the steep winter slopes. Of singing songs with the tiny red robins, and riding our ponies across the high fields.

And in those memories, Mother is the prettiest woman ever—long black waves cascade down her back, almond-shaped eyes set in a delicate round face, a permanent rosy glow on her cheeks. A most beautiful woman, outside and in, for her physical attraction matched her charming personality. She radiated a liveliness, a lightheartedness that made you want to be around her in the hope some of that natural delight would rub off on you.

No wonder the house was always filled with people when Mother was around. She'd made everybody feel welcome, just by being herself.

"Lhamo, I wish you wouldn't spoil our guests as much—we never seem to have a moment for ourselves." I still see Father wrapping his arms around Mother, complaining about the many visitors overstaying their course. But then again, he never complained about the first-rate prices paid by the eager traders for our horses—Mother's charming ways had played a part in that too.

Yes, Mother was great with people and with horses. I didn't realize how special that was, a woman riding and handling horses. Not until the day after her death, when I went out to the stables to fetch my pony—when I learned women aren't supposed to be around horses in that way.

"No more riding, Nordun." Father's eyes had been red and raw, and he locked the barn door. That had been the end. No more riding for me.

Sure, we slipped out a few times anyway—my little pony and me. But somehow Father always seemed to know, giving me that look of disappointment, wrapping its guilt around my little heart. My fingers fold around the reins—my heart still shrinks when I think of it. I so much wanted to ride, but the glaring hurt in my father's lightless eyes was too much for my tiny shoulders to bear.

Imagine my reaction when Father told me we'd be riding to see my grandmother that day. I had been the first in the stables, not even letting him finish his tea. Never did I suspect it would be my last ride on my pony. A bitter taste fills my mouth. I lift my face to the sun and her the golden rays fade my bleakest thoughts. *No use going there again.*

"Over here!" Sangmo's voice sounds from afar, and I crane my neck. There she is, her stallion already clattering into the canyon leading into the lower valley. She waves and halts at the adjacent creek. Time to let the horses drink and rest for a while.

At last, some shade. A soft breeze sways the dragon spruces that border the gorge. My horse dashes into the crystal-clear inlet. A pair of ruddy shell ducks takes off, flapping their white and green wings in bewilderment. They're as stunned as I am—I haven't even dismounted yet.

The water rushes a rawness between my tingling toes and I throw back my strung-out shoulders. Soreness stifles my limbs—I'm not used to riding, and certainly not at this pace. Still... I'm almost afraid to admit it, but it feels right being back in the saddle. Almost kind of freeing, despite my initial fear.

My eyes closed, there's nothing but the rustling of the spring, and the wind whispering my name. I stretch my arms and an incredible lightness unfolds in my being. In this very moment, I don't want to be anywhere else but under this warming sky, surrounded by these magnificent mountains with the cool water swirling around my weary ankles. I'm at peace, right here, right now.

"You're a natural on the horse," Sangmo calls to me from the shade. I open my eyes, turn around, and laugh. She must be joking.

"You think so?" I rub my legs. *Sure doesn't feel like it.*

"Oh yes." She throws her head to one side, a bold smile on her lips. "Runs in the family." She beckons me to come in the shade. "Too hot, sister."

Sangmo's hands rummage through her bag and she pulls out a tsampa ball. My senses satisfied, I pick on it anyway. Ghedun puts his head to rest on a patch of hardy gray moss and dozes off.

"I haven't been around horses much." I run my sleeve over my heated face.

"Hmm..." Sangmo sinks her teeth into a fleshy peach. "I can imagine after what happened to your mother." Her lips smack. "Still, that can change." She pauses. Her eyes dart from our prancing horses to Ghedun and back. "I heard about the divination."

She heard. I bite my lip. Even Sangmo heard about the prophecy—as always, I am the last one out of the dark. Sangmo leans back and puts her arm behind her head.

"Does it bother you?" She glances at me. I shrug as my mind searches for a response. Does it?

"I would love to tell you it doesn't." With a lazy gesture I throw the left-over tsampa towards the water. A frisky white-throated dipper comes flurrying out of nowhere and snatches the morsel before it hits the shore. Delighted with its catch, the bird hops onto a bolder to devour it in one go.

"Why would it?" Sangmo's eyebrows raise to her hairline. "Being a horse master." She snickers. "Me, I would be delighted."

I laugh. "I know you would." I shift my weight backwards. "Some think it's a false divination." Dolma's warning, still fresh in mind, leaves a stale taste on my palate.

"Why false?" Sangmo reaches for a fine twig and chews it to clean her teeth. "If you ask me, it's a great divination. Got no doubts about that." She runs her tongue around her teeth and spits the husk on the ground.

"So, you think it's possible? I pull up my knees and hug my legs. I stare at the midges, dancing across the water. Could it be?

"Of course it is." Sangmo sounds sure. "Many women from outside handle horses. Karma told me so." She straightens herself and starts telling me all about Karma's travels and his encounters with outsiders on the trade roads. I listen in amazement about how foreign women own things they can buy and sell, how they have other people working for them, and how women even own other people. My eyes widen. Yes, they own slaves.

"Karma says so." Sangmo leans in, a hand on one knee. "And by the way, just because it hasn't been done here, doesn't mean you can't do it." Her hand brushes the crumbs off her shirt and jumps up to gather the horses.

My mouth opens to respond, but my mind draws a sudden blank. I glance around, trying to decide what to do next. Say something? Do something? *Best to just go now and stop thinking about all of this.*

Ghedun's woken up by now, stretching his limbs. As he prepares himself to mount his horse again, his movements remain cautious. The ride takes a lot out of him. I slip on my sandals and hurry over to the elderly monk.

"We will rest a little more, Gen-la." I take the bridle of his horse, but he won't have it.

"Time to go." He rests his clawed fist on my shoulders. "Don't worry about me. You follow Sangmo, I'll tag along."

Sangmo's stallion prances up and down the stream, showing off his fabulous physique.

"Hey sis!" Sangmo mounts with the biggest grin. "Who says women can't ride and horses can't fly?" Her laughter echoes, bouncing off on all sides of the gorge. Her stallion rises and speeds off, drenching me in a cloud of sparkly white spray.

"She's a wild one." Ghedun shakes his head. "Good thing that doesn't run in the family, eh?" He prompts his horse in a calm trot and waves his hand to follow.

I wipe my forehead with the back of my sleeve. *No way.* I grab the reins and haul myself on the mare.

Sure, it feels good being on a horse again, but that doesn't mean I'm going to trot around in the wild all day. I've devoted my life to the path for the benefit of all sentient beings. I'm a nun.

My mare spurs off, the reins burn in my sweaty palm. I'm so close now. No more foolish thoughts of horses—or men. Once I have Father's word, I'm returning to my sisters to fulfill my destiny—as a nun.

Ten

The sun has reached its highest point as we descend to the lower valley where farmed land replaces the wide-open fields of grass. Small dwellings dot the stretches of burgeoning crop. The barley seed sown not long ago weaves in an amber glow over the fields. Women load their baskets with the first fresh cabbages—the early crop, tender green.

Sangmo's stallion boots up the hill in front of us. It sure shows no lust for rest. Straining to recognize the surroundings, I slow my mare at every home we pass. Alas, my eyes spot nothing familiar. My temples throb—the heat is getting to me. I focus on the road ahead. How the valley has changed. Or is it me not remembering? After all, it has been so long.

We follow in Sangmo's trail. My stomach tightens. This hill. Could it be? I look up as Sangmo has stopped. Are the stables there? My mind frenzies. How come I don't remember?

My mare halts next to Sangmo's stallion with a skittish snort. My eyes search down the slope. *There it is.* Tucked in a dense hem of purple and green, the stables lay hidden below. I can just about spot the homestead's flat roof, a darkened square among the silver sway of tall pines. My fingers tangle in my horse's manes. *My home.* For a moment, all is quiet, and I catch my breath.

Ghedun turns to me, his eyebrows raised.

"I'm good." I smile, but really, am I?

"Let's go." He steers his horse down the hill. My mare follows. Sangmo's stallion closes the row.

I can't keep my eyes off the homestead. My mind dashes around. Somehow it looks bigger than I remember. Much greener, too. Will the house still be the same?

Now the outhouses and stables come into sight. And the paddocks with the horses. My pulse quickens. *My pony.* My stubborn childhood friend, will he still be here? Will he recognize me? A sudden urge to spur on my horse rushes through me, but I hold back. *Easy.* My heart pounds against my ribcage. This is not the time to rush.

A slight turn to the left. Yes, there it is—the path leading up to the main gate. Blood rushes in my ears. The memory of Mother and me skipping along this path floods my mind. The towering trees were smaller back then, and the path not that long, and there were bramble bushes, those prickly ones, all along here. So often I've wrestled with the thorny bushes, but always came home claiming victory. Ripped sleeves and ruby streaked arms full of juicy berries, how sweet the taste. Yes, it's all coming back.

The silvery foliage of lacebark pines lines the entrance to the main gate, a cooling canopy as we ride through. Our canter relaxed, I shift to the back. My eyes take everything in, as if for the first time. A tall figure steps out of the muted shade. I squeeze the reins and my mare balks. *It's Father.* My heartbeat stalls as he moves into view.

"Ghedun-la." He greets the old monk with a bow. "Tashi delek."

"Palden, old friend." Ghedun slides from his horse. "You were hiding on us." He receives the khata with a gracious smile.

"Too hot." Father leads Ghedun into the shade.

I've frozen on my mare, sweat trickling down my neck. I can't move, only stare. Father, as tall as I remember, but his frame frail and hunched. My heart sinks. This is not what I wanted to see.

"Nordun." Ghedun's stern voice summons me, and I slide off my mare.

Next to Ghedun, Father's still an impressive figure—but he's nothing like the man I remember. Mother's death wreaked havoc at the time, streaking his long hair white overnight. The fire in his eyes died with the love of his life, and his bright, cheerful demeanor changed into a surly mien. Being with Father became a strain. The years clearly have shown him no mercy and I wonder if he's found some of it back, for it must be still there, deep down inside.

I can't recall how long I lived with Father after my mother's parting. A few turnings of the moon, maybe even longer? These weren't happy times. Father drifted away from me when I needed him most. His once so gentle manner became uncompromising, not only towards me. Servants left, new ones came and went again. The house, once bursting with laughter, became silent, and shadows took the place where men once sat. Too engrossed in his own harrowing grief, he could not bear to see it, let alone deal with me.

Tears burn behind my eyelids. My fingernails dig into the palm of my hand.

This is what the madness of love lost does to all—bringing even the strongest of men to their knees, driving them to abandon their own blood.

I straighten my shoulders as my mind returns to the now. Worldly love, no matter how pure, in the end always brings suffering. My hands relax and I take a sharp breath. My sisters are right. *Better not to get attached to worldly love, better to devote yourself to the dharma.* A nun's life is a good life.

And with those thoughts, I step forward to face the man I once cherished as my father, but who feels like a stranger to me now.

Eleven

"Father." The white scarf flutters before me. I struggle to find the right words to greet him. So often I've imagined this moment, in which I knew exactly what to do, what to say. Calm and collected, I would accept Father's welcome. I would thank him for giving me a life dedicated to the Dharma, and then Father would hug me and be my father again. Be the father from before, the father that loved me, the father that didn't banish me from his life.

That's how I envision it—always. But now...

A sudden rush of anger seethes within the hollow where my sunken heart used to be. *I was a child, barely six years old... how could you leave me when I needed you most?* Blatant blame boils in my chest, rumbling and raging to erupt, to spit its scorching wildfire, as blazing hot as any dragon ever flamed. *How could you abandon me to bear my grief alone?*

A howling hurricane of emotions ravages my body. Shameful thoughts of outrage and rebuke soar through my mind. *How dare you stop loving me, your only child?* My mouth opens to let it spill over, for this fuming inferno is more than my being can contain.

No! I clench my jaws and claw my fists as my body comes to its boiling point. *No!* My temples throb, my head about to split. I close my eyes, for I can't face my rage, but I can't give in either. This is not how I'm meeting with my father. This is not who I want to be. This is the desperate reaction of a helpless six-year-old, not the dignified response of a grown woman, and a dedicated practitioner on Buddha's path.

In a frenzied shame I douse my fury, my temper, and watch it sizzle, blow off steam, and dwindle into ashen. I didn't come here to reopen the wounds of a man torn apart by love lost. I did not come to rip Father's world apart.

Wisdom and compassion in every situation—that is what the Buddha taught us, and that is how I want to be. Dechen told me, wisdom and compassion are the two wings of a bird that you need to take flight and stay on course to wherever you want to go. The wisdom to see clearly, to see the true nature of all things to be. And compassion to recognize that we, all beings, are connected, and that we all experience suffering in this life. No being is without.

Wisdom and compassion, the qualities needed to live an honest and awakened life. My eyes open, and the storm passes. And so it is, wise and compassionate. I'm going to do Dechen proud.

And with that thought, I bow my head and surrender to the man before me. The man that loved me once; the man who's still my father.

"Welcome," he says, and slips the silk around my neck.

Welcome. Not welcome home. A twinge of disappointment tweaks at my insides. He is correct though—the monastery's my true home now.

"Thank you." I look up and flinch. A harsh glare meets my eyes, a dark shield to ward off the pain. Like a cornered warrior, all toughened up, Father has raised his armor to hide behind when life feels too shattering and lonely. No, time has not softened Father. Nor has time given him the wisdom to deal with his heartbreak.

"You didn't have to come." The frown above his eyes deepens. His hands hold on to the ends of the khata.

"I know." I lift my chin. "I was called to." I swallow. "And I
wanted to see you." The words slip from my lips before I know
it. A sudden pang stretches across my heart, and a little love
rises within it.

There. I said it. *I wanted to see you.* Sweat beads on my
forehead. It's true. For now I see, whatever Father did, he
did out of sheer desperation. He doesn't understand there's
another way to deal with his pain. The past, what happened
between us, it doesn't matter anymore. He's my father, and I
needed to see him. A great calm spins its fragile treads of grace
through my being. I reach out to receive the khata. He drops
his hands to his side.

"You shouldn't have." He falters. "But as Dechen let you
come, I'm happy to receive you." His eyes dart over Sangmo.
"All of you." He wraps the third shawl around her neck.

As if that's a sign, two servants rush out of nowhere and
take the horses to the stables. Prancing and bucking, Sangmo's
stallion won't have any of it. She has to haul in the rebelling
animal herself.

My feet follow Father's to the big house. It stands as grand
as ever, with polished wooden columns gleaming in the blaring
light of the midday sun.

My hands slide over the lavish embellishments around the
front. My feet hop over the threshold. Yes, it's still steep. I
rest my fingers on one of the many notches and my eyes go
over the inside of the door post. There it is. A row of small
markings. My fingertip rubs the one on top, the last notch
mother made, the mark that showed how much I'd grown. I
sigh. My forehead finds rest on the door post. Was I really that
small?

The familiar sounds of feet stamping and pots clattering
welcome me as I walk up, my hands gliding along the timber
banister. Warming aromas of fried dough, spiced meat, and
sweet fruit draw me through the lacquered corridor. Yes, this is
the feeling of home, our home, the home Mother always took

such a pride in. My feet float over to the kitchen where she used to cook up a storm, working her wonders there too.

"Nordun." Father's voice calls me. "Come in." He gestures for me to join him—not in the kitchen, but in the formal room. The room my parents used to receive the important visitors, like the heads of the tribes and the traders from the East. The room I wasn't allowed to enter, unless Father told me to.

Only after the visitors had gone would Father take me to that room, showing me the many curiosities they had left. Shiny stones in red, green, blue, dark yellow and brown—carved in the most peculiar of shapes. Rolls of the finest fabric, embroidered with vibrant flowers and odd animals, and intricate patterns woven through. Not warm like the coarse wool we wear, but flimsy and light. Delicate, my mother used to say, refined beauty. And sour fruits, coated in sugar that tickled my tongue. And once even a round cage with a pair of squeaking birds—but our tsampa was not to their liking. They died after just a few days.

I sink in the plush seat between Ghedun and Sangmo and observe that nothing has changed, except for the servants who are swift to set the plates down, dish after dish. Steaming meat, freshly cooked in broth, on the bone. A splendid array of mixed vegetables cured and arranged by color, with a choice of spicy sauce on the side. Golden fried momos, pasty buns, hearty noodles in thick soup, and cut squares of buttered bread in silver baskets. Curls of dried cheese, a variety of mixed nuts, sliced and cubed fruit, and freshly stirred yogurt—the dishes keep on coming, until there's no place left to put them. A feast for the senses, just as I remember, just like home.

What a welcome—I take it all in. Nothing was ever too good for our visitors in this house. *Visitors.* My mind takes a wrong turn. Visitors—this is Father's way of dealing with us. I'm welcomed as a visitor in my own home. *A visitor.* I'm a guest to my own father, a formal guest, not family—not anymore. My stomach pitches.

Tiredness takes my bones and I sag back in my seat. My ribs tighten, my breath shallows. I wipe my mouth with my sleeve. Cold sweat sets on my upper lip. It's too hot in here.

"Eat." Sangmo sinks her teeth in a juicy peach. "These are delicious." She hands me one. I decline.

"Not hungry," I say. My fingers fumble in the dense weave of my seat. She rolls the peach beside my bowl.

"Then keep it for later." She winks, and I throw her a faint smile. That girl sure loves her midnight snacks.

I glance over to Father and Ghedun, my ears picking up fragments of their animated conversation. The flourishing horse-trade and the planned expansion of the stables. How the horses bred here are in tremendous demand. And that all thanks to Tennah and his sons. *Tennah?*

My hands tremble as I reach for my cup. That's caught my attention. When I was a child, Father and his only brother had a contentious relationship. The details, I don't know, but Tennah was never welcome in this house. Not then. Now he lives here? With his sons running the stables?

Oh well, it's probably a good thing Father has reconciled with his brother. At least he has some family again, for from all I see, he's written me off. *A formal visitor.*

My eyelids drop. A dull ache settles in my chest. The rich aromas of the food, once so appetizing, now turn my stomach. I swallow again. Bitter bile lashes at the back of my throat. My fingers grip the corner of the table. Fresh air, that's what I need. Maybe a wash too. I have to go.

I clear my throat and shift off my seat. With a humble bow towards my company, I excuse myself. My feet fly down the stairs, my hands push the heavy door. *Fresh air!* I fling my arms aside and let my lungs delight. An immense weight I never noticed lifts off my shoulders, and the nausea ebbs away. With another sharp breath in and out, I steady myself. I'm fine, all fine.

My heels turn in the gravel, and my eyes dart up to the house. Weird. I pull my scarf tight. Must be all the traveling and excitement—or rather disappointment—that's worn me down. What did I expect, anyway? A grand welcome from my father? Well, at least he received us with the utmost respect.

Respect. A stone plummets right in my stomach. That's exactly where it hurts. Respect, but no love, not even a shred of fatherly affection—not in his words, not in his ways. I blink and fight back the tears. Coming all this way, desperate for his approval. My lips pinch and my thoughts cry out. Dechen was right. What a fool I've been. First thing tomorrow morning, we'll head back. With any luck, I'll be joining my sisters for evening prayer again.

The clattering of hooves resounds in my ear. The smell of fluffed up hay, greased leather and sweaty horse hides reeks from everywhere. *My pony.* Is he still here—and if so, will he recognize me? Hope lifts my heart from its darkened hiding, and with a spring in my step, I make my way to the outer stables behind the main house.

I've got a great feeling about this—a great feeling for once.

Twelve

Rows of sturdy stables line up behind the main house. New outhouses, massive barns. The stables were prosperous when I was a child, but they were nothing like this. The horse trade must really have taken off under the guidance of Uncle and his sons.

I stall for a moment. There're no horses out in the fields, and it would never be allowed in the paddock. I turn left. It must be in the old stable, the one where our family horses used to be. With an assured step, I turn left. My eyes spot the old crimson barn door.

The door slides as reluctant as it was back then. I hunch my shoulder behind the rusted latch. It screeches opens; the spiky smell of fresh grass itches my nose. The mellow afternoon sun lights the entrance of the barn but doesn't have the strength to shine the entire way through. I peer towards the end. No horse to be seen. I purse my lips and blow a high whistle.

For a few moments all is dead quiet in the barn, then—a loud, spirited whinny echoes from way back. A huge reshuffling of fodder and hay follows, and I leap. There he is! Too tiny to stick his head over the stable door, but not too small to voice a massive welcome. I scurry over to the last stable and swing open the door. *My pony.* My arms find his stocky frame.

"You're here." I rest my cheek on his neck, and my hands curl in his manes. He snorts and shoves a velvety nose against my shoulder. "Trying to push me over, are you?" I chuckle; it's a game we used to play. "Well, I'm taller now."

he didn't forget me. My hands run over his fur, soft and shiny. Clear eyes, clipped manes, a glossy coat and the roundest belly—somebody's taking great care of this little one. Father? I pick a few strands of hay out of the wiry manes, and I wonder.

"Why are you in here, little one?" My fingers scratch between his twirling ears—he always loved it. "Don't you hate inside?"

My mind fills with memories of those endless summer days, dashing through the meadows, with seas of poppies, red and blue, reaching all the way up to my pony's wobbling potbelly, and even higher, tickling my toes. I can't contain my smile. "Come." With my hand on his neck, we walk out the door.

"Keep that pony in." A shrill yell stops me in my tracks. A swift silhouette surfaces from the corner of my eyes. I freeze. A thin man steps out. Not a servant, for he stands too tall. Besides, a servant would never address me in this manner. A vague family resemblance shows as he moves closer. Sleek black hair with a noticeable line of gray on his temples, slanted eyes set in an elongated, drawn face, and pasty, wafer-thin lips. Nothing like Father, even so, something tells me it's him. *Tennah.* Goosebumps roll over my arms.

"Well, well, look who's back." His voice is a sticky, sweet tone. "So nice to see you, all grown up." He parts his lips and pearly-gray flashes through the gloomy shade.

"Uncle." I clasp my arms. What's going on here? My body's gone rigid and I can't feel my feet.

"Yes, you remember?" He sucks in his cheeks and a strange grin curls around his mouth.

My fingers wring the cord around my wrist.

"As far as I remember, we've never met." I square my stiff shoulders and rearrange my thoughts. Why won't my body move?

"Oh, we met." A sneaky gaze glides over me, taking me in from head to toe. "It was on that unfortunate day. You were only a child." I duck my chin. If he's my uncle, then why does this feel so uncomfortable?

"I heard you're doing well at the monastery." He moves in and I shuffle back. The pale light reflects his cold, empty stare.

"Yes, Uncle." I steady myself against the stable door. My eyes dart over his shoulder. I never heard the bang of the door. How come it's shut now?

"Your father's pleased." He smirks and pushes a greasy strand of hair aside with his bony fingers. "He made the right decision. It's no good, a man raising a young girl by himself." He clacks his tongue. "Especially a wild one like you." My jaw drops. Wow, that was an indecent sneer.

I push my elbows into the stable door and dig my nails deeper into my palms. My eyes search for a gracious exit, but he's not budging and keeps harping on it in that vile tone of his. About how devastated Father was, incapable of running the stables. How quickly business had died, and how he and his sons had come to the rescue, reviving the stables in their glory and even exceeding beyond everybody's wildest dreams.

I stand there, my body numb, and Uncle blabbing on. My thoughts try to recall, but it makes little sense. Yes, Father was struck with grief, and he couldn't deal with me. But incapable of running the stables? Sure, after Mother's passing, most guests had stayed away, but had it really been that bad? My mind struggles to stitch the fragments of our past together, but my memories are frayed, and the thread of common sense won't hold.

"Don't the stables look excellent?" He forces himself closer into my field of vision.

"Yes, Uncle." I shuffle back, my hand on my pony. He huffs, his hooves tossing up hay.

"With my sons becoming head of the stables, your father will take up his rest." His face is too near, and his sour breath stains my nostrils. What is going on?

His voice vanishes into a distant descent, and I can't hear a thing. My knees buckle and black dots form in my eyes. *Om Tare.* This feels very wrong. My hands grip the solid door, but it's no use, my legs won't hold me any longer. I hit the floor, dragging my pony along.

Darkness envelops me, as swift as the twilight in mid-winter, when the day turns to night in the blink of an eye. I gag as the putrid stench of eggs, gone rotten under a blistering sun, pervades the air.

A fierce hiss roars between the walls, and a burning breath scorches my cheeks. I heave and look up. My mind falters for a moment as my eyes take in the vision in front of me; every part of me halts while my thoughts are catching up. There, in the same place where Uncle just stood, the crude scaled body of a massive cobra rises, rearing its monstrous head.

Looped in a luminous green, the ferocious viper pulsates a bone-chilling hiss, piercing my eardrums with the most harrowing growl. Its forked tongue slithers between shimmering white fangs, and in his elliptical eyes resides a living, amber-streaked marble. His colossal head sways in hypnosis above me—left, right, left, right. He's ready to strike.

My blood thunders through my veins. This can't be. I've never seen anything like this before. My mind tumbles, my fingers claw into the fodder. My eyes rattle around, looking for Uncle. He's gone, and I have nowhere to go.

I blink, trying to make sense of my vision. This monster, so grotesque—for sure, it can't be real. My hand hauls a fist full of hay. I've got to get a grip on my thought. It's an illusion, an obscuration of the mind. *Only a trained mind can overcome the obstacles on the path.* I swallow hard as Dechen's words ring in my ears. *Focus.*

I draw a sharp breath and let the rancid reek of decay and death blaze through my nostrils. The biting burn soars through me, shuddering me to the core, and clearing the daze from my mind. *Focus.* My fingers twist the cord my sisters tied on my wrist. They are here to remind me. Stay on the Buddhist path, and there is nothing to fear. *Focus.* Stay on the path. The thread twists again, and Tara's mantra flows from my lips. *Oṃ tāre tu tāre ture soha.* I call upon the mother of all Buddha's with all my being, all that is in the inside of me. *Om Tare, please lift the veil of this dreaded delusion, for I have nowhere to hide.*

A ferocious green blazes from above and blinds my being. My body stretches in the flurry of forage. My nails scratch the earth-beaten floor. Once again I call upon Tara; the only one who can help me now. *Please lift the veil, for I have nothing to fear.*

The stable doors bang, splinters fly, and a sudden gust of air rushes through. I throw my arms over my head as hay, fodder, and dust plummet down. Time stands still—or so it feels—and a thundering silence slashes through me. All becomes weightless, airless, and breathless. The pressure sears through my chest, ripping my lungs from my ribcage. I fling my head up and a startling lightning crashes from the darkness above. The sky tears open into an infinite, piercing yonder. A thunder-clap follows, and a fuming column of festering ashen and gravel coils down, swallowing the cobra with a blood-curling shriek in the bright void of blazing blue.

It's gone. Dust settles around me. My eyes stare in bewilderment at the beams, at the ceiling. My mind baffles, for there is nothing, not even a trace left. The silence is deafening. I rub my eyes and scurry up. My pony's squeezed into the corner, his ears flat on his head. It was not my imagination—the poor thing saw something too.

The barn doors wide open, the stable shows a proper mess. Hay prickles all over. I shake the chaff from my robe. Something happened here, for my pony's still riddled with dread. My knees still tremble. It wasn't only my imagination, it wasn't only in my mind. And where's Uncle gone to? His vile glare still glooms all around.

"Come on, boy." I shiver and lead my pony out of the barn into the pallid light of a weak afternoon sun. Something's wrong here. Dechen, Dolma, and even Father—I should have listened to them.

My heart quivers.

I shouldn't have come.

Thirteen

S angmo waves from the courtyard with a smile that lightens up the dim and overcast end of the day.

"See you found your little friend." She ruffles my pony's mane. "I bet it was quite a rascal in its younger years."

I manage a brittle laugh. "Yeah." My voice wavers as I glance at the barn once more. Better not tell Sangmo or anybody else. They might think I've gone mad.

"You good?" She frowns and slips a bridle on the pony. "You look like you're about to run off, you little devil." He neighs as if he knows she's onto him. My hand glides over his neck. This little one still steals my heart.

"I just met Uncle." I clear my throat. "And I think something's off." My feet shuffle in the gravel and my mind sways. Maybe I should tell her?

"Oh, for sure if he's anything like his sons." Sangmo's eyes narrow. "I tell you, they're definitely off." With a resolute tug she ties my pony to the tree. "I just saw them training a horse." Her tone deepens. "No good. Pure abuse."

Abuse? "What do you mean?" I frown. "There's no abuse around the horses here."

Father would never allow that. He's always had the gentlest of hand. Sturdy, yes, but abuse? No way. Sangmo sucks in her cheeks. Something in that paddock has upset her, something that's not good. A sudden worry rumbles through my insides. I've got to get to the pen. Right now.

"Did they see you?" I'm ready to run over, but my feet stall, deliberating what to do.

"Nope." Sangmo put her hands on her hips. "But I came very close to jumping in." She wrinkles her nose.

"Let's go." My heels turn and I stride off. "I've got to see for myself."

The paddock, like the formal room, was a no-go area for me as a child. Here the horses are trained from their first walk with a bridle to the saddle. Only on Father's hand could I go in. Otherwise, I'd stand peeping between the beams with my faithful friend on my side.

"Wait." Sangmo's futile cry gets lost on me, as something urges me to the pen. I'm running as fast as my robes allow me to. There it is, the pen. Sangmo is right—it's not good.

A black stallion, drenched in sweat, stomps his hooves in fury. Eyes fevered, nostrils snorting wide, he spins around, trembling with fear. A rope around two of his legs restrains the horse from galloping, bucking, of any natural movement, making him limp, tied to the ground. A lanky young man stands wide-legged, watching with a whip dangling at his side. Two other youngsters hang over the fence, hollering their amused cries at him.

Crack! Sand flies up and the stallion balks at the blow. The men hoot, the horse brays in ire. His anguished look soars through the hallows of my heart. I recoil as his pain packs its punches right into my stomach. My mind bolts with a blinding rage. Tying up a horse's legs and using a whip? I don't think so! I duck under the beams and shoot into the paddock.

"Are you mad?" I jerk the whip out of the man's hand and heave. The man staggers back. The lash lands with a fling at his feet.

"What the...?" He grows as his eyes set on me. A rough glance and surprised recognition follow. "Well, well, if that isn't our cousin, the nun." He throws a nasty smirk at me and sets his hands on his narrow hips. "Or should I say the great horse master to-be?" His flinty eyes size me up from head to toe. "You've got some nerve coming into my paddock." He turns to the pair hanging over the beam and makes a vile face. The three of them holler.

"Your paddock?" My arms cross my chest. These must be my cousins, the ones that will take over the stables. Rage roars through my limbs. These bullies, they are to continue Father's legacy? This can't be happening. No way!

I blink at the man in front of me, my eyes set on the whip at his feet. This man's a brute, nothing like Father at all. Father has a gentle hand, forging a genuine bond with his horses. This guy's a bully, torturing horses into submission. My fists clench. Father would never have that; it goes against everything he stands for.

"Your paddock?" I meet his harsh gaze.

"Yes, my paddock." He purses his lips, and his spit lands right in front of my feet. "Don't you know horses are meant to be broken?" He rolls back his shoulders. "Some horse master you are." He bares his teeth. "You're just a woman—there's no place for you here." He turns to his companions and his boots kick up dust. "And if you weren't a nun, I would have my way with you right now, eh boys!" The cousins snicker as their brother hops over the beams. "Let's go before she cries for her papa."

And off they go, their crude laughter trailing behind them. My hands tremble and cold sweat prickles my neck. My sleeve swipes at my forehead. What just happened here?

The horse. I turn around. Sangmo's already over at the stallion, calming him down. She's good like that—she has the same confident manner as Father. She unties his legs, and the horse shudders, taking a leap on all fours.

"He needs water." Sangmo walks the weary stallion over to the courtyard. I pick up the whip and stagger behind her, as shaken as the horse.

"You amaze me." She slaps my back as the horse quenches his thirst. "Yesterday you were afraid to ride a tame mare, and now you are jumping in the paddock with a cracking whip, a crazy cousin, and a wild stallion."

Her laughter eases my tension. My hands steady and I roll my head in my neck.

"I wonder what you're up to next." She giggles, and I rub my eyes. I don't know either. Unease sets where the tension has left, hurling itself deep inside of me. A tingle shoots through my spine.

"Time for tea." Sangmo ties up the horse and walks me over to the main house. The kitchen's deserted. Looks like Uncle and his sons have their quarters at another part of the stables. Good.

Sangmo fires up the smoldering stove with a sturdy log. I open the tea box and I glance around. The plush seats lined up around the stove, the low, maroon lacquered tables around the wall, the stacks of polished bowls set on the wooden shelves, everything's still in place, just as Mother left it. The kitchen truly was the heart of our home where the three of us started our day with tsampa and piping hot tea—my father's favorite—and ended the day with a wholesome thenthuk, the dish my mother made so well. We even spent most of our nights here, huddled around the stove, especially in wintertime when the snow was mighty high. Yes, all the things are still there, but the place I used to know is missing. Where's the laughter and joy that bounced from these walls? Where's the warmth, the affection, the deep love that bound us together? A lonesome blue seeps through the windows, and the simmering stove muffles a jaded hiss. I blink. My eyes don't deceive me. How empty this kitchen.

The tea releases her earthy aroma as I crumble it into the boiling pot. The highest quality tea, as it has always been.

Sangmo hands me a washcloth. I press it to my sweaty face. The comfort of the coarse fabric on my cheeks, its warmth spreading to my limbs calms me down, but won't wipe away the restlessness that dwells in my mind. What a day. First seeing Father after so long, then meeting Uncle and these cousins of mine. The heavy thump of leather boots approaches in the hallway and I halt my thoughts.

"I heard you made quite a spectacle of yourself." Father dooms on the threshold of the kitchen with his tone of voice so rough it makes me flinch.

A spectacle? I feel the blood drain out of my face. My eyes narrow. There he stands, my father, feet wide apart. The cloth drops, and anger rises from the very bottom of my being.

"A spectacle?" I shriek. "A spectacle?" In an instant, I dunk and scoop the whip from the floor.

"Nordun!" Sangmo raises her hands. It's too late. The leather lash lands with a crack at Father's feet.

"You should have seen the spectacle in the pen." Tears scorch around my eyes. "Your paddock, your horse, and a whip?" My hands fly up in the air. "And tied up legs?" My words thunder down, and a violent storm breaches between us. "What has become of this place? What happened to you, Father?" My voice breaks. "You used to have such a gentle hand." My rage reverses to a profound sadness as the desolate image of my father, a frail old man suddenly standing speechless, blurs before me.

"A whip." I whisper now. "That's not you, and I remember you well." I search for Father, for a glimpse of understanding in his eyes. "You taught me to respect the wild nature of the horses, admire their strength and grace, not beat it down."

His face, before faded into a paled ashen, now turns a crimson red. His lips pinch, his wide jaw sets. Not a word comes from his mouth.

"You never tied their legs, for you trusted yourself and the horses to bond, to establish a relationship based on mutual respect." I swallow. "What happened to that trust, Father? What happened to you, hurting the ones you hold so dear?"

The glare in his eyes harbors a harrowing distance. There's not a trace of recognition from the father I once knew.

My heart sinks and I hang my head. I give up, making no attempt to wipe the tears dripping down my face. With a sob, I turn away. *I've lost it.* My face flushes with the shade of shame, and my hands press against my burning cheeks. I've lost my calm in front of Father. Deep sadness mingles with profound regret. This is not how I want to act. This is not who I want to be.

"You better leave tomorrow." Father's voice rumbles from afar.

I turn and face him, for I know that behind his hard-boiled facade hides a loving man, a father who once cared for his daughter, his little girl. He's had years of loneliness and grief, years to forge his armor, years to raise the highest of walls around his broken heart. My eyes search for it, for a crack in that wall, for the tiniest tear in his hardened shell. But there's nothing. Not a glimmer of the dimmest light shining through. My mind suspends in those empty eyes. Lost. He's lost to me and most of all, he's lost to himself.

"Go home, Nordun." He lowers his gaze and turns his back on me. "You already got what you came for." With his shoulders hunched, he barges out.

Home. My knees buckle and I sink down at the stove. With the cloth before my eyes, I bury my face in the heat of shame, hurt, and regret. This is not what I wanted, not for Father, and not for me. I've caused nothing but pain and embarrassment. He's right. I got what I wanted. I'll go home tomorrow, home to my sisters and my grandmother.

She was right. I shouldn't have come.

Fourteen

"Enough?" I toss a few blankets on the bed, making sure we stay warm tonight. Sangmo and I sleep in my old room tonight—the room Father expelled me to after Mother died. Or at least, that's what it had felt like to me. I used to sleep with Mother in the kitchen or all three of us slept in my parents' bed. Warm, cozy. But after Mother's passing, Father had a bed made for me alone, and put it in this room.

Sangmo rearranges the blankets. The room fits only one bed. A single window looks out at the old barn. My hands slide along the ledge, and my thoughts drift out to the night sky. Hard to believe I actually fit through this tiny window once. My gateway to freedom. I snuck out many times, mostly at night, to find solace with my pony. Father must have known. The way he picked the hay out of my hair in the morning. He never mentioned it, but the sorrow in his eyes said enough.

I make my prostrations and remove my outer robe. Sangmo sits on the edge of the bed, braiding her long locks.

"I'm sorry things got so awkward today." I slip under the blanket.

"Awkward?" Sangmo smiles and swings the braid over her shoulder. "I guess life at the monastery is more serene." She squeezes herself cross-legged beside me.

"I don't fit in here." Time to get honest with myself. I roll onto my side, one hand under my head.

"Well, you didn't look for a place here, did you?" Sangmo tips her head to the side. "You're taking full vows." She fishes a peach from her pocket.

"Even if I wasn't a nun, I wouldn't know how to fit in here," I say. "Especially as a woman." I sigh. My fingers fumble with a strand of loose hair.

"Oh, from what I've seen today, you're doing just fine." She sinks her teeth into the peach with a vengeance. "The way you dove into the pen." She chuckles, and a trickle of juicy pink drips down her chin.

"You're different." I say. "You're confident, sure of yourself." I look at Sangmo, it's in her bold smile, her fearless eyes. "You're capable of doing anything, going anywhere."

She loosens her belt and her skirt slips to the floor.

"Ah, it's in my blood." Her lips smack and she stretches her legs. "It's all about walking the thin line between what's allowed and what's not, in the family, and out here." She wriggles her toes and turns to me. "And sometimes I step over that line—a little—to see how far I can go." Her teeth scrape the bare pit. Her eyes flash into a mischievous smile.

"Hmmm." My mind mulls over her words. Not that different from my life at the monastery, really. Only those rules I am familiar with. Set by the most precious Teacher, and explained by Dechen, I hold these dear to my heart. They help me become a better practitioner, a better person. But the rules out here? I don't have a clue.

"It works for me." Sangmo shrugs. "For now, at least." She points her feet. "I guess I'll be married off someday, and then it's a whole different game." Her arms stretch above her head, and she lets out an enormous yawn.

"And you're fine with that?" I lean back. Sangmo and marriage? I'm not so sure.

"We'll see. We never know what our karma is." Sangmo rubs her arms. "My hunting and horse-riding days could be over any time when the family wishes." She pauses and sucks in her cheeks. "But then again, maybe I'll marry a kind man, one who allows me my little pleasures." She shrugs. "In the end it's not for me to decide, so why worry about it?" She slips next to me.

I lift my face to catch a glimpse of the heavens spreading their velvety drapes outside my tiny window. All is calm, with a swollen moon amidst an infinite twinkle of stars.

Sangmo's asleep in no time, but her remarks about marriage keep churning in my mind. Obedience to a husband, hoping he might be kind. I shiver and pull the blanket tight. That's how things are for women. That's how things have always been, and it always feels wrong.

Sure, it's karma, being born in a woman's body, a lesser, weaker body, I have no doubt about that. It requires great willpower to achieve anything as a woman, but it's not impossible. Dechen told me so. With diligence and determination, women can be excellent Buddhist practitioners, just like men. And there're plenty of outstanding examples to prove it.

My fingers rub the knot my sisters tied on my wrist and my thoughts go back to the day Dechen told us the story of Tara, our savioress, a long time ago. The twins had already heard it a million times, but wanted to hear it again. They loved to deliver their comments, or rather "discuss the possibilities of other views," as Tsomo put it so well, so Dechen spoke once again.

Of how Tara was born as a princess in a mighty palace, but showed no interest in worldly matters. Instead, she devoted herself to the Buddha and his teachings. She practiced with diligence, and developed a deep compassion that impressed the monks at the temple nearby. They told her they would pray she be reborn as a man, so she could be a proper teacher, and spread the Buddha's words.

"The fools!" Pema had thrown up her hands in a dismissive gesture, and Tsomo had shaken her head. I was glued to Dechen's lips, wanting to hear more.

So, the princess thanked the monks and informed them that there was no distinction between the male and the female, for nothing existed in reality. Therefore, she wished to remain in female form to serve all the sentient beings.

"And right she was!" Tsomo added, as her perpetual frown lifted at a moment, every time again. Me? I could only laugh, for what did I know? My sisters were far more accomplished, even then, and all I wanted was to hear the end of the story, how Tara came to be.

Now, because of her excellent practice, the princess generated the pure selfless mind. She wanted all beings to be happy and be free of suffering. She even rejected the idea of complete enlightenment and joining all Buddhas in nirvana. No, the noble princess vowed to keep her feminine form and work for the benefit of all beings right here in samsara. And so she became Tara, the savioress of all.

When Dechen first told the story, I could not believe my ears. This courageous princess, how good, how selfless she wished to stay in this wretched, worldly existence. And how brave to do this as a woman? Right there and then, my deepest wishes surfaced from my young and tender heart. This was what I want too. To live my life for the benefit of all sentient beings, just like Tara. And Dechen told me I could!

"You're still young, my child." Her hands cradled my face, and she looked me straight in my eyes. "But I want you to understand that there is no difference between a man and a woman, for our body is only form." Her eyes flashed the most golden of amber, and pure love shone through. "The difference exists only in our foolish mind. With time, practice, and willpower, you will come to see for sure that there's nothing a woman can't achieve." Her hand stroked my cheek.

"And with the purest intention, you too can help sentient beings, just like Tara."

I toss and turn; my intention is good, if only I could be diligent in my practice. My eyes prick and I wipe my nose. If only I could save a few sentient beings suffering here in samsara, only now. Like the tormented stallion in the paddock this afternoon. My stomach turns as I think of all the other horses in the stables, too. The poor creatures. How they must endure the same cruel fate at the hands of my cousins.

And Father. How he lets his heart be hostage to his grief, forcing him to back away from love and embrace the utter despair. My body folds. The sorrow is too much for me right now, and I shudder. *Oṃ Tare.* How I wish I could help him, too.

Oh, come on, I can hardly save myself. And the shameful way I acted towards my father only this afternoon. I curl my body into the night and pray for sleep to come until the morning breaks.

Oṃ Tare. Tomorrow I'll go home.

Fifteen

Blood! A scream awakens me, submerging from the deep. I jolt up, panting for air. Beads of cold sweat lash down my temples. *The dream.* It came back to haunt me. This time, even worse. No brightly colored mares or dancing dakinis, no laughter up in the sky. Instead, there're black stallions and blood—so much blood pouring down on me. Surely I'll drown.

I press my forehead to my knees. Nausea takes over. *Fresh air.* My feet find the edge of the bed, sliding onto the hard-wooden floor. My hands reach the window, and I rest my chin on the ledge. A cool breeze caresses my cheeks, creeping into my nostrils. *Focus.* I set my eyes on the crystal-clear sky that holds a bright yellow moon in an embrace of black and midnight blue. *Focus.* My lungs tingle as the crisp air works its wonders, and the rush of anxiety ebbs away. I've made it once again.

So much blood. I close my eyes as the dream fades to the distance, but I can still see myself standing there. It was at the base of these very mountains, with a herd of wild stallions galloping by. Their brays high, clouds of silver streamed from their vigorous breath—or at least, so I thought. As they came closer, their pearly gray spray darkened into a coral and crimson. Blood gushing from their mouths. Blood coiling in thick trails from their widened nostrils, like serpents crawling their course down, down at my feet.

Blood splattered its raging heat against my ankles, and the horses soared further and further away. A terrible fear invaded my body, and a mute scream arose in my throat. I tried to move, wading through, but the blood kept on gushing, sucking me into the ground. And as the last stallion disappeared in the blue yonder, the earth opened up in a terrifying roar. An infinite abyss beneath my feet stared right at me, and I crashed into an eternity of nothingness, never finding my solid ground again.

I made it. Ache throbs a dull reminder in my temples. For sure, it's the suffering stallion in the paddock this afternoon that triggered this nightmare. I know little about training horses, but that was pure torture. I roll my neck. A sigh soars from my chest. So much pain in this place. A desperate hollow fills my lungs. What to do?

My eyes settle on the string, my sisters' reminder to keep faith with boundless compassion and discerning wisdom, no matter what. The bright red blurs. Have I ever cried as much as these last days? I rub my eyelids. My sisters would know what to do. They have unwavering confidence. Why can't I have more faith, even in me?

Prayer and meditation—that will clear the turmoil in my restless mind. It always does. I reach for my outer robe.

A slight snore escapes from under the blanket. Sangmo won't wake from my stumbling around. I tiptoe out of the room with everybody fast asleep.

First through the long, empty hallway. This house used to feel like a gentle hug, a grounding embrace. Now it's a chilling encounter. I pull my scarf up as I sneak up to the second floor. My feet avoid the first step up on the landing; it creaks—my body still remembers.

I halt at the threshold as I scout in the moonlight, shining bright and unambiguous. Fresh flowers in huge vases embrace the shrine in elegance. Zesty incense smolders in polished copper cups, and clear butter reflects in the flickering wicks set in a pair of hefty silver lamps. This room is in immaculate condition. I smile at my rising hope. Has Father finally found solace in the Buddhist teachings? He never showed much interest in the prayer room. It had always been my mother's delight.

Three prostrations. My fingertips glide over the maroon clothed books at the side. If only mother saw I'm able to read these books by now. I sink down on the small mat that used to be mine. My eyes close, the prayer beads a cool touch to my palm. *Oṃ tāre tu tāre ture soha.* My mind turns to Tara and a great calm descends. Silence fills my being. Yes, prayer and meditation are my refuge, again and again.

A tender glow pats my cheeks ever so lightly. It feels like a draft but warm, a comfort. Did I not close the door? I thought I did.

I open my eyes, and my gaze hazes. A cloud of green floats around. I squint and the mist deepens into a rich green, like the precious shade of imperial jade. And there, in the midst of it, the image of Green Tara emerges, like a splendid vision, right here in the room.

My body chills, my beads halt. *This can't be.* My eyes must betray me. This can't be the Mother of Liberation appearing. Not to me.

Beautiful jewels adorn her, and the most precious of silken drapes around her body as she sits on a moon disc, on top of a thousand-petaled lotus, a flower throne, pure and white. Her right hand stretches open to me, in a gesture of giving. Her left hand gestures the symbol of skillful means and wisdom as she joins her index finger and thumb in a circle. The stem of a blue utpala flower rests in both her hands. I blink again and rejoice in the image of Tara right here, in front of me.

She floats closer and I still hold my breath. She settles at arm-length from me. My head light, I lean back. My fingers dig into the rug and I steady myself. I must be dreaming. A melodious voice fills the room.

"You called me so I'm here." Like a song, it sings around and around.

My mouth opens, but I'm too stunned to react. It is Tara, and she's speaking—to me. *To me.* I heard the stories—Tara appearing to beings who call her in their time of need. But they're always the stories of advanced practitioners, not beginners with a faith as fragile as mine.

"Tara." A breath exhales from within me. My heart quivers, my thoughts scramble to understand.

"Yes, you called." Her voice speaks straight to my heart. "I'm here."

My hands search for my beads—I can't find them. Yes, I called with all of my heart.

"Why me?" I bow my head. "I know so little, and my practice is poor." My voice trails off, and I shake my head. *Why me?*

"Ah yes, your wisdom needs to ripen." Her gaze meets mine, and there is only love between us. "But your desire to help is strong enough to act. There's no need to wait."

A dreadful admiration holds within me, and I can only stare.

"For inside of you beats a wild, persistent, and most of all loving heart." She pours her words straight into my being, filling me with a honeylike warmth. "The genuine desire to help sentient beings, and that's what counts, Nordun. Wisdom will grow, but only if you act on your heart's desire right now."

My head spins. What is she talking about? Me, a loving heart? My eyes widen, and the prayer beads find their way into my sweaty palm.

"Only by acting will you get experience." The blue flower sways its petals in her hands. "And in time, with profound reflection, this will grow into the wisdom you crave."

My mouth opens again, but closes without words. I have nothing sensible to say.

"Don't sit around waiting, woman." Her voice becomes stern. "You have everything you need and more. You've had more study and guidance than most women and men ever will."

Her eyes burn within me, and my mind fevers. What is she talking about? I still can't believe.

"It is good to be serious about study and meditation." Her image expands as she continues to speak. "But remember that practice is taking action in the world." Her vision fills up the space in front of me. "You can help all sentient beings right now, Nordun. Nothing's stopping you, for male or female, monastic or lay person, it's only form, and nothing exists, nothing is real."

My shoulders drop. A flush appears on my face.

"No more excuses—you are ready to do whatever is needed." Her gaze and voice pierce right through me. "Act from your heart, with the purest intention."

I swallow hard. Act from my heart? But my heart holds no courage, it only wants to run and hide.

"But..." My mouth opens, and again there's no need to speak, for I already know what to do—the right intention will help me act in the right way.

"Yes, you see." Her rich jade glow loses its luster. "Act from a pure heart, and all good things will be done."

I lean forwards. *Don't go!* She vanishes in front of me as my whole being begs her to stay.

"Be aware, for this human lifetime is fleeting." The brilliant hue evaporates into thin slivers of frosted green. "Act from your heart and act swiftly."

Act from the heart and act swiftly. I shudder. *Om Tare.*

What did I set in motion with my foolish desire? *Om Tare.*

What is happening to me?

Sixteen

The golden morning sun hits the window ledge. Her warming beams stroke the top of my head. I squint, and my eyelashes tickle my cheeks. I take a moment to realize I'm in my old room. I stretch my lazy limbs and rub the remains of a deep sleep from my eyes. A flimsy fog lifts with reluctance. My old room. I roll my neck back and forth, and my jaws release a huge yawn. Stiffness has crept itself to my bones. Two days in the saddle, only to return today.

Something's stirring in my being. A disquieting, ever so still. Must be sleep that hasn't left yet. Sweat pricks down my collar. *Too hot.* I shove the woolen blanket aside. Prayer first, for a good start of the day, and a fortunate journey returning home.

Where's my robe? I toss the blanket. No robe to be seen. Maybe Sangmo has taken it out to air? It's quite dirty after all the riding. I tuck a few loose strands back in my braids. My fingertips brush the collar of my shirt. *Huh?* I rest my hand on the collar, glancing down. *My robe.* I'm already dressed.

Tara. A green apparition floats through my thoughts, passing in a slow motion. I shake my head. I must have been dreaming.

My hands smoothen the coarse crumpled fabric. *Act from your heart.* Tara's melodious voice echoes from the walls. *Act swiftly.* The sweat in my neck turns to a chill, and a quiver runs down my spine. I'm dressed. I wasn't dreaming.

For a moment, the sun touches me, and everything in the room is in suspension. All turns a crystal clear. Flimsy particles of dust drift on golden rays. The grainy fabric of my shirt grazes my neck. A thin veil of perspiration forms on my face. The faint clatter of hasty hooves resounds from outside. A door creaks at the far end of the house. The world's on-hold while my mind has to come to terms with last night—Tara appeared, and she spoke. *To me.*

A sudden knock rattles on the door. "Nordun, your father awaits you." I veer up at the tone of Ghedun's voice, strong and determined, and Tara's words settle down, finding its home into the tender hollows of my heart.

I slide off the bed and sprint to open the door. Ghedun's outside, his back stooped, his hands clasp a cane. The long ride has taken its toll.

"Sorry Gen-la." I rush back into the room. "I just need a moment." I fold the blanket on the bed and wipe the sweat off my forehead.

"You didn't sleep well?" He swings his cane forward and steps closer, a worry crossing his face.

My cheeks flush. I must be a mess. My hands straighten my robe. This has to do; I can't let him wait. My eyes rest on his stick. The fingers clawed, the joints swollen, my heart aches for the elderly monk.

"Sorry Gen-la." My voice wavers. "I made you come all the way here—for nothing." I bow my head at my foolish, selfish deeds.

"Oh, Nordun." His voice calm, his twisted hands wrestle the stick. "Nobody made me, I offered myself. When Dechen told me, I thought it would be good for you and your father to meet." He leans forward on his cane.

"But I've brought nothing but heartache to Father." I stare at my bare toes. I've brought nothing but hurt and anger. For what? "My behavior's been selfish, and it has done nobody any good." I glance up.

He still stands there, unmoving.

"Now, now, my child." A sulk sets on his forehead. I know that one. He's not letting me off the hook.

"Don't be foolish. Much good has come from your journey." His words are kind, but there's a sternness in his tone that he's not trying to hide. "You met your grandfather's kin, and they finally made peace with it all. And yes, you need to talk to your father—for what happened between the two of you must be mended, and there's still time."

I hang my head, my hands clasp together. Ghedun's right, as usual. How wise he is. Meeting Grandfather's side of the family has been good, especially getting to know Sangmo. My spirits lift. This hasn't been all bad.

"You're finally experiencing life outside the monastery." Ghedun puts his full weight on the cane. "And to me, that has always been the best practice there is." A thoughtful smile crosses between us. "This is how we make progress on the path, Nordun. Sometimes through opportunity, sometimes through challenge." My toes curl, as if they want to dig in the wood. Yes, challenging is has been, that's for sure.

He lifts his cane and lets it land with a little thump back on the timber. "Now you know what challenges, what obscurations your mind holds. If you go back, your practice will be much more focused, much richer."

If. My mind stumbles. Gen-la said "If." My hands unfold and I straighten the sleeves of my shirt. For sure, there's no if. I'm returning to the monastery. Today.

"Your father is waiting." Ghedun shifts his weight from the cane and turns.

"Yes, Gen-la." My ribs tighten. *Father.* It's time. My feet drag behind Ghedun as we walk down the hall. How can I face Father after that disgraceful outburst from yesterday?

"You know what to do." Ghedun nods as we reach the kitchen. He walks away. My hands grip the doorpost. Why doesn't he stay?

No tea on the stove, only a stale whiff in the air. It's dead quiet in this deserted kitchen. The weight of sadness presses down into my chest. My eyes search for Father, my mind for the memory of what once was. This kitchen, once the lively heart of the house. *There're only shadows where men used to be.*

He's in the furthest corner. A chuba wrapped around his once muscular frame, he sits unmoving, his head resting against the wall.

"Nordun." His flat voice reaches me. His hand gestures for me to sit.

"Father." I lower myself on the opposite seat. The dusk lights the lines on his face, forever etched by despair. He puts up his hand.

"This is not how I wanted us to meet." He leans forward. His hands draw on the low table between us. "I didn't mean to." He pauses and his hand rubs his forehead. "The way you reacted yesterday, with the horse."

I cringe, as I recall my obstinate disrespect. My head bows, and I wait for his reprimand to come crashing down. I wait long, and I wait in vain. There's nothing but a somber silence.

"Nordun, you are so much like your mother," he finally says, and I come up for air. "Her spirited nature, her deep love for the horse, I see her in you, and it's so clear." A distant melancholy has taken his eyes. "The memory of her... I'm so sorry, my child, it all got to me as you came back to here." His voice chokes, and his hands grip the side of the table.

That's it. I shift back in my seat. *The memory of Mother.* That is it.

"So that's why you sent me away." I sound as small as I was way back then. "Because I remind you of Mother too much." A wistful calm comes over me. All those years, I wondered. Was

I too wild, too obstinate? Was I too much? Now I know—I wasn't too much. Her memory was.

"No, no, my child!" Panic floods Father's face. A pained expression meets my gaze. "How can you think that of me?" His hands reach over the table. "I brought you to your grandmother because you needed a safe place, a secure home to grow up in." He clears his throat, and red rims his eyes. "After your mother's passing, it was difficult—she was the heart of our family and with losing her, I lost myself." The muscles in his jaw tighten, a gloom glances his eyes. "But you, you were my little one, the only thing that was left to me. I needed to protect you, get you away from the horses." His voice pitches. "I needed to keep you safe."

My mouth turns dry. Keep me safe? Blood rushes to my head. From horses? What does he mean?

"But Mother drowned," I hear myself say. She'd been bathing in the river and slipped. She must have hit her head on a boulder. It was an accident. That's what I was told.

"Yes, she drowned." Father stoops. "She drowned because of the horse she rode on that dreadful day." His eyes close. His head drops in his hands. "We found her lifeless body washed up on the banks of the river. Nobody saw, but the horse must have leaped into the water, trampling her as she fell off." His hands run over his ashen face, his eyes aloof, like a ghost. "I told her not to ride alone that day, not on that horse." The lines in his face deepen. His hands clasp in a powerless fist.

I think I hear what he's saying, but I don't understand. Mother died because of a horse? *That can't be.*

"Horses are wild creatures, unpredictable, no matter how well trained." Father's sorrow looks upon me. "And you, my little one, you loved horses and riding more than anything in this world." His hands form a steeple. "I know it makes little sense to you, but I had to protect you, get you away from here." He rests his chin on his folded hand. "And yes, I needed to preserve the very last, the most precious piece I had left of my love."

My gaze blurs. My thoughts swirl so fast I can hardly follow. *My mother was killed by a horse.* Father wanted to keep me safe. Sending me from here had been the most sensible thing to him, and the monastery had been the safest place he knew. My senses fail me. Father's words have knocked the wind out of me. A saddened stillness wraps around us.

All those years I thought he didn't love me, that he had become maddened with grief. How mistaken I was, judging Father like that. Tears burn their way through my eyelids, streaking my cheeks with their heated confusion. I was wrong, but then again, he abandoned me, his only child, when I needed him most. I was tiny, with a heart shattered into a thousand pieces. And he never even came to visit me. Not even once.

Focus. The blur fades. Father did what he thought was right. Still, he should have known. The bitter taste of blame engulfs my mouth. He's my father. He should have known. I swallow hard but relentless remains of resentment keep seeping back up my throat. I take a deep breath. *No use.*

"I'm sorry I doubted your love for me," I say, and I mean it. What else is there to say? No need to go into accusations, no need to drag up our past pain—not now.

"It's all my fault." Father tries to catch my gaze, but I can't face him. "I didn't know how to explain—you were so young—and later, I just got lost in here." His fingers tap his temples. "Fortunately, my brother and his sons came to the rescue."

I shoot up straight. *His brother?* "Really?" Uncle and those bullies. It can't be.

"They're doing an outstanding job." He waves his hand. "The stables are in excellent condition, and the trade is booming." His chin points over at the window.

"Sure, all looks great from the outside, but at what price?" I grip the table. "Their ways are brutal—it goes against everything you stand for." My body tenses. A fierce headache sets in.

"Sorry, Nordun." Father sounds far away. "I've had my chance for a successor, but alas, my karma changed." He turns and rests his hands next to mine. "My unborn son—your brother—passed with your mother."

My heart takes a dive and tries to find a way out of my ribcage. *A brother?*

"Mother was with child?" My hands find Father's. "I'm so sorry."

"Your mother was convinced it was a boy," Father says with eerie calm. "She was right." A slight smile breaks on his lips. "Your mother was always right, you know?" His large hands envelop mine. "She told me early on you would be a handful—and look at us now."

Our eyes lock and my heart soars through mid-air. I clutch his hands and look straight into his immense ocean of sorrow, and keep staring in the depth of him. There, amid all the despair, a tiny flicker surfaces, a glimmer of hope is shining through. All those years of mourning, of remorse, of regret—and he still can't find his way, his words to express. My smile meets his. This is enough for me, at least for now.

"I guess the monastery didn't do me any good, then?" My smile turns into a grin, and my being delights in this very moment.

"Ah, don't say that," he's quick to reply. "You're an educated woman now." Pride graces his face.

"Well, that sure doesn't show." I flinch. "Lashing out to my father like that." My embarrassment is seeking a way out through my cheeks. "I couldn't control myself, not when I saw the suffering of a beautiful, innocent being." My breath shallows. "I truly felt its anguish." My hands draw to the flat bone of my chest. "I smelt its fear, its agony slicing right through my being." I take a sharp breath. *Focus.* No need to lose myself again.

"You've always been close to horses." Father smiles. "Not only to that ugly thing there in the stables." He points towards the barn.

My pony. Yes, he was everything to me back then.

"It looks great." My fingers fumble with the edge of my sleeves. I get it. Father's avoiding the matter of Uncle and the succession of the stables. Yet, he brought up my love for horses. My pulse speeds up. I can't let this go.

"So, there's no other option for the succession of the stables?" I steal a glance his way. "I mean, Uncle, his sons, they are brutes. You must have seen it." I wiggle in my seat. "You can't let them have their nasty ways." I bite my lip. A fast beat rushes the blood through my veins.

"You're talking about the prophecy." Father's face vanishes behind a staunch mask I can't read. "Who told you?" He leans back, and my head is about to explode.

"Dolma." I hesitate. "You believe it might be?" An unexpected exhale spills from my chest. Not that I would ever would. For sure, the conversation with Sangmo last night that stirred this in my mind. For sure, I never would.

"Don't even think about it." A shadow falls over his firm facade. "There're no women being horse masters. Never have been, never will be." His eyebrows pull close. His huge hand rubs the back of his neck.

"So the divination was false?" Now I'm the one trying to catch his gaze, for his words didn't convince me.

"It has to be." His restless stare settles over my shoulder. "Though the ngakpa was very sure."

The ngakpa. I know him. He lives in the village nearby. Father and I visited him once for divination. It was the day before we rode out.

"But let me tell you, your mother, she was great at training horses." Little cracks show through his toughened disguise.

"With such grace and ease." He lifts his chin. "I'll tell you that."
He leans in, and a fierce pride ignites in his eyes.

"You come from a fine line of strong women, my child." The
last trace of his toughened cover crumbles as he dares to admit.
"I wouldn't be surprised if the ngakpa was right."

A lightness breaks in my chest as father's face glows with
genuine love, as he remembers her, without the pain, without
the despair. This is him, this is the father I remember. *He's deep
down there, but it's him.*

"Still, my child, I can't let you." His voice raw, he reaches for
my hand. "I already lost your mother; I can't bear losing you
too." His strong fingers grip mine with a startling desperation.

But you already lost me, for you put me away. The voice in
my head is feeble, but the words thunder through my mind.
Focus! I blink as blame and shame mingle; these thoughts, let
them pass. They're not mine. I hang my head for I recognize,
deep down inside, I still hang onto the sour resentment of that
lonely girl, abandoned with a broken heart, the little girl I once
was.

Father's hands squeeze mine tight. What's left for us now?

"I understand, but..." I pause as one of the stable boys rushes
in.

"Palden-la." He gulps as he's out of breath. "You are
requested in the paddock."

With a grumble Father gets up. "I'll be right back." The
heavy thud of his boots fades in the hallway. I rest my head
against the wall.

A fine line of strong women. A deep breath eases the tension
that has locked in my neck. Yes, I do come from a line of strong
women. Dechen's an excellent practitioner and a respected
abbess. My mother was brilliant here at the stables, with the
horses and the trade. My thoughts turn a corner against me.
An acquainted insecurity passes by.

And what about me? Where do I fit in this line of strong
women? I'm not the great practitioner I strive to be—not even

by far. I'm bouncing from fear to excitement and back. I'm all over the place since I left the monastery. I even lashed out at Father. And the dreams came back to haunt me, more frightful than before.

Act from the heart and act swiftly, Mother Tara was sure to encourage me, but here I am, feeling nothing but small, insignificant really. Let's face it, I spared the stallion a lashing from the whip yesterday, but the suffering here will go on after I'm gone. I shudder at the thought. If only I could. *Tara.* Was it really her?

A breeze of fresh air bursts through the kitchen, the tangy smell of fresh greens follows a panting breath. Sangmo dashes in.

"Uh, those cousins of yours are nasty pieces of work." She bolts from the doorway. "I watched them in the stables." Her nose wrinkles and her eyes narrow to the smallest of crescent moons. "Can't stand them, and I don't want to be around them." She crosses her arms and puts herself in front of me. "We either do something, or we leave right now."

I look at Sangmo, her bag slung around her shoulders. *Do something or we leave.* This girl makes no bones about what's on her mind, and she sure doesn't hesitate to act upon it. *Act swiftly.* Tara's words drum in my ears, spreading a feverish yet exciting warmth through my body. That's it! I veer up. *No more excuses.* This is my chance. It's my turn to show my strength.

"Then let's do something about it!" I hear myself say. *What? Yes!* A fierce roar of newfound courage ripples through me. It's my time now to be strong, to follow through on my deepest desire. It's my time to serve all sentient beings, to keep them from harm.

"That's the spirit." Sangmo's smile reaches from cheek to cheek. "But first tea, I'm parched, and hungry too." She plops on a seat.

I stumble up, dazed, stunned at my daring declaration. Do what? *What am I going to do?*

A cheery tune hums from the corridor. I peep around the corner. It's gen Ghedun, sneaking out of the hallway, swinging his cane in a rhythmical rap. The tips of my ears burn; for sure, he must have heard the whole conversation. I look again. No, I'm not mistaken. There's a mighty spring in the old monk's steps.

Seventeen

The nutty aroma of roasted barley fills the kitchen. I knead a little more tea in to make it firm—it's the finest tsampa, the best of tea. My palate delights as I lick my fingers. Yes, the food has always been nothing but the best quality here at the stables. At least these standards haven't degenerated.

The anxious stallion in the paddock sprints through my thoughts again. My stomach throws up a protest. Beads of sweat pearl on my upper lip.

"Any idea how we go about this?" I turn to Sangmo as she seizes up a fresh peach in her hand.

"Well, you claim the stables to get rid of these cousins of yours." Sangmo takes a juicy bite and wipes her mouth with her sleeve. "Since your father is still the current horse master, you marry a good man and let him make the claim." She pauses for a moment, smacking her lips. "Or..." She cocks her head to the side. "You can claim the position yourself as the first option is not available at the moment." With a wide grin, she swallows. "Right?" I clear my throat. *Marriage.* No, that's not what I had in mind.

"Yeah, well." My fingers crumble the tsampa. Somehow my appetite's nowhere to be found. "Some fine options I have." The first one is definitely out of the question. That leaves the second one... "I don't want to take the position myself."

Sango's eyebrows raise. "You wouldn't have to." She runs her tongue over her teeth. "You could revert the stables back to your father—he's more than capable, if you ask me. He just needs some help." She hauls the boiling tea over and pours me another cup.

"What do I need to do to claim the stables?" I take a slow sip and examine Sangmo over the rim of my cup. She knows these things.

"You'll have to bring back a wild horse, tamed." Father strides into the kitchen. I flinch. I never heard him coming.

"Father." I twist on my seat. "We just..." He raises his hands.

"I don't want to hear about it." He looks at me, his eyes carrying that dark gloom again. Sangmo hastens to pour him a fresh cup of tea.

"Here you are." She hands it to him with a pleasing smile. "Fresh bread is on its way." She dusts the flour off her skirt. "But please, Palden, why don't you tell us in the meantime—about how to go about bringing a wild horse and all." She glances at me. "I would love to know."

Sangmo! I can see what she's doing. Father can too. He doesn't seem to mind, though. He sits down, his shoulders hunched, and blows the steam off his cup.

"The new horse master—even if he was my son—can only claim the succession to the stables by bringing in fresh blood." He sounds weary, but I detect a tinge of intrigued attention in his tone. "A fresh stallion of the highest standards." His eyes dart over to Sangmo, who's pounding the flour with a vengeance. "Not by trade, but by catching it in the wild and working with it himself."

Sangmo raises her eyebrows. I shake my head in dismissal. A wild horse. No way.

"Ah, well." Sangmo sucks in her cheeks. "That's not impossible to do." Her eyebrows raise.

"Don't look at me." I frown. "I can't even control a tamed mare." Point made.

"It's not about control." Father's fingers draw along the rim of his cup. "On the contrary, it's all about mutual respect and trust." He chooses his words with care. "The horse is a force of nature to be reckoned with. It will always be stronger than us humans, as the horse draws its physical strength from its innate connection to its spirit." He raises his teacup to his lips and pauses. "It's about connecting with the wild nature of the horse and communicating respect." He takes a sip. A drop strays along his moustache. "Only then you're able to forge a bond and use that strength to mutual benefit. Respect the horse's wild nature and it will respect you." The dark dusk ebbs in his eyes, and a dawn draws in the glowing amber again. Father knows horses. A softness touches my heart. And the way he talks about them—that's the father I know.

"It's something few people understand." His face mellows, and his eyes won't leave me. "Fruitful relationships are based on mutual trust—you can't afford to spend your time and energy always looking over your shoulder." He puts down his cup. "But most of it is about recognizing your own nature and trusting yourself. If you don't know yourself, don't have confidence in yourself, how can you genuinely connect and trust the other? Animal or human alike." His eyes and his words, the sincerity of the man before me awes me. *To know and trust yourself.* How wonderful would that be?

"Yep." Sangmo, for once, puts on a serious face. "Animals sense it in an instant. We humans, however, are slow to catch on."

I lean back for a moment, letting their words sink in. I've got no experience with all this. Father and Sangmo—they understand the wild.

"Where did you get your horse at the time?" I pull myself upright.

"In the mountains up North," Father says and gulps down his tea. "But nowadays, they are not that easy to find."

Sangmo hurries over to pour him another one, swinging the kettle high.

"What it really comes down to is going up there and letting them find you." Father's head shows to the North. "They're up high, but it's coming to summer now. It's the best time to succeed."

Anxiety and anticipation swell within me, competing for a safe place within my chest. *The North*. Sangmo's eyes shine. I see what's she's thinking about.

"Now I've told you, so let it rest." Father's voice turns stern. "I mean it, both of you."

Sangmo peers into the flaming stove. I glance away.

"Yes, Father." In the corner of my eyes, I see Sangmo, and she's not even trying to hide her excitement. My stomach knots. *What am I going to do?*

"Good." Father squares his shoulders. A renewed zest has come over him. "All that talking, and still no breakfast." He waves his hand at Sangmo. "So where's that bread you promised me?" The ease is back in his voice. I jump out of my seat.

"Coming." I grab the butter. Sangmo piles up the fired bread.

"You know, gen Ghedun needs rest." Father's fingers tap the stack with approval. "Why don't you stay for the day?" His posture's upright, but his voice wavers a tad bit. "I've got some work this morning, but we could spend time together later on."

His eyes gleam that golden amber again and I let it stream in, warming the hollows of my heart.

"I would like that." I mean it. Besides, I could sure need a day off riding. I rub my legs. The aches have only worsened from all that sitting around.

"I've got some oil for that somewhere." Father laughs and butters a crust. "But it's better you ride it out over the next few days." I pull a loose tread from the hem of my sleeve.

"Just my thoughts, sister." Sangmo pinches my neck. "More practice in the saddle will do you good." She slides beside me. A few flat breads roll on the table. "Eat up, you'll need it."

By the look of her, she's already got our day planned.

I resign to buttering and chewing the bread while Sangmo and Father chat away—about horses, training and the trade, and hunting, of course. I only listen with half an ear. My stomach's settled, but my mind's churning over our conversation.

The sun's up high as Father leaves us, but not without warning us one more time.

"Don't let me hear anymore talk about claims and wild horses again," He sighs. "It's no use, Nordun." His eyes shoot over to Sangmo. "You too."

My fingers trace the crumbs on the table. Sangmo stacks the empty dishes and pinches her lips.

"Yes, Father." I hold my breath as he steps out into the hall.

The iron latch scrapes the wood frame, and Sangmo and I both leap from our seats.

"Well?" My heart pounds in my chest, like a frenzied animal rattling to get out.

"I'll come with you!" Sangmo claps her hands. "Where do we start?"

A rush of adrenaline shoots through my body. Nervousness, excitement—I don't know what I'm feeling at this moment. My emotions are bouncing all over the place.

"The ngakpa." I blurt out. "He did the divination at the time of my birth." I take a moment to catch my breath. "He can guide us, and he's near." My mind runs ahead. His house is the first one in the village, I think.

"Good." Sangmo's quick to clear the dishes. "Ready?"

I steady my trembling hands on the side of the table. A nervous laugh escapes from my throat. Sangmo must be joking. *Ready? Me?*

Will I ever be?

Eighteen

A blaring sun beams high in the sky, beating her blazing rays down our path as Sangmo and I walk to the edge of the village. So hot already, and summer is yet to arrive. First house on the left—I've been here before. Father took me before he brought me to Dechen. I didn't understand why we'd visited this strange Buddhist lama, who was not a monk, nor a layperson either. It was years later, when I studied Buddhist philosophy and its rituals, that I came to understand the ngakpa's role in it all.

The ngakpa's house is as I remember it—a white-washed enclosure, a myriad of colorful prayer flags fluttering from large poles at the entrance and a neatly kept courtyard. A tallish woman stands in the doorway.

"Nordun-la, so good to see you again." She steps out. "It's been a long time."

Do I know her? Beaded black eyes pry into a tawny face. Thin lips draw in a slender smile. Her raven hair is swept back in a glossy bun. I search, but my mind bears no memory of her.

She takes my hand and guides me in, her long nails scratching the back of my hand ever so slightly. "He's preparing. Please sit down." A charred stench lingers from the kettle on the stove. "Have some tea."

I fiddle with my prayer beads. Nerves have taken my stomach, leaving no room for more tea. Waiting has never been one of my strong points. Dechen was always fast to remark. A brief pang of regret stretches across my chest. *Dechen.* What would she say if she saw me sitting here, having a very different destination than home on my mind?

Sangmo rummages through the bag we brought. Some fresh fruit, a brick of tea and a ball of butter we snatched from the kitchen—offerings for the ngakpa. She catches my eye and throws me one of her swift, bold winks. My heart smiles and relaxes in my chest.

A bell rings, a drum resounds from the room next door, signaling the end of the preparations.

"He asked for you." The woman's hands wave at the door.

I gulp down my tea and a sour taste hits my palate. Sangmo gags as she puts down her cup. "Here." We hurry through the hallway. I pull two sleek white scarves out of my sleeve. "Now we're ready."

My hand slides the curtain and my eyes peer into the dark. Herbaceous swirls of incense tickle my nostrils. I sneeze. A thin red cloth, adorned with auspicious signs, obscures a tiny window. A single butter lamp flickers its faint light across. Lengthy shadows draw on the small shrine in the middle. Wrathful deities with twisted bodies on faded thangkas bedeck the rough timber walls of the room.

I shuffle ahead while taking in the eerie images. My knees buckle. *Focus.* There's the ngakpa seated on the left side of the shrine in the meditation position, his eyes closed. A stoic expression veils his wrinkled face. His long hair is coiled up in twisted locks. A red and white scarf drapes over his wiry shoulders. Yes, this is the ngakpa I visited so long ago.

I lower myself three times, with Sangmo behind me. My hands tremble, but with a meticulous precision I stack the offering in front of the shrine, and wrap our khatas around it.

Without saying a word, the ngakpa beckons us to sit. Clammy sweat pricks around my neck. This feels unreal. I should be on the ride home now, not requesting guidance for a very different journey ahead.

"It is good of you to come." The ngakpa's raspy voice resonates in the dense space between us. "The journey on your mind is not lightly to be undertaken." He opens his eyes, and a flash of clear blue pierces through. *He knows.* Sangmo presses her knee against mine.

His hands reach across the small table and touch the top of our heads, a welcoming blessing.

"The last time we sat here, you were also going on a journey." His blue gaze mellows on me. "I am happy to see the journey was fruitful." A reassuring smile breaks through the unnerving serenity on his face. His hands unfold a golden-threaded cloth, and two pearly bone dice roll out. I lean in, anxious not to touch the table. Strange symbols are etched on all sides of the dice.

"Let's pray we may see the next journey too." His hands fold, his head lowers. The dark coils sway, throwing a shifting shade over his face. His lips mumble. I can't hear the exact words but recognize the invocation by the rhythm of it—prayers to the Three Jewels, Palden Lhamo, and other Dharma protectors. A profound stillness settles inside of me. Sangmo shifts in her seat.

He sits motionless, in a deep meditative state. It seems as nothing is happening, but I know what the ngakpa's doing. He's requesting the deities to reveal the answers to us. He sighs and looks up. A deep, obscure indigo blurs his eyes. The dice click, a muffled sound in his closed palm. With a decisive throw, he spins the bright bones onto the cloth.

My body tenses. All eyes are on the burnished signs. AH TSA—the symbols are revealed to us. My eyes narrow, my mind searches in vain. Only the ngakpa knows what the symbols mean.

"Ah Tsa." His low voice vibrates in the room. His bony hand finds a crimson clothed book at the edge of the table. "How fortunate the result will be." The dark blue fades from his eyes and the sharpest of cerulean shoots through. "If you work with only steadfastness and carefulness of mind." The corners of his mouth turn up. "How fortunate all activity will turn out, be it traveling as well as giving."

My heart skips a beat. A vast relief saturates my being. This sounds good. If I guard my mind, my journey—where I'm going—will be blessed.

"You will receive the company of the spirits of nature." He flips open the book, and his fingertips turn the loose leaves. "And all be revealed, some in the North and some in the East."

North and East? A clammy sweat pearls on my forehead. My mind fevers. That's not where my monastery is. It's where the mountains are, where Father caught his first wild horse. I glance at Sangmo. Our eyes meet and we both understand; it's a done deal. I'm going for the horse. My heart quivers. But honestly, did I expect any other outcome? It's why I'm here after all.

The ngakpa's fingers trace the scribbled lines. He turns the page with determination. Then a few more.

"Yes." He mumbles and scrapes his throat. "There are some minor enemies, but no real danger."

Enemies. A chill drafts by. I shiver. That must be Uncle and my cousins. For sure, they'll not be pleased with my plans.

"There's a trivial presence of an air illness of the mind." The ngakpa speaks with certainty. My cheeks flush with the heat of shame. *He knows.*

"A slight doubt from the mind is not bad as long as you put full trust in yourself and the ancestors." He nods at me. My jaw tightens. See, there it is again. My fickle mind, always scattered, always wandering, never to be sure.

"And water." His gaze sets on the page. His stained nail scratches the table right next to the page. "Any activity involving water will be unfavorable as the water spirit is restless. Most restless."

Mother. My insides take a blow and sweat breaks on my upper lip again. I've feared the water ever since my mother's passing.

"But again, all will be auspicious if you leave without hesitation, and the right preparations are met." His hands draw together, his fingers intertwine. Then he lists his instructions. I listen close.

The preparations are extensive—from hanging prayer flags to doing ritual offerings to the Dharma Protectors, in particular the green deities. Unusual herbs and incense are needed. My fingers mess with the cord on my wrist. We have none of these items with us.

"Khandro-la will help you," the ngakpa says. "She's gathered all necessities for you." With the utmost care, he wraps his book.

Khandro-la? My eyes widen. She already prepared the offerings? *How?* I look over at Sangmo. She shrugs and wipes her nose.

The ngakpa's hands stretch to touch both our heads. His eyes close. It's our time to leave. We get up and make our way out. Just as I reach for the door, his raspy voice vibrates from the walls.

"And go without a word about your undertaking, all of you." His ominous tone ripples through the room. "As it is one that has not been done yet—ever—and will set in motion what is not always favorable for others."

A rawness hinges onto my bones and my heels halt, turning in the carpet. The ngakpa's silent silhouette's where we left it. Did he just speak?

"Come." Sangmo tugs at my elbow. "Let's pray Khando's offerings are better than her singed tea."

Sangmo! My hand slaps hers, and we step into the corridor. My feet drag as we head to the kitchen. The divination weighs heavy my heart. All will go well if I keep my mind steady and avoid water. And leave without hesitation. I can do that, right?

A swollen orange sun accompanies us as we make our way back to the stables. All preparations have been made. Our work is done for now.

"How are we going to do this?" I hook Sangmo's elbow. "We can't just run off." I halt. A pebble has lodged itself between my toes and my sandal.

"First, we'll head back to the camp." Sangmo steadies me as I hop on one foot. "The family will help. They'll know what to do, how to get you the horse."

The family. *Karma*. Emerald eyes surface from the furthest corner of my mind. My lips pinch. *Don't be silly*. I shake my sandal and oust Karma from my thoughts. The family, that's a great idea.

"And gen Ghedun?" I wiggle my toes. "What to do about him?" A little gravel rolls out.

"Hmmm, yes." Sangmo wrinkles her nose. "We'll tell him you want to spend some more time with the family, with Grandfather being so old." Her voice sounds certain, as always.

My eyes settle in the distance where the sun sinks behind the highest peak, spreading a burnished auburn over the ridge. Ghedun's no fool, and I'm not good at hiding a truth.

"I'm not sure." I draw my gaze back and look at Sangmo. Her brown eyes blaze with confidence. If only I had a little of that.

"I am." She squeezes my shoulders and my heart lifts. I might not have her confidence—yet—but I have her on my side.

"So it's a deal." She bares her teeth in a massive grin.

"It's a deal." My insides stir up a small protest, but it's no use. The dice have been cast.

We'll set off tomorrow morning, with no word to anyone about the journey ahead. Not to Father, not to Ghedun. This is what we'll do.

Nineteen

D usk hasn't driven the darkness from the night, yet I'm already wide awake. Crumbs of sleep tease the corners of my eyes as my body begs for another rest. I've been twisting and turning all night, even though last evening was more than I could ever wish for. Father treated us to a scrumptious meal and, with the honest conversations we shared, the genuine warmth of his company—it truly felt like I was home again.

A slight draft grazes the tip of my nose. I pull the blanket closer. My body curls. It was only one evening. I close my eyes and sorrow washes over me. Once I'm gone the horses will suffer at my cousins' hands, like I was never here. And Father will be alone again with his paralyzing grief, only able to look away, to turn his back on the stables, on our home that once was so dear to him, so dear to us. *I can't let this happen.* But can I hide my plans from him?

A snore rumbles from under the blanket. Sangmo's still fast asleep. We talked half the night. If it weren't for her, I would have gone back to the monastery today. Still, I wonder if Ghedun will let us. I roll over and stare at the beams above. No use, sleep has left for today. My feet slide out, my toes scrape the timber boards. The kitchen will be warmer. I slip on my robe and tiptoe out of the door.

"You're early." Father's seated in his corner. A servant skitters by.

"So are you." I join him and bask my bare feet in the glowing heat of the roaring stove.

"I always am," he says. "Don't you remember?" He rests his hand on my arm.

"I do." My face lifts at the recollection of him and me so long ago. "And you used to hoist me out of the blankets in the morning, pretending to search for me everywhere." We share a laugh.

"I sure did." He hands me his cup. How sweet that memory.

I get up before he can to serve him. "Please, let me." He's my father after all.

A mild steam rises from the kettle. Dawn slides through the windows on its delicate hues of ocher and blue. The quiet ease between Father and me saddens my being. All those years we were apart. This is how it could have been. I blink. A little tea spills over the rim. This is how it should have been.

"Come sit." Father reaches in his shirt and pulls out a string. "These were your mother's. Now they are yours."

Mother's beads. Imperial jade, a most exquisite, rich luster and soothing to the touch. Mother always carried them with her. It was here in this kitchen, she taught me my first prayers as she turned these very beads between my fingers. Later, she gave me a string of my own.

"Small beads for small fingers," she said. "Made from special wood from a far away land." She had rubbed the string between the palms of her hands, and a sweet, creamy, and warm fragrance had filled the air. But being the wild child I was back then, hiding in the hay and dashing through the fields, I'd lost them within no time. I was so careless with everything.

My cheeks flush at the cool caress of the jade around my neck. "Thank you, Father." I only whisper and rest my hands on the beads. "This means a lot." Father's eyes redden.

"You have no idea how proud I am." He clears his throat. "You're doing well in your studies, Ghedun tells me, and your heart's in the right place." His hand envelops mine. "I have no doubt you'll become an excellent practitioner under Dechen's guidance." I swallow hard and our hands blur before my eyes. *If only he knew my true plans.*

A cadent thud arrives from the hallway.

"Please Gen-la." I clear my seat as Ghedun steps in. His eyes bright, his back straight, the day's rest did him well.

A youngster rushes in to serve us. Father and Ghedun continue their conversation from yesterday, talking about horses, trade and politics, all worldly matters beyond my grasp. I force myself to eat as restlessness is stirring my insides. Or is it the truth of my actual destination today that I'm trying to hide?

The last of my tea slushes down my throat. I excuse myself to say goodbye to my pony and wait outside. This way they won't see me fret.

A strong wind strikes as I stride across the courtyard. My step wavers at the old barn door. The hiss of the viper stirs in my mind. *Don't be silly.* My hands hesitate on the iron latch. *Om Tare.* With one sharp slide, I open the door. My little friend welcomes me with a lively whinny.

"Happy to see you too." I hop over to his stable. A wet nose pokes at my side. "No play today, sorry." He slobbers the small tsampa ball I've snuck out from the kitchen and snorts with content. My hands rub his bristly manes. So many times, I came here, holding my heart as it spilled over with grief. The presence of his stocky frame, its round and warming belly, it always felt enlivening. This time is no different. One last pat on his neck. "I'll be back soon." It tosses up some hay as I close the stable door.

"Not if you keep up this crawling pace!" Sangmo calls through the barn. "Been looking all over for you." She leans against the door. "Ready?"

"Not really." I tilt my head and squint. Morning has broken through with a spirited yellow among a stark cerulean blue. "Guess there's no turning back now."

"Nope." Sangmo throws her arm around my middle. "And you're making everybody wait, as usual." She chuckles and ushers me out of the barn.

White smoke swells into a cloudless sky. The poignant scent of fresh greens swirls through the courtyard. Ghedun has lit weisang, burning freshly cut pine and juniper branches to pray for a blessing. My lungs inhale the zesty vapor. The billowing column rises straight towards the heavens, despite the strong wind. It's an auspicious sign. *Om Tare.* All will be fine for today.

"I'll come to see you soon." Father gives me a knee up my mare. "I won't make that mistake again." He leads my horse down the lane towards the gate where Ghedun and Sangmo wait. My fingers tangle the reins. I bite my lip. I'm not used to saying goodbyes.

"I'll miss you." I say. I didn't know the words were there. A hot burn wells in the back of my eyes. *Not now.*

"You coming here, it meant everything to me." Father pats my horse on the neck. "Just promise me one thing, my child." His voice breaks, and I lean in. "The monastery is your true home now, it's where you belong." His hands find mine; a dark gloom meets my eyes. "Forget about the prophecy. Don't even let it cross your mind anymore." His strong fingers urge me. "Promise me, Nordun." He won't let go. I have no choice.

"I promise." I swallow hard. A lump lodges itself in my throat. I'm not used to stomaching lies, either.

"Good." Lightness spreads on his face. The amber shine graces his eyes again. "And don't let Sangmo drag you into any mischief." He waves his hand at her and throws her a wink.

Somehow I must have convinced him. Relief washes over me, but it won't dissolve the stains of my shameful dishonesty. Lies are lies, even if they are intended for the good.

My heels spur on my mare. It takes a few times before she trots into a reluctant canter. I pat her on the neck, sure she must feel my hesitation to set off.

With the sun on our back, we mount the hills. Ghedun leads the party, with Sangmo and me following close. I shift in the saddle. The oil Father has given me doesn't fulfill its promise. My legs ache, but not as much as my heart. *Lies.* I need to get back. Soon.

Ghedun's horse picks up a fast gallop. Sangmo rides on my side.

"You're good?" She throws me a worried look. I grimace.

"Nothing a few days in the saddle won't cure," I say. Sangmo lets out a holler.

"Let's go then." She spurs on her stallion without looking back and flies straight down the hill into the open meadows.

My mare follows with a leap as if it's her last ride. I shoot forward and my hands grip the flow of manes. A strange, yet delightful excitement bursts through my body. We're off! To wherever that might be.

Twenty

W̶e keep a good pace through the rolling meadows down the valley. A flock of frisky shrike-babblers hops from branch to branch, welcoming us with a joyous call. A mild breeze has replaced the gale, rushing the promise of a warm day through the budding trees. I loosen the scarf around my head. Soon we'll enter the gorge, leading to the higher mountains on our right. And then? Back home? I glance at Sangmo. Seems like we're still on track.

Ghedun's horse prances as he slows to a steady canter. He turns in the saddle.

"So, where to now?" His eyes pry at us. "What's your plan?"

What does he mean? My mare balks as I clamp the reins too tight.

"You think I didn't hear?" He sounds stern, but there's a twinkle of mischief gloating in his eyes. "The lost daughter visiting the ngakpa in the village." My heart skips a beat. "Word gets around here faster than the blink of an eye, Nordun."

"I trust you made the right preparations?" He draws his cap over his eyes. "Good." He doesn't wait for me to answer. "We're heading left here, towards Dawu." He turns his horse. "Follow me."

Dawu? Now? My mind picks at the puzzle Ghedun just threw in front of my feet. Somebody told him about our visit

to the ngakpa, but who? Father? I cringe at the thought of
him catching me in a lie. And now Ghedun leads us to Dawu.
What's in Dawu? And why is he helping us?

More pieces of a puzzle, and they're not fitting. My mind
frenzies. I've never been to Dawu. It's a tiny village on the road
to Dartsedo, where many of the traders come from. Why go on
the road to Dartsedo? Sure, I'm not supposed to buy a horse
but catch one myself. Makes no sense.

"Come on!" Sangmo's horse dashes after Ghedun's.

I spur on my mare. Both of them are bolting by now. The
speed we go leaves me panting. It takes all my strength to
stay on my mare. I look beside me. I can't believe Sangmo's
chewing a peach.

"Trust him." Sangmo's loose tresses dance in the wind. "He
knows what he's doing."

"I do," I yell over to her, my voice fighting the wind. *What
else can I do?*

"Soon enough." Sangmo spits the pit aside. "We'll find out
soon enough." She grins. Carefree. Why can't I be more like
Sangmo? Nothing seems to bother her while I fret over every
little thing these days. I arch my sore back. There's the path to
Dawu. At least the ride will get a little less rough.

We ride on until the sun's drawing the smallest shades of the
day. Ghedun signals to stop at a shallow creek. Before I have the
chance to slide off, my mare leaps into the stream, leaving me
soaking wet at the bank of the creek. I frown, deciding whether
to scold the horse or to enjoy the unexpected, invigorating
bath.

"They always give you exactly what you need." Sangmo
scoops the cool water over her face. "Don't they?!" She's a
jokester.

"If you say so." I wring the end of my robe. Her boundless
optimism—how she's growing on me. I spread the provision
while Sangmo has a fire lit in the blink of an eye. That woman
can do just about anything.

Lunch at the banks of the creek's a welcoming break. My body aches even more than this morning. I stretch, waiting for the tea to boil and Ghedun curls up in the shade of a few dragon spruces. My heart goes out to him—how his body must hurt, even more than my young, healthy limbs. And still he rides for days at an end, all because of me. How fortunate I am with his company. Sangmo stirs the tea. Gratitude spreads its fluffy wings all over my chest. Yes, how blessed to be with these people.

Mosquitos dance on the water, enjoying the warmth of the midday sun at its peak. Flashing blue wings skim the surface of the water—a lone flycatcher chases the insects for its lunch. After few futile attempts, it joins its dozing buddies in the shade of the trees.

"Here, let me." I take the kettle from Sangmo. Sweat lashes down my back as I pour the tea.

"Nordun, come sit." Ghedun made a place for me between him and Sangmo. "Too hot, you need a rest." Sangmo licks her fingers, butter drips along all sides. I'm hungry, but can't wait. I have to ask.

"So, what's in Dawu?" I hand Ghedun a small cup of yogurt. He doesn't react. With the utmost precision, he smears the yogurt on his bread. I shift to the front as he chews in silence.

"Patience is a great virtue." Ghedun's voice is steady. He winks at me.

It is a virtue, and it's not one of mine. That's a fact.

"We're going to Dawu to meet up with Sonam, one of your Father's oldest friends." He sips his tea. "His family lives in the mountains. You will stay with them to learn about horses." My jaw drops. Am I hearing this right? I'm to stay in the mountains, with a family I don't know?

Sangmo leans in. "We're going to the Four Sisters then." She smacks her lips at my stunned face. *Four Sisters?*

"Yes, Sonam's family lives near The Four Sisters Mountain. You'll both spend some time there." He looks at Sangmo. "I take it you want to come."

"Of course." Sangmo pinches my arm. "I'm not leaving my sister." My fingers fumble with the hem of her sleeve. That's Ghedun's plan?

"Your father got his first wild stallion from there." Ghedun's fingers clean his cup from the last traces of yoghurt. "There are still a good few ones up there. It's your best chance to succeed, but not before learning about the great wild."

"But..." I opened my mouth but close it again. Ghedun's right, I know nothing about wild horses. I can't even mount a tame one by myself.

"You see, Nordun, if you want to be an equal, if you want the wild horse to respect you, you have to understand its true nature." Ghedun stretches his legs and leans back. "The only way to understand wild horses is to familiarize yourself with their surroundings. Only then you can truly acknowledge and respect their power, their greatness."

Of course, Ghedun knows all about horses. I never realized, but he was a horseman once, before he became a monk.

"Sonam's family will take good care of you." He draws his cap further over his head. "With their help you'll bring back a horse."

My thoughts stall. My mouth goes dry. *The wild.* Nomads. I have to learn the way of the wild. That's his plan. My body caves. My arms find their hold on my knees and wrap around.

"Can't I stay with my own relatives to learn?" I glance aside. Surely my family will teach me. They would be happy to.

"You can." Ghedun turns towards me. "They are good people but they're too close." He sighs. "Tennah is most keen on seeing you fail. He doesn't know yet, but will find out soon enough. The further you stay away, the better."

My stomach tightens. *Uncle.* He hadn't crossed my mind today. He won't be pleased if I return to the stables with a horse.

"Hey, I'm here." Sangmo interrupts my thoughts. "And I'm family, sister." Her arms hold me close. I guess Ghedun's reasoning makes sense, and I'm not alone. I've got Sangmo after all.

"Yes, you are." I lean into her. "And I'm so grateful for that." Sangmo gives me an extra squeeze.

"You'll do just fine." She pinches my cheek. "The wild, it runs in our family, in our blood after all."

My eyes prick. I'm not so sure it runs in me. Still, I'm trying, and I have the best support.

Ghedun hands me his cup and I pour another round of tea.

"Thank you, Gen-la." My fragile voice doesn't measure up to my vast gratitude. "You're putting yourself in a difficult position for me." I glance at the stooped posture from the corners of my eyes. He does, going against Father and Dechen's wishes. I butter another chunk of bread for all of us.

"We all have our reason, Nordun." Ghedun's eyes set in the distance. "Long time ago, when I was asked to guard your grandmother, I failed, and I swore that wouldn't happen again. Not to me." He shakes his head.

"I thought it would be good for her when the family decided on the monastery. I was sure I could do a better job guarding her there." His hands draw over his face. "How wrong I was." His voice wavers. "To see her struggle... So many times, I had to bring her back to Dolma, to the monastery—even in the middle of the night."

My mind jolts. What? The bread slips from my fingers. My grandmother, the abbess, we all look up to. She struggled? No way! There's no one as devoted to the dharma as she is.

"Sure, in the end she settled and excelled, but not because of my doing." He rubs his chin. "She had no choice but to surrender. It would have killed her if she didn't." His gaze

settles on his cup now. His fingers ring around the rim. My
mind churns at his words. My hand trembles as I scoop up the
fallen bread. Soiled. No good.

"I often wondered if I did the right thing by aiding the
family, keeping her in. After all, what family keeps their
daughter away from her newborn baby girl?" His firm jaws set
and bleak regret flashes over his face. My heart hurts for the two
of them—my grandmother and her appointed guard—the
cruelty of the choices put before them. I hasten to butter
another piece for Ghedun.

"Your mother, she was beautiful." He takes the bread. His
eyes avoid me. "She was everything the family could wish for."
My mother.

"Gen-la, you knew my mother?" My voice pitches. Dechen
and my mother, they never met again. At least, that's what I
always thought.

"Oh yes, I did." Now he looks at me, and it must be the
memory of mother that softens the stark regret on his face.
"Dechen asked me to keep an eye on her for I could, you see."
My lips pinch. Yes, even as a monk, Ghedun has the freedom
to go about, unlike us nuns.

"I saw your mother blossom." His fingers tear a piece of
the bread and dip it into the frothy foam. "Especially when
she married your father, the one she loved most." He swirls
the crust around. "He gave her the one thing she needed—her
freedom." The bread soaks and sinks into the cup. *Freedom.*
My eyes narrow as the sun turns a corner.

"It's what we all need." He stirs the cup, the bread all gone.
"So you see, I have my own reasons to be here right now." He
empties his cup in one gulp. I smile. It's the way Father takes
his bread and tea too.

We eat in silence. All life has withdrawn, seeking the shade.
There's only the rushing of the water floating through the air.
Too hot this afternoon.

My mind won't settle with Ghedun's unexpected revelation, but I get it. He wants to give me the chance to make my own choice. No matter what. He must have seen me fretting.

"You'll be fine." His reassuring look meets me.

I shrug, my insecurity weighing heavy on my shoulders. "I've been in the monastery most of my life," I say. "The world out here is different. I feel different." The right words won't come. And there are tears again at the back of my eyes, waiting for the chance to burst through. How can I explain I feel lost and out of place, even with my own family?

"Yes, I've seen your struggles these past days." Ghedun nods. "But it's only when we are called to the challenge, when we have to tread the unknown grounds that we really get to understand ourselves and the true power we hold."

I'm losing the battle, and tears streak my cheeks. *You fool, you thought you could hide it, but they've all seen you struggling.* My thoughts turn against me, and my heart feels smaller than ever.

"All you need is time." Ghedun takes another sip of tea. "Time and guidance to trust yourself and gain confidence out here." His gaze floats over the fleeting creek. "You'll be in excellent hands with Sonam's family." He empties his cup and wipes the crumbs from his shirt. "You'll see."

I bow my head. My sleeve's soaked, and Ghedun's words make their home in my heart. No use agonizing about it any further. After all, what do I know about this world?

Sangmo serves Ghedun another cup. I wrap the unfinished food. We'll probably need the remaining provision. I rub my aching limbs once more. I'll get plenty of chance to ride it out. That's for sure.

Twenty-One

C louds of granite-gray thunder over the road ahead. A deafening uproar hits my ears. Bells ring, hooves stamp, and hoarse shouts spur on a horde—a caravan's approaching. Ghedun steers his stallion off the road and we follow.

"We better let them pass," he says. "Never seen one before?"

My eyes widen at this colorful cacophony of men and beasts, sounds and smells. Urged on by the lahdo, the traders travel by on their sturdy horses—a convoy of mules, yaks, and human porters staggers by in a blur of dust. The precious cargo of first-class tea, sown in yak-skin cases, and bamboo tubes are piled on their backs.

"Where are they heading?" I pat my prancing mare.

"They're on their way from Ya'an to Chamdo or even Lhasa." Ghedun cranes his neck. "If it's Lhasa, they'll be on the road for many moons ahead."

Lhasa. My jaw slacks as I take in the enormity of what I'm witnessing. The heat's intense at this time of the day. Streams of sweat gush down the porters' faces, wispy steam rises from the animal's frames. Walking all the way to Lhasa, tracking into the higher mountain ranges, where the steep, snowy peaks and glacier ridges reach into the heavens. With no shelter for the night, and this enormous load to carry, my heart shrinks at the thought of this arduous and lengthy undertaking.

"But the cold has not gone yet." I shake my head. "And the paths might be snowed up."

"Yes, and some of them, animals and humans, won't make it." Ghedun shakes his head. "But we want to sip our daily cups of tea, don't we?" He steers his horse further to the roadside, away from the passing parade of dirt, sweat, and suffering.

My daily cup of tea. I swallow. It's brought in this way—on the backs of humans and animals, through the hardship of other sentient beings. How come I've never thought about my tea, or where it comes from? It's been provided for. How ignorant of me. How far removed from this harsh reality I've lived. Nothing to worry about, taken care of by Dechen and my sisters. A privileged life, and desperately unprepared for what lies ahead.

Even now I'm sheltered and provided for by my faithful companions. Nevertheless, I've caught myself off balance too many times these past days. How feeble, how frail I grew up to be. No more of that. I lift my chin and force myself to face what's right in front of me. Opening my eyes and my heart to this cruelty of life will strengthen me, encouraging me to keep on the path for the benefit of all.

Even when the dust settles and the outcries will fade, their agonizing ordeal won't be over. For this is samsara, the circle of life, death, and rebirth, a suffering without an end. I take a deep breath, my mare leaps ahead. The road's wide open again.

A rich shade of orange and gold stretches over the fields at our arrival in Dawu. Ghedun leads us through a vast courtyard. This must be Sonam's house. My knees snap as my feet hit the ground. My hand grips in the sweaty fur of my mare. It's been the longest stretch I've ever been on horseback. I didn't do too bad, even though the raw reddened marks in the palms of my hand prove otherwise.

Carved columns, a decorated front, vast outhouses behind it, we've arrived at the house of a wealthy man. Quite a difference from some of the ramshackle dwellings we've passed on this road. This stark contrast strikes my mind—how come I've never noticed inequality like this before? Grime cakes my sleeve as I draw it over my face. The ride, all the impressions along the way, it's beaten me down. My legs tremble, and a heavy hammer pounds in my head.

A servant takes over the reins. At least my mare will get a good rest. Ghedun has already stepped, and Sangmo urges me to follow. Fatigue seizes me without mercy and I stumble in.

The welcoming in the house is as copious as expected from an old friend. Rows of steaming spicy dishes, fresh dairy products, and sweet fruits cover the low tables in a formal room. My body plunks in the first plush seat near the doorway. No expenses are spared, but Father's friend is nowhere to be seen.

"Sonam will be in later." Ghedun nods at servants to pour the tea. "Let's not let this good food go to waste."

Seems like Ghedun knows this house well. Sangmo's already chewing on a peach. The clatter of dishes and smacking of lips fills the room. The long ride's been left behind.

Sonam's arrival is soon announced, though, as boots stomp in the hallway, and a jolly voice cries out. "Welcome, welcome, my good friends."

A robust man strides in. His arms wide open, he greets Ghedun like a long-lost friend.

"Sonam, thank you for your lavish welcome." Ghedun's eyes delight at the man's sight. "You didn't have to go to so much trouble, especially on such a short notice." He points at the abundance of food.

"How could I not?" White teeth blink under a bushy moustache. "It's been far too long." He slaps Ghedun on the back.

"Little Nordun-la, look at you." The man beams. "All grown up."

I jump from my seat with a humble bow.

"Sit, sit," he urges me. "You don't remember me, do you?" He strokes his moustache. Tall, broad shoulders, a head full of boisterous curls and a somewhat crazy, yet sophisticated air around him.

"I'm sorry," I say. "I don't think so." My whisper's followed by Sonam's roaring laugh.

"Thought so." His fingers run through his pepper-streaked hair. "Time has not been kind to us." He winks at Ghedun. "But you're all here, safe and sound, and I'm happy. Please dig in." His long coat lands in the back and he sits between Ghedun and Sangmo, exclaiming again how happy he is to see us all. I sit back and relax. Although it's my first time here, something feels familiar, and I even dare say it feels good to be here.

The dishes keep coming and chang replaces the tea. The men—and even Sangmo—talk animated about the latest journeys, the trade, and the foreseen troubles on the borders. Their voices dwindle. My eyelids feel heavy. Snug in my corner, I drift off. My attention's caught as the conversation turns to the reason for our visit. The tone lowers. Sonam looks at me, his eyebrows drawn over his eyes.

"But she's a nun." He turns to Ghedun. "And you want her to go up North?"

I veer up with the flash of heat rising from my neck to my face. Sonam's questioning my plans. He's doubting me. This is not good.

"Yes, I do." Ghedun's calm composure is reassuring as ever.

I straighten my back and meet Sonam's eyes. There's no trace of a doubt in them, only joy sparking from deep within.

"Alright then, little Nordun-la." He rubs his moustache and grins at me, radiating an almost tangible brashness. "I'll take you, we'll set off tomorrow, you and me."

His hands raise and chang flows from his cup. "And tonight we toast to good friends and even better fortune!"

Twenty-Two

W ith an enormous yawn, I jump out of the bed, my body rested and refreshed. Sangmo was right. There's only a little soreness left. The early night did me good, asleep before my head even hit the mattress. The dreams stayed away, and I didn't even hear Sangmo come in. My outer robe slips over my shirt. I'll find my way to the prayer room, no problem.

On tiptoes, I slink through the dim corridor, past the kitchen and the adjoining formal room.

"Nordun, come in," Ghedun's voice calls from the kitchen. I was sure he would still be asleep. After all, Sonam and he were drinking all night, as men do. I guess morning prayers have to wait.

His eyes bright, his posture upright, the old man looks very much awake. The long day's riding and brief night's sleep have left no trace on him. I pour him another cup of tea while I take one for myself. The creamy brew melts on my palate.

"Yes, Sonam knows his tea." Ghedun savors his cup. "He enjoys the best of things." My eyes dart around the kitchen. Turned bowls stack on the shelves, all sizes available, the gleam of polished wood. Dozens of kettles and cauldrons line behind it, engraved, the hardest of steel. Even the colorful rugs with intricate patterns on the seats and the floor, the highest quality wool and weave. Yes, it's obvious that Father's friend only settles for the best.

"Nordun, I'm returning today." Ghedun sips his tea again. Today? My hands clench around my cup. Why so soon? A sharp breath steadies my wavering thoughts. *Focus.* I'll be fine. Ghedun has faith in me.

"I understand." I bow my head. "I'll miss your company and your excellent advice."

His hand taps my shoulder. "The time out here will do you good," he says. "You'll learn to trust yourself, what you feel beneath the surface of things, rather than what appears to be." He puts his hand on his heart. "Silence your mind, listen to what speaks from within, and all will be well."

My ribs tighten. I'm such a stranger to what is within me. My mind, yes, my unruly mind I'm familiar with, but what comes from within scares me, I have to admit. I don't want to know.

"Rely on your inner senses," Ghedun adds. "Deep down you know what needs to be done."

"Yes, Gen-la." I press my hands to my heart. He believes in me, and so I will.

Sonam breezes through the door. His arms full, he drops a colorful load of cloth on the table.

"I trust you to take good care of her." Ghedun puts on a serious face. "She's the family's most prized possession." His eyes gleam as Sonam throws him a smirk.

"You know better than to ask me that." Sonam's face is all smiles. He's a jokester, like Sangmo. I veer up and pour us all another cup of tea.

"Still, there're the robes." He points at the load he's brought in. "Better to change into lay clothes, Nordun. Easier and safer to travel."

Lay clothes? My body winces at the thought. No way I'm wearing lay clothes. I'm a nun and nuns wear robes. Sure, some nuns wear lay clothes when they work on the land. Few also wear lay clothes when traveling, but Dechen never does—she insists. We nuns wear our robes at all times. Dechen has never worn lay clothes since she became a nun. My lips pinch. My arms cross in front of my chest. Then again, Dechen never rides a horse either, let alone has plans to catch one that is wild.

I turn to Ghedun for guidance. He nods in agreement. *What?* Does he think I don't want to be a nun anymore? My eyes flash at the table. My vision blurs at the bright heap.

"Clothes mean nothing, Nordun." Ghedun's voice sounds from the distance. I look up. No way!

"But Gen-la." My voice breaks. How can he say that? Sure, he himself wears his robes all the time.

"Yes, to the outside word a nun is defined by her robes," Ghedun says. "But does the definition of others, how they perceive us, really matter to us?" He shifts to the front of his seat. "It's our intention that counts." He leans forward and catches my cagy gaze. "And only you hold your true intention. Turn within and listen to what is needed. You yourself will know."

I avert my eyes. *No way.* My mind turns a nasty corner.

"Don't let your ego with its misconceptions or even other people's misconceptions of how things should be or how you should look like, stand in your way." Ghedun's words pierce through the fragile fabric of my mind. "Try to let go of what you think you should be, for it's only form."

Let go? All I can do is sit here and fumble with the red string on my wrist. My dear sisters, what would they do?

"There are many ways to accomplish your goals, there are many ways to serve." Ghedun reaches out. "A new way has opened, and things will fall into place if you surrender your ego and act from your heart."

These words. I never thought I would hear this from Ghedun, yet I could have known. This man is the living proof of all he speaks about. There are many ways to serve the Dharma, and Ghedun has forged his own. He surrendered his lay life when it was needed to serve Dechen—I bet he never wavered once to follow what was calling him. And he believes in me. Who am I to doubt his words?

I'll wear lay clothes—for now, for it serves me best. I'm a nun, even without robes, for my heart is pure. I'll do what's needed for the benefit of all.

"Yes, gen-la." I close my eyes.

"Good, we'll leave you to it." Both men leave, and someone closes the door.

Lay clothes. My hands sift through the pile Sonam left for me on the table. Smooth silk and fluffy fur twines round my fingers. How different from the coarse woolen of my robes. My mind lingers. Simple is the best. A plain shirt and dress will do for me.

"You need a hand with changing." Sangmo's head pops around the door. I didn't hear it open. "Some great stuff over here." Her hands throw up a vibrant storm. "Might even get myself one." She delights in a purple, flimsy, sleeveless dress that finds her way around her middle.

"I do need your help." I hold up a plain chuba in a modest hue, like the undergrowth of moss in mid-winter, protecting the earth from frostbite in an unassuming manner.

"Yep, and not only with the clothes." Sangmo pinches my arm. My heart expands at her candid anticipation, and I can't help but hug her.

She's a true sister, and even though she's not a monastic, in a weird way she's so much like my other sisters, the twins.

Twenty-Three

H ere I am, heading further in the mountains on horseback in lay clothes, searching for a wild horse with two people I haven't even known for five days. And all because I needed to visit my father. What was I thinking? There they are, Sangmo and Sonam, chatting away on their horses, trotting ahead of me.

"All good?" Sonam slows his stallion beside me. I nod. He must have sensed my soaring sentiment.

"Soon we'll head North." He points to the left where a magnificent mountain range displays her crystal crusted peaks in the golden glare of the morning sun. *The sheer height of it!*

"From what I'm seeing, you're doing great on the horse." A sparkle comes to his eyes. "Like your mother, I see you've got her beads."

My fingertips slide over the jade string around my neck.

"Yes." I tilt my head to him. "Did you know my mother well?" A bark of laughter rolls my way.

"Palden didn't tell?" He looks like he's about to chew his moustache. He's gloating.

"Tell what?" I frown and turn over to face him full on.

"He didn't, right?" Sonam's smile curls around the edges of his moustache.

"No," I say. "But you can." My voice pitches at the last words. A swift curiosity shoves the remains of gloomy sentiment over the steep edges of my mind.

"Oh, I will." He chuckles. "Next stop." He spurs on his horse to catch up with Sangmo's. I'm left to wonder in a trail of dust. *Hmm*. Patience. I guess I'll find out soon enough.

We ride until the shadows have shriveled to their smallest shape with the sun at its peak. A shallow inlet, hemmed with lush shrubs and budding seedlings, provides the perfect shelter for rest. This time I'm ahead of my mare, and my feet stay dry before she dashes in the creek.

"So, your wife's from Rongdrak." Sangmo hauls fresh water while Sonam and I gather a few branches for the fire.

"Yes." Sonam blows a smoldering flame over the dry twigs. "Where all the most beautiful girls hail from." He sits down and leans back. A green sprig sways from under his moustache.

"Oh, I've learned that story." Sangmo crumbles a piece of the tea brick. "It's true then?" A strong, earthy fragrance rises from the kettle.

I throw in a few more twigs and stretch my limbs. The pile's blazing by now.

"What story?" I make my way into the shade next to Sonam.

"Well." Sangmo stirs the kettle and puts it down again. "Once a phoenix flew over the Rongdrak Morre mountains and liked its landscape so much that it stayed." She squats next to the fire and pokes it again. "Later on, the phoenix turned itself into a thousand beautiful young girls to bring hope and laughter to Rongdrak, right?" Her eyes shoot over at Sonam.

"Right." Sonam's fingers pry a satchel of tsampa. "And that's why women from Rongdrak are the most beautiful ones."

I snicker. A phoenix turning into graceful girls—just the thought of it. People told some amazing stories a long time ago.

"She's pretty then." Sangmo's gaze sets on Sonam with a curious determination. "Your wife." Sonam smiles and shakes the fine barley flour in his cup.

"She is," he finally says. The thin twig moves to the corners of his mouth. His eyes narrow. "But no-one was ever more beautiful than your mother, Nordun." He turns to me and hands me the bag.

"So tell me." My pulse races. *Strange.* I steady my hands. There must be some story here. Otherwise he would have told me this morning.

The kettle hisses, and Sangmo adds milk to the boil.

Sonam's voice lowers. "We were actually promised to marry." *What?*

"Marry?" My eyes widen. "You and my mother?" My fingers sink in the tsampa. "All she ever told me is that she married Father a week after they met." My hand cramps. "It was supposed to be love at first sight." The tsampa spills over. A thin white layer covers my shirt.

"True." Sonam glances at me. His cheeks carry a flush. "When your mother met Palden, it was love at first sight." His sturdy hand holds up the cup and Sangmo pours tea over the tsampa. "I know, because I was there, introducing my wife-to-be to my best friend."

I gasp.

"What?" I fall silent. The kettle clatters on the soggy grass.

"Well, yeah." Sonam's lips release the swinging green from the corner of his mouth. His fingers He works the tsampa through the piping hot tea.

"There's a long history between our families, so they arranged for Lhamo and me to marry." He blows his fingers to cool them down. "I recognize a good woman when I see one." A tiny smirk escapes his lips. "And I'll tell you, Lhamo was everything a man could wish for. She was young though, very young—and I was—well, let's say I still had my looks." He smiles, and his hand glides over his moustache.

"Ah, you still do." Sangmo swings the kettle. "And you know it." She throws a quick wink his way.

"So what happened?" I say. I can't believe this. How come I've never heard this story before?

"My best friend, your father, arrived for the wedding preparations, and I didn't think twice about introducing them." Sonam sighs. "Big mistake—they fell in love the moment they laid eyes on each other." He pops a small tsampa ball in his mouth.

"That must have been awkward." Sangmo sucks in her cheeks and puts the kettle back on the fire.

"Well, no, as Palden was—still is—a noble man and the best friend one can wish for." Sonam's lips smack. "He would never let it on, of course." He shakes his head.

"And Mother?" I wipe my shirt and wrap my arms around my knees. First the story, then I'll eat.

"She was... well, unsettled like any young girl is before her wedding." He runs his tongue over his teeth. "She tried to hide it, even so, I realized—she would not be happy with me." He pauses. His eyebrows draw near. "And I would lose my best friend, for Palden would have stayed away out of courtesy—he would have." His fingers knead another tsampa ball. "Yes, many a man would have seized her to elope, but not Palden." He sniffs. "Your father's too much of an honorable man." He smiles at me.

An honorable man. Right here, right now, I want to hug Sonam for what he just said about Father.

"And what did you do?" Her eyes still on Sonam, Sangmo pours us another round of tea.

"I told Palden I changed my mind and asked him to take my place." Sonam shrugs. "Sure, my family was disappointed, but it wasn't the first time I had let them down." He swirls the tea around, and his eyes settle on me. "And your mother's family was all too willing to oblige. Palden's from excellent stock, so no complaints there." He empties his cup in one go.

"Still." My thoughts run over the story. "That must have caused some upheaval in the families." Breaking a promise to marry. That's not something families take lightly.

"Ah, it ruffled some feathers, but it all worked out fine." He puts down his cup. Sangmo hastens to pour him more tea.

"And in the end, I got myself another one." He throws his head back and winks at Sangmo. "This time a real wild one if you know what I mean." *A nomad girl.*

"She's not with you, your wife." I regret it the moment the words spill from my lips. I'm prying into his private life. That's disrespectful.

"Nope, but that's her choice." A shadow moves across his eyes. "Still, she's the best wife a man like me can ever wish for." He gobbles down his tea and excuses himself, disappearing in the dense greens.

"That's some story." Sangmo swirls the kettle around. "And you didn't know this before?" She cleans her bowl with her fingers.

"No." I peer into my tea. "But then again, there're a lot of things I never knew." I sip the last bit as I digest all Sonam spoke of, and something tells me there's a lot more to Father's friend that meets the eye.

It will come to me, as all comes in time, I guess.

Twenty-Four

"Up here." Sonam guides us off the path. "There's the track into the mountains." I crane my neck. No way, that murky, narrow trail?

"Is there a reason we don't stay on the main path?" I shift to the back of the saddle. Surely there's an easier way of going up to Rongdrak? There must be.

"It's kind of a short-cut." He sounds nonchalant. "Besides, it's much more interesting taking the path less travelled, don't you think?" He laughs. *Not funny.*

"Follow me." He waves. "You'll be fine." His horse tramples the low hanging shrubs and takes the lead on the trail.

"I'll close the row." Sangmo halts her horse for me to pass. That cheerful, encouraging smile—he's in her element here. I'm not.

Hand raw, I swipe the sweat from my face—with the day only half gone, I'm already a right mess. Ah well, at least I haven't fallen off my mare, and the ache has almost left me. My spirits lift as I steer my horse onto the trail. If only my cramped fingers would relax. I flex my hand. Not yet, but soon.

The trail spirals down. Tall, bushy foliage fends off the sunlight, big dewdrops drip from the leafy stalks on the slippery rocks. A musky smell lingers, a dense and moist atmosphere wraps around. My eyes focus on Sonam's horse

ahead. Salty beads of sweat on my upper lip mingle with the
sticky sweetness of honeyed air.

I duck. Too late. The overhanging vegetation left its clammy
trail on my face. A heaviness creeps in my body, my stomach
throws up a protest. I'm not good in confined spaces. *Focus.*
My toes spread in my sandals. My knees press in my mare's
flanks. It helps—my body grounds and falls into the rhythm of
horse hooves clapping with caution on the moss-covered trail.
We ride on in the dead quiet of the day. I've lost track of the
sun. For long, the only sound is my breath panting in my ears.

And then—with no sign ahead—the track widens. A breath
of fresh air surges and verdant pastures emerge in the softest
rays of a tangy afternoon. A diligent stream cuts through open
grassland. Burnished brushwood and hardy scrubs hem the
small, scattered dwellings that dot along base of the mountain
range. Relief rises from deep within me. My mare snorts as my
hands ease the tight reins.

"You're still there?" Sonam turns, looking over at Sangmo
and me. "Never knew you young women could be quiet for
such a lengthy period." He grimaces, the jokester again.

"Oh, don't worry." Sangmo's horse speeds behind me.
"There's much more about us young women you'll never
know." Her daring laugh rolls over my shoulders. "Right,
Nordun?!" She passes me by.

I wiggle my toes. This talk—about men and women—it's
not for me. Good thing there's people coming. Two fellow
travelers on horseback—a monk and a layman—are coming
our way. Sangmo and I slow down our trot while Sonam stops
for a moment to familiarize himself with them. They're no
doubt exchanging the latest news on the road.

"Looks like we've got a clear passage to Rongdrak." Sonam
catches up with us after a while.

"Did you expect any difficulties, then?" The moment I
ask, I feel like the fool. How naïve of me. An isolated trail
like this, with one man accompanying two young, defenseless

women—much can happen. Sorrowful stories of robbers and tricksters, and of ruthless foreign raiders, not only Mongols, are known, especially in the areas here. And there're the spirits of nature to be respected. We might disturb them without even being aware. *Om Tare.* Landslides, torrential rains, vast floods and hailstorms that come out of nowhere—we must take the utmost care in traveling through this landscape. My fingers search for my beads. The mountain gods have been favorable to us, but that can change any time. Better not to take any chances. *Om Tare.*

The trail flows along winding river banks, through the abundance of budding meadows, with flowers peeping towards bloom. The mild breeze releases the warming scent of the earth. A quiet content seeps into my body, and my mind empties herself with light and ease. As the shadows lengthen, we make another stop to rest and refresh. We won't reach Rongdrak tonight. Tomorrow's another day's ride, so we need to pace ourselves and our horses.

A flaming crimson brims over the mountain range and still we ride on. I've surrendered my thoughts to the present and to whatever's planned by my companions. Sonam and Sangmo know where we're heading, that's obvious. They've been chatting on and off all afternoon, engaging in small talk and loud laughter. I'm more than content to trail along. What do I know about trade, travel, and horses anyway? Then again, I'll have to learn, and quickly too, if I want to succeed.

"Over there." Sonam gestures over the far side of the river. A denser forest looms on the other side.

"We cross the river?" My hands clutch and my mare halts in an instant.

"It's not deep." Sangmo's stallion dashes straight into the stream. *Water.* Fear wraps itself around my ribcage. Bitter bile runs up my throat. *Om Tare.* I stare at the fleeting river. *Focus.*

"Take your time." Sonam stands beside me. "I'll stand with you 'til you're ready." He understands.

My mare prances as she knows of no fear. *Put full trust in yourself and the ancestors.* The ngakpa's words echo through the hollows of my heart. He told about my restless mind, like the water spirits are restless in here. Yet, his divination was clear—I'll succeed. All the right preparations are done. All I have to do is steady my mind.

My eyes dive into the depths of the water before me. It's crystal clear, and even shallow. What is there to fear? *Focus.* I take a sharp breath and look at Sonam. I'm in good company.

"I'm ready." My knees spur on my horse. It needs no encouragement. A silver spray surrounds us as it splashes through. I only dare to breathe once its hooves scrape the banks on the other side. I made it—yet again.

Light flickers in the woodland. A bolted gate hides between tall trees and a falling twilight. Two shadows emerge on either side to pull it open. It slams behind us as soon as we've entered. *What is this place?*

"Sonam-la, long time no see." A man raises his torch. Sonam slides off his horse to embrace the man as if he's his brother.

"You've come at the right time." He gestures to the bustle around the house. Shifty silhouettes of men, beasts, and their belongings crowd the courtyard. Sonam gives orders to a man in a language I don't understand. A strange mix of reserve and excitement rushes through me. What a different world we've entered.

Sonam's arms usher us straight through the hallway towards the overwhelming clatter of bowls and jabber of men. The dim-lit kitchen is packed. Small groups of men eat, drink, and there's laughter all around. Two women rush with generous bowls of steaming thenthuk. Hands pass around large dishes of spicy meat cooked on the bone. At the sight of Sonam, the woman clears a space for us next to the stove.

My eyes feast on the variety of people around me, and my palate delights on the hearty soup served on the spot. I noticed straight away as we entered the kitchen—few women besides

Sangmo, me, and the servants. The murmur of the men gets louder as chang's served beside tea.

"Do you know where they're from?" I lean into Sangmo, sitting snug behind a sizeable pile of cooked meat.

"Nope." Her hand wipes her mouth and reaches for another piece. "Haven't seen outsiders much, have you?"

I haven't. My eyes peer through the hazy smoke and my mind wonders at the sight of their strange faces and especially their odd clothes. Some I recognize from the traders that visited the stables, when I was young—the loose sleeves that flutter all around, and the bright patterns that dazzle in the dim light.

"No chang for you two, I guess." The woman serving pours Sonam's cup to the brim. Sonam raises his hand.

"Nope, I promised to keep them safe." He gulps down his drink and lifts his cup for another filling.

Once the food's finished, most of the men retreat to the back. "Talking trade," Sonam says when I ask him, but Sangmo rolls her eyes.

"What?" I raise my eyebrows.

"I'll tell you later," Sangmo says and hands me a slice of her peach. I decline, too full. I blink as the smoke stings my eyes—or is it plain sleep emerging after a day that's been too long?

"Time to rest." Sonam wipes his hands on his trousers as he gets up. "These ladies will show you." His chin points at the two servants clearing the dishes by now.

"Thank you." My eyelids drop. Evening prayer will be short.

"Good." Sangmo cocks her head at Sonam. Her braid's untangled, her long locks cascade down over her back. "And you?"

He pauses for a moment and turns on his heels to face her.

"Don't worry, I'll be right over." He rubs his moustache. "You can be sure of that."

Twenty-Five

F eet scuffle on the earth-beaten floor, a cool breeze blows
in. Cloth rustles and something heavy drags beside my
mat. A muted thud—a door closes. I surface from a deep and
dreamless sleep. A zesty tang hits my nostrils, fine particles
of dust tickle my throat. *Pepper. Meat. Food.* I blink and
scout around. The stockroom. Sangmo and I were put in the
stockroom last night.

Enormous bags stuffed with produce and bundles of goods
line the wall. Dried strips of meat hang with bundles of fresh
greens from rusty hooks. Pots, pans, and cups in all sizes are
stacked on crude, crooked shelves. I wipe my runny nose and
turn on my side. Sangmo's snore sounds from deep under
the blanket. I heard her get up last night, but I didn't hear
her return to bed. A big yawn escapes from my insides, and
my arms stretch above my head. The ache has left my bones.
Sangmo was right—all I had to do was ride it out.

I scramble up and find my beads. Finally, some time for
a decent morning prayer. I lower my body three times on
the blanket. My eyes catch the red string on my wrist. Yes,
my journey has been blessed with safe travels and caring
companions to guide me.

My thoughts float back to the river crossing. A familiar
shiver runs up my spine. My body still holds fear at the

sight of water, yet my mind celebrates the minor victory from yesterday. A smile accompanies the conquest of my thought. *Today's victory can be tomorrow's defeat.* Dechen's stern warning rings in my ears. My dearest grandmother, always with me to guide my way.

A slight tension creeps up from the bottom of my neck, right along my jaws. Yes, I did succeed yesterday, but will stay vigilant and guard my thoughts and actions. Nothing's a guarantee in this samsaric life, and everything is always changing.

My fingers turn the knot—my home, so far away. I guess class's about to start. A tinge of regret tugs at my heartstrings. *No use.* I steady my back against the wall. My eyes close and my mind opens. The hallowed words flow from my lips. Yes, these words have grounded me for the last decade, and so they will now. My whole being falls into the intimate rhythm of prayer and time slips away.

Sangmo hasn't moved a muscle. I lean in as I say the last of my prayer. A healthy glow on her cheeks, tiny beads of pearly sweat on her upper lip—does she have a fever? I hold my breath and my hand touches her forehead. In a flash, her hand flings from under the blanket. She gets a hold of my wrist and a big belly laugh follows.

"*Hey!*" I jump up. Sangmo's wide eyes greet me. No fever, for sure.

"Good morning to you too." Her bright voice sings around. "Can't believe I slept this late." She yawns and rolls to the side.

"Well, at least you look rested." She does. A healthy blush on her cheeks, a lively glow in her eyes—there's something particularly radiant about her this morning.

"I am." She sits up. "And I'm starving." Her hands rumble through her pockets. Her long locks swirl all over the place.

"No peach in sight, then?" I chuckle.

Sangmo's always storing snacks; this time no different. She cracks her teeth on a candied nut and offers me one. I take it.

The honey glazed almond looks delicious, but I put it in my pocket. My palate's parched. "Tea first."

There's only the stale stench of last night's visitors lingering in the kitchen. Judging by the clamor and commotion outside, everybody's eager to get on the way. We should head soon too, but Sonam's nowhere to be seen.

A servant rushes in—a different one from last night. Her hands flurry around and within no time we're set with tea and a variety of leftovers from last night.

"These women make one great thenthuk." Sangmo slurps her overflowing bowl. "Must be the meat."

My lips smack with approval. This soup has the great hearty bite you expect from a good thenthuk, and leaves an unexpected tangy aftertaste. Delicious.

"It's the water." Sonam scurries into the kitchen, energetic and jolly as ever. "The water here that makes it all taste good." He grabs an empty cup from the shelf. "You two slept well?" He sits down beside us, the sweet arom of chang surrounding us.

"I did." Sangmo smirks over the rim of her bowl. "You look like you've been enjoying yourself." He puts on a grimace.

"Sure thing." He throws Sangmo a wink.

"The perks of doing trade," I say and pour Sonam a cup of tea.

"More like the perks of being a man." Sangmo takes on a teasing tone.

Sonam swigs down his tea and raises his cup for another one.

"We'll wait for the others to clear the courtyard," he says. "And then we're off, another day in the saddle."

I pull the cloth in front of the window aside and squint at the cool blue morning hue. The fine fog carries a chill through the courtyard where men are loading their packs, and beasts are kicking up a fuss in protest. Looks like the place's clearing out.

"These travelers." I turn around. "They're not part of a larger group?" Why travel in such a small and vulnerable party when you can be part of a bigger, safer caravan? And why take such a winding trail when there's an easier path to the destination?

"Nope." Sonam slurps the last of his tea. "They're small traders, being their own boss." His fingers crumble a slice of bread into a large bowl of thenthuk.

"Why not take the regular path?" I lower the cloth. Sonam takes his time to finish his thenthuk.

"Well." He cleans his bowl out with his thumb. "If we use the main path, we have to trade according to the rules over there." He looks up at me. "Out here we set our own rules." His eyes narrow. "You get what I mean."

The rules over there. I get what Sonam means. Taking the main path means passing the posts and paying the required tax. Taking these back trails, traveling in small, unregistered groups, the traders avoid these charges. They take more risks but keep more profit.

"They're avoiding the duty stations." I blow the foam on my tea aside. *They're smugglers.*

"Exactly." Sonam clicks his tongue. "We're looking out for ourselves and our families. We give some, and we keep some." His lips smack at the last pieces of meat.

We. He said we. So he's in the illegal trade too. *Ouch.* The hot tea singes my lip. That's dangerous. The penalties for smuggling are severe, even death. I steal a glance at Sonam. He's Father's best friend. Would Father... No way, Father's an honorable man. Sonam said so himself. My fingers ring around my cup. But then again, things have changed at the stables, and people change too.

A sudden cry roars outside. Something—or someone—crashes in the gravel. Sangmo and I are at the window at the same time. Two men roll around in a scud of sand and shale. Silver blades flash and the crowd hollers. The long knives are drawn! Sangmo gasps, her hand in front of her mouth. I grip the window seal.

"Stay here." Sonam long coat trails behind him as he flies out of the door.

"Sonam, don't!" Sangmo turns to the empty doorway. She shakes her head. "No good."

We both hold our breath, but before Sonam has even reached the courtyard, two stocky watchmen bolt from the gate. With a few knockouts, the brawl is settled. Swiftly, adequately.

"What's that all about?" Sangmo cocks her head as Sonam steps back into the kitchen. Unfazed, he sits down to finish his tea.

"The loser from last night didn't pay up." He shrugs and my mind jumps. *Loser?* Loser in trade? My eyebrows raise. I turn to Sangmo.

"Gambling." She puts her hand on my shoulder. "Harmless."

Gambling? Here? Last night? Smugglers, gamblers—what is this place? My eyes dart to Sonam, my father's best friend. Him too?

"It's men's idea of fun," Sangmo adds. She probably sees my distraught. "Nothing to worry about."

My mouth opens, but my thoughts suspend. I clutch my sweaty palms. What's there to say? Sonam's life, Sonam's responsibility. Things out here are different. People are different. Sangmo's right. Nothing for me to concern myself with. My eyes lower. Anyway, Sonam's been nothing but good to me. He's going out of his way to help me, so who am I to judge?

"Let's get a move on." Sonam clears his throat. "With any luck, we might make it before nightfall."

"Yes." I throw him an appreciative smile. "We'll follow you."

Twenty-Six

A ll day the three of us travel through the valleys of luscious green, rippling streams and swaying pines. Scattered farms sit in the shade of the flowering trees, growing their budding crops at the bottom of the hills. Black tents of nomadic families are tucked away in the pleats of the mountains, their cattle grazing on the rolling dales. With the homesteads increasing in size and the fields releasing prosperous produce, it's obvious this area thrives.

A full day in the saddle—not too long ago I would have cringed at the mere thought of it, but now that the ache has left, I'm actually enjoying the ride. The cadence of the continuous trot calms my mind and the vastness of this scenery, it's soothing and invigorating at the same time.

A cool breeze draws the afternoon to a close. As we enter a bountiful vale, an odd series of tall steeples pop up in the landscape. I stand in my stirrups to see. Watchtowers? Stacked with stone and mud, they must be at least forty men tall. Looks like there're spread all across—some are near houses, others stand in solitude on the hillsides afar.

"What's this?" I spur on my mare and join Sangmo and Sonam in front of me.

"We've come to the Valley of the Towers." Sonam slows his horse for a moment. "From now on, these are everywhere, even past Rongdrak."

Coming closer, I see the pillars vary in shape, from four to even eight sides, and with windows from tight slits to broad nooks. All of them have entrances high up though, with wooden ladders balancing against the sides. Some are under construction, sludge and stones piled up beside them.

"Never saw them before." Sangmo halts beside me. "Wonder what they're for. I mean, they're not very easy to get into." Her eyes glide up.

"Oh, there're many stories going around." Sonam steers his horse next to us. "Some say these towers dispel evil and invite good luck." He snorts and swipes his nose. "I guess they're practical storage in peaceful times and decent defense in times of turmoil." His chin points at the top of the tower we pass. "People here light beacon-fires to warn each other if trouble's approaching." I can see that, alright. So high up, these towers can hold lots of goods and give a splendid view over the plains.

"People here are well off." Sonam's eyes go over the land. "These towers also show off the wealth of these folks." He smirks as he spurs on his horse. "Ah well, some like to flaunt their gold, others their stone." His roaring laughter follows, and I can't help but smile. Yep, that's a typical remark for Sonam. How well one gets to know another when one travels together.

The curious towers throw their lengthening shadows upon us as we pass from valley to valley. Prayer has been my constant companion, as dusk is the perfect time to appease all. The hallowed stream of words also takes my mind off the returning ache in my back. I was too optimistic, thinking I could actually ride all day without my body. Despite my gentle inducements, my mare slowed too—she must feel the same.

A fire blazes in the distance, up the steep mountain slope. It's there, Sonam's family camp. Steeped in darkness, we conquer the hill up to the camp. My heart aches for my mare. With a quick slide, I dismount and pat her clammy neck. Her huge eyelids tremble, little drips on her lashes. Tiredness has taken the both of us.

"Thank you for carrying me this long distance." The briny steam from her fur penetrates my nostrils. It's the retched smell of hardship; a surge of gratitude engulfs my being. These days on horseback—especially witnessing the caravan and traders on the way—have given me a whole new appreciation of the beasts that carry our human burden. Their suffering in this samsaric existence is immense. My fingers twist in my horse's manes. If ever, it has strengthened my determination. I have no choice but to redeem my childhood home of evil.

"Here, let me." A small boy bobs around. A huge mop of tangled black curls crowns his jolly face. "You go in." This must be one of Sonam's sons.

"Thank you." My knees buckle as he turns the mare.

The main tent is in full light. A sturdy woman marches out to meet us.

"Nordun-la, I've been expecting you." Her hands extend to mine. "I'm Zinzin, it's good to have you here." Gentle eyes and a heartfelt smile meet me. Whatever doubts I had about meeting Sonam's family, his wife has erased them with her warm welcome.

"I see you brought company." Her strong hands squeeze mine tight, and her eyes soften as she looks over my shoulder at Sonam. My toes curl in my sandals. That expression of affection and admiration—the same way my mother used to look at Father—of two people sharing the deepest of connection. My eyes cast to the ground. This intimate display of lover's affection—will I ever get comfortable with it?

"What took you so long?" Her arms slide around Sonam's middle.

"Oh woman!" One toddler hopping in his arms and a little girl hanging from his trousers, the rest of Sonam's words gets lost on me as he stumbles into the crowded tent.

Heat lashes in my face, the stove's fired up to the boil. Big pots hiss and drench the air in blaring steam and the scrumptious aroma of savory meat. Milk tea bubbles, and flat bread piles on the side. A simple, wholesome meal is waiting to be devoured.

"Sit, sit!" A young woman with rosy cheeks urges us around the stove. Little children fly off in all directions. Her protruding belly peeps out from under her black yak hair coat as she hauls the tea from the fire. Sangmo's quick to take the kettle off her hands.

"Please, let me." Sangmo pours the cups while the young woman lathers chunks of bread with a generous, creamy butter. My stomach rumbles with relief as the warm dough hits my palate, and butter drips along my hands.

Surrounded by chewing and chatting, I sit back and rest my head. Like my family's tent, this one is also packed. Sacks of grains and stacks of blankets line along the walls. Small children crawl over the place; woolen carpets and thick sheepskins are arranged to sit and sleep. A larger bundle of blankets rises up and down in the far corner. Somebody's sound asleep.

"Father." Zinzin leans over with a bowl of soup. "He's not feeling well today—old age." Her face strains with worry, and her sorrow becomes mine. I will remember her father in my prayers over the next few days.

Prayer. Guilt cramps across my ribcage. How little time I've taken. My head lowers at the sight of a simple shrine, lit in the dim left corner. The golden mask of a small Buddha statue glows in the flicker of a single butter lamp. I didn't even prostrate to the Buddha as I entered, only thinking of my rest and food. How quickly I've slipped into the behavior of lay people; just as easily as I slipped into their clothes.

Smouldering dung bites into my eyes, and I blink the battling tears. My appetite's vanished; my hands wring round the bowl.

"Don't mind us talking. We've got a lot to catch up." Zinzin rests her hand on my forearm. "Why don't you take your sleep?" Her chin points to the corner. "It's the perfect quiet spot for you right now."

"I'm sorry." My voice drowns in the lively chatter of my company. "I'm not used to traveling, not used to all of this." I haul myself up and excuse myself.

Zinzin follows close and puts a thick rug down. "Not to worry, you'll get used to it soon enough." She smoothens a blanket and tucks me in as if I'm one of her little ones. "And no need to hurry, either."

Twenty-Seven

I ce water slushes over the kettle; angry steams hisses up from the smoldering stove. I rub my raw palms. I might not be as handy as Sangmo yet, but I'm getting there. The good night's sleep has done me wonders. Waking at dawn, I took my time for morning prayers, and now I'm refreshed, ready for the day.

"Thank you for everything." I turn to Zinzin and wring a wet cloth in my hands.

"Oh, we love to have you." She untangles her long locks and spreads the ends of her hair between her fingers.

"Time's leaving its mark." She pulls a few pearly strands out of her otherwise deep black tresses and sighs.

I crumble a few pieces of the tea brick and glance up to her. There's not a trace that reveals her age or worry in her soft, round face this morning. She knots the strands around her finger and tosses them into the fire with a vengeance.

"There." She grins and turns my way. "You really are the spitting image of your mother, Nordun. Same gentle, caring manners, and the same beautiful smile."

"You knew my mother?" My fingers tighten the grip on the knife. Of course, they would have met. Sonam used to be Father's best friend. Must have been awkward, though.

"Oh, yes." Zinzin points to the entrance of the tent. "And thanks to her, I've got this man over here." Sonam barges in as we speak, with Sangmo on his trail.

"You're talking about me, woman?" He beats the dust off his boots and jumps over to the stove. "Can't be anything but good then." He plops down, and the zof freshly cut grass spreads around.

"Oh, for sure." Zinzin throws me a wink. "He might not always be there, but he takes care of us—like a decent man does." She waves her hand at Sangmo. "Come in, girl." Her eyes narrow. "You look like you could use something hot to drink."

Face faded, shoulders hunched, the ghost of Sangmo lingers in the entrance.

"Thanks." Sangmo shakes the grass off her skirt. "It is chilly outside." She moves next to the heat, silent, aloof.

"You good?" I hand her a cup of tea. She shrugs and wraps her hands around the cup.

"Nothing a cup of tea can't clear." Her eyes dart around the tent. "I'm fine." She sips from her mug. I pick a few wet blades of green off her back and squeeze her shoulder. That's Sangmo, always taking care of the animals before she takes care of herself.

A weak sun peeps through the cracks of the tent. The score of children has woken and lets us know. Sonam's got a number of them tumbling over his knees and shoulders—I'm not sure which ones are his. Their enthusiastic shrieks are extended to Sangmo and me. A little boy climbs on Sangmo's knee and stretches his chubby little fingers for a sip of her tea. A tiny girl pulls my skirt for attention. I smoothen her fluffy hair. The young woman who served us last night wipes the girl's grubby face with the slip of her dress.

"Sorry." She straightens out the girl's frumpy clothes. "She's always such a mess, like her father." She puts her hands on her protruding stomach and flashes a smile. "I sure hope this one looks more like me in that manner."

The girl, a bit more presentable now, extends her arms to her mother.

"Oh no." The young woman puts her hands to her sides. "I can only carry one." She presses one hand on her lower back and uses the other to urge the little one to sit near the stove.

Boisterous laughter fills the tent as the children gather around to be fed. Cups bang and milk spills over. They sure make their breakfast into a bash. Free-spirited and easy-going, how they remind me of my sisters. Not their loud noise, but the unpretentious way of their being.

A twinge of homesickness touches my heart. Despite the kindness of my current company, I miss my sisters. Being with them is so effortless, nothing like the awkwardness I feel around here. Sentiment lodges a lump in my throat. *Here we go again*. I shake my head and turn my thoughts. This is my choice. No use reminiscing. With a swing from the hips, I haul the kettle from the stove. "Who's thirsty?" A dozen little hands raise.

Fed and flying high, the young horde heads into the bleak morning outside. Sangmo piles the dirty dishes. I gather the leftovers and sit down to eat. Peace has returned to the tent; even the roaring stove has quietened down, releasing her warmth with a soothing hum. Sonam's gone again. Zinzin puts her feet to the stove. The baby at her chest murmurs, and milky bubbles form around its teeny mouth.

"Would you mind?" Zinzin hands me the baby. I open my arms—I don't mind at all. I hold the little one snug in my arms, her eyes closed, her body soft and warm. My fingertips stroke the furry down on her head. She lets out a snuffle. My sleeve touches her peachy cheek and her long eyelashes lift. A pair of big brown eyes stare at me, startled, like a little deer lost. My arms tense. She's going to cry. No one's left in the tent but Zinzin's father, fast asleep. I rest my eyes on the little one again and my heart takes a breather as she throws the widest smile I've ever seen from such a small mouth. Total trust and unconditional love have wiped the alarming look off her chubby face. She's completely surrendered herself to my care with ease and delight.

My heart explodes at the sight of her joy, effortless and full of content. I swipe my eyes with the back of my hand. *Silly me.* Even the laughter of a baby bringing me to tears. What's wrong with me these days?

The little one takes my finger and suckles it. The gummy ridges of her milky teeth coming through and scratch the tip.

"Hungry then?" I dip my finger in the frothy tea for her to taste. An instant giggle is followed by a slight burb. Her eyes follow me. I repeat the ritual with her quiet consent. It's a done deal; this little one's got me wrapped around her little finger.

Her appetite for milk tea is quickly satisfied. Her eyelids close and she drifts off to sleep. A slight wheeze rises from her chest. Holding this little creature who's a complete stranger to me, yet she trusts me with all of her being—my heart glows in the intimate silence between us.

For sure, I've come here to learn the ways of the wild here, about horses and how to connect. But right now, life's teaching me about my own nature, and about precious human connections. Gratitude and apprehension mingle within me, releasing a sigh from my lips. I should be out there with Sangmo and the others, but really, all I want to do is to sit here and be still.

My last thought is not going to materialize, though. A burst of fresh air surges through the tent. Sangmo's back and the sunniest of yellow rays accompany her bright face. The morning chill has gone. Sangmo's back to her cheeky self again.

"Are you hiding from us and the work?" Two buckets swing from her arms. "There's milking to be done." She plants one of the buckets in front of me. Its bottom bangs on the earth beaten floor.

"The dris are waiting, and from what I've seen, this is your perfect introduction into the wild." Sangmo's tease says it all. These dris are rough, nothing like the few docile dzomos at the monastery. It's going to be quite a start.

I rise, careful not to wake the baby, and lay her down in her basket beside the stove.

"Let's do this." My hands grip the bucket. I'm almost convinced by the steady sound of my voice.

Our sandals slide across the wet meadow. In the corners of my eyes, I spot Zinzin and Sonam, talking behind the main tent. From the back, I see Zinzin throwing up her hands.

"They were here." Zinzin's hands anchor on her sides. "They asked... wanting to know all about..." Her voice lowers, inaudible to me. Sonam stands there, looking away. I can't see his face.

"Don't worry about it, woman." He shuffles his feet. "I'll take care of it." His hands touch her shoulders, but she shakes them off.

Are they fighting? My fingers fumble, the bucket slips from my hands.

"If you don't, I'll have to." Zinzin's voice pitches. It looks like she's ready to storm off. Sonam grabs her by the arm and draws her near. He turns and catches me watching the two of them. I duck and stumble. He must have seen me. *Too nosy for my own good.* I cringe and shoot away.

"Any idea?" I pant and catch up with Sangmo. She pulls up her nose and shrugs.

"Probably a little tiff between husband and wife." A shadow passes over her face. "Not that I'm familiar with that." Her bucket clatters to the ground. She plants her hands to her sides. "Don't know about it and don't want to know."

Her tone of voice, it almost bites. I step back. What's wrong with her? I bend down and pick up her bucket. My hands hesitate, and I glance up. A sudden smile breaks across her face. Her laughter lightens up the air in an instant. Good, she was only joking.

"Come on." The cheeky twinkle has found his way back to her eyes. "I can still see the bottom of that." She takes the bucket from me with a swing. "No more talking until it's full to the brim."

I grin and agree. It's time we—or should I say I?—get some work done here.

Twenty-Eight

V ast bodies rise from the mist that hugs the lower grasslands. Long coats sway in awaited anticipation. My eyes widen at the sight of the rowdy herd, huddled together in a grunting protest. My heart drops in the empty bucket. All these dris need to be milked. A head pops up between the wandering mass. It's Yeshe, the young woman with the rosy cheeks who turns out to be Zinzin's niece.

"Happy to have extra hands." She rubs her protruding stomach. "This little one is getting heavier by the day."

Yeshe must have been up long before breakfast, driving the dris near the tent and collecting the dung to dry. I'm sure Sangmo helped her. Sh's great like that, always looking out to lend a hand. The delight in Yeshe's eyes as we walk up to her touches me. If anything, I'm grateful to be of help to her.

My eyes go over the restless herd. I swing the bucket. Where to begin?

"Here, take this one." Yeshe points to a smaller dri. "It's used to me, and docile."

Like any livestock, dris tend to attach to one person handling them. I better prepare myself for a scuffle. The dri groans its objection to me as I approach. Its horns probe my leg. I swallow hard and seize it up, running my thoughts around its burly frame. It smells my foolish anxiety. Maybe if I'm fast enough...

I slide under the dri's body. My fingers hasten to part the long skirt of hairs around its teats. The dri sways its body from side to side. It has no intention of giving its milk to this stranger—not without a scuffle. I steady my forehead against its hardened belly. And why would it? After all, its milk belongs to its newborn calf, not to me. The newborn, however, is separated from its mother early in the morning. It's kept away for most of the day, preventing it from suckling all the milk. No wonder this dri's not pleased.

Sweat pricks down my neck. I strain my arms, legs, and all my limbs to reach the hidden teats. My heart pulses a dull throb through my temples. The dri twists and turns, its hooves churn in the mud. The muscles ripple under its dense coat—it's ready to charge off.

Mud splatters against my ankles as the dri stamps and snorts, whacking its raggedy tresses to my clammy forehead. Hooves stamp in the corner of my eyes, and black spots dot my vision from out of nowhere. My one hand grips the bucket, the other gets lost in strands of coarse hair. Too late. I tumble and land on my back, clutching the bucket all the way.

A foul stench hits my nostrils. I grasp for air. The agitated dri just steps aside. My mind buckles. What happened? The dri didn't even touch me!

Still hanging on the bucket, I stagger from the stinking muck. Yeshe and Sangmo are rolling around laughing by now. At least someone's amused. *How stupid I must look right now.* I cringe. There's nowhere to hide. My hands wipe the slimy filth off my dress. It's no use.

"Don't worry about it." Yeshe's hands reach for my bucket, but I clamp it tight. *No way.* I raise my chin. An apologetic smile pleats on my lips. I'm not giving up on this simple task. Her amusing simper softens to an encouraging nod.

"It's just that it's used to me." She takes the dri by the horns. "Try to settle down inside." Yeshe points for me to try again. "Go easy on her, but mostly go easy on yourself. That will do the trick."

I hesitate, but put my hand on the furry back once more. My thoughts go to the dzomos at our monastery, docile and tiny compared to this rugged beast. My fingers slide over her muscles, thick ropes running over backbone and sides. Sturdy and solid, its strength throbs under my palms and my thoughts turn from anxiety to admiration. Surely, I can never outdo this magnificent creature by force. Not that I would ever consider it, for violence has never been in my nature. Yes, I'm stubborn and selfish, and set in my own ways, but I don't have a violent bone in my body. No, if the dri allows me to—only then can I milk it.

I bow my head, admiring and admonishing its obvious strength. My thoughts and my heart go out to this beautiful creature, nourishing us every single day with the milk that we deprive of her newborn. And to its calf, destined for a similar existence of suffering, giving us milk and even its own meat, skin, and bones to nourish and protect us in this life. My fingers dig deeper into its muggy, waxen fur. How we humans take this selfless sacrifice for granted. How ignorant we are.

These magnificent creatures... their endless cycle of suffering spins in front of me. Their profound misery in this samsaric existence sweeps through the deepest hollows of my heart. The intense pain leaves me breathless for a moment. A trail of bitter bile rushes in my mouth. As it settles in my stomach, a salving balm to soothe all suffering pours from my lips. *Om mani padme hung.* Without a sound, the prayer cascades from my being, invoking the blessings of Chenrezig, the embodiment of compassion for all. *Om mani padme hung.*

A few shallow breaths out ease some of the tension. I shake my hands. Not all, but it's a beginning. I bend beside its massive body yet again and let the mantra flow between us.

Loving kindness, a boundless compassion for all suffering beings has seized me, leaving no place for anxiety or thoughts of struggle to co-exist. I place the bucket and stretch for the dri's slippery teats. My hands stroke along its surprisingly soft, furry underbelly. This time there's no rushing or trembling of fear. There's only the humble touch of compassion, an honest plea for permission. *If you will allow me.* All of me reaches out.

The dri sways and shudders, swirling its damp tresses around my grimy forearms. My fingers wring around, trying to be gentle. The first spray of oily milk hits the long hairs around the utter, sending the milk dripping along to the ground. Not good, a waste. My shoulders drop. *Focus.* A sharp breath in. Again. The second spray hits the bucket with a triumphant splash. *Yes!* A weight lifts off my shoulder. It's only a few drops, but there's milk in the bucket and I'm still standing. A tiny smile curls around my lips.

With short spurts I fill part of my bucket, and my prayer flows, thanking the dri for a generous gift and wishing for the benefit of all. My cheeks burn and the grime cakes my face. I raise myself and turn to Yeshe. *I did it!* My fingers scratch the dri behind its ears.

"You did good." Yeshe peers into my bucket. "And if you want some more practice, go ahead. They're all yours." With an enthusiastic wave, she gestures at the rest of the gruntling group.

"No problem." My eyes go around the field. "Happy to be of help and fill this one up." And I am—if I can only find a smaller dri to milk.

We end up filling our buckets to the top. Stiff fingers and sore arms come with it too—it's not only my mind that needs practice, my body's not up for this hard labor out here. Not yet.

I waddle back to the tent, a full bucket on my hips. Sangmo's off to feed the calves. That leaves Yeshe and me to boil and skim the creamy milk, making it into yogurt, cheese, and butter.

Zinzin pours the rich liquid into a heavy cauldron set on the roaring stove. Does this woman ever get a rest?

"Nordun, sit." Zinzin laughs as I drag my weary body into the tent.

"Have some fresh milk and rest for a while." She stirs the boiling mass, a large wooden spoon in her hands. A sweet, comforting aroma drifts from the pot. My fingers tremble around the cup Yeshe passes me. Oh my—this is only the beginning. Women's work here is never done. After boiling milk and churning part of it into butter, there's fetching fresh water and cooking lunch to do. The rest of our afternoon is filled with skimming, pressing, and drying, the laborious process of cheese-making. And of course, there're the dogs to feed, dry yak dung to collect, and fresh yak dung to be dried. Not to mention clothes to be washed and other chores to be done.

By now the youngsters drop in, packing the tent with their lively laugher. Good thing there's many to help, even if they're small hands. By the end of the afternoon, there's dinner to cook, calves to collect, and then a second round of milking—all done by the women and the older children here.

I stare into the flicker of the stove. My mind wanders to my sisters on the mountain. They've finished prayers and class by now. Lunch is next and then work in the gardens—but nothing as backbreaking as the work the women here do.

The fire hisses a loud protest. The stench of scorched milk hits my nose. Yeshe scoops a few loads of boiling milk into a pot aside to let it settle into yogurt. She heaves, one hand on her bulging belly. Milk slushes over the rim—tiredness has gotten to me. I shoot up. *How can I sit here, daydreaming with others working right in front of me?* I flinch at my idle behavior.

"Here, let me do that." I take the pot of her hands and swing it back onto the fire.

"I'm worn out today." She smoothens her skirt. "This baby's ready to arrive." She arches her back, and a weary smile graces her petite face.

"You better rest." Zinzin's determined voice resounds from the back. "You've got some hard work ahead of you, girl."

Yeshe yawns and stretches herself. "Oh, if it's anything like the last one, I'll be fine." And with those words she waddles to the back of the tent.

Milk splashes over the handles, scalding the back of my hand. I squirm. That's sure to blister.

"Stay there." Zinzin shoves the lid on the cauldron. "I'll get you a wet cloth for that." She dashes out.

"No need," I call after her. "It's nothing." My hand hurts, but it's nothing—nothing compared to what these women go through, day after day. It's a hard life, being a wife and mother, but what do I know? Dechen, Dolma, even my sisters, they warned me about the hardship of lay women's lives, and now I get to experience it myself. It will do me good—Ghedun said so himself. Life out here in the world is the best practice ever. Once I'm back home with my sisters, I'll treasure it even more.

A little one latches himself onto my skirt. His chubby cheeks blow bubbles, his grubby face gleams with sheer delight. My heart spreads its wings and takes flight, wishing to be nowhere but here, in this place, this very moment—and so do I.

Twenty-Nine

A luminous waxing moon reigns over the indigo sky. A thousand twinkling stars accompany her as she moves through the night to her fullest. It's been a long day at the camp. The second round of milking was easier. Fortunately, I'm a decent cook. At least I'm of use here in the kitchen. Everybody's fed. The yaks wander the hills and the stove murmurs a comforting heat for all who've gathered around. Shadows of men on the right take stock of their trade while sipping their tea. Women on the left spin the wool and chat away the day. Children scatter around, curling up wherever they feel like sleeping. It's a large family. I'm still not sure who's who.

Zinzin throws a few slabs of dung in the stove. No way she's going to cook again?

"I'm making Father's medicine," she says. "He's not been up today." The baby's in her arms, a worn pouch is in her hands—and the worried look's back, lining her lovely face.

"Let me, please." I take the pouch and crush some of the dried leaves in the palm of my hands. A crisp zest permeates the air as the crumbles soak the boiling water.

"It only needs a little." Zinzin puts the baby on her breast. I nod, and a slight smile comes to my lips. Gently, my hands rock the pot back and forth. *No stirring, only simmering. Let the plants do their work.* That's what Choezem, our amchi at the monastery, says when she hands us our medicine. The water stains a vibrant viridian as the leaves release their shades of potent healing. An acrimonious aroma whiffs up. It's ready to be taken.

"I'll bring it." I strain the liquid in a cup, making sure the soaked leaves stay behind. The brew settles within moments, revealing the bottom of the cup. Yes, it's all clear.

"He needs a little help with it." Zinzin wipes the little one's mouth with her sleeve. "His strength has left him." Her hands tap the baby's back. Defeat has settled on her shoulders.

"I'll take care of him." I move over to the right side. A heap of woolen blankets covers Father's frail frame. A wheezy cough rattles in his chest.

My arms support his bony body as he slides up to take the cup. My hand wipes the veil of perspiration from his forehead. A pair of fevered eyes seek me as I put the cup to his parched lips. A few strained sips follow. Then a few more. The tremor in the man's body seems to ease. The healing liquid does its work. A lightness moves in me, holding this fragile human so close. At least I'm able to ease some of his suffering, even if it's only to help him drink.

I bend to rearrange his blankets, making sure he's comfortable for the night. His hand raises at the jade beads around my neck. Of course, prayer to Sangye Menla, the Medicine Buddha. This will be of benefit to him—and to all who need the healing. I slide the string off my neck and crouch beside him. His thin fingers burn in mine. I lower my head—if only my sisters were here, we could all do the powerful Medicine Buddha prayer. The whole ritual requires at least two or three accomplished practitioners.

My mind wavers. What can I do? I'm only one, and not very skilled yet. As my thoughts wander, Father's heated hands pull mine tight. A serene glow draws in his feverish eyes and meets mine in the midst of his suffering. My heart cracks open, and tears swell in the furthest corners of my eyes. He's found the courage to surrender to his faith. Who am I—a strong, healthy human being—to doubt even the smallest thing I can do?

Traces of bitter medicine and sour sickness mingle, a stale stench rises in the air. *Namo Gurubhyah, Namo Buddhaya, Namo Dharmaya, Namo Sanghaya.* My mind focuses, my heart expands and presses against my ribcage, wanting to go beyond the boundaries of her human bondage. My faith surges as I start chanting, letting my practice—no matter how feeble or fragile—purify some of the disease, pain, and suffering of this man and of all.

Teyata Om Bekanze Bekanze Mahabekanze Radza Sumudgate Soha. I invoke the Medicine Buddha with his mantra, visualizing his body, the shade of most precious lapis lazuli in my mind's eye. Clothed in the robes of a monk, he sits on a multicolored lotus. His hands cradle a gilded bowl with healing blue nectar, the salvation of all that is ill. Emerging from the depths of my being, the Buddha's benevolence descends upon the two of us, enveloping us in the purest love—as only a Buddha can. *Teyata Om Bekanze Mahabekanze Radza Sumudgate Soha.*

My being suspends between the here and the now. My heart pleads. *Please release all pain and disease from this man's body, relieve his suffering and purify all the bad karma collected over his countless lifetimes.* My mind steady, I call out—again and again, until the Medicine Buddha's cup bubbles and blue hue beams from the glistening bowl. The clearest of cerulean rises among the golden and cascades down through the crown of the ailing man, brimming his body and mind with the boldest of blue. The nectar spreads beyond and banishes all illness, spirit harm, and all negative karma that might be. *Teyata Om Bekanze Mahabekanze Radza Sumudgate Soha.*

The beads click and my heart stretches into infinity, holding the ailing man in front of me and all beings in the realms—humans, animals, tormented spirits, and hell-beings alike. A magnificent rainbow dives from the heavens, blazing in shades of stark sapphire and treasured turquoise. Lost in time and space, I plead to the mighty Medicine Buddha to pour his healing nectar to cleanse the suffering of all. *Teyata Om Bekanze Mahabekanze Radza Sumudgate Soha.* Over and over again, I plead until my prayers are heard.

The healing rays billow and bulge in front of my being, discarding the wretched misery that takes hold in us all. Only when the last traces of illness and insanity are banished away does the Medicine Buddha's image fade from my mind and dissolve into the timeless space far beyond.

I'm left to rest in uncontrived awareness with the old man, now fast asleep. With a heart full of renewed hope, I conclude the dedication. *May the merits of the past, present, and future that I have collected liberate all sentient being from their sicknesses and may sentient beings never get sick.* And so it is.

"That was powerful," Zinzin whispers as I join her at the stove. "Few can do what you just did, for Father, for all sentient beings." She hands me a cup of warm milk. Her face still holds a shadow of sadness, but there's also a tinge of relief shining through, a lightness for something has cleared.

"Oh, it's nothing, really, compared to what you do." I sit beside her. My body bristles with renewed zest. "You're raising a wonderful family with mighty determination, and it all comes so natural to you." I shrug. "To be and act with confidence in this world, well, I'm quite lost out here." I lift my chin to find an encouraging hint in Zinzin's eyes.

"You know, many of us feel lost, and I guess in a way we all are." Zinzin's voice lowers. "We have no choice as our children choose us, so we make do with what we have." Her arms cradle her baby at her chest.

"But I know what I just saw—your heart holds a boundless compassion, and that's something not many of us possess." Zinzin's eyes gleam as she rocks the baby back and forth. "It will be of immense help to you out here, in all you've set out to do."

I sip the sweet milk and savor Zinzin's words. A boundless compassion. But how's that going to help me catch a wild horse? I wipe my nose.

"You want to become the master of your father's stables, don't you?" Zinzin's eyes burn on me with a sudden, fierce curiosity.

Do I? My hands hug my knees. "Not really," I hear myself say. "But I do want to rid the stables of my brutal cousins." And that's true. "Even if it means I'll get a wild horse tamed." My lips pinch. A light quiver turns my stomach.

"What happens after that? No idea." And that's true too. I'm a nun, striving to live my life for the benefit of all. My shoulders drop. *A wild horse tamed.*

"Best to take it one step at the time." Zinzin nods. "You know, it's not that difficult, bringing a wild horse back. I've seen many men do it, so why not you?" Her fingers grip around my wrist, and a daring twinkle flashes between us. "You've found the courage to venture out here. Now you have to follow through."

I blink. Courage, if only.

"We'll show you our way." Zinzin leans in. "But there are no tricks." Her eyes narrow as I peer at her. No tricks? "Only a genuine connection like the one you just make with Father will bring results."

My thoughts turn to the man sleeping in the corner, resting in his ailing.

"See this baby, innocent and pure." Zinzin's fingers stroke the sleeping child's head. "New to this world, and naïve, we say, yet in an instant she senses if our intentions are good or whether we have harm in mind."

My gaze sets on the little one, fast asleep in Zinzin's arms. Surely, she must have felt my panic this morning, but she surrendered to me with her unconditional love. I'm sure, she also must have felt my intentions were pure. With a smile, I take the little girl from Zinzin's arms. So small yet so smart.

"Nature can't be fooled, Nordun." Zinzin clutches our blankets, ready for the night. "To forge a genuine bond, your heart has to be truthful. Nature can't be fooled."

Thirty

To be honest, I dread the nights ever since the nightmares have returned to haunt me. Fortunately, the long days in the saddle exhaust me to where I'm already asleep before my head hits the pillow. And now I turn to Tara in the evening, with the hope in my heart that the fighting vision stays away. It works, for this morning too I wake up rested well after a night of dreamless sleep.

Seems to me this tent is for ever bustling. Children jump around, men stamp their boots, and women circle around a blazing stove that never seems to die down. And yes, the tea's always ready to pour. It's delightful to witness this harmonious collusion of lives, for it all plays out well. But my being craves for quietude, a little time alone. I guess my only chance here is in the early morning, but by the sound of it, I'm not getting any of it today. Even before I open my eyes, there's Zinzin, calling me from afar.

"Nordun, have some tea." She busies around my blanket. "You're going up the mountains this morning—we've lost some yaks."

The haze in my mind lifts. *Yaks? Lost?* I scramble up and fold my blanket. All's quiet in the early dusk, there's only the mellow glow of the stove. Even Sangmo's still fast asleep.

The flickering butter lamp reveals a few empty blankets. Zinzin's oldest sons are already up. Three hasty prostrations in front of the small shrine and a brief morning prayer will have to do for now. I stumble to join Zinzin and Sonam at the stove, the heat a welcoming relief to my stiff back and aching limbs.

"The wolves have been around last night." Sonam peers from over his cup. "I've heard them, even though they sounded way out." He soaks a piece of yesterday's bread in his milk. "The boys are already up to check, but we've probably got some yaks gone astray." He slobbers the moist bread with his fingers, mumbling on. "So, the boys are heading up the mountains to get them, and you're joining them." Traces of milk run on his chin.

I stretch my hands for some warmth. I understand. Time for more riding practice.

"You'll enjoy it." Zinzin hands me milk and bread, too. "It's quite different ground up there and driving unruly yaks is, well..." She bends to fire up the stove. "Let's just say it will be a challenge." The pungent smell of burning dung hits my nose. My mouth turns dry in an instant. *A challenge.*

I fumble with the bread—soggy crumbs sink to the bottom of my cup. My eyes trace them floating down. *A challenge.* If Zinzin finds it a challenge, it must be really tough.

"Oh, you'll be fine." **Sangmo's snuck up to me from behind. She hugs my hunched shoulders.** The smell of green is all around. "You've been on a horse before, and you handled some wild dris." She's beaming her wide smile again.

"For sure." I say, but the tone in my feeble voice is not so certain. I gulp down my milk and lick the mushy bits with my fingers. *Ready.*

A chilly breeze blows through the tent, a refreshing change from the stale stench of scorched dung. It's Norbu, the eldest son, bouncing in. On his tail's his younger brother Rinchen, both the spitting image of their father—tall, with a head full of curls, and the same boisterous air around them. Leaving a trail of wet grass, the young men race each other to the stove.

"Boys!" Zinzin's voice carries a scold at her sons for their rowdy behavior. Sonam's throwing a look of approval only a proud father can. The scuffle has woken up the little ones and in an instant, the tent fills with enthusiastic smacking, slurping, and chewing.

"It's fantastic up there." Rinchen gobbles down his milk. "Let's hope we'll find them alive." He wipes his mouth with the back of his hand.

A chill moves up my spine. I try to steer my mind from the worst we might encounter. I've seen it before. Every springtime the wolves try to seize the easy prey, the newborn calves. Often they succeed, leaving the mauled carcass for us to find. Such a terrible ordeal for both the calf and the wolf. I don't know what's worse, being born helpless or being born a predator. It's in their nature, and a terrible karma.

"Let's go." Richen slaps his brother on the back and jumps up. "I bet the yaks are waiting for us up there."

Crystal beads reflect the morning rays, as the dew's holding on the grass with a stubborn delight.

"It's a glorious morning to go up." Norbu points his chin at the jagged mountain range, displaying her peaks with pride against the cloudless blue. My mare's snorting, prancing up and down. Even she seems to be keen to go.

"Up you go." Sonam gives me a leg up the mare. "The boys will take good care of you." He pats my horse on her neck.

A tiny spur from my heels, and my mare's off in the trail of the others, galloping across the open grasslands to the rocky plains way up ahead. I crane my neck but need all my attention to get into the rhythm of the canter. *Focus.*

The soggy grass squishes, releasing a zesty scent from under fast treading hooves. My hands grip the reins tight. A startled red deer leaps into the grayish firs as we dash by. Those boys—or should I say men, for they are—are used to it, but I'm not. That speed!

We dash uphill, the sun on our right. The wet grassland thins out and rocky grounds pave our way. Hard edged boulders are strewn around tufted buckhorn bushes and hardy grass; the clatter of hooves echoes around. It takes all my strength to keep up, but Norbu doesn't slow down. He keeps a good racing pace for Richen and me to follow.

At last, we hold. My mare shudders. I heave to catch my breath. Two curious pikas pop up their furry heads from under a lone juniper bush at the edge of the open plateau. This must be the place Sonam was talking about. Richen was right, the scenery is breathtaking; a vast plain encircled by magnificent mountain peaks unfolds right in front of us. With the dazzling morning sun throwing her silver beams over the snowy tops, the elevation bathes in a glistering gray. Massive standing stones throw ghostly shadows over the pearly plane. A small lake right in the middle reflects the clear blue sky in her deep turquoise, mirror-like surface.

A shudder rushes up my back as I take in the plateau. Yes, beautiful, yet eerie at the same time. Somehow, the immense silence of the plane makes my skin crawl. I shiver as my temples throb a dull ache around my head. A hauling wind sweeps through the elevation with a ferocity that cuts my breath. What is this place?

A single string of frayed prayer flags flutters from the pillar of washed-out bones and eroded mani stones marking the entrance. The brothers dismount from their horses to circumambulate. I follow to do the same.

"We better appease the spirits of the mountains." Norbu ties a white silk around the bleached horns at the top. My icy fingertips touch my prayer beads, and steam rises from my lips. *Om Mani Padme Hung*. Where did this sudden cold come from?

We proceed and our horses trot with a certain care. Norbu points to a small inlet, carved way out in the solid cliff.

"There used to be a hermit living there, long time ago," he says. I peer at the desolate mountain cove, set austere and remote. Yes, devoid of any distraction, this bleak dwelling is the perfect place to practice. The hostility of the environment adds a grim reminder of our miserable existence here in samsara.

I draw my scarf close as the wind pierces my eyelids. Strange, such an amount of turbulence, yet there's not a cloud in the sky. The brothers seem to be undaunted by the gale, their horses scampering ahead, the flaps of their chubas trailing after them. What a forlorn place—not even a few scattered tufts of resilient green to be seen. My hands clasp the reins tighter. Why would the yaks go out here?

Norbu halts at the lake; its crescent shape pulses a peculiar deep greenish blue.

"Better go slow." His voice lowers. "The nāga lives here."

A nāga. My heart shrinks at the possibility of a serpent here. That might explain why the yaks went astray. A nāga might have lured them all the way out here. Surely if there's one, it will never allow us to take the yaks back. My gaze fixes at the profound depth, radiating a calm blue—so tranquil yet so deceptive.

Our horses line in single file as we move across the barren expanse. Pearly bones, marked by fierce predators and scorched by the blistering sun, scatter around. In the distance a lone vulture circles a snowy peak. Its lengthy, ragged wings slice with a vengeance through the sharp gale. Cold sweat forms on my forehead. Are we treading charnel grounds? *Focus.* I steady my shallow breath as Dechen's words ring in my ears. *Only a steady, well-trained mind will be capable of warding off the obstacles you will meet out there.* We ride on.

"There they are." Rinchen's voice reveals a relief. I squint. Yes, there are four gray dots in the distance. Four yaks. Their long coats float on the wind, like ethereal shadows drifting ahead of us. Somehow they seem unfazed and unmoving, how strange. The mantra of compassion flows from my lips. *Om Mani Padme Hung.* How lucky we are. How lucky they are.

We steer our horses around the yaks. The wind ceases at once. The animals, calm and compliant, are in great shape. There's no mark on their sturdy frames that reveals they left their homes late last night.

"Mom's going to be delighted." Norbu instructs us with a dead calm and we retreat at an unhurried pace.

Om Mani Padme Hung. My mind turns to prayer as we drive the complacent animals past the crescent lake. It's not until we circumambulate the pile of bones again, that my lungs breathe with ease.

"We're good to go." Norbu turns to me. My shoulders drop. *Good.* The yaks grunt. It must be their sign to become their unruly and unwilling selves again. Our horses form a tight line driving the yaks, but being back on familiar ground, the animals throw up a tussle; no way are they in the mood to go home.

My arms tire, my eyes strain—it takes all my strength and focus to follow Norbu's directions to steer and lock. The brothers move like the wind, agile and flexible on their horses' backs. I'm more like a stiff log of a tree, cumbersome and definitely clumsy. My palms are raw, my knees numb—this riding's great practice for me.

My bumbling holds up the swift brothers, for sure, but we make it before the sun's at its highest point, all in one piece.

"I'm sorry I slowed you down." I steer my horse next to Norbu's.

"No problem," Norbu says, and a gentle smile peeps from under his hat. "Nothing wrong with being careful." He holds his horse and dismounts.

"With yaks like that, it's easy to get injured—the cattle and yourself." He turns to hold my mare, and I dismount. "Besides, we'd rather ride up there than do the chores waiting for us down here, right, Rinchen?" His brother joins us and bellows out the same laugh I've gotten to know from Sonam so well.

"Right!" Rinchen takes all three horses by the reins. "Tomorrow again?" He smirks as he sees me rubbing my reddened palms.

"Tomorrow again," I say.

And I mean it. After all, this experience has turned out to be great practice—for my body and for my mind.

Thirty-One

How good to see Zinzin's father sitting outside the tent, his face turned to the sun. Spinning a mani-wheel with content, he's even got some color back on his sunken cheeks. I slip the beads off my neck and crouch beside him for a while. His fragile smile meets mine and the warm mid-day air envelops us in a balmy breeze. My thoughts drift away on the mantras flowing from my lips. Despite the bustle around the tent, infinite peace and tranquility are ours. If only for a moment, we've created our own serene sanctuary and I feel home—home within myself.

"Nordun." Yeshe's sweet voice puts me right back amidst the lunchtime tumult. No rest for the weary here, as the work is never done. I hurry in and dish the steaming thenthuk out to the hungry bunch. The enormous pot is filled to the brim, but my serving spoon scrapes the bottom in no time. These folks can eat!

"So how about some horse-handling this afternoon?" Sonam cleans his bowl with his thumb. "Norbu's training a horse to the saddle."

I throw a few hands full of salt in the simmering kettle and nod. I don't even have to think about it. It's why I came here, after all.

Norbu's great with horses. I realized that while riding with him this morning. Observing Norbu in the paddock this afternoon, the way he plays with the young horse, is pure joy. The shiny brown mare is already used to the bridle. It prances around him as he stands in the middle, reining her in. A colorful wool saddle rug hangs over his left arm. He coaxes the mare to sniff it, making her familiar with the touch and smell.

"Notice how calm Norbu is, first building up trust." Sonam joins me and we watch Norbu from the edge of the pen. "Out in nature, predators jump on the horse from above, the same spot where we place the saddle on its back." His chin points to the pen. "Even though this mare is born and bred here at the camp, she still carries that natural instinct of the wild. She will panic and throw up a fight if you don't let her get familiar with the saddle first."

The mare sniffs out the piece of fabric on Norbu's arm. Pushing the wool with her nose, she nibbles the small rug.

"Well then." Norbu pats the horse's neck. "Let's give this a try." He folds the rug over the horse's neck and slides it down to where the saddle will be placed.

The mare's ears point as she jerks the rope. Dust flies up as she circles around the rug on her back. She shudders a few times, and the rug slides. Norbu pacifies her in a mellow voice.

"You've seen this before." Sonam nods in approval. "Your father used to train horses like this all the time." His eyebrows raise. "Sure, your mother was a great horse trainer too, if he gave her the chance." A muffled chortle follows.

"I have." My eyes fix on the mare. My mind searches deep, for I know they are there, hidden in the vault I make for myself, stored away when I was left alone with too much grief to bear. Memories of those carefree childhood days at the stables, of those long, warm summer days that never seemed to end. Riding my pony in the rolling meadows with Mother beside me. A warm glow spreads through my body as the memories become clear.

My eyes close and for a moment I'm there, at that very summer, back at the stables, with Mother in the pen. The sunlight catches her shiny black locks. Her face beams as she holds a long leash. A gorgeous stallion prances from left to right as a golden amber gleams on its fur.

Come on, Nordun. Father's white shirt is wide open. His arms stretch out to me. Up I go, onto the horse's back. Strong hands walk with me, holding me tight, making me feel safe and loved, so secure.

In the distance, I hear a horse snort. My breath slows and the memories flee. My eyes blink as tears loom on the edge. Too late. I avert my heated face.

"You're so much like her." Sonam rests his hand on my shoulder. His voice wavers. "I'm so sorry, Nordun." He clears his throat.

"I didn't know about his demise, about the troubles at the stables." He draws a hand over his face and his mouth twists. "But I should have—I should have kept in touch. He's been the best of my friends." He tips his hat back and meets my eyes. A hint of shame flickers through.

"It's just that things became sort of strained after your mother's death, you know." His feet shuffle in the sand. "I guess deep down I blamed him, your father, for her accident, for letting her ride a wild stallion alone like that." His eyes narrow and he looks away. My hands wring around the pole.

"I never told him, but he felt it anyway." He takes in a sharp breath. "So he kept his distance, and I did too." His stare hardens. A vein strains in his neck. "I've let your father down bad, Nordun." He shakes his head. "I swear I'll make it up to him, to you both." His fingers dig in my shoulder and my hand slides over, covering not even half of his. This immense, somewhat madcap man—there's so much more to him than meets the eye.

I turn to face him full on. "You already have, Sonam. You took me in."

"Oh, that's nothing." His other hand grips mine. "I have no doubt you will succeed, even your mother..." His words stall and my fingernails dig into the wood. *Even my mother, what?* He doesn't finish his sentence though. His heels turn and he's dashing off to Zinzin, calling him over from the other side. I never even heard her.

"Hey, you." Sangmo springs her ever enthusiastic self at me, pushing Sonam's words to the back of my mind. "Driving yaks, handling horses, you're doing great."

I laugh and pinch her forearm.

"You're not leaving me already, are you?" I mean it. Sangmo's presence has been immensely reassuring.

"Nope." Sangmo's smile says it all. "I'm with you all the way." She takes my hand and looks me straight in the eye. "No matter how much time you need, I'm here, you know that."

My heart bursts at the sight of her honesty and I lean in. "I know," I say. "I know." Her warm hands in mine, her unconditional support... *This family is your sanctuary.* Grandfather's brother's parting words come to my mind. No matter the outcome of my journey, how fortunate I am to have all these wonderful, loving people, my new family on my side.

"Nordun." Norbu's voice calls me back to the pen. "Would you mind?" He strokes the mare's neck. His hand points to the saddle in the corner.

"Sure." The wood frame's light on my arm. The mare eyes me up with suspicion as I join in the pen.

"It's a devil, this one." Norbu keeps patting the mare's neck as he puts her nose to the saddle in my arms. A loud sniff and an even louder breeze. Does she sense what's coming?

"Take your time." Norbu's calm tone encourages the mare as she pokes the frame with her nose.

He turns to me. "And you too."

My eyes widen. My hands sweat, fumbling around the edge of the frame. Does he expect me to saddle this mare?

"Sure, you can." Norbu meets my startled look with a gentle smile. "You've had the perfect training—with all that meditation and compassion at the monastery. You've got the patience and right mind to connect with a horse."

He's right. In theory, I've had the best education on the benefits of patience and compassion, how it connects us to the nature of others and the suffering of sentient beings. However, I'm awkward with others—and myself—out here in the world.

"Let her know you're here." Norbu takes the saddle from me and slides it over his arm.

I take the lead. I stroke the mare's neck, gliding all the way down its back. The horse shudders and huffs. How beautiful, her smooth fur like a golden gleam in the sun. And yes, a devil, poking her velvety nose into my side and probing my balance. I walk with it around the pen a few times. The mare strides, the saddle rug is on her back and my confidence is soaring. I'm in the pen with a wild horse. Yes, this is going well.

At Norbu's sign, I stroll to the middle. Time to put the saddle on. I hold the lead, one hand stroking the mare's neck. Norbu slides the wooden frame over the woolen rug with ease.

I hold my breath as the saddle lands. The mare's nostrils flare, her muscles ripple under my smooth strokes. The mare's body tenses, and her eyes bulge. She breezes and my heart races. *She's going to buck.* Panic flushes through my arms and I tighten my grip on the lead, pulling it close.

In an instant, the mare neighs and jolts on all fours. Front legs soar in the air. *Hoo!* I let out a yell, and my feet stumble back to steady myself. Alas, I tumble and land flat on my back, the lead still in my hand. The dust settles. I look around, dazed. *Ouch.* That hurts—my back and my pride.

"Come on." Norbu's hand stretches in front of me. Without hesitation, I take his offer to pull me up. His grip is firm and secure. The mare just stands there, unfazed. The saddle's still on her back, be it pushed aside.

"I'm sorry," I mutter and hand Norbu the lead. How stupid am I to react like that? Pulling the lead in a panic—everybody knows it makes a horse jump.

"Oh no, you're not getting away with that." Norbu's suppressed smile says it all. "The horse is clever; she sensed you waver and saw her chance." He scratches the mare behind her ears.

"It's in a horse's nature to test you, so you'll try again right now." He slips his hand over mine, securing the lead between our hands and starts walking the pen, around and around. Sweat trickles down my neck. I'm a mess and must look like a fool, but I keep walking. He's right, I can't give up now.

"Now you walk her for a while." His fingers release mine. "And don't forget to breathe." He winks and walks away, leaving me with the mare in the middle of the pen.

My knees sag, but I straighten my back and keep walking under Norbu's watchful eye. How could I ever have this done without his help? I even dare to breathe again as the mare ambles around with the saddle, still trying to probe me—again and again.

"Now you've felt it yourself." Norbu ties up the horse. "A slight hesitation, and the horse is off." He takes the saddle and hands it to me. "It just takes a bit of confidence on your side." *Confidence.* Where did I hear that before?

"Don't worry, we'll practice some more." He tips back his hat. His brown eyes smile at mine. "Trust me, you'll be fine." His encouraging words, the way he handles the horse with kindness... lightness seizes my being. How lucky am I to have his help?

My lengthy shadow accompanies me on my way back to the tent. What an eventful day it has been. The memory of Mother drifts back in my mind, of training wild horses with Father, and me being around her in the pen. I was so small back then, yet knew of no fear.

A memory like that, buried so deep, and resurfacing in an instant when needed. It sure makes me wonder—will my original courage resurface like that too, when called for?

Thirty-Two

S oft murmurs call out from another deep and dreamless
sleep. I stretch and surface, delighted with the good night's
sleep. It must be the work in the outdoors that relaxes me the
moment my body hits the mat. The tent flap rustles, and feet
slip over the carpet, a patter on the earth beaten floor. Who's
up so early? I hold my breath, trying to identify the muffled
conversation.

"You've only just arrived," A faint voice, definitely female,
hisses. *Zinzin*. It's Zinzin and Sonam talking outside.

I raise myself on my elbows, careful not to wake Sangmo
beside me. Why are they up so early? The two of them whisper,
too hushed to make out their words. The tone of their voices
is strained, though. Not good. I pop up my head. Shifty
silhouettes move along, stealthy, in and out of the tent.

I lower myself again. Something's up. Should I go over to
help? Then again, it might be a personal matter. Their heated
conversation behind the tent two days ago sits fresh in my
mind. Sonam caught me eavesdropping. I cringe and pull the
blanket. How embarrassing that was! I'll let them be. More
sleep is good.

But I can't. My curiosity—and sincere concern—are getting
the better of me. I keep listening, my eyes closed. A faint neigh,
wet grass squishes under hooves. Somebody's getting a horse

ready. *Sonam*. Sonam's leaving. I shoot up. No way. Leaving without saying goodbye? Something's up. It must be urgent.

I throw on my sandals and tiptoe to the entrance. My heart pounds in my chest. My hands on the bearskin, I waver.

"I'll be back soon." Sonam's voice, I was right—he's leaving. My face flustered, I step outside. The grass squeaks under my feet. The icy drops between my toes stop me in my tracks.

"Nordun, you're up." Sonam's horse is all packed, and he's got the reins in his hands. Zinzin's huddled in a blanket beside him.

"You're leaving?" My shoulders drop. I already have the answer. "Sorry to see you go so soon." I shiver and throw my arms around myself, shifting from one foot to the other.

"Don't worry, you'll be fine." Sonam slides his arm around Zinzin and pulls her close. "You're in a good place here," he adds, his voice hoarse.

"And we love having you." Zinzin's honest smile eases me. I avert my eyes.

"You better go now. It's a long ride," she says. A long ride to where? I glance up, but I'm not asking. It's private, that's obvious.

"I'll pass the word to your father." Sonam smirks. "Even though Ghedun already told him you're in excellent hands, he'll still be worrying." He mounts and shifts in the saddle. "That's Palden for you, such a big wuss. Too soft for his own good, but the best friend a man can ask for." Sonam's words warm my insides, defying the biting cold that has latched onto me. I pat his horse on the neck.

"Thank you. For everything." A willful presence meets my eyes.

"Listen Nordun, whatever is said, there's no such thing as a false divination." Sonam leans over. "Your mother knew it, and she was sure one day the stables would be yours. It's your father who doubted the prophecy, but only after losing the love of his life." His eyes flare at me. I take a step back.

"He did well putting you in the care of Dechen, a mighty woman who he knew would instill the right attitude in you. I'm sure she taught you there's nothing a woman can't achieve if she puts her mind to it. So there you are." His horse prances, eager to fly off. "Think about that now!" He pulls the reins tight and his stallion boots away, leaving me speechless, frozen to the ground.

Mother was sure I would lead the stables. I would stand there for another eternity if not for Zinzin, taking my icy hands in hers, urging me into the tent.

"We might as well start the day." She pokes the dormant stove while I try to get my head around what Sonam just said. *Father only started doubting after mother's death.* Fire crackles and within no time the cooker's ablaze, casting a warming glow in the tent. With a hungry baby on her breast, Zinzin sags down beside the cooker, an absent look on her paled face.

"This baby, so hungry all the time." Zinzin shakes her head. "I'm grateful for another healthy child, but I'm drained." Cold to the bone, I haul the big kettle on the stove. How selfish of me to stand around. A fresh cup of tea will do both of us good.

"What's going on?" Sangmo's awake. A blanket thrown over her shoulders, she joins us at the stove.

"Sonam left." I hand Zinzin a cup of warm milk. The tea takes too long to boil; she needs something hot right now.

Helpful as ever, Sangmo takes over the tea, splashing the rest of the milk in the kettle.

"When will he be back?" Her eyes go over to Zinzin, whose hands wring around her cup.

"We're fine." She sighs. "We always are. He'll be back in his own time." She sips her milk. I clean out the churn and put the butter in, waiting for the tea to boil.

"Still." I squat beside the stove, the churn between my hands. "You must miss him when he's at the homestead." The words are out. *Not good!* I'm prying. I cast my eyes down.

"It's fine," Zinzin says. "We're both used to it by now." The placid tone in her voice assures me she doesn't mind me asking. "I missed myself more when I was at his home." Sangmo and I both turn to Zinzin at the same time.

"You lived at the homestead?" Sangmo's voice pitches.

"Yes." Zinzin lets out a laugh. "It that such a surprise?" She takes another sip of milk. Her arm rocks the little one back and forth. Still stunned, I point to Sangmo to pour the tea in the churner.

"I was there for about seven years." Zinzin sighs. "Seven long years." Sangmo's eyebrows raise at me. She churns the tea. I nod. So Zinzin was living with Sonam at the homestead, but now she's living here, in the tent, with their children, away from her husband. That's unusual, to say the least.

"But you returned to the camp," Sangmo says. I clear my throat and throw her a sharp look. That's none of our concern. Sangmo, however, ignores me.

"How so?" She casually pours the butter tea back into the kettle. My toes curl in their sandals and I veer up to get some cups.

"It was hard to be a good wife, to live in one place." Zinzin's lips press tight. "I missed the open spaces, the higher grounds." A longing smile graces her face. "Endless sky above me, solid earth beneath me, in tune with the pace of nature—I can't live without it." Zinzin pauses as Sangmo pours us all tea.

"I can imagine." Sangmo shakes her head. "I don't do well between solid walls either." She puts her hand on Zinzin's arm as she sits down beside her.

"It's not something we can explain." Sangmo turns to me. "It's in our nature."

Zinzin nods, her eyes close for a moment and I take the snoozing baby from her arms.

"Silly me, I was so young when I married Sonam." Her voice sounds far away. "Even younger than you girls are. In love with a tall, handsome stranger, what did I know about life?" She rubs her eyes. "Living in that big house was hard on me, and whenever the yearning would get too much, Sonam would bring me here." A sudden sadness sets around her lips. "He's always been so good to me, but it wasn't enough. It only made me long for the open spaces more."

Zinzin's honest revelation weaves a delicate silence between us, an intimacy I think only women do share.

"Three healthy boys we had, Sonam and me, but then I lost a few precious ones." Her voice wavers. My arms pull the sleeping bundle tight against my chest. "And with that, my lust for life. I even lost interest in my beautiful boys, ignoring their call for me, staying in bed all day." She stares in the fire now, but her gaze looks inside. "I was losing my body, my hair, my strength, and for sure, I was losing my mind."

My heart sinks at her, telling the sorrow she went through. The woman before me, vibrant and strong, I can't imagine her losing any of it, let alone her mind.

"But then, after many losses, a healthy daughter came." Her eyes light up and she raises her hands. "Holding that beautiful baby girl, tiny yet full of life, I knew I had no choice." She puts her head in her hands. "No matter how much I loved Sonam, it was either going home to the mountains or die." Her hands draw over her face. She straightens her back. "It was as simple as that."

Sangmo gets up and pours us more tea. "I've heard it before," she says. "People like us, we need to move with the sun and the stars, and the wind on our faces."

I blow the foam to the side of the cup. My thoughts drift to my sisters on our mountain. Many of them are from nomad families, but I've never heard them talk about this longing. Sure, some go away from time to time to meditate and practice in the open, with Dechen's permission of course. They always return, claiming it makes their practice stronger. I never thought much about my sisters going off into the wild. I sway the little one in my arms, her bundled up body warm and snug to my chest. There're many things I never thought about at the monastery, and many things I see differently now.

"You were young and in love," Sangmo tilts her head to one side, a mischievous smile on her face.

"What do we know anyway, right Nordun?" She puts the kettle down and gives me a quick wink. "We learn by doing and get up again when we fall." I chuckle. Somehow Sangmo has the gift of lighting the air.

"We sure do." The sadness ebbs from Zinzin's eyes, revealing an earthy brown within them, as solid as oak. "We learn by living and I became a stronger woman, living outside my family, confined to four walls." She gulps her cup down in one go and puts it down. "I learned who I was and what I needed to thrive—not just to survive." Her eyes flare up. She puts her hands on her knees.

"They were a tough seven years." She tilts her chin and rubs her knees. "The battle inside of me, it wore me down, but it's in times of battle that we build our strength. I learned what was needed for me and my children to thrive—so the battle served its purpose." She turns to me with a serene yet determined calm. "But it was following through on it, acknowledging that deep connection to my true nature, and returning to where I belong. The following through, that turned out to be the most difficult."

I take a sip of my tea as my thoughts taste the truth of Zinzin's words. Yes, that must have been rough, leaving the husband you love, taking the children away from their father, almost impossible.

"I was lucky. Sonam's the best, for he saw that if he didn't let me go, I would wither away in his arms." A pensive smile curls her lips. "He's quite the wanderer himself, but I allow him his pleasures." Her voice picks up. She throws a stealthy glance at Sangmo, who's working the dough for breakfast by now.

"His heart is mine and he'll always return home, to me and the children—he always does." She bends over and she takes the sleeping baby from me. She draws her close, humming a soothing tune.

Sangmo pounds the dough with a heated face and dogged determination. I think of Sonam and our stay at that dubious inn. The drinking, the gambling, the smuggling—yes, he's wild in his own way. Zinzin knows she can't change him, so she lets him. Just like Sonam knows he can't change her, so he gives her space. With mutual respect and unconditional love as their common ground, they've both found their own way of living with each other. My fingertips draw over the baby's furry crown. That's quite something, I guess.

I smoothen the scarf around Zinzin's shoulders. *The battle served its purpose.* It shows, for she's got that look of content, that knowing she's home. My chest tightens and for a moment I envy her. How I long for ease like that, finding what is needed of me, knowing my true home. I thought I knew—for so long the monastery was my home, but now, everything's changing.

Your mother knew it. Even I can feel it in my bones.

Thirty-Three

I lift my face to the morning sky. A pale yellow disk struggles behind shredded hues of stubborn blue and gray. With Yeshe still in bed, we're down a good woman on milking this morning. At least we got up early, no time to waste. My heart goes out to her with her baby due any day now. Jinpa, her husband is still on the way, so Rinchen went over to the nearest monastery to get prayers done.

Om mani padme hung. The beads slide through my fingers. More prayers are needed, as the birth of new life is always a precarious time—for mother and child. Not that I know much about it. I've only seen a handful of babes being born—sisters who had an unexpected pregnancy, and a wandering nun who came to stay with us until birth. *Om mani padme hung.* The suffering of childbirth and raising a family, to me it's a wonder how lay women can think becoming a mother is a blessing. It is a sure way of accepting their karma, I guess.

"Let's go." Sango bounces out of the tent. Her arms swing a few buckets on their way. *Om mani padme hung.* I tuck the beads under my shirt. My mind continues the prayer, my feet follow her to the lower grass land. We're in luck. Norbu has already driven the dris together. Their low grunting sound greets us, a protest to our intrusion of their private morning graze.

"Some more training this afternoon?" Norbu slides off his horse with that ease I envy. "Now that we've got the saddle on, it's time for a rider—perfect preparation for you." He tips his hat back and squints at the mellow morning sun, finally able to break through.

"Oh, yes." I swallow the rising fear and put on my bravest face. *Mounting that horse.* My knees go weak, but I will not give in. I've got the perfect person to help me.

"Thank you for the opportunity." And I mean it—with Sonam and Jinpa gone, Norbu's carrying the responsibility of the camp. He's got a lot of work to do and isn't obliged to waste any of his precious time on me.

"Any time." He waves and walks off with the horse. Sangmo's smug laughter comes from behind.

"He likes you." Sangmo's hips push a sturdy dri around.

"I like him too," I say. "It's good of him to help me." *Om mani padme hung.* The words keep flowing from my mind as my eyes scout for a smaller dri.

"No, I mean in that way." Sangmo turns to me with a brazen smile. An instant heat rises up my cheeks. *No way.*

"You think?" I try on a casual tone. I've found my dri. Now lining her up the right way is next.

"It's in his eyes." Sangmo's nose wrinkles. *Eyes.* An emerald green flashes before me, a reminder of someone else. *Karma.* The flutter's back from deep below. Sangmo's voice gets lost in the noisy grunting of the dris as I drift to the night at the river, and to Karma with his quiet, powerful presence. *Stop it.*

My fingers stiffen around the dri's utter. Sweat pricks on my neck. I will not give in to this illusion. *Focus.* With all my effort, I steer my thoughts away. *Om mani padme hung.*

A sweet whiff rises. The first spray of warm milk splashes in the bucket. *Om mani padme hung.* Another gulf of cream switches in the bucket. See, this is going well. I'll let these silly thoughts drift by, paying no heed to them at all.

"Hey." Sangmo leans over, her bucket already half full. "You're not listening to any of what I'm saying." Her bold smile turns into a frown.

"Sorry." My sleeve's already soaked as I keep wiping the sweat off my face. "Got to concentrate. Don't want to land in the muck again." We both laugh, for we know it's probably true.

"You're taking this far too serious." She positions herself under the next dri, a solid gray one. "Cheer up a bit, or it will be a long and dreary day." Her voice sounds stern from under the dri, but I detect a little laughter in there. She can't be serious, but she is.

"Let's sing a milking song. It makes the heart light and the milk flow." She sets in a tune with the most melodious voice. "Milking the young dri, who's yellow butter I offer to the Gods." My hands suspend between the utter and the bucket as her happiness fills my ears.

"Milking the young dri, when feeding on the meadows, the young man feels happy." She sings on. Never would I have guessed Sangmo had such a lovely voice. A loud one, yes, but so musical, no.

"Come on." Sangmo's tone isn't taking no for an answer. So we sing, even though I would rather keep on praying. "Milking the young dri..." And, as always, Sangmo's right. My voice isn't as pleasant as hers, and I'm often out of tune, but humming in harmony sure makes my heart sing. Our hands move at the rhythm of the song, our buckets fill up as fast as the early morning sun warms up the thick, foggy air.

"See, told you so." Sangmo carries the last bucket to the edge of the pen. "A tune eases the work."

I rub my sweaty palms on my skirt. We did good. The buckets are full to the rim, and I even enjoyed it. I can't believe it's only two days ago I stood here with the same bucket—it was loaded with fear. Now it's a bucket filled with milk. I pick the newly formed callus on the palm of my hands and wonder why I feared milking dris. Silly me. I mean, what was the worst thing that could happen, anyway? Yes, I landed in the muck. So what?

"Let's go." Sangmo's already way ahead of me. Her long tresses trail behind her. The tangy smell of fresh green floats on a breeze. I pick up two buckets. My hands tremble, but my mind's tireless as ever. So what's the worst thing that could happen with the young horse in the pen? I was around wild horses all the time as a child. What's there to fear?

My stomach clenches. It crushes all the lightness from the song with a sure sense of anxiety. My mind's off to make sense of it all. This is not the way to deal with fear, for whatever it is, it's not real. Dechen told us young nuns long ago, in one of our first classes. She asked us, "Who's afraid of the dark at night?" And most of us raised our hand. What's not to fear for a little girl when you're alone and can't see?

"Everything is a creation of our own mind, including our fear," she said, walking around the room. "Our mind loves playing games with us. It makes up many excuses why we should be afraid. This way our mind keeps us trapped, and not only in the dark."

Back then I didn't understand. The dark night on our mountain remained something scary for a long, long time. Later I realized, our mind wants us to stay safe and secure. It doesn't want us to go out and venture into something unfamiliar, something we don't know. So our mind makes up fear as an excuse to stay in, to keep us in the place we know as comfortable and secure. Yes, very foolish, yet most effective. I halt a moment, my fingers numb.

"I'll help, Ani-la." Two tiny hands grab one of my buckets. A chirpy smile looks up at me. Lhadun, Zinzin's youngest daughter, has come to my rescue. The gaping hole in her mouth where her two front teeth are supposed to be makes her even cuter than she already is. She's off with the bucket, hoisting it between her little legs without spilling a drop. My heart expands at the sight of her. How can one not feel delight in such endearing company?

As I step into the tent, my mood gets even better. Yeshe's up, feverish but clearly enjoying a cup of fresh milk.

"So good to have you two around." She throws me a grateful glance as I pour the milk in the cauldron to boil. "I hope you'll be here when the little one arrives; it won't be long now." She arches her back.

"No worries." Sangmo fills Yeshe's cup once more. "I'm not going anywhere." That's Sangmo, always looking out for others.

My chest tightens. I wish I could say the same, but I can't forget why I'm here. I honestly don't know when I'll be leaving. Sure, I can handle the dris now. I even enjoyed being out there this morning.

Golden foam ripples on the spoon as I scoop it off the boiling milk to set it apart. This rich cream is going to make delicious butter. I lick my fingers and press the cover tight. If only I could find the same ease and joy in handling that young horse. That joy that for a few moments filled my being this morning. The joy that everybody seems to have so naturally around here.

"Somebody's waiting for you, Nordun." Yeshe's sweet voice calls me from my thoughts. The cracks in my hands are still tender. I swipe them with a rag and jump up.

It's Norbu, a saddle over his arm. "It's time." The tranquil reassurance in his voice puts me at ease. I put down the rag. Yes, it's time.

Thirty-Four

Norbu ducks into the pen. I follow. The mare's already kicking up dust.

"You know what happened yesterday, don't you?" Norbu tilts his head at me. I bite my lip.

"I pulled the lead to control." My shoulders tense, I rub my neck. The midday sun's scorching every piece of undisposed skin it can get to. "That's a no-no," I add. Everybody who's been around horses knows.

"Yes, horses need leadership." He hands me the halter, a serious look on his face. "But it's all about that certain feel to them, like an invisible connection."

I slide my hand through the halter, the leather cool to the touch. A certain feel?

"It's like holding a small bird in your hand." Norbu points the palm of his hand towards me. "You hold it too firm, it suffocates." He folds his hand into a fist. I stare at it, his fingernails black rimmed and frayed.

"You don't hold it firm enough, it flies away." His hardened palm stretches out to me. Yes, I u.

"Either way, a horse will balk." A jolly grin replaces the gravity on his face. "Because horses can't fly, right?" My shoulders sag and my anxious thoughts back down. Norbu's good at making people feel at ease.

"Right." I thank him with a smile for his company at this very moment.

"Tell me." Norbu turns. "What do you see?" The young mare prances around. It snorts and neighs in content.

"Look at her." Norbu's eyes are on the horse. "Observe her world."

I gaze at the mare. Dust tickles my throat. She flings her head up and down, and her long shiny manes follow in a gilded slow motion. Her wide nostrils heave ever so slightly. Tail held high, ears pointing around, the mare prances with zest as her bright eyes keep us in sight at all times. Oh yes, this horse's showing off for us.

"See how it's eyeing us up?" Norbu points his chin. "In a clever way."

I lean forward a bit; my fingers wring the leather. A musky smell comes up from under my sweaty palms. The mare's hooves paw in the sand. Sleek muscles ripple along her flanks, displaying power and strength while challenging us—almost in a playful manner.

"This mare's young and ready to be entertained." Norbu laughs. "Let's see what we can do today."

I lean back on the pole. Norbu moves to the middle. The mare starts circling him at once. She keeps her eyes on him, while twisting and turning her agile frame.

"Now watch how inquisitive she is." Norbu's so at ease in the center there. The mare is frolicking and circling around.

"See how the inside ear is directed at me, trying to find me?" He lifts his chin to the horse's ears. "The outside ear is listening to the rest, but the inside ear is pointed towards me." A pleased look comes to his face. "I've got her attention."

My eyes widen. Yes, he does. I dig in my heels. How does he do that?

The mare circles again but moves in to Norbu, until she's close. Norbu squares his shoulders and relaxes his arms at his side. I see what he's doing. He lets the horse come to him at her own pace.

It works. The mare's almost at Norbu's shoulder now. My pulse quickens. My back pushes in the pole.

The horse bends its head at Norbu, curious to size him up. Norbu turns his left shoulder towards her and steps away. Just a few steps. The mare stretches her neck. Hooves crush as it follows. I hold my breath. A tightness tingles through my chest. There she goes, following him again.

"Good." Norbu says, his voice soft. "Now we reward her." He strokes the mare's forehead.

"Again." His heels turn in the sand and he steps away with the same relaxed manner, the same ease in his moves. Again, the horse follows, even closer now.

"You can't chase a horse." Norbu makes eye contact with the mare. "They're faster and stronger than any man will ever be." His hands slide down the mare's neck in a gentle assurance. "So you make the horse chase you by arousing their natural curiosity and reward them for checking you out."

By now the mare has her head bend at Norbu, a display of trust. He puts on the halter. It takes him no effort at all. When he looks up at me, my heart sinks. I know what's coming. My hands dig into the rough timber pole. A small splinter lodges itself under my fingernail.

"Your turn." His hopeful smile is almost convincing, but my mouth runs dry at the thought of my turn.

"Get the horse's attention like I did." He moves away and ducks the rope. "Then again, everybody has their own manner. You'll see, you have your own way of connecting with it."

My mind's running circles with the mare in the pen. *My own way.* Sounds easy and yet. I clear my throat as Norbu nods for me to step in.

"My own way. I'm not sure what that is." My voice sounds smaller than I want it to be. Where's my sliver of confidence when I need it the most?

"Well, you know what isn't your way." Norbu puts his hands on his hips. "Don't you?" The sour stench of fear hits my nostrils. The lash of a leather whip cracks in my ears as anxious eyes bulge before me. A surge of adrenaline shoots through my body—that's not my way.

"Most people don't understand the inner world of a horse." Norbu leans back. "It's closely tied to their outer word, to nature." His hands fold and his face assumes that serious expression again.

"Of course the horse is going to buck when you force something on its back—it's the place where big cats attack, so it's in its nature to react." I nod, Sonam told me yesterday. It's so logical, but I had never seen it in that way.

"Of course the horse is going to kick when you hit its sides—it's the place where doglike animals attack, so it's going to balk before running off," he adds. "If not, the horse will have its insides torn out, that's for sure." My eyes search for the mare. This all makes sense, and still...

"Put yourself in the horse's place and go from there." Norbu straightens his back to the pole and my heart pounds against my ribcage.

"She's curious and playful by nature, so it shouldn't be difficult." Norbu's trying hard to loosen me up. Did I just hear a nudge of teasing in his voice?

My feet shuffle to the middle, my eyes seek the mare. There she is, circling around me in a prancing pace. What now? My mind searches, but there's only my epic land from yesterday coming through. Yep, that was embarrassing. I wonder if she remembers. This horse is smart, so I'm sure she does. Unwillingly, a smile comes to my lips.

"Remember me?" My lips move, my voice a mellow plea. "Yes, that landing was quite embarrassing, so let's not do that again."

The mare's inner ear locks onto me. Enormous eyes gleam a sharp alert. She keeps circling, with a trot that seems feather light, yet pure strength radiates from a vigorous frame.

One ear twirls towards me. Yes, I have her attention. My mind keeps searching. What can I give to connect? My eyes close for a moment. Sweat trickles down the back of my neck. I settle my hands on my stomach. With a sigh, my breath lands in my hands. My mind clears and my being becomes a void space within, empty and ready to receive. My eyes open again, and the mare's curious stare is on me. I tilt my head to the side to meet an open gaze and see—there's nothing to fear. There's only the mare and me.

I bow. "I'm here, I see you," I say, and I don't know whether it's meant for the mare or for me, but it works. A comforting calm moves within me as the horse bends her head to me. *That's it.* She wants to be seen.

I square my shoulders, my heels head away. I walk on a few steps. My heart leaps; hooves squish in the sand behind. She's following me. My shoulders drop and I meet her. My hand slides down to the soft fuzz of her muzzling lips. A huffing breath vibrates from open nostrils. She nudges my side as her ears swipe away.

"Yes, there we are." The words hide under my breath. The mare stands next to me, head down, ready to connect.

I slide the halter over her head and rest my hands on her neck. The mare shakes, solid muscles swelling under her a gleaming fur. My warm hands fuse into her energy, into her play. A surge of confidence rushes through. My fingers click the lead from the halter and my heart drums in my chest. Delight surrounds me as the mare dances in a cloud of dust. Darting legs move in an elated canter, from left to right and back again, and all the while she keeps a big, bold gaze on me.

"Yes, I see you!" My voice pitches at this audacious display of the wild and the free. Laughter fills my ears, and all tension pours from my limbs. We've made it—our first connection. There is nothing to fear, not from the mare, not from me.

The horse returns to my side, pushing me with her wet, velvety nose. Her curiosity is still aroused. Norbu walks up to join us, and the mare twitches her ears, playful but a bit more at edge. My fingers fold around the bridle and click on the lead. With a sharp neigh she raises an alert. I guess the horse is mirroring me.

Norbu takes the lead. He pats the mare on its neck, but it's me she keeps in her sight.

"That's it." Norbu nods. "Now ask her permission to mount."

Mount? Salty sweat trickles down my upper lip. I wipe the veil of grime from my eyes.

"There's always a chance she'll buck—it's in her nature." Norbu glances at me. "But that's fine, for you've experienced how comfy the muck is here." His lips pinch in an attempt to suppress a grimace. *How nice.*

"Well thank you," I say. "You sure keep the spirits up." My hands glide over the horse's smooth hide and rest where the saddle's supposed to go. Norbu nods and gives me a leg up.

With the lightest touch possible, I shift my upper body over the mare's back. The weak tissue of my stomach leans against the mare's hardened spine. I rest my cheek against her upper side and put just enough pressure for the horse to feel me. A rapid heartbeat throbs through the veins beneath the fur, and a briny scent surrounds the two of us. The mare snorts and shifts from left to right and back, only a little. I hold my breath as we rock, back and forth, in synch, until the horse's confident with my weight. Norbu's right. This horse is all up to play with me.

The mare stands at ease, ears all twirls, and a slight puff breezes from her nostrils. Sweat lashes down my back now, but I don't care. I'm here and still on the horse. My head light, my hands move down her sides. I glance at Norbu from the corners of my eyes. He smiles and his arm moves up. I get it. Time to mount.

My body veers to the front. My shirt stretches over my chest. My right knee pulls over the mare's spine and down. My breath shallows as my ribs clamp around my lungs. As light as my body allows me, I shift my weight over, my legs dangling from her sides. The mare reacts in an instant, turning her ears, one to me, the other one out. Hooves scrape and legs prance coolly. My hands secure themselves in tangled manes. With a deep breath in I straighten myself in one go.

My eyes find Norbu's over the mare's head. My vision blurs—Norbu's proud smile says it all. The mare and me, we're fine.

I just mounted an untamed horse.

Thirty-Five

"It's good to see you like this." Sangmo swings two buckets from her hips as she joins us in the pen. "Instead of a scared little bird hopping around on a horseback, you're actually riding." Her eyes beam with solid pride. "That's the spirit."

Her candid delight lifts my heart. All afternoon we've been working hard, Norbu, the horse and me. And with success. We even got the mare to canter around the pen with me in the saddle. Fatigue has set in my body, but my spirit's soaring—as is my confidence. This afternoon taught me so much—about the horse and about myself.

"Yep, you've taken a gigantic leap." Norbu reigns in the mare.

"I still have a lot to learn, though." I slide down and scratch the horse behind her ears. "And somehow it feels like time's running out." It does. A vague sense of urgency has lodged itself in my stomach after Yeshe's remark about being here at the time of birth. My thoughts hamper. The mare nibbles at my sleeve.

"One step at a time." Norbu's voice sounds reassuring, as always. "No use rushing out of panic or fear." He turns to lead the horse out of the pen.

"Listen to your intuition like you did this afternoon, and you'll be fine." He tilts his head to the side and tries to catch my eye.

"Thank you." I meet his gaze. *Gold.* An intense blush spreads over my already heated face. Radiant speckles of the brightest golden shimmer from the deep as the sunlight captures his eyes. *How beautiful.* How come I never noticed before? My gaze averts to the mare. I cover my face with the back of my sleeve, pretending to wipe the grime.

"I couldn't have done it without your help." My voice trails off. Did he notice my stare?

"My pleasure." He tips his hat in his familiar way. "I see Sangmo's got you lined up for more work." He waves his hand at us and walks off. The mare's hooves clap away in an enthusiastic tread.

"You're a fast learner." Sangmo hands me a bucket. "I told you so. It's in your blood." My hands beat my skirt. The dirt, the dust, it's a permanent thing here.

"Now let's see if the dris enjoy your company as much as Norbu did this afternoon." Sangmo strolls out of the pen, nonchalance folding over her face. "You know what to do by now."

My mouth opens. Did Sangmo just say what I think she said? The cheekiness of her. I pinch my lips. There's no way I'm going to even respond to that.

Still light-headed from this afternoon's training, I float alongside Sangmo, bouncing her bucket on our way to the dris. Lucky me, to have people around me whose faith in me is stronger than I've ever been able to find in myself.

The handle of the bucket rattles between my fingers. My thoughts go back to all the good. To all those times my rigid fingers couldn't command the pen over paper, and Tsomo was there to practice with me. All those times the prayers we had to learn by heart strolled straight out of my memory, and Pema was there to chant with me, guiding me through the rhythm of the stanza. A pang of longing stretches across my heart. How I miss them, my sisters in solitude. My eyes search the distance. I wonder, where are they now?

The shadows lengthen, and the wind spurs a staunch chill to the humid air. The sky rolls a billowing silver and pearl, a likely forebode to oncoming thunder. Sangmo and I milk all the dris before evening falls upon us. There's no grunting or pushing or shoving this time. The cattle seem too placid this evening. Is it me getting used to the animals or something else?

"Might be the weather changing." Sangmo scouts the distance. "Animals sense more than we do, but you're right." She points to two huge black and tan mastiffs, their colossal bodies lazing around the herd. "Even the dogs are more quiet than usual."

Our buckets filled to the brim, we're welcomed by the outcries of the unruly mob of youngsters and the roaring hiss of the fired-up stove. Little Lhadun's hands are swift to help me, busying her rowdy siblings away from the sizzling cauldron, making sure nobody gets burned.

"Sit." Zinzin hands me a cup and a nob of butter on my hand. I smear the rich cream along my fingers, patting my face. The merciless sun has left its angry marks on me. My lips are parched, my cheeks streaked from the scorching rays and my prickly sweat. Rubbing the rest on the rough patches on my palms, I look at the score of children.

"You've had your hands full too," I say. Whatever's up with the animals being quiet tonight, it doesn't seem to bother the children. I lean back and sip my cup. The milk needs to be boiled, but it will have to wait; my aching limbs have decided.

"Oh, children have their days." Zinzin pours me another cup. Her eyes dart to the women's side of the tent. Something's up. I lean in. Zinzin nods. It's Yeshe, tossing and turning under a blanket in the far corner.

"The baby should come soon." Zinzin lowers her voice. "She's too fevered, not good."

My hands reach for my beads. "Anything I can do?" I slide the string from my neck. Usually pristine and shiny, the jade beads are now dulled by a thin cloak of filth and sweat. *Oṃ Tāre Tu Tāre Ture Soha*. The beads slide through my fingers, and my heart cracks open, for Yeshe and all women carrying the perilous burden of childbirth. My lips plead upon Tara for Yeshe's wellbeing and the speedy arrival of a healthy newborn.

"Not much any of us can do." Zinzin rakes up the fire. The blaze lights the lines of worry around her tired eyes. "We've requested the amchi to come before night falls."

The amchi. Choezem, the amchi of our monastery, she would know what to do now. I close my eyes. My mind strays on the remote mountaintop. *Oṃ Tāre Tu Tāre Ture Soha*.

To no avail. The amchi can't make it before nightfall, and Yeshe's taken a turn for the worse. The fever burns her up, and we cool her ailing body with wet cloths. I try to get her to drink. Her heated breath reeks sour. My ribs tighten around me, a stone entrenches itself in my stomach. *This is not good*. Her eyes turn away, while her body withers in relentless agony. A muffled groan escapes from her heaving chest. It's Yeshe's spirit, intending to leave with her fading strength. She's slipping away from us, and the baby still doesn't want to come out.

It's the longest night I've ever known. Yeshe's voice, ripping through the dark tent only a few moments ago, has become an incoherent moaning. Her shattered body, cold and clammy now, fights a losing battle for herself and for her baby's life. Zinzin's face is beaten and bruised with sorrow, a flood of panic rises in me. *This can't be happening*. I grip my smudgy beads and fold Yeshe's stiff fingers in my shivering hands. *Oṃ Tāre Tu Tāre Ture Soha*. Together we pray, or at least I pray, trying to hold on, to keep Yeshe's spirit close to us. *Oṃ Tāre Tu Tāre Ture Soha*. A plea cries out from the desperate hollows of my heart.

Time gets lost and I call out to Tara, crossing states of mind
I've never known before. It's only when a cold gush hits my
face—the amchi rushes in—that I resurface. A tranquil mind
settles into a quivering body.

With the amchi here, the birth instantly gains momentum.
Herbs are boiled, a reviving aroma clears the stale sickness from
the tent. The amchi bathes Yeshe's soaked body in the zesty
liquid. The medicinal brew stains a crimson red. Her body
contracts with a vengeance. The veins in her neck swell, like
snakes crawling out of the darkest of woodwork. A rush of
renewed spirit shoots through. In a last resort, her body urges
with all its strength left inside. Her eyes wide with desperation,
she surrenders with a final agonizing howl. The baby's out.

Relief and anxiety rise in the air. Zinzin throws a blanket
around the newborn, her feet fly to the stove. Warmth is what
it needs right now. Yeshe's hands, all night fevered and rigid,
now lay cold and wilted in mine. I heave as my body trembles
beyond my control, and rub her hands in a futile effort to bring
the life back into them. Numbness takes over and my mind
blanks out. I stare at my palms. Tiny trickles of blood swerve
in front of my eyes.

"Here, let me." Sangmo sits beside me, a cup in her hands.
She tilts Yeshe's head to get her to drink. The amber liquid
seeps with reluctance along the corners of Yeshe's lifeless lips.

"Come on." Sangmo pours the elixir. The amchi packs
Yeshe's hemorrhaging body in steaming pouches of herbs. The
pungent odor of medicine hits my nostrils, jolting my mind
back to this moment in time. *The baby.* An erratic awareness
comes over me. I shoot up. *Zinzin.*

She cradles the bundled blanket in her arms and stands there,
motionless. From her hunched stance I can tell something is
not right. *It's too quiet.* I move over. My feet stumble, afraid of
what I might see. Her eyes avert mine as she hands me the tiny
bundle. My fingers tremble as I fold the blanket to the side. *Oh,
he's gorgeous.*

Little black curls, greased and sticky, crown on its head. Long eyelashes rim his soft blue veined eyelids. A peachy blush tints on his chubby cheeks, the color of rosebud on his heart-shaped lips. So serene. Tiny hands clutched close, his body still in the fetal position. So beautiful, but so quiet. I look up to an intense anguish. Zinzin hangs her head in defeat.

"Please, you take care of him." Her voice chokes. "Yeshe needs me right now." She leaves me at the stove, the little lifeless body of the newborn in my arms. I gasp. The understanding of what just happened sinks in with a terrifying speed. A shiver runs up my spine. I close the blanket and clutch it to my chest—so tight, as if I could squeeze the life back into it. I walk outside. My legs carry us to the river, where a prayer flows from my lips.

Dawn's about to break through. Sheets of silver-gray unfold along an opal sun. All's quiet—the world holds her breath after waking up from the worst nightmare ever imagined. My knees drop into the banks of the river. I unwrap the blanket above the fleeting stream. This boy so small, still so warm. I lower his body down the river and the crystal-clear water washes all over him. Thin cloths of blood and translucent phlegm drift away as my hands trace his fine face, his fleshy cheeks, his rounded belly, his short legs and plump feet. All the while I pray, and the hallow stream of words guides the precious life out of this tiny body, turning it slowly but inevitably from warm pink to icy blue.

The glow of gratitude warms my being. At least I'm able to pray. My hands tingle. I dry the little body with my scarf. This brief life, fortunate to come into this loving family. This fleeting life, fortunate to be leaving samsaric existence swiftly again. Blessed it is.

I fold the blanket around the baby and wrap it close. Now consciousness has left, this body's no more than an empty vessel, yet it needs to be treated with respect. The bundle presses to my chest as I walk back to the camp. No need to hesitate. This time I know what to do.

My eyes squint against the rising sun, and I search for Norbu. Together we'll ride to the nearest monastery. New life came, but it swiftly departed.

We need to lay this tiny body to rest.

Thirty-Six

The camp's fully awake, but the usual cacophony of buzzle and hustle is lacking this morning. All's gone quiet for the mummer of prayer humming around. Zinzin's packing the offerings of butter, tsampa, yogurt, dried fruit, salt, sugar, tea, and a new wool blanket. Norbu's getting our horses, and Sangmo hurried out to add fresh milk to bring to the monks. The amchi's still with Yeshe, but I'm afraid to ask. With the tiny bundle strapped to my back, I wait in the chalky morning light, my toes wet in my sandals. I slide the prayer beads through my weary fingers. This is all I can do in this troubled moment.

I pull back a bit as Norbu brings the horses around. He's leading the young mare. I shake my head. It hasn't been ridden outside of the pen. A protest is on my lips, but I swallow it. *Everything in life's an opportunity to practice.* Dechen's words ring in my ears. It's what she used to tell me when things got rough, like the time the twins left for a visit home once and I missed them too much.

"Nordun, our entire lifetime is a practice," Dechen said when she found me crying my eyes out, hiding in the furthers corner of the hall. "Every moment, especially the difficult ones, gives us the opportunity to practice. We only improve if we appreciate these moments and meet them just as they are—over and over again."

I knew she was right, but at that moment, I missed the twins so much. It ripped my little tender heart apart. Dechen understood as she let me sleep in her room that night. I sigh. Thoughts of home only play on the heavy sadness for Yeshe's loss. I turn my mind to the task at hand and meet the moment full on—and let the sorrow be.

I stare at Norbu and blink. Thoughtful eyes seek me beneath the rim of his hat. He reaches out to me, and I take the reins.

"The horse's up to it." Norbu's voice is soft but sure. "And so are you." I lay my hand on the mare's neck; a steady throb pulses beneath a tawny coat. A relaxed snort accompanies a welcoming bump in my side. It too is calm today. It's like Sangmo said, animals sense much more than we do.

A leg up from Norbu and I'm in the saddle. The offerings are piled up in his saddlebags. The little bundle is secure on my back. We're ready to go.

Sangmo and Zinzin watch in silence as we leave the camp at a walking pace. Speeding off is not appropriate right now. Thick white smoke curls around us, tears sting my eyes. Rinchen lit cedar and juniper branches, an appeal for a fortunate journey, but most of all a clearing of the evil, dirt, and death that looted precious new life here last night. Lingering traces of the smolder fill my lungs, the spicy aroma refreshing, invigorating. May it please the mountain god to support us on our ride. *Om mani padme hung.* The mare follows tame in Norbu's trail.

As soon as we're out of sight of the camp, the horses change into a gentle gallop. Down the rolling hills we ride, into the open valley with the stone towers watching over the farmers working tireless on their fields. The land's abundant here, with the second crop coming through and the golden-brown hay strewn around the dwellings to dry. A mellow breeze has replaced the gloomy gray with an endless bright blue. The meadows are coming up to full bloom. Summer awaits.

Our horses dash through the river, white and silver spray around. We've hit the lowest point to join the small gravel path leading straight through the gorge. Norbu slows his horse and turns to me. He tips his hat back. I nod my head in approval. With my mind on prayer and my eyes focused on Norbu leading the way, the aftermath of the trying night has no place left in my being. The mare must feel it too, for it's almost a joy to ride. I'm good—we're good.

"The road will lead us straight over those hills." Norbu points ahead.

I lean to the front. Patches of lush green hem swaying fields of golden grain. There seems to be no end to this rich valley. With our horses in a steady canter, we ride on with no rest as we carry a pressing and precious load.

White-chalked chortens stand like proud beacons in a sea of green. Withered mani stones are strewn along. The monastery must be near. I crane my neck. Yes, there it is—a rooftop, crowned with prayer flags, hides in the dense green of the gorge. Norbu's horse slows to a walking pace. He takes a narrow path leading to the sheltered monastery. My mare follows without hesitation. Tiny pebbles grind under her hooves as we descend the overgrown and winding trail.

The crisp rustle of leaves announces our arrival. An elderly monk is waiting at the gate. Long straws of incense smolder in his hands. Norbu holds my mare as I slide down with care, the tiny bundle strapped in the scarf to my back. As the monk approaches, our prayers meet—we both know this part so well. No words, only khatas are exchanged, and I untie my scarf. The monk presses the precious package in his arms and my eyes cast to the ground. Guided by sacred chant and opulent smoke, the monk walks off to a place that will remain unknown to us all.

Norbu and I make our way to the temple. The wooden planks creak under our feet as we enter the hall. A drawn back curtain reveals a small but lavishly decorated prayer room. Countless rows of butter lamps cast their flames into the cool dark. My eyes wander to the precious thangka's painted in gold, colorful clad statues of Buddha's and deities, and an immense vivid statue of Padmasambhava, The Precious Teacher in the middle of the room. Lions hold his seat, and his face—white with a reddish hue—carries a wrathful expression. A lotus crown adorns his head and precious brocades drape around his body. His right hand holds a vajra, his left hand a skull cup with a long life-vase. This shrine is dedicated to Guru Rinpoche, the Lotus-Born who brought the Buddhist teachings to our lands. *Om Ah Hung Guru Benza Pema Siddhi Hung.* The magnificent image of The Precious Teacher opens my heart and my lips form the Guru's mantra. *Om Ah Hung Guru Benza Pema Siddhi Hung.*

We lower ourselves three times to ground. With utmost precision, I arrange the offerings of food and other goods on the shrine while Norbu attends to the lighting of butter lamps. The vibration of the guru's chant swirls through the air. I cover the offerings with a crisp white khata and go around the shrine three times. Norbu's lit the last of the lamps—one hundred and eight flickering wicks to guide the baby's spirit into the next life. Our task is completed. Norbu's hand rests on my shoulder as we step out into the glare of the midday sun.

"Come in, come in." An enthusiastic wave comes from a side door. A young monk begs us to the kitchen. "Surely you're up for some tea." I am, we've been riding since the early morning and with the sun at her highest now, my palate is parched. The monastery's kitchen is deserted for the young monk.

"Sit, sit." The monk's jolly face bobs on top of his lank robe. "It's about ready." I sink into a seat near the stove. A wave of weariness swipes through my body. Norbu's shoulders hunch and a shadow has dropped on his face. I guess the trying night is catching up with him too. With thenthuk simmering on the stove and tea steaming in the cups in front of us, we sit in silence, Norbu and I. The haunting events of the night pass by.

"Ani-la." A deep voice resounds from the doorway. "What brings you here so far from home?" The old monk leans against the doorpost. *Ani-la*. My chin drops to my chest. Somehow he must have guessed I'm a nun. I crumple under the frown of the young monk. Yes, I'm a nun even though I don't wear the robes.

"Visiting relatives, Gen-la." I swallow. My fingers trace the rim of my cup. It's not the place nor the time to explain what I'm actually doing here.

"Did your abbess give you permission?" The elderly monk's drawn finger points at my clothes. "Like this?" A harsh squint. "Nuns should be in robes, in the monastery, not wandering around."

A blush spreads on my face. His words hurt, for I know their truth.

"She's well protected, Gen-la." Norbu gives me a stealthy glance and, although his words are directed at the old monk, I know they're meant for me. That's Norbu, always trying to put my mind at ease. With trembling hands, I take the bowl of thenthuk from the young monk's merciful hands.

The elderly monk, however, will not let me off the hook. "It's a waste." His lips blow over his thenthuk. "This life's too dear." I don't dare to face him, but he turns directly at me.

"Do I need to remind you of the example our precious teachers gave us?" His eyes shoot up to the young monk serving us. "And you?" The young monk ducks to the stove—he knows what's coming. "Do I?" The old monk's voice is harsh now.

"Just think of how rare it is—this precious human life. It's like a vast ocean on which a yoke is floating, right on the surface." He pauses. A trickle of thenthuk spills from the corner of his mouth.

"And then there's a blind turtle in this ocean that comes up once every thousand years." The monk's eyes flash across the room and rest for a moment with each of us.

"Now, what would be the odds of that blind turtle putting its neck through that very yoke?" His voice rises. "Exactly!" He puts down his bowl. A bang resonates through the kitchen. "That's how rare it is to get this precious human life."

By now the blush has spread across my neck, down my chest. Sweats pricks the back of my neck. *I know!* I know this all, and I want to tell him. *I know!* I'm not wasting my time.

Instead, I bite my lip. "Yes, Gen-la." My feeble voice has the right amount of respect. No need to defend myself, for this monk means well. I glance at Norbu, gulping down his thenthuk. My stomach throws up a protest as I follow his example, but it's the only way to get out of here right now.

"Thank you for everything, Gen-la." Norbu veers up. He takes a deep bow to both monks. I hasten to collect the cups and bowls, offering to give a hand with the dishes.

"No need." The old monk's hand dismisses me with a wave. "You go on your way now." He clutches his tattered bone beads.

"But do remember, Ani-la." The monk's eyes burn on my forehead. I avert my eyes to the ground. "Even though a nun can never reach the state that monks can—for your bodies are defiled—anything's better than a lay woman's life." His jaw clenches as he huffs. "Let today be a lesson for you."

My eyes widen. My head jerks back. Did I hear that right? Did he think... Did he think the baby was mine? The scorn look on the monk's face says it all—it's no use for me to answer. I cast down my eyes again and bow. No use to go against a mind made up.

The mare must sense my agitated mind. It prances and sways its body from left to right as we head back up the path. I'm not reigning the horse in, for it's been so good until now. I'll let it go a bit, play with it, going back and forth. Our little game demands my attention even more, making it a good practice. A smile comes to my face. It's like the mind training Dechen taught us with diligence—being attentive in the moments and meet them, one moment at a time.

"I really admire that in you." Norbu steers his horse next to me. We've reached the wider road again. "You put everything you've learned into use, regardless of the situation." A mellow smile curls from under his hat.

"Whether it's an obstinate monk or a boisterous horse that crosses your way—your focus, your connection in the moment, your confidence to act on your intuition—it's all there." Norbu's candid words bring a glow to my cheeks. I never noticed he'd been watching me close.

"Well, thank you." I sneeze. A fine dust whirls in my nose. And I mean it, thanks to his kind patience my confidence is growing. I feel it myself.

"It's all there, Nordun, you've got everything you need." He spurs on his horse and I gasp as my mare makes a sudden jump to follow. My hands dig into the long-tangled manes. I've got this. I steady myself.

At full gallop, we speed back to the camp. No stops on the way back either, as there's work to be done.

It's a timid evening at the camp, as expected. Yeshe's still in bed, but she'll make it. It was a close call. With enough horse training done for the day, I join Sangmo and milk the dris.

A strange contentment has settled in me. All will be fine. There's no need to hurry. I'll meet the moments as they come, one by one.

The dusk sets her purple haze over the grass lands. The last flares of coral and orange polish the crystal crust on the mountain ridge. Sangmo hums her song, and milk splashes in buckets. The canter of a horse sounds from afar. My eyes dart to the higher meadow.

The silhouette of a lone rider approaches from over the hill, and my heart skips a beat. I haven't seen him up close yet, but I already know.

It's Karma. He's here.

Thirty-Seven

"Karma!" Sangmo's yell echoes over the wide grass land. She's spotted her brother too.

My hands rest on the dri's utter. A surge of blood rushes through my ears. I wasn't mistaken. It's Karma. *He's here.*

His horse boots down the hill, slashing through the shreds of mauve at a frightening speed. I grip the handle of my bucket and hoist myself up. Sangmo leaps out of the pen and throws her arms around her brother, giving him ample chance to jump off his horse. My feet move towards them, my mind dragging behind. *He's here.*

"Now that's a welcome." Karma wrestles himself out of Sangmo's embrace. "Missed me, sis?" He puts her at arm's length. His tall physique towers above her.

"Missed you?" Sangmo's still bouncing. "I seldom ever see you at home, and now you're all the way out here." Her eyes widen. "Is Grandfather alright?" Her cheerful smile turns tense.

"Of course he is." Karma wraps his hand around her shoulder. "Everybody's fine and sending their regards, especially Grandfather." His green glare meets my stunned stare over Sangmo's shoulder. *He's here.* A familiar flutter rustles in my stomach. My heels dig in the sand.

"That's wonderful to hear." My hands swing the bucket against my hip. I try hard not to look away. What do I say? A sea of silence surges between us. A wave of heat creeps up my neck.

"What's up then?" Sangmo's anxious tone drowns in the stillness. "You didn't come all this way to say hello, did you?" She cocks her head to the side.

"How well you know me." He reigns in his horse, but his eyes are on me. He must have been in the saddle for days to get here. What would be so urgent that he rides all the way out here?

"I've come for Nordun." His tone is nonchalant, but the emerald in his eyes ebbs to a deeper shade of sage. I take a step back. My pulse jumps.

"Me?" My grip on the bucket tightens, and the smooth handle cuts into the raw of my palms. Me? Why?

Before I have the chance to ask, Zinzin joins in. She greets Karma with her usual warm heartedness.

"Welcome brother." A long khata weaves from her hands. "Good to see you made it." Others join and welcomes are exchanged. Sangmo takes the bags of his horse; filled with food and wool—gifts to Zinzin and her family.

"Please, no need for this." Zinzin waves. "Your sisters are our sisters." It's a futile refusal however, as Karma gestures us to take the bags to the tent.

"The family is grateful." He nods as Rinchen takes the reins of his horse. "As yourself, we value our family's relations."

Good relations? Did I hear that right? Our families know each other well? With a head full of questions, I wander back to the main tent. The bags pull their full weight on my arms. My knees wobble. It's been a long day, but my mind's on edge, curious as ever.

Sangmo and I finish the milking. Company or not, the dris can't wait. Fueled by our eagerness to join Karma and Zinzin, our hands work as fast as they can. With Lhadun as my little helper, the load's not that heavy. I can't feel my fingers anymore and focus on the bucket below to calm in my wondering mind—it doesn't work. My heart pounds in my chest. *He's here.*

"I see the two of you are doing just fine." Karma sits at the stove with little ones climbing all over him. He too seems to fit right in. Despite his relaxed manner, there's slight tension drawn around the corners of his mouth. It betrays a sense of urgency. *Something's up.*

Zinzin beckons me to come sit next to her. Richen takes the children to the side. *I was right.* A stone lodges in my stomach. Karma draws closer, and a restless flicker meets my eyes.

"Your uncle's gotten word where you are." His voice barely makes it above the hiss of the stove. "And what you're intending to do."

Uncle knows. My thoughts twirl with the red rope around my wrist.

"News travels like lightning over these mountains," he says, as if he can read my mind. "We need to move on."

Move on? I shake my head. No way, it's too soon. My mouth opens.

"But I just came here," I say. I hold my breath and my eyes flash to Norbu. "Right?" Norbu will understand—he knows I still have a lot to learn.

Norbu stays silent, his eyes avoiding me. I swallow. A tiny lump of disappointment has lodged in the back of my throat. Why is he not pleading my case?

"And I'm safe here." I press my lips together. A sour sting burns at the edge of my tongue. Sure, Uncle will not come here. I pull up my knees and hug them tight. And what if he came? What could he do? I blink. My eyes fix on the roaring stove. Nothing, for sure.

"We know." Zinzin leans into me. The sweet smell of babies and milk hints in her hair. "Just hear Karma out." She rests her hand on my knees.

"Nordun." Karma's voice wavers. It's almost not noticeable, but it's enough—every fiber of my being is on edge. "There's something else." He pauses for a moment and rubs his neck. "Your father's brother, he's evil." Karma shifts in his seat. "He is one that sucks the life out of all living beings he comes across."

Evil. The image of Uncle flashes before me. A bitter aftertaste drives the sour from my palate.

"He will harm you if he gets a chance." Karma's voice urges me and my heart wants to hide at the intense tone in his speech. His jaws tighten. "Your sisters told me."

My hands drop to my feet.

"My sisters?" I shoot up. "Pema and Tsomo?"

Karma nods and in his eyes cloud vast shadows of slated gray and willow green. My stomach knots.

"They requested me to keep you safe." His eyes shoot to my wrist. *The blessing cord.* The red string blurs in front of my eyes—it's not only a reminder of the Buddhist path. My sisters tied a protection cord to keep me from whatever harm comes my way.

Karma's words leave a dead quiet upon us. There's only the gentle gush of tea poured in empty cups as even the stove has ceased its angry hiss.

He shifts in his seat yet again and diverts his gaze. *Something's really wrong.*

"Your mother's death," he says almost inaudibly. The shadow of night draws over his averted face. "It was your uncle who caused your mother's death, Nordun." A startling midwinter cold crashes down on me. *Mother.* My mind freezes. My heart withers.

"Your uncle put a nāga curse on the horse." His voice is nothing but a whisper; it's not safe to speak of these things out loud. "That's why the horse staggered and tramped your mother; it was frightened by a snake." Karma's words cause a stir among our company, but I can't move. Zinzin's hand, still on my knees, now grips me tight. A snake curse. *Om mani.*

"Sonam was right then." Zinzin heaves. "He always thought there was something suspicious about her death." *A snake spell.* Karma's revelation rips through my mind with a lightning thunder.

"But how?" My mouth opens and closes again. The relentless pounding in my ears won't stop. "He's only a human. My voice falls as my mind flies off. *Father.* His once solid frame so frail, his shining eyes now sunken and lackluster, the eerie atmosphere I couldn't put my finger on. *He's one that sucks the life out of everybody.* Father's demise. It must be Uncle's doing, too.

I shiver, the cold seeps through the marrow of my bones. *He will harm you if he gets a chance.* Uncle's leery look as I met him in the stable, the giant viper appearing, the whirlwind in the stable, him vanishing on me. *Could it be him?* Piece by piece, it joins together. I wasn't losing my mind; it was uncle's doing. But how?

"Humans can access great powers." Karma's voice picks up. "Even beyond our realm."

My hands draw up my sleeves. True, but spells are practiced by spiritual practitioners, by those who have gone through rigorous training, after they've been disciplined in using it for the greater good of all. My eyes seek for answers. I meet Karma's veiled gaze.

"We don't know how." He leans in. "That's not important for now." Everything in his body tells me he's about to jump up. "Your sisters saw it; we have to go."

They saw it. My sisters' premonitions are always correct.

"You know we love to have you here." Zinzin's words cut through my bewilderment. She folds my hands in hers. "But I think Karma's right."

I stare at her. Worry traces around her eyes again. My heart hits rock bottom. The truth of it all slowly sinks in. I've always trusted my dear sisters, and always for the good. It's not the time to question. This time I'll have to go—once more. I rest my chin on my knees and my eyes at the smoldering stove. My sisters saw it. It's time to go.

"I'll come with you." Norbu's tone is persistent. "I'll make sure you get to the Four Sisters Mountain and back." He leans forward, his hands on his knees. His honest concern lifts my heart, if only a little.

"That's very kind of you." Karma glances over at Zinzin. "But you can't be missed here, with Sonam gone." My shoulders drop. Yes, Norbu is needed here.

"I'm going with Nordun." Karma sits back. "We'll leave early tomorrow."

My heart skips a beat. Tomorrow. *So soon.*

"I'll stay here." Sangmo draws closer to the stove. "With Yeshe in bed and so." She clears her throat and turns to Zinzin. "If that's fine with you."

Zinzin's face lightens. "You're more than welcome to." Her hands relax on my knees.

My nails dig into the grip of my hand. No Sangmo. Tears burn behind my eyelids. *Not now.* This is not the time to be selfish. She's needed here. I let the anxiety drift away.

That's it then. Sangmo pours a last round of tea. I wave my hand. My body can't handle any more. My hands search my beads. *Om Tara.* The day's been too long.

"I wish you would come," I say as we retreat to our blankets. It's a whisper to Sangmo, next to me in the dark.

"I know, but you've got this." She pinches my arm. "Besides, Karma's coming." Her faith in her brother is as solid as a rock.

"Hmmm..." *Karma.* I bet my sisters pressed him hard to come. They can be very convincing. They're like a pair of mastiffs, those two. Once they've got you cornered, they won't let go. I crawl deeper under the blanket.

Then again, Karma doesn't strike me as the type that lets himself be seized. His quiet confidence, the determination in those unusually bright emerald eyes. *No way.* The annoying flutter's back. *Not now.* I grumble to my lingering thoughts, and I roll on my side. *Not now.*

And for once, my mind complies with my plea and surrenders to a dreamless sleep.

Thirty-Eight

*T*ara. Her benign gaze fades in the distance as I awaken.
I blink, wanting to hold on to her, but alas, she's gone.
Om Tara. It was her, letting me know she's always present.
A stillness unfolds within me. A crystal clear illuminates my
mind. Time for prayer.

I haul the blanket over my shoulders. My feet tiptoe to the
shrine. The butter lamp's lit, the incense's fuming. My knees
sink in the dense weave of the wool and my whole being settles
as I relish the peaceful aftermath of Tara's visit.

"You're up." Karma's voice pulls me out of meditation.
"Good, you're packed?" My limbs dazed, I scramble up,
pulling my blanket tight.

"Packed?" I shrug. "Uh, I have nothing but my bag."

Meeting my confusion, Karma grins. His shirt open, the
flicker of the single lamp reveals a tanned, muscular chest. I
avert my eyes. Too late. He's already caught my stare, and no
doubt the heat that bursts in my cheeks.

"Don't worry," he says, relaxed as ever. "I'll take care of it."

And off he is. I'm left standing, being the fool, as usual. I
cringe. We're off to a splendid start.

The tent wakes with a lazy rumble. Heavy blankets are
shoved aside, lazy feet shuffle in and out, and empty cups
clatter for thirsty mouths to quench. Yeshe's sipping her tea

near the stove. Her face pallid, a red rim around her eyes. I join her and take her icy hands in mine. My heart goes out to her and together we sit with her grief—raw, honest, and open. No use denying what happened. No use masking any of it.

"Thank you," Yeshe says. "For all." Her voice dim, I squeeze her hands.

"You're welcome," I say. "It's good to see you up." Her shoulders are drawn and her eyes stare into nowhere.

"My body's strong." Her voice shivers with sadness. "It's my minds that calls for more time." I nod. She's right. Grief demands its own time, for it leads us to a deep realization, an understanding beyond our individual loss.

Grief teaches us the most essential truth of our lives in our darkest moments—the truth of impermanence and the cause of our suffering. Like this little human life that came to us yesterday and left within a single moment—we know it's blessed, fulfilling its karma and moving out of this samsaric existence so soon. Still, we attach to this tiny life with our emotions, having high expectations of how it all should be. And then, when everything changes, we hold on to our hopes with an ignorant determination, causing our own hurt, our own pain. Oh, how foolish we humans are.

I get up and pour us another tea. By now the buzz is at all-time high—in and outside the tent. Arms stretch out, feet tumble, skirts are pulled, and voices cry aloud. I'm not moving though, for my heart tells me all I need to do right now is sit here and be still. I glance at Yeshe. A hint of rosy red has set on her sunken cheeks.

"Eat some." Zinzin slides me a bowl of tsampa. "You'll need it on the way." She sits beside me, the baby on her breast. *Om mani padme hung.* Our beads click in sync and for a few moments she's with me in our own little world. All is well.

"I know you think you're not ready." Zinzin puts the baby over her shoulder. "But I'll tell you—you so are."

I glance at her, my thoughts still in prayer.

"We women, we are always ready as we are strong minded and able-bodied—no matter what they tell us." Zinzin's jaw sets, her intense gaze meets my eyes.

"We are capable of anything, for our bodies carry new life and our minds stand the horrifying loss of it." Her voice steady, she rocks the baby back and forth. "Now that's strength, that's pure strength, so don't believe for a moment you're not ready for it, Nordun."

Zinzin's words hit home with me, for they resonate with Dechen's words, only in a different voice. Gratitude rises, a warmth fills my being. How fortunate I am to be with her.

"Thank you," I say. "It's been only a few days, but I've learned so much, and not only about horses." Our eyes meet again and my vision blurs.

"We're here for each other," Zinzin says. The soothing scent of her, of sweet milk and happy babies, lingers around. "It's in everything we are." *We're family.* I understand.

"And we'll be here when you come back with the horse." Sangmo plunks herself beside me. The tangy fragrance of fresh grass mingles in. "And nothing less than a magnificent one, promise?" I smile, seeing the semi-serious expression she's trying on.

"Promise." The tone of my voice is solid. How could I refuse?

"Good!" She slaps my knee. "Then you're off the hook with the milking this morning." That's Sangmo, always lighting up the day.

"And I think somebody's waiting for you outside." Her hand waves and I turn to see. It's Norbu, his head popping in the entrance. I guess it's my time to leave.

I tie my bag across my chest—nuns always travel light—and ignore the tautness setting in. With Sangmo's arm wrapped around me, I stride outside.

Norbu's waiting. The young mare prances behind him, all shiny and saddled up. He tips his hat. "It's all yours." The horse's front hooves crush the sand. A loud neigh drifts out; sounds like it agrees with him.

"Oh no." I flinch. "I can't." This horse, it's too much.

Norbu shakes his head. He's not having any of it. He presents me with the reins; his hands fold around mine.

"I'll bring her back to you," I say. "I promise." Still, it's too much.

"No need." His fingers search and slide between mine. "But I am looking forward to your return." He tilts his chin. A golden amber glows under the rim of his hat. *It's in his eyes.* My heart soars. My palms sweat.

"Thank you." I grip the reins tight. "For everything." Norbu nods, a gentle understanding. His fingers slip from mine and he gives me a knee up onto the mare.

All set, I meet Karma. His stallion cavorts behind the main tent. Side by side our horses march out of the camp. My heart's dragging at its feet.

"Wait!" A teeny voice lets out a big yell. I hold my mare and turn. Little Lhadun rushes our way, bright green ribbons flurry from her hands. She squeals and ties them to the brittles of our horses. "For good luck." Her eyes twinkle. Her tiny hands raise to me. "Come back soon." My heart expands as our fingers touch.

"I will," I say. "That's a promise." A precious little girl inside and out, that's what she is. I take a last look at the camp. Sangmo's head sticks out from between the dris. A last wave. I spur on my mare and we're off.

Karma's horse flies off as soon as we hit the open field. My mare leaps and bolts in its trail. My mind jolts. This speed! The Four Sisters Mountain is at least a two to three-day ride. There's no way we can keep this pace up all the way. I wonder what Karma's plan is. I pant as the pace cuts off my breath. *I have no idea to where I'm going.* Yes, The Four Sisters Mountain, but I don't even know where it is.

My hands clench the mare's flying manes. I try to steady myself and my wobbly mind. Ever since I left the monastery, I've been on somebody's trail, following along. First Ghedun-la and the sisters and Sangmo. My head hurts. Then Sonam, Zinzin and Norbu, and now I'm lagging behind Karma. My eyes focus on his horse, dashing ahead. Everybody's been great, but honestly, what am I doing?

As if he senses my worry, Karma slows his stallion.

"You're good?" He steers next to me.

"I'm not used to the pace yet." I heave, out of breath. "For sure, we can't keep this up all the way?" I straighten my back.

"Don't worry." Karma pats his horse on the neck. "I'm just letting it blow off steam, otherwise it'll be restless all day." He loosens the reins, and the horse cavorts again. "See?" Powerful muscles bulge under the stallion' shiny coat, its energy high. Of course, that makes sense.

"I'll tell you all you want to know." He shifts to the front of the saddle. "About horses and all." He pauses and his eyes set on the horizon. "But we need to get ahead today, so let's ride steady 'til midday, good?"

Not awaiting my answer, he's off again. The scent of the summer after a rain fall trails behind him; thick clumps of wet grassland fly around. In an impulse, I throw myself over my mare's neck. What else can I do but hold on?

Midday doesn't come soon enough for me. Descending from the higher grasslands of Rongdrak to the lower sloped terraced farmlands, I'm struggling to keep up with Karma as our horses' hooves bash through the narrow canyon at a frightening speed. The pace he sets rattles the bones in my body. By the time we dismount, there's not a piece of my skeleton left in its original place. My knees buckle as my feet hit the bank of the creek. A cool silver spray soaks my skirt. I'm stuck for a moment. Our horses splash in the stream.

Karma puts his bags in the shade of a large pine. I stumble and search some dry wood and twigs for a fire. We've got plenty of food, and even fresh milk, courtesy of Sangmo who must have surprised a dri exceedingly early this morning. Silently we work our way to a kettle of simmering milk tea, accompanied by tsampa, butter, and strips of dried yak meat.

"Excellent tea." Karma blows the steam of his cup; an approving slurp follows. I take it as an opening. We haven't exchanged a word since the ride this morning. Maybe he's just as awkward with the situation as me?

"Thank you." I fill his cup to the rim and put the kettle on the smoldering fire. "For accompanying me to wherever we go." I sit down beside him. "I know my sisters can be persistent." My stiff fingers dig in the tsampa and try to form a proper ball.

"They didn't have to ask." He glances aside and takes another sip. His eyes meet me over the rim of his cup. "You're a brave woman, sister." A rush of blood surges to my head. My temples throb. *Brave.* He thinks I'm brave. If only he knew.

"Not really." My voice breaks. "To be honest, I have no idea what I'm doing." My shoulders drop. In the distance my horse neighs.

"Well." Karma pops a tsampa ball in his mouth. "From what I see, you're doing just fine with Norbu teaching you about horses and all." His jaws chew. In the corner of this mouth peeps a knowing grin. *Really?* I'm sure my face can't be any more flushed than this.

"Uh, yes." My fingers fumble. The tsampa won't stick. "Norbu's been very kind." A mess forms all over my shirt.

"Sorry." He puts down his cup, but he can't hide his masked chuckle. "I shouldn't be teasing you like this." He gets up and pours us another cup, an apologetic gesture on his behalf.

My hands beat the crumbs off my skirt. I draw a deep breath and I scold myself. *Get yourself together.* It's ridiculous how easily I'm thrown off by his cheeky remark.

"You're allowed to." I look up to meet his stare. "We're family after all."

His eyes narrow and he averts them a bit too fast. "We are." He gulps down his tea. "Even though not in the way you think."

I lean back, my eyebrows raised. We're not family?

"I'll tell you about that some other time," he adds before I can ask. "Right now, let me tell you about the road ahead." He starts talking about how we'll take divergent roads to our destination, but my mind wanders away with what he just said.

They didn't have to ask. And we're not family after all. *Not in the way you think.* I don't know what it is, but something tells me this trip to the Four Sisters Mountains is going to be much more interesting than I could have ever imagined.

And we're not even midway.

Thirty-Nine

All day we ride, mercifully not at the bone-breaking speed at which we left the camp. The path we're taking after noon demands a slower pace. Karma leads us on narrow, winding trails, away from the main path, away from any abodes. Better not to be seen, he said. I wonder what that means, but who am I to question? He's travelled, and I'm not.

With only a few stops to let the horses drink and quench our own thirst, we ride on. Karma, becoming more talkative, points out markers in the landscape and tells me about horses, travel, and trade. I listen, taking it all in while I focus on the trail ahead. It seems he's more at ease with us. So am I.

An auburn sun hails the dusk with a lilac streaked sky as she sinks behind the mountain ridge. Karma's fast to find a safe spot for the night. A ridged cave, hemmed with tall spruces, up from our trail. I make the fire at the entrance, while Karma takes care of the horses. I scout around. We could see all the valley from here, all that's coming and going, if the darkness wasn't falling so soon.

"Here's some cushioning for the night." Karma sweeps a pile of the dry leaves my way. He installs himself at the entrance of the grotto, the fire crackling between him and me. His fingers lace behind his head and he leans into the moss-covered wall.

His eyes gaze into the now stark dark blue. He seems right at home.

"Sleep in caves a lot?" I let the tea simmer for a while and sit back. A wispy breeze sweeps through, carrying the wood-smoke outside—simply perfect. The prayer beads slide through my fingers, thankful for the day coming to a close.

"For sure." He turns sideways to face me. "I always try to avoid the lodgings on the way." He reaches for a few twigs. "I prefer to spend the night under the stars than with those savages at the inns." He shrugs. "I guess that's all I need; a wide-open space to lie down my body and a bit of fresh air to clear my mind."

He draws up his sleeves and pokes the fire with a few more twigs. The flames lick up to the ceiling and I see it—a curious, miniature marking on the inner side of his right arm forearm. My fingers stall, the string going slack in my hand. *What's that?* I lean forward ever so slightly, but he's already noticed my stare. I can almost hear him think. Will I?

"Can I ask what it is?" I tilt my head to the side, my eyes still on his arm. He shoves his sleeve back up again and shows me from across the fire. It's a small drawing—intricate black lines in the shape of a tiny head. I lean in closer. There's a pair of swirling curls on top of it. A smile builds on my face as I make out the marking. Antlers. A deer. It's the head of a deer.

"How gorgeous." The lines are so crisp, as if they were drawn yesterday. "Where did you get it?" I can't keep my eyes off the miniature etched in Karma's arm.

"I don't know." The crackling of the fire attempts to drown his voice. "It was already on me when Grandfather found me." *Found?* I look up. My wide eyes meet his green stare.

"What do you mean?" I draw back a bit. "Found?" My fingers slip from my beads.

"Yes, found." He pauses a moment and looks at the marking, rubbing it with his thumb. "Grandfather found me, many years ago on the trade route East." He pulls down his sleeve. "He doesn't know where it comes from either."

What?

My mind—calm and content only a moment ago—is gaining full speed. I feel myself staring at him. It's not respectful, but I just can't believe what I'm hearing.

"Grandfather found you?" I shake my head. "On the trade road?" How is that possible? Sure, I've heard of small babies being found. Unwanted babies placed near people's houses to be discovered soon. We even discovered a tiny baby girl in the barn of our monastery not too long ago. But way out on the trade road?

"Well, that's the story." His eyes gaze into the fire. "Grandfather found me as a young boy, wandering in a stream along the caravan route. My clothes torn, sick, ailing, I don't remember." He looks up. Flaming orange tongues reflect in his somber, distant gaze. "Grandfather took me home as grandson. I've been most fortunate ever since." I sit back, my mouth and eyes wide open, while trying to piece his words together. *Found.*

"Well." I shrug. "That explains your tall posture." *And your stunning emerald eyes.* I don't know whether I blurt out this ridiculous remark to lighten the air or to calm my own nerves, but it works. He bursts out in laughter and offers a strained yet genuine smile.

"Yes, I do look different." He rubs his forehead. "And somehow, I am different. I mean, I feel different?" He hesitates. "You understand what I mean." His eyes lighten to that frosty shade of green that covers the grasslands on a dewy spring morning. My heart softens and I nod. I do understand what he means.

I stroke the cool jade of the beads and my mind dwells back to the stables, to Father and Mother, to those happy times when the summer never seemed to end. Even though I grew up with Dechen, my grandmother, there's always that subtle, lingering longing for home, that elusive distance, always there, even when others seem so close. Yes, I understand what it is to have a longing for a home that never was.

"So we're not blood relatives." I lean back on my elbows.

"No, we're not." He tilts his head to the side. His words spark between the flickering flames. "Does that make a difference?" We stare at it as it swells between us—a silence filled with expectations—of what? My heart quivers and I straighten my back.

"I don't think so." My mouth spills the truth before I want to. "For somehow you and I, we're connected anyway." I bite my lip. *Where did that come from?* The blaze of the fire scorches my cheeks.

"Yes, we are." His intensity of him relaxes and a gentle glow of tender green meets me, holding the innermost of my being in his eyes. No, it doesn't matter we're not relatives, yet it makes all the difference—and we both realize it does.

A sudden burst erupts before me. The pervading stench of scorched milk hits the air. I jump up. The tea! With a sweep, I take the pot off. Too late, it's spilled.

A little less tea than we're used to, we eat in the stillness that has settled between us. It's comfortable but lined with a fine edge of something—I think it's a kind of daring excitement, for that's what's stirring deep inside of me.

And as the tranquil night wraps our cave into an indigo veil, we retreat to our blankets. With Karma securing the entrance and the fire smoldering between us, I drift off. My evening prayer's cut short by a persuasive weariness my body can't resist.

Sleep arrives at alarming speed, so I expect it to be restful. Little do I know.

I shoot up, eyes wide open. My body's thrown into a rude awakening. The haunting nightmare's back—again. Thick streams of blood quicken around my ankles. Sweat lashes down my back. My hands clasp my chest. I try hard to subdue my heaving breath and not to wake Karma. No use, he's already at my side.

"Just breathe." He hunches beside me, a slight concern in his voice.

"Sorry." My fingernails dig into the weave of the blanket. My eyes frenzy around the cave. *I can't get out!* My mind bounces off the wall and my lungs are on the verge of exploding.

"It's fine, I'm a light sleeper anyway," Karma says and fetches some water. "Here, drink." He steadies the cup in my trembling hands.

The cool water lashes at the back of my throat. The last traces of smoldering sprigs sting my nostril. My heart's pounding in my chest. *Focus.* Slowly, I come up and resurface into the now. An icy shiver rushes down my spine. Karma wraps my scarf around me.

"You have dreams too." I gulp a sharp breath. He fills my cup again and urges me to drink.

"I've had them ever since I can remember."

He sits beside me, his presence exuding that calm confidence I envy. Without me asking, he says, "Mine are dreams of wide-open spaces, of flat grasslands and a clear blue sky. Of eagles soaring and deer hooves clapping." His voice echoes from within. "And of tongues that speak in a language foreign to me."

I draw up my legs and hug my knees. My being eases at his pure presence. The warmth of his body and his honest sharing radiate in comfort beside me. Fine threads of a fragile intimacy weave between us into a closeness of minds, into one I've never felt before. He's so near to me for the first time, and somehow it feels like he always has been.

"Do you believe they mean something?" My hands search for my beads. "Your dreams?" I don't want to pry, but can't help myself. I've been wondering for years if mine have.

"Could be," he says and moves even closer. "I've had them for as long as I remember." He pauses. He slides his fingers across the rim of the cup. "You?"

"Some say our minds are a storeroom of all the karmic energies we've accumulated in the past." My eyes rest on his slender, firm hands. "And that dreams are the way for our conscious to bring a message through." I stare at his tanned wrists, the veins running along them.

"Makes sense." He twirls the cup between his hands. "But if so, I don't understand what the message is here. You?" He tucks my sliding scarf under my toes.

"Me neither." My fingers turn on the beads. "But this nightmare somehow feels like an urge to move on, to speed up to whatever is calling me." An ominous tightening hinges over my chest.

"I've sensed it too." A grimace twists his mouth. "In fact, I felt it the night we met, and it hasn't left the air ever since." He slides his hand over my back and gets up. "We better get some sleep." My heart pounds in my chest again. *The night we met.* I slip under my blanket.

My dreams. He felt it too. If I only understood the meaning of all, if it only would make sense. *Only the clear mind has the ability to understand, to realise things.* Dreams mean nothing, Dechen told me. And if they do, we humans can't understand them. Our minds are clouded with expectations, fears, and ignorance—we can't see clear. How often she reminded me of that. A clear mind, if only.

My mind pleads to the dark. Let sleep come fast and be without disturbance.

My prayers are heard. A deep sleep arrives before troubling thoughts get the chance to move back in.

Dawn tumbles into the cave, spreading her bluish haze around my mat. Twigs crackle and a comfy draft passes by. Karma's got a fire lit. His tall frame leans at the edge of the cave, overlooking the valley.

"Looks like a good day," he says as I crawl from under my blanket. "With any luck, we'll reach our destination tonight." He sounds at ease, but his stance is tense.

I join him at the edge, the blanket wrapped around me. The breeze picks up, ripples of turquoise stray through a sky of vast gray. Karma glances at me, and I nod.

I feel it too. It's in the air.

We'd better go.

Forty

We ride into the early morning, cloaked in a strange, elusive hush. There's no wind whispering, no leaves or petals that rustle, there's not even a birdsong humming around. There's only our horses' hooves clapping in sync through the valley with Karma's stallion striding ahead.

My mare follows in a careful step, ears pointed to the back. A barren chasm on the left, a moss-grown ridge on the right—the steep, winding path dictates our steady pace. For now, my aching limbs relish this rather easy tempo, but will we reach the Four Sisters Mountain by tonight?

The Four Sisters Mountain. My thoughts wander back to the mountaintop I know so well, to Ghedun and how he first told us the story of the Four Sisters sitting in his hut. We used to sneak out to him to listen to his tales, my sisters and me, when we were younger, later not so much anymore. Ghedun would feed us tea and tsampa, and sometimes slides of dried meat—his favorite snack and the sisters' favorites too.

One day he told us of a valley where a wicked spirit harassed the poor locals, bringing battles on them, and natural disasters, and many other calamities too. A brave local man, older already, had taken up the courage to fight the evil one, but the poor man had died doing so. Now this heroic man had four daughters, and the youngest, the most beautiful one, was set on revenge. She fought the spirit several times, all by herself. Finally, her true love, a young man from the village, joined her. And yes, they defeated the spirit. Hurray, we all had cheered.

But the story was not over yet. It took at least two more cups of tea for Ghedun to finish it. Yes, all looked fine, but the evil spirit planned his revenge.

First, he convinced the Goddess of the Water to flood the entire valley. All four sisters were enraged and got up to help. They saw their youngest sister could never handle it alone. And of course, then all the men stepped in to help too.

"At last!" Pema snorted, and I hit her over the head for her remark. "Shhh!" I was so enthralled by the story. The three oldest sisters fought with a vengeance but were defeated. My heart sunk, and I think Pema and Tsomo's hearts too—although they would never admit it.

Nevertheless, to help their youngest sister and the locals in their fight against the evil, the three sisters turned themselves into three magnificent mountains. They lashed themselves on top of the spirit. They fought hard, but the youngest sister saw they were losing the fight. So she turned herself into the most stunning massif, with cascading glaciers and all. She launched on the chest of the evil spirit and stayed down, crushing him for good.

When the lover saw what the youngest sister had done, his heart broke, and he wept with enormous grief. Then he transformed himself into a dazzling white cloud and rose on the peaks of the massif to stay there for eternity, hanging around the top of the mountain—an enduring wish to stay with his love.

How this story captivated me. Such a heroic deed from the sisters, and what a beautiful love between this youngest sister and her man. But of course, Pema and Tsomo had to tear into the story with their questions, like they always did.

Where were all the locals in this, leaving the four sisters to fight alone? And that man turning himself into a cloud because of true love, what a nonsense, they ridiculed. Surely there were enough pretty women around? He could get himself another woman, just as attractive. No, the sisters didn't buy into the love story, as usual. I did though, for I had seen what the loss of true love can do to a man. Or to a woman, but I said nothing, for Pema and Tsomo have a knowing way about them, and they're always right.

Like they saw Uncle's hand in my mother's death. The weight in my stomach crawls up along my ribcage. My mind churns the way our horses' hooves grind the gravel. I have no doubts about what the sisters see, but how did Uncle get a nāga spell? Who is helping him, I wonder? If he is one that sucks the life out of the people around him, does that explain Father's gaunt appearance? Will Uncle come after us?

My eyes fix on Karma, but my thoughts spin out of control by now, round and round, worrying about what's coming. When we're at the Four Sisters Mountain, what do I do? Yes, I can ride an untamed horse now, but...

A sudden loud yelp resounds from beneath. The sound of horse hooves scrambling in panic follows. Gravel cascades down into the abyss, and I gasp. My mare lost its grip on the narrow, rocky path. A surge of anxiety rouses through me. In reflex, I duck, and my fingers claw into the manes as my mare jostles and pushes through.

"Whoa!" Karma's voice pitches. His horse halts in an instant. The last gravel hits the bottom of the steep gorge.

"I'm fine." My eyes cast down on my mare. "We're fine." *Focus.* The smell of salt and sweat urges through my nostrils. My hands run through the coat of slick on its neck. The horse is no less shaken than I am.

"Let's stop for a moment." Karma sounds determined. "Steady yourself and your mare." I raise myself but don't dare to face him. I wince at my own stupidity, of not paying attention.

"That happens when you scatter your thoughts in front of your horse's hooves." Karma turns his stallion on the precarious path to face me. "What were you thinking of, anyway?" His inquisitive, tender twinkle meets my eyes.

"Oh, what not?" I blurt out. I might as well be honest. "Mostly about what will happen when we get to the Four Sisters Mountains." I clear my throat. Better spill it out. "I have no idea what is coming, and it worries me." My sweaty palms slither along the tarry leather of the reins.

"Of course you don't," Karma says. "Nobody knows." The airy tone in his voice surprises me. "We don't know what has been before, and we don't know what's ahead." A cooling breeze blows through, carrying the soothing scent of sweet earth churned under a summer sun. I look up. His horse dribbles back and forth as he sits there, so at ease.

"True, we don't understand what karma we've created." I stretch my fingers from the reins. "We don't see what's lying around in our karmic storehouse to ripen and what's about to come to fruition—good or bad." I tip my head to the gray yonder, torn to shreds by a pearly blue. "Still I wonder, still I worry, against my better judgement, I still do." With a sigh, I face Karma again.

"Yep." He rubs his chin. "Worry's pointless, for this moment is all we can ever perceive. So how about focusing on this moment again, and act with our best intentions." That playful sparkle in his eyes—is he provoking me, if only a little?

"Focus in the moment with a good intention." I try to meet Karma's stare, but I just can't. All those years of training in the monastery, all those precious lessons, and here I am. My gaze darts over his shoulder. A lone blackbird skirts along a frayed fern.

"And to act quickly, of course," Karma says. "Seize the opportunity, the moment as it presents itself." Karma spreads his fingers and clasps his fist, as if he's trying to catch the air.

"To act quickly." I face him full on. *To act quickly.* Where did I hear that before?

"Yes, to do something." A crystal glint ignites in his eyes. "And not just stall." He hesitates for a moment. "Mind you, we can't stall, for if we choose to ignore the moment, or if we question everything that's being presented to us—sort of like you're doing now—that's also acting." He leans to the front; his hands rest on his horse's neck. "But that's kind of lazy and arrogant, I think."

My eyes widen. *Lazy and arrogant?* Does he think I'm lazy? And arrogant? My mouth opens, ready to protest, but he waves his hand.

"Just hear me out," he says. "We question the moment that's in front of us because we think this moment should be different. We already had our expectations of this moment, and—of course—they are not met." A slow smile builds on his face, and I let his words land within me.

"So now we doubt the moment and what the moment asks of us because it doesn't meet our expectations—like we know better. That's quite arrogant of us, isn't it?" He lets out a big laugh. "And we don't know better, because it's not up to us, is it?" My heart sinks with his words within me. It's what Dechen always told me. It's like that, but in different words.

"Instead," he adds, having my undivided attention. "If we turn inside, with no expectations of how this moment should be, then we know exactly what the moment is, and what it asks of us." He rolls his shoulders and stretches his body. "So yes, it's lazy if we don't do something about it, and it's also arrogant if we keep questioning it."

My mind wraps itself around his words, and I have to admit, he has a point.

"That's an interesting take on it." I let my mind grind on his explanation. Lazy if we procrastinate, arrogant if we question the moment, for we already know. My body shifts to the front of my saddle. "I'll sit with this for a while." And I mean it, for it's quite an interesting point of view.

"To be clear, Nordun, you've ventured all the way out here." His hand motions over our immense surrounding, but his eyes stay hooked on me. "You're acting on what calls you, and that's anything but lazy or ignorant." His gaze fades into a verdant green, and my heart holds on its breath. *How incredible.*

"I'm fortunate." I whisper. "With everybody helping me—everywhere I go." I bite my lip.

"And a fine horse that takes you anywhere, so please don't let it trip over your thoughts again." Karma's muffled chuckle tiptoes along as his stallion turns on the narrow track with a tiny tap from his heels.

"Got it." I sound more relieved than I am. Karma raises his hand in a salute in front of me, and I can almost imagine his mocking smile.

With the scanty, twisting trail and dense overgrowth demanding all of our attention, we ride on in a comfortable silence, keeping the pace as best as we can to Karma's content.

"We'll stay at an inn tonight," Karma says as the late midday sun moves a shadow across the peaks. "I don't like it, but we need the information."

I frown. "Information about what?" I stretch the ache in my limbs. About wild horses, or where they may be?

"About whether they have arrived yet." He doesn't speak their names, but I understand. My stomach churns. What if they have?

A massive lodging lies ahead in the deep orange sunset. I've seen nothing like it before. Two stone watchtowers rise over a wooden beamed guesthouse, each lighting one side of the enormous inn. In the sinking shadows I detect countless outbuildings, wood, and stone alike. The outcries of people and beasts of burden cram the cobbled courtyard.

My eyes widen at the sight of strange faces, hats, and hairstyles. The harsh sounds of tongues I've never heard before chafing my ears. Music and laughter drift alongside. It's overwhelming, this strange yet curious gathering of everything new. The aroma in the dining area is familiar and settles my rumbling stomach—there's a good hearty thenthuk simmering on the stove.

"I'll get us some food and a place to sleep." Karma beckons me to the furthest corner, out of sight. "Sit tight." And I do as I watch the spectacle in front of me. Travelers, traders, agents, and officers of all kinds mingle. Everything imaginable is happening here—eating, drinking, buying, selling, bartering, entertaining, and no doubt gambling too.

I rest my head against the wall and cast my eyes over the intriguing company. Seems by the look of some of the casually clad women going around—as I'm embarrassed to witness—a lot more than the usual entertainment is happening too. I close my eyes for a moment and let the tiredness wash over me. As I'm about to drift off, Karma's back.

"Nordun." His urgent tone rushes through me. "They're here. We've got to move."

Forty-One

"Seems two fellows arrived moments before us." Karma's eyes shoot over the crowd. Good thing it's shady in here. "They're asking around about a traveling nun." A nasty nausea hits my insides. That must be them.

"My cousins. Not Uncle?" I shrink at the thought of him.

"Don't know." Karma shrugs. "I think he sent his sons to take care of it." There's a sharp edge to his voice that reflects in his eyes. A fierce viridian flashes in the dim of the room.

"They'll eat in here." He grabs my hand and pulls me up. "I've gotten us a place to sleep." I throw my scarf over my head. His strong arm shields my pounding chest as we dart across the courtyard into a smaller building.

"What now?" I catch my breath. The stale smell of moldy food and spilled chang hits my nostrils. My eyes adjust to the dark. Massive bags and smaller bundles pile against the pealing plaster of shoddy walls, a few stained mats cover a corner, clothes heap up all around—this must be the servant's quarters. The iron latch clangs. It's secure.

"We're good here." Karma tosses his bags on one of the mats. "Sit and eat some. I'll be back with something to drink." He's calm, but that livid look in his eyes betrays him. "Lock up behind me." The door is ajar, he's gone.

I lean into the wall and steady my trembling knees. *They're here.* My mind dwells in an empty space. I stumble over to the mat, give in to the overwhelm and heave. Cold sweat runs down my temples and the sour taste engulfs my mouth. I can't control the shaking. I need to eat. My hands rumble around Karma's bag.

Tsampa crumbles in my mouth. A layer of fat and sweet and salt lines my palate. My strength and senses return. They don't know we're here—my cousins. I close my eyes. We're fine. All we can do is hide and wait out the night here. And pray. *Om Tare.* The beads slide between my greasy fingers.

"You didn't lock the door." Karma's voice echoes from the dark. I jump up. I must have dozed off. "Here's some fresh tea." His hands fold mine around a warm cup.

"I've found a way to distract them." He sinks beside me on the mat. The reek of chang surrounds him—and something else, something sweet I can't place.

"I'll be gone for most of the night, but you have to trust me." His breath has trouble keeping up with the speed of his words. "If I'm not back at dawn, take the horse and go into the middle valley, like we talked about." He pauses for a moment and takes a sip of my tea.

"Keep the mountains on your right side. Past the monastery, there's a trail leading up to the first mountain." Another gulp of tea. "I've packed your horse." He veers up to speed off again.

My mouth opens, but the words won't come out. Panic floods my veins. In a reflex I grab his arm, his muscles flex under my fingers. "How will I find you?" The darkness smothers my voice.

"I'll come for you, Nordun," he says. "I promise." A whisper, his lips brush my cheeks, a tender caress, and he's gone. A vast void fills the tiny room as I'm left, stunned by his unexpected touch and departure.

My mind's back into the empty space again and I return to the dark. This isn't happening. *Focus.* I crawl into the thin mat.

My hands draw a coarse wool blanket from the side. Everything inside me screams—*stay awake*—but I can't.

My body curls to a ball and I call upon Tara to turn my thoughts before total panic seizes me. My plea is heard. *Om Tare.* My body sinks into the mat and my mind falls into a dreamless sleep.

Rain dabbles on the roof, a muffled murmur passes by. The door's open a peek and a little light finds my eyes. I'm awake, but Karma isn't here.

There are only the ghostly silhouettes of beasts and baggage hiding in the courtyard. It's not dawn yet, but soon a silver gray will lift the shaded black. I sling my bag across my chest and shiver. Karma didn't return. I'll have to go. He said so. *Focus.* I gather my scarf close and skulk across the yard.

One glance at the main house—the door's ajar. Light pours out. They must have gone on all night. I turn away, but my curiosity draws me back. Is Karma in there?

Another glance at the house. The door's still open. My curiosity gets the better of me and my feet are in the hallway. My back slides along the wooden banister. I hide behind the wide doorpost, a perfect view into the room. It's as crowded as it was when I left. Bodies slough over benches, tables, and each other, voices sing and croak out loud. I lean in further. *There they are.* An iron fist squeezes around my heart. There they are—my cousins, amid the mob, drunk, and perched over a large round table.

Dice are scattered, cups stacked and broken everywhere. One of them is asleep, the other's trying his hand at the dice once more, his face in a foolish grimace. *Good.* I draw a breath and roll my head back. The state they're in, they won't be able to mount a horse.

My eyes scout their rowdy companions. *Karma.* On the opposite side of the table, his long hair tossed over his shoulders, his back to me. *There he is.* A woman on his knee, another around his neck, his arms thrown around them. One whispers in his ear, the other one's hands slide along this broad shoulders. *Really?* My heart takes a dive into the ground.

My heels dig into the dirt and I stumble out. What was I thinking? Of course, he's a man, and men drink, and gamble, and enjoy the company of women at every chance they get. *You fool!* I swallow to control my heaving breath and my unruly mind, but neither one's abiding. *My horse.* I shoot to the side. There it is, my mare's all saddled up, a bag tied to the side.

Well, at least he prepared it like he said he would. My heart pounds in my chest. I steady myself on steppingstone and mount my mare. *Let's get out of here.*

As my mare hits the trail Karma told me about, a soft golden dawn rips through the sky. A blue ribbon weaves through the pearly shades of gray, and a soft rain sprinkles on my face. What an auspicious sign to the journey ahead. I press my knees into the mare. A gentle nudge to my loyal companion, and off it is—we're on our way.

It's a brief ride to the middle valley and as we enter the gorge, they already bask in the first beams of morning sun—the magnificent Four Sisters Mountains lie ahead. With snowy peaks covered in a crystal crusting, the mountain range dazzles like a proud beacon above the lower valley. I halt for a moment and blink, content with having my breath and my mind back at my possession. I pet my mare on the neck. We've made it this far.

A crisp breeze rustles through the pines, hemming the narrow path into the valley. With my mare prancing in a placid trot, we move onto the secluded part of the trail. The chirpy morning tune from the earliest birds calls to the world full of cheer. A pair of picas probes from under the thorny shrubs, foraging to feed their no doubt countless young. Peaceful and quiet, with my eyes on the path and Tara on my mind, I've left the inn and all its rowdy visitors behind.

It takes a good while before the dense gray sway of the pines turns into open green and luscious flatland. Coming into the full morning sun, thin strands of smoke spiral up from afar. It's the weisang from the valley's monastery, a warm and encouraging welcome to all who pass. My heart leaps and I spur on my mare—time for a decent morning prayer, and with any luck, a cup of tea.

"So sorry, Ani-la." An old woman greets me as I arrive to the monastery's gate. "The monks are not in today." Her back bend, her beady eyes peer at me. "But please come in." She strokes my mare and feeds it a little crumb of whatever she had in her pocket as she takes us down a modest yard. "You must be hungry."

I smile. She heard my stomach grumble.

The oily aroma of fried bread welcomes me into the kitchen. I stop mid track. The spread of dishes set out on the low tables is amazing; so much food, and fresh too. My eyebrows raise and I turn to the old women. A toothless smile graces her face.

"I'm so sorry, sister," I say. "Did I come at an inconvenient time?" For sure, she must expect a large group of people soon. The woman's smile widens to the creases around her eyes.

"No no, Ani-la, please sit." Her wrinkled hands wave at a comfy seat near the stove. "I was expecting you."

My mind puzzles, my body pops into the seat. The weisang, the food—and she called me Ani-la. How does she know I'm a nun?

"Please, eat," she says and pours me tea. Still stunned, I sink my teeth into a chunk of bread. The briny salve of creamy butter, the tangy zest of fresh yogurt, the zing of spiced veal, the honey-glaze of dried apricots—my palate savors it all. Still, I wonder and would love to know.

"How...?" I look up, but she's gone. I lean back to glance into the hallway, but she's nowhere there. Outside, there's the placid neigh of my mare. The woman's taking care of another guest. I glance over the simple kitchen. The bowls stacked on the shelves, the tidy pots of herbs and spices all in a row.

So familiar, yet so far away. There's something of immense comfort to me, sitting in a monastery's kitchen.

"Don't forget to see the oracle..." I didn't hear her coming, but she's stepped into the kitchen again. "... as you're going up to the Oldest Sister." A bundle of offerings in her hands, her eyes meet mine. A flash of recognition, a tingle shoots through my arms. *She knows.* I open my mouth, only to close it again. No use. I better stop probing and take the moment as it is.

"Thank you, sister." I bow my head. "For everything." She presses the bundle in my hands, and a pungent aroma weaves through the coarse knit. A comfy glow spreads across my chest as I leave the kitchen. It's time to go up the mountain, but not before one last preparation.

It's marked right outside the monastery's gate, a pile of washed-out mani stones and bleached ribbons that once wore the vibrant colors of rainbows. I offer my bundle on the ancient altar of the mountain god and as the herbs smolder, I plead the deity of these lands. *Please grant me permission and success in my endeavors on your precious soil.* A delicate tranquility lingers within me.

I close my eyes as the days pass through my mind. So many people, so many events, all leading up to this very moment. Now I stand here, alone to face the vast blue yonder. For the first time in my life, it's all up to me. Only me. Alone.

A lively whinny, my mare's waiting.

"You're right," I turn to mount. "It's time. Let's go."

Forty-Two

Nourished and content, I ride on, leaving the fragrant forest of swaying cypress and willow pines behind. The trail runs into the sun-soaked flower meadows covering the foot of the mountain range, the Oldest Sister being the first peak on my right. Although she's the smallest of the four, she stands proud, looking magnificent. The abundant blossoms of white clover and purple-pink heather scatter on her steep slopes. It's the perfect place for the pheasants to hide their young from the jaws and claws of the fierce predators there.

With the midday sun reaching her peak, we cross the meadows, the intoxicating fragrance of wildflowers all around. Tiny streams of snow water trickle down the slopes, all flowing to the major river winding along the gorge. Crags and boulders dot the landscape as we clamber higher. The wind screeches along the rugged slopes and rustling sea buckthorn bushes. A pair of deer claps away, the crushing of pebbles under their hooves. With my mare as my sole companion, I ride on, calm and alert.

I stop for a moment and my eyes wander across the valley. The horses, where would they be? The grasslands on the slope of the mountains are my best bet, Karma said, plenty of grass and water. I shift to the front of the saddle and scan the slopes, knowing that a wild herd travels around.

The horses graze and roam across the range. I'll have to keep wandering along, looking for signs of hoofprints, any unusual disturbances in the shrubs and trees, droppings—anything that might indicate the presence of horses. Could be a herd or even a lone horse, Karma said. Many times, rebellious young stallions get ostracized from the group for having challenged their peers too often without success.

We wander all day, my mare and me. Even though we keep an effortless pace, the search in the scorching heat sumps our energy. Fortunately, the bounty of streams and waterfalls provide refreshing shelter. My bag's filled with food, enough to stay out for a few of days, so there's no need to hurry. Yet there's this vague sense of urgency dwelling within me, the one I've had all along. My body's tensing her limbs with a numbing tingle. It's getting stronger—I can't afford to rest for too long. We circle the slopes again. There are no horses.

Evening falls with a spectacular show of burnished orange, red, and yellow flaring around the mighty peaks. It's time to secure a place for my mare and me to spend the night. I spur it on a narrow trail leading to the higher grounds. It balks and puts one foot in front of the other with great reluctance. I spur again. No use. The mare senses what I didn't see—we've come onto charnel grounds, the base of a sky burial.

It's here where the people of this valley and around put the bodies of their deceased down to be devoured by vultures, the biggest act of generosity and compassion for all living beings. There are no scavengers circling, no traces of bodies or bones left, but the flat rocks are stained a bloody brown. That gives it away. *Om Mani Padme Hung.* My mare halts and I dismount to pray for a while.

Gratitude glows within me as I sit in this bleak and barren place. Death is familiar ground to me as I often visited the homes of the deceased to pray with my sisters to support the souls of the deceased and the families left behind in this samsara. For forty-nine days we pray. If the conditions of a rebirth are not favorable, the soul of the dead will suffer immensely in the bardos for that time. Despite watching all the sorrow and grief from the ones left behind, I've always been thankful to be in their presence, to be of benefit to them. How different now, sitting here, alone, not knowing what to do next.

A shiver runs up my spine as the sky twirls. Billowing clouds of darkened gray drift in an eerie still sky. A dense weariness dispels the gratitude that filled my entire being at prayer. I draw my scarf close. Fatigue tingles my limbs. My thoughts, still with my sisters, are slowly turning against me. Pema and Tsomo, they always know what to do. My chest tightens as I think of my new friends, of Sangmo, Sonam, Zinzin and little Lhadun, Norbu, Yeshe, and especially Karma, all at home with themselves in this world.

My heart sags to my stomach and I lean back on the boulder. I'm so awkward out here. The thought of it makes me cringe. Sure, I got a little better over the last few days, but look at me now, overwhelmed by my own emotions again.

My head tips back at the darkening sky. So far from the untrained mind Dechen was talking about, so far from taming a wild horse. I breathe in and let my lungs expand until they hurt. What was I thinking?

A sudden gush of wind hits the ground. Dust, gravel, and dirt swirl up in a twister.

"Whoa!" I clutch the reins. My mare brays and balks, ears pointed backwards, ready to take off.

Luminous green flashes in the midst of the whirling dust. I blink. A figure appears in a ring of blazing flames. My mind blanks at the ferocious presence of twirling green, wearing nothing but bone-ornaments on bare skin. This is not my beloved Tara, the mother who saves all. No, this savage presence wields a knife that's hooked, and a skull cup brimming with blood. *It's a dakini.*

I shrink away as the apparition whirls her way, dancing with her right leg raised while she extends her left leg toward me. A khatvanga staff leans in the crook of her left arm, swaying from left to right. My mind races with my speeding pulse. *Karma dakini*. It's the fearless dakini of action accomplishing wisdom appearing here in front of me. *Om mani!* How can that be?

"So, back in your thoughts again?" she shrieks and her eyes smolder at me. "How's that working out for you?" A squealing laughter peals out—she's mocking me. I blink again, for I can't believe what I see. "Want some?" She wields her knife at me, its edge so close to my cheek I can feel the draft.

"At least it will cut your disturbing emotions and false concepts." She bares her teeth and hisses. "Because the way you're going now is nowhere, sister, so you might as well."

I'm frozen, my back pressed against the rock's edge. All I can do is stare at this ferocious sky-goer. Never have I seen a dakini before. Yes, painted on thangkas, but not for real.

Her body, fiery green, emits the ruby rays of all accomplishing wisdom. The blistering heat around her is almost unbearable, even on this chilly night.

"You know by now, with all the studying you have done, that the powerful emotions of a woman are nothing other than wisdom." She wields her knife again, and it drafts too close. "You fear your emotions so much you try to thwart them." Sarcasm spikes her voice, the look of contempt glazes her eyes. "How ignorant of you, little girl." She snorts with contempt as she averts her gaze from me.

I sink down, my head to my chest. My vision blurs. Yes, I know, Dechen's told me so many times. It's useless battling my own emotions. "Let them roll by, like clouds in the sky," she said. "Observe them in a non-attached way and learn from them." But I couldn't and still can't. And here I am, in the face of all-accomplishing wisdom, grasping at my emotions like a dog chewing its own tail.

"Clarity only comes when you see the pattern and the nature of your emotions." The dakini's voice softens, and a husk rims the edge of her tone. "Want to stop them? You'd be mad denying yourself the wisdom in it!" My nails press into the flesh of my hands so hard it hurts.

"What you see, sister, what you see?" She hops around me, teasing me, challenging me. "I know what I see! Expectations, self-blame, and resentment—and too much disappointment to go around!" Her words shoot the sharpest of searing arrows at me, straight into my heart.

"Look at you, look what your restless mind is creating—thinking, talking yourself down, and keeping no other company than fear." My breath quickens. Her truth slaps me hard in my face.

"Drop it!" Her words rip the tensed space between us. "Drop the fear, drop the anxiety—there's nothing to fear or worry about in inner space," she snaps. "Be open to what unfolds, as you've done your entire journey until now."

My mouth opens but all I can do is listen and stare at the dakini, blazing and raging on.

"Here you are—despite your doubts and fears, despite your expectations of how it should be." Her staff slams the ground, a lightning beam crashes. "You surrendered yourself—for there is none, you understand that well." Her head bobs, her eyes narrow into slits of a verdigris crescent waning, peering right into the void within me.

"And you've trusted the guidance of your inner nature—the guidance of compassion." Her hooked knife points at me, slashing a circle in the air. I flinch at her strike. Compassion as my guidance. *Me?* She must be mistaken.

"That's not really..." I'm startled by my own voice, for I honestly feel it's not like that. "I've come across incredible amount of support—everywhere I go I'm guided, supported, encouraged." I swallow hard. I have been most fortunate with all.

"And why do you think that is?" She bobbles her head from side to side. "It's because deep down—under all that doubt and insecurity—you, sister, have never ceased the solid connection to your true nature." Her knife draws to her side, and she raises the overflowing skull, bristling with blood. "That's what makes you surrender yourself at the moment—that's what makes you act with compassion, and that's what will make you succeed. Look at it!"

Her voice fades as the unforeseen events from the past weeks fly by. The prophecy, the visit to my family, the suffering of Father and the horses at the stables, changing into lay clothes to travel on, learning the ways of the wild at the camp; and now I'm here, all alone. Yes, my every move was guided by compassion, for the benefit of all. And everything has led me here. A tinge of confusion tugs at my heartstrings. Even that silly mess with Karma—it has led me here. I hang my head. All the anxiety, all the insecurity, over what?

"Want to meet the horse? Want to succeed?" Her voice shrieks again. "Drop the anxiety, Nordun, for there's nothing to fear in inner space." And just as I dare to face her, she dashes herself away with a swift spin in the air. The echo of her howling laugh fades further until she's completely gone.

My limbs won't move. I slouch against the boulder. What just happened here? My mare prods its nose into my side. Sweat sticks to my fingers. *The karma dakini.* She spoke. Her truth tore through my inside. I crouch. My stomach's gone weak. *Focus.* I swallow the traces of bile in my mouth.

Cold night air spins around me. The wind spurs me on. Stars scintillate a pearly white in a vast purple hue. In the distance the thunder claps. My mare scrapes its hooves, sensing it too. It's going to pour out of the heavens soon—we'd better seek shelter.

Forty-Three

A gain, I'm lucky as a small hollow, carved into a sheltered plateau, reveals itself up on the slope. It's the perfect cave to spend the night. With my mare secured, I scout the cavern for critters or even bigger predators. A dry and protected shelter is always sought after in the mountains, for humans and animals alike.

A small fire warms my body, but my mind's still out there in the evening chill, grasping at straws. *The Karma dakini.* It's time to put my being at ease with prayer, at least until the blaze smolders away.

No rain, no thunder—the storm never arrived. A shroud of charcoal and cobalt hides a full moon and cloaks the cave in darkness. The night is quiet. I lay my body to rest after prayer, for the day has been too long and sleep is on its arrival.

A shrill neigh from my mare rings out, followed by the crackling of dry pine needles—I open my eyes, but there's only the dark. The shape of my craggy cave and its moss-covered entrance emerges. Nothing's out there, yet a sense of unease creeps in.

A slight draft caresses my cheeks. I pull my blanket around my shoulders. The sound of pebbles crunching under horse's hooves echoes out; my mare's getting restless. I veer up and peer out. I can barely see as shadows shift against the now bright silver moon.

A sudden roll of thunder strikes and lightning crashes at the entrance of my hideaway. In the flash, I see my mare wrestling with its restraint. It's throwing all fours in the air. I jump up but too late. The rope has snapped, and the horse dashes off with a loud bray. Hooves clatter on granite, echoing into the eerie abyss

A deluge of anxiety waves through my body as a foul stench pervades the cave. A bone-chilling hiss pulsates from the walls. *It's there!* It's right at the entry. I shudder at its sight. A fiery amber glows in the dark, a slippery scaled skin gleams in the light of a silver moon. My eyes scoot around—the viper from the barn. It's back and I have no way to run out or hide. Panic surges within me, and as the giant snake rises and roars its monstrous head, my knees buckle and give in.

Gravel grates my palms as I claw my way back further into the cave. *This can't be.* I blink again. My frantic sight must deceive me. For sure, this is the work of Uncle. My mind leaps to the barn and back. It's a spell, and the phantom of Uncle is trying to reign my mind. My back presses hard against the rock-ribbed wall. *Focus.* It's not real.

This snake, with its fiery eyes, horrid stink, and terrifying hiss, it looks alive and real—yet I have to realize it's not. It's a spell. My sisters saw it, so that must be it. It's a spell, and now it's the time for me to see it clear.

Drop the anxiety, there is nothing to fear in inner space! That's what she said—the words of Karma dakini swirl in my mind. This demonic snake, seething and slithering—it's only the fear and anxiety created in my own mind. Nothing else. I grasp my wrist, the prayer bead and the red string intertwined. What to do? Useless to fight. Besides, violence is not in my nature.

Surrender yourself at the moment. Karma dakini's words shriek in my ears. *Look at it!* I turn to the snake, gulping hard at the monster I see. The viper's head sways back and forth, as it's sizing me up.

It's an illusion. I want to see it; I want to believe. My nails squeeze in the flesh of my hands. Another tidal wave of panic swells within me, drowning every bit of my fragile faith from within.

Act with compassion, and you succeed. The dakini's words soar through the void in my mind. *Compassion. Surrender.* There are nothing but hollow words resounding within my hopeless being. My mind has left me. Please tell me, how do I understand?

Another burst of lightning crashes through the cavern. The hush of the cobra's hiss is daunting, announcing the moment before the strike. My body shakes beyond my control, and I rest my head in my trembling hands. I don't dare to look any further—there's no way out.

A green veil blurs my vision. The dakini's hooked knife slashes at me, cutting circles in the air while the cup in her hand simmers and thick blood coils down. With the sharp arrow of her blazing truth, she pierces a gaping hole in my desolate mind. I gasp as the meaning of her unfolds before me. *It's the practice of chöd!*

The skull cup, the cutting, the slashing of the knife—that's what the dakini showed me, the practice of chöd. Cutting away the outer demons and inner demons, and slashing through the false perceptions of the self, by offering your own body to all, demons, and gods alike. *Chöd!* It's the practice of the ultimate surrender through infinitive compassion, the beggar's offering when there's nothing left but the body to give. *Compassion. Surrender.* So chöd it is.

I lift my head and my heart and fold my hands in prayer. The usual drum, bell, and thighbone trumpet needed to perform the ritual of chöd are missing, so I'll have to perform the practice with the only thing that's left with me—my own body.

The snake's slimy skull hovers over me. Foul saliva drips from edged fangs, a crude-scaled, slippery carcass loops through the rustling leaves. My teeth clatter at the first words of the prayer. *Focus.* I turn inwards and sit with my quivering heart until a soft light ignites from the deep and glows into a comforting warmth. I let it expand into glorious rays that push beyond all imaginary boundaries, making all that is around me sacred and safe. My mind and lips fall in sync and the words of the prayer flow. The entire cave is ablaze with my light and love. Let the feast begin.

I clap the bone trumpet three times in my mind's eye, inviting the viper with my best intentions to do good.

"Please, I'm here for you," I beg the monster in front of me. "I'm here—come on over to feast." My heart reaches out, extending my invitation to all the destructive forces of demons, spirits, and evil ghosts in this realm. All monstrous torments, all suffering, and all ill come to wander in front of me. I continue to ask, extending my plea to my uncle, the one that killed my mother, and now is trying to harm me.

"Come on over, Uncle." I call out to him and to all harm that surrounds him. "I wish to do something good for you, please hurry." I request them to crowd my mind. Gaunt, ashen phantasms, red seethed with anger, hideous deformations of body and mind. They all flock together, a great ghoulish gathering of evil, sickness, and disease right here with me in this horrendous samsara.

These creatures, helpless in their misery, they too are stuck in this cyclic existence, just like me. They too are good in nature, yes they are. I know for sure. A flood of empathy rushes through me as even more beings appear. These creatures don't have the capacity to free themselves from the hate and rage that has taken possession of them. They have no means and no ability to control themselves, they're defenseless and in need—unlike me. These destitute beings deserve all of my loving kindness and compassion. I can help them, these wretched ones. I can feed their hunger and quench their thirst. And I will.

The tender hollows of my heart stretch beyond to hold all of them, all these unfortunate creatures. I call upon all Buddhas, to all great masters, protectors, and helpers to help me carry out my good intention, my deepest wish. My physical body dwells here in the cave, but my heart resides at the top of the sacred Mount Meru, together with the Buddhas, saints and sages. Good and evil, all came along here at my invitation. All are gathered together to take part in a magnificent feast.

With sincere intention, I declare my body to be offered, devoured by all beings—good and evil. *I wish to feed you all, to nourish you all with goodness and compassion. Please come.* My heart cries out with my deepest wish—and my body softens. My skin dissolves, my flesh melts, and every bone in my body crumbles, transforming me into the most desirable elixir, a nourishing mix enticing all.

A luminous sky radiates around Mount Meeru and rainbows of the brightest colors exude from my mixture, boiling with sweetness and releasing an enticing aroma in the air. Dakinis soar with skull cups in their hands, scooping and serving my scrumptious solution to the great gathering around me. The evil and the good, they all feed ferociously on me, satisfying their huge hunger with my body's delicious taste. They are so clear to me now, nourishing themselves—the Buddha's, the saints, the ghouls, and all demons. Even the cobra and my uncle are feasting on me.

I'm gifting my body, selfless and with delight in my heart. I let all beings dine on me until their hunger is stilled and all their needs are met. Coming to the final offering, with nothing left of me to devour, I bend my head in total surrender. The fear that once dwelled within me has succumbed to my unconditional love and compassion for all.

A lightness settles my being, and all the shadows are gone. The worries, the doubts, the anxiety and fears within me, even the monster of a snake out here, not a trace is left. I've slashed through it all, like the dakini told me. I've cut the attachment to my body and my self with the unconditional love for all. There's no more being of me, only a crystal clear inner space with nothing to fear.

Tears well up behind my eyelids. I let them cool my heated cheeks. They're tears of pure joy. All that's left now is to be still and rest in uncontrived and exuberant awareness.

The twilight foreshadows the imminent rising of the sun. The night must be coming to an end. I don't know how long I've been sitting here, relishing the calm that's rooted within me. Time seems to be suspended, a crease between the here and now.

As I lay my head down, sleep comes to me as it never came before—it's a sleep I'm not afraid to wake up from, a sleep full of hope.

Forty-Four

The brief night has left no traces on me. Waking up at the first light of a pink dawn, it's still there—that feeling of utmost completeness and an almost fierce serenity. I get up, my body light and relaxed. Pine needles and dry leaves strewn across are the only reminders of whatever happened here last night.

The edge of the cave, with the softest of sunlight just coming in, is the perfect spot for my morning prayer. I set myself on a bolder overlooking the gorge. The wind strokes the loose strands of my hair. Memories of the past days flee, and I shake my head. No use thinking about it anymore. I'm here, right now, and that's all there is.

I bask in gratitude, and I bow my head in prayer. The anxiety once seated so deep is gone. Somehow, I've laid down my fears, accepting the insecurity of whatever is coming. A sure trust has taken its place, for I know now—nothing's certain, and all is open, and all will change. This is samsara. My fingers slide the prayer beads around, an homage to the new day. I'm here for the benefit of all.

A pair of brow-cheeked laughing thrushes flock together in their morning song. The sun peeks over the top of the mountain range; it won't be long until her golden rays will caress the alpine meadows in the vale. After morning prayer,

I still my hunger with left-over bread. Savoring the warming sun and my peace, there's no urge at all, but it might be time to look for my mare.

I crumble a crust of bread in my pocket, some encouragement for the horse to come. And just as I sling my bag over my shoulder—ready to go—the familiar clatter of hooves reaches on the path. My mare's back, and by the sound of it, she brought company.

A gorgeous stallion parades behind my mare. A real beauty of a stallion, with solid muscles rolling beneath a glossy chestnut brown coat. Still young but already carrying the signs of pure strength, his slender body protrudes an air of pride and power. Eyes alert, ears pointing forward, he tosses his wild mane around as if to say, "Look at me, I'm here." There's a brass boldness in the stallion's eyes. Kind of the way my mare eyed me up in the paddock, but so much more provocative. I hold my breath—he's truly a wild one. *Stay calm.*

"Well, hello again." I turn to my mare. My heart leaps and I slow my breath. "Hungry?" I feed her the crumbs and stroke her neck. "I see you brought a friend." My horse neighs and shakes her frame. "Sure, I think he's handsome, too."

I laugh, for what would Sangmo and Norbu say when they saw me now, talking to the horse? Ah well, I'm acting from my heart, for that's all I can do.

I lean against the rock overlooking the valley, feeding my mare a little more. The stallion's eyes are on me, ears going back and forth. He's checking out the situation, but mostly me. How do I get the stallion to come without chasing it? Maybe I shouldn't put myself in a corner like this, leaning against a boulder. After all, he's wild and has a mighty set of teeth.

My chest tightens. I've seen horses bite. *Focus.* A sharp breath clears the old anxiety wanting to creep back in. No need to go that way. The stallion will come when he's ready—or not.

My hands slide down my mare's forehead, down the soft fuzz of her lips. She nibbles a bit as I take the halter and walk with her to the side. There I tie the mare up, feeding her some more bread, keeping all my attention on her. It works—the stallion's hooves grind pebbles as he joins us, one foot before the other. His interest is stirred. Now what? Norbu would know.

Norbu. I press my lips together and straighten myself. My shoulders squared, I walk away, my back turned to the stallion. Just a few steps. A moment later, there are hesitant crunches on the gravel. The stallion follows! The bread's sticky in my sweaty palm. I take another few steps. Another few crunches follow—he's behind me. I drop my shoulders and turn on my heels—a piece of bread in my stretched hand. Ever so promptly, the stallion snatches it, producing a loud smack from his greedy lips.

"I get it." I meet his eye, where there's a keen brown gleam. "You're interested." I make a slow turn. Shoulders firm, I walk on, repeating the ritual Norbu taught me. Chomping hooves, he's following again! And when the last piece of bread is gone, I stride to my bag and feed my mare some more.

The stallion keeps trailing, ensuring a distance between us. Safe for him and safe for me. My mind's going around—how and when to get the halter on? My hands search in the bag. I'm sure Karma packed one. Yes, there it is.

I slide the leather straps over my arm and stuff another hand full of bread in my pocket. My heels grind in the gravel. The stallion's nostrils widen—*too fast.* I've moved too fast—there's no connection yet. My pulse quickens. I hold my breath and feed my mare more bread. I've got to slow down.

Connection, it's all about connection, remember? My fingers fumble with the mare's halter. My mind buzzes around. How to connect from the heart when I'm so in my thoughts? *Focus.*

"I get it." I soften my gaze, ready to meet the stallion again. Resting my hands on my lower body, I bow my head. *Connect from the heart.* My eyes close and a warm breath flows in, expanding my chest, awakening my heart. As I exhale, my breath drops in my hands. My heart surges wide open, ready to give it my all. My mind's swept clear. *I'm here, ready to receive.*

I open my eyes and raise my palm to the stallion. Some more bread.

"I'm here, I see you." I meet his eye and he shakes his head, sweeping the bread off my hand. A huffing bray clouds from his nostrils. He nudges at me. His ears swipe sideways, brazen and bold. My mouth opens. Of course, he's up to play!

"Oh, I see you." I laugh. "I see what you're up to." Another frisky bray, he frolics from left to right. That brash spirit of his, he's up to playing this game all day long. My arms reach out to stroke his forehead, mindlessly sharing in his delight.

Whoa! My hands float in mid-air. A slight hesitation—a quiver from the heart. For a moment I freeze, but all melts away as his head butts into my somewhat shaky hand. A surge of energy shoots through my arms—we've connected.

"Yes, here we are," I say, breathless, my eyes on the horse. Another piece of bread gets muzzled as the halter slides over his head. He curves his neck as my hand strokes down his manes. I take a small step back, some space to take it all in. What strength, what grace, all right here under my touch.

The lead from the stallion's halter swings in my hands as I pack the bag on my mare. "Time to go." My voice's cheerful and steady, but my mind wavers ever so slightly, ready to question every move I make—again. Am I going too fast again? My nose wrinkles. *I got this.* With a sweep of newly found courage, the anxious thought is whipped aside.

"Let's go." The leads from the horses burn in my hand as my feet shuffle down the narrow trail. Hooves slap a cheerful rhythm on the gravel, almost in sync. The pair's following. *Yes!* A smile builds on my face. I pick up a steady pace and we walk on, past the charnel grounds, through where the winding streams flow along.

The trail widens, the lush grasslands are calling us, the last sparkles of glittering dew enticing our way. I ignore the slight quiver in my stomach and mount my mare. Careful not to let my excitement get the best of me, I put all my attention on the trail ahead. With the stallion following on the lead, we ride down, the sun on our back.

And so we track through the flowering meadows. The sweet smell of summer flowers brings the bumble of bees, accompanying us on our way with their hum. It's not long before the sun peaks high over the rugged massif. The horses prance, showing no patience at the sight of the crystal-clear water running through the base of the gorge. Time to rest, refresh. Might be careless, but I let them dash into the fleeting creek.

A few wry pines are the perfect spot to catch some shade, their dry needles a cushy seat. I know I should eat, but I'm not hungry. My fingers pick a tsampa ball apart as my thoughts ponder the next step. Tightness nestles itself in my chest again, just thinking about mounting the stallion. With Norbu's help it would be doable, but how to do this by myself?

My eyes go over the sprawling river. Plenty of boulders to serve as a steppingstone. My stomach rumbles. Also, plenty of rocks to land on when thrown off a horse. My mind wavers again. The cool beads slide across my fingers. *Oṃ Tare.* I've come so far with Tara's help. I put my complete trust in her.

A faint breeze caresses my face. *Act from a pure heart and all good things will be done.* Tara's truth flows on my breath. A wrinkle appears between the here and the now, and a moment of complete stillness crashes down on me. In the distance the horse hooves splash, and the water fleets. *All will be fine.*

I blink. The horses dart into my vision, circling around in the fine spray of opal and white. Their sheer joy and pure strength spread a glorious glow against the bluest of skies. What a magnificence, these creatures, being at home right here in the wild, belonging to nothing or nobody but themselves.

Threads of a golden sun meet the silver spray spun on the water—a bright beam flashes through. My whole being jolts. *Home. Belonging to nobody.* That's it! That's what it takes to proceed.

"Time to move on." The water churns an invigorating prod around my ankles as I join the horses in the creek. I pack my mare and tie her lead loosely to the pine. "Just wait for a while." I feed her the remains of my tsampa ball and she seems content. *All is well.* Next step.

The stallion probes around us. My trembling fingers take his lead and tie it into a rein. I know—or at least think I know—how to do this. Everything inside me is clear, and yet. My hand slides over his drenched flank. *Permission to mount.*

"So here we are." I lead the horse to a flat boulder. My knees sag a bit as I step on the stone. *Focus.* My hand strokes his neck, down his flank, towards his belly. My eyes never leave the sight of his ears. They're twirling. A good sign.

"I know you don't have to do this, for you are free. You are your own," I say in a whisper. His ears twirl and he lets out the softest of brays. I've got his attention.

"You owe me nothing, we both know, but I'm asking you anyway." My heart beats a drum in my ears so loud now, I can hardly hear my own words. My hands are on the stallion's upper back, the place where I'm supposed to mount. Tiny beads of sweat trickle down, loose strands stick to my temples. *Focus.*

"I'm asking your permission to mount." My cheek rests on his warm hide. "To let me ride home on your back." He shakes his head, and his long manes sway against my cheek. My breath shallows and my hands put a little more pressure there. Will he? A brisk bray. The stallion's veins throb under my sweaty fingers. I pull in another sharp breath.

"I promise I'll let you go once we're home." My voice is steady and confident, my cheek still rests on his neck. "I'll set you free, free to go, that I promise." My mouth dry, I swallow and straighten my back. "I will." One hand on his back, my other slides through his coarse, tangled manes. "You have my word." I bit my cracked lip. Will it work?

"Let's do this," I say, more to myself than to him. Both my hands on his back, I draw myself over, putting just enough pressure for him to feel me leaning on his hardened spine. Another bray, louder now. A nervous prance, he shifts back and forth.

"We're fine here, aren't we?" A quiver shoots under my belly as he halts. His muscles snake along his spine. He scrapes his hooves and shifts his weight from left to right. Again he brays and picks up his sway in a lively manner. His spine presses against my belly. I feel his body relaxing underneath mine.

I smile, for I know this game by now. I hang my full weight off him. We rock together as he sets the pace, back and forth and back. The stallion and me, getting in synch, getting confident with each other. It takes a while before he stands at ease, shaking himself. Another spirited bray flows from his nostrils. One ear turns to me, the other one goes outwards.

"That's my sign." I move my weight to the front and pull my right leg over the horse's back. He prances right away again, swinging from left to right.

My hands reach for the reins. *Easy!* A sudden tension soars through my body. *Focus.* I swallow and let the anxiety pass with a low hiss from within. That's it. My hands slide through the manes and I straighten myself. My legs sway from his sides. *I'm up.*

An immense surge of relief passes, and my shoulders sag. The stallion shakes himself with a vigor, and a smile breaks on my lips.

"I understand." My voice pitches. "You're in charge." And it's the truth—he is and always will be, for he's the wild one.

But for now, we're fine and we're on our way.

We're going home.

Forty-Five

Getting out of the valley with two spirited horses, what was I thinking? The stallion, not used to being steered, frolics all over the place. My mare prances at his tail. I have no idea how to handle two horses, but I somehow sense—ah, there's my intuition!—the only way forward is to play along. So I let these energetic animals go out a bit and reign them in with a gentle hand when needed.

My limbs exhausted, I'm balancing between a slip and a slide of the stallion's back as he makes his rapid moves. But my mind's elated, for we're moving—zigzagging and slow—and getting ahead; we're on our way home. I don't want to think about the long days in the saddle, or even what awaits us at the end of this valley. For now, I savor being with the horses, relishing in their delight.

Time travels a lot faster than we do. A tangerine sun sets on the towering peaks, dragging her last long shadows behind us. In the distance, the tops of the pines wave their welcome into the woodlands. The monastery will come up after that. It might be a good idea to seek shelter there. Staying at the inn or another guesthouse will raise too many questions. After all, I'm travelling alone.

I'll come for you. Disappointment yanks across my chest. Karma drinking and gambling, two questionable women around his neck—so much for a promise. No use waiting. I set my eyes on the dense forest ahead. I'm on my own, and I'm doing fine.

I duck with the rustle of fine branches waving above me. The woodland wraps around. Sharp and sweet, almost like lemons, the refreshing fragrance of young pines in the late midday sun lingers under the dark shades. A few windy bends and we're almost out in the open. The monastery awaits.

I squint as the forest releases us into the rosy glaze of the late afternoon. A sudden snort resounds, hooves scrape in the sand. *That's not from my horses.* I halt. My mare bumps her head against my stallion's flank. There, in the midst of the bright glare, a steed rises in front of me. My heart stops and jump-starts the next moment. *It's him!* My cousin, the nasty one, from the pen.

A cruel smirk curls on his lips as he coils a long whip around his arm. The leather tip hits the ground with a whack as he lets it fall. My stallion stiffens. His ears fling behind him. My mare brays and bumps her head on my side.

"So you thought you were going to get home with that horse?" He raises his hand. The lash draws up. And the blood drains from my veins. "As far as I can see, you're going nowhere." My eyes fix on the tip of the leather. I can't move. A cry of anguish gets stuck in my throat. If he cracks it, I'm gone.

A rich purple shade billows through the auburn dusk. A swift wind swells around us. Dust and sand swirl up our horses' legs and the shadows darken. My mare tears on the lead as I pull her tight. My stallion's muscles ripple underneath me; he's ready to balk on all fours.

"Put that whip down—very slowly." A voice, calm and clear, resounds out of nowhere. "Now." A tall silhouette moves from the forest. A lone rider, two eyes glow underneath a rimmed hat.

It can't be. I blink. But it is. *Father!* My heart leaps, my mind moves into a blank. It's Father, coming out from the trees. It's really him.

"Don't be a fool, you old man!" A harsh sneer slices from the younger man's mouth towards the woodland. Silver flashes from underneath a chuba. Father's drawn a knife—not long, but blinkingly sharp.

I flinch. Father used to have a mighty throw. Never missed, as I remember. My eyes shoot over to my cousin. His arm is still raised.

"You're the fool, young man." Father's clenched fist rests along his leg. "By now you should know you can't win from a man who has nothing to lose."

His quiet tone, his determination, it makes me shudder. My gaze flings from one to the other and back.

My cousin's arm doesn't lower. Father shakes his head. The knife flickers. *No!*

"You see, if a man carries his demons with him long enough, they take over." Father steers his stallion forward. "That's what happened to me." His horse halts. Father's mouth twists in his ashen face.

"I let the demons take over until there was nothing left in me—not even life." He pauses. His hand tips his hat back. The last blush of a coral sun reveals a bright and gallant gaze. *Nothing left in me.* My heart surges at the valor in his eyes, even though the meaning of his words bruises my very being.

"No life, no fear." Father's words tear through the tense threat the young man poses in front of us, ripping it into flimsy, meaningless scraps within the blink of an eye. "So you better go now." My mind boggles at the showdown in front of me.

The young man's arm wavers. His flinty eyes narrow and his face betrays his loss. His shoulder drops, and his lips pinch. *Ptooey!* Spit splatters in front of my feet. He throws a last vicious glance around. His horse turns on its hind legs, jolted by a violent tug, and he speeds off, the long whip trailing along.

My mare brays. Her hooves stamp in the sand. My stallion balks on all fours. His solid frame stirs as he lands on his front legs. I duck. My hands grip the manes. I'm fine, I've been here before. As dust and gravel settle around us, I turn to Father, standing unmoving. His eyes trace the disappearing dot on the horizon like a hawk regretting his prey.

For a moment, all is quiet, even the pines stall their sway in the breeze. It all happens too fast.

"You came." My face flushes. It's all the words I can manage for now. *He came.*

"Oh my child, how could I not?" Father hangs his head, his shoulders hunch.

My heart quivers as I see. There's no victory in this man, only a weighted mingle of sadness and shame.

"I've been a coward, letting my grief control me for all those years, turning my back on everybody out of fear I would lose even more." His voice is thick with emotion. "When you came to see me, I couldn't deny it anymore. Your true nature, my child, it showed through your immense compassion for the horse." He looks up and I meet him amidst his intense regret.

"But I let my fear reign again and I send you away for the second time, afraid of what might happen to you—to us—if I didn't." He clenches his fists.

He understands. My heart slows, my hands sink into my stallion's manes. Father understands what was calling me, that distant longing within me, always there. It was within my heart, my true nature calling me. I didn't understand, but Father did—all along. He knew the prophecy was right.

"Oh, Nordun, I could see my own wrong, but I didn't want to admit it." He shakes his head. "And then I heard you were going out for a wild horse to save the stables, to save our home." His hand draws over his face. Pain, shame, sorrow, regret, all flashes before me in an ugly glare.

"How I've failed you as a father." His voice cracks. "You didn't question, you didn't hesitate, you answered the call of your heart with an unwavering 'yes' while all the while I had been hiding, wallowing in sorrow, creating only more misery, for myself and the ones around me." His eyes shoot up at me, a bright amber flares. My heart skips a beat. If he only knew of my struggles, of my insecurity.

"You showed courage when all I did was give up, on you, on me, on everything and everybody." His shoulders square and he tilts his chin. "I knew I had to end this senseless struggle in me, or I would lose it all—and especially you—for good." He pulls in a deep breath and I stall mine as my heart cracks open at the sincerity of his words.

"So you meant it when you said you had nothing left to lose." My voice sounds so frail at the sight of this brave man, my father, hearing him say and admit what we both knew deep inside, all along.

"I did." The fiery amber in his eyes gleams with tears, held back at the verge, but not afraid to be seen. "I turned my back on you, my only child, and send you away—not once, but twice." His voice fades in a thick haze of sadness and remorse. "So how could I not come after deserting you too many times?"

A lightness bursts in my chest, dizzying me through my whole being. *Father knows.* My hands grip the manes, and my stallion shakes his frame. I wasn't sure if he did, but he just told me in these very words. He abandoned me—and regrets it after all.

My vision blurs. Still, I meet his eyes. They mirror mine with a glimmer of hope. I lift my head ever so slightly. Words won't come, for they are not needed. Father's here. He's here for me now. That's all that matters.

A profound understanding rises within me, and my hand reaches out. He bends over, clasping it tight.

"I'm so happy you came." With these words, I bridge the immeasurable distance between us. It's settled. This is all that needed to be said.

"I see you brought one fine specimen of a horse with you." Father clears his throat. "Or actually two. You did well." He leans in to inspect the horses with an approving eye.

"Thank you, I was lucky." I mean it. Somehow, I had little to do with it all.

"Maybe." Father lowers his head. A joyful glimmer peeps from under the rim. "Or it could be something that runs in the family, don't you think?" He tips his hat and faces me full on, emitting the pride and unconditional love only a father can, that which my heart has yearned for ever since he left.

I try, but I can't hold it. A sob escapes from the back of my throat.

"Could be." I avert my eyes. My hand is quick to swipe my cheek.

"It's been a long day." Father's hand squeezes mine. "Let's see if there's room at the monastery." He takes the lead from my mare. "Here, let me for a while."

Together we ride, side by side, with the last of the sun sinking in streaks of cobalt and crimson. Evening has tumbled upon us; the night will follow soon.

As always, tea is ready, and a scrumptious meal to accompany it. The old woman who runs the kitchen has outdone herself again. My stomach rumbles at the savory smell of the hearty thenthuk. I'm famished and thankful as the servings are big and not few.

Father and I eat in silence. With my appetite satisfied, and the elation of the day settled in, I lean back. *Father's here.* I rub my eyes, as I still can't believe it. He's sitting here with me, drinking his tea. He travelled at least five days. How did he know?

"Father," I say. "Who told you?" I sip my tea. His eyes clear, his posture upright, he seems full of energy. He nods as he puts his bowl to his mouth, finishing the last of the thenthuk. Somehow the long journey doesn't seem to have bothered him at all.

"Karma." Father wipes his mouth with the back of his hand.

Karma. I flinch as the hot tea scorches the tip of my tongue.

"He came after he brought your sisters home." He puts down his cup and sadness lines his mouth. "Needless to say, I was livid at first, but deep down I already knew. I just didn't want to see, for I feared what could happen." He rests his hands on his knees.

"He told me what your sisters revealed." The amber in his eyes darkens to a charred honey-brown. A tightness stretches over my ribs. *Father knows about Uncle.* How that hurts. I had been wondering, but didn't want to ask.

"Of course I refused to believe him at first. I mean, my only brother." He rubs his neck. "But when Tennah and the boys disappeared, I knew for sure."

My jaw drops. "They're gone?" Where would Uncle be? Surely he would not... I call off the search for I don't want to go there. *Focus.* I rest my head against the wall. My fingers ring around my cup.

"Yes, they left in a hurry." More tea gets poured. "I haven't seen them on the way—except for the one coward this afternoon." His eyes light up with a certain pleasure.

"You handled him well," I say, leaving out the part where I was convinced he would throw his knife.

"I've been around them long enough to know he wouldn't have the guts." He slurps his tea, and an approving burp follows.

With the last of the tea and thenthuk devoured, we sit back in a quiet contentment.

"Time to rest. We've got a long journey ahead of us." Father gets up, a little slow. "I'm sure Ani-la will have a room for me." He grabs a blanket from the corner. "Here, you'll sleep in the kitchen, nice and warm." And off he is, without a goodnight. That's the father I remember, always on the go.

The night is brief, or at least so it feels. As soon as I lay down my head, I wake a moment later. The stove seethes a gentle good morning with sweet simmering milk. A toothless smile greets me with a cup filled to the brim.

"So sorry, Ani-la." I scramble up from the seat. "Let me help you." My feet hasten over to the stove, my thoughts rushing to catch up. How rude of me to sleep while she's working.

"No need, no need." Her voice creaks. "I'm happy to have visitors as the monks are gone for too long." She hands me a cloth. "Here, the water's behind the kitchen." With a bow, I take the cloth and hurry outside to freshen up. My hair hangs loose, sleep itches in my eyes. I must look a mess.

All tidied up and refreshed, Father's finishing his breakfast.

"I'll get my horse ready." There's an uplifting air in his voice. "You'll take care of your wild bunch?" My heart delights. *My wild bunch*. Yes, a wild bunch they are.

"I will." I had hoped for morning prayer, but Father's set to go. A piece of bread and a cup of tea, and we're off.

With Father heading the way out of the valley, my stallion's showing his true nature. Competing his way for the lead, pacing up and down, left and right, he seeks any chance to pass Father's horse. Reining him in has no effect. This horse is a natural leader, and he's claiming his stake.

"Well, this promises to be an exciting ride." Father roars with laughter. "And we're only just starting." He turns in his saddle. "Best way to let him lead. He'll get tired soon enough." He waves and the stallion passes with speed.

"Somehow I don't think so." I wrestle the reins to keep him from flying off. "But at least we'll be home soon as he sets the pace." We both laugh. It will be a long way home.

A mellow morning sun unwinds in the blue yonder. There's not a cloud in the sky. With the road wide open now, the horses pick up their pace.

"From here on its straight to Rongdrak." Father points ahead. "Two days, if we're lucky."

Two days to Zinzin's camp. Then another three days to the stables. I haven't thought about the journey ahead yet.

I didn't want to, as my quest for the stallion demanded all my attention. Now this is accomplished, I have to face what's next. With Uncle gone, and the cousins too, the position of horse master will be mine. My stomach knots slightly at the thought of it, but somehow I don't think Uncle and my cousins will show up again. Then again, one never knows. My mind slips away from me. And then what to do? Stay at the stables with Father? Sure Father's more than capable of running the stables himself. My home's on the mountaintop, with Dechen and my beloved sisters. It's where I belong, right?

I'm sure Father senses what's going on, for he interrupts my restless thoughts.

"You know, Nordun." He slows down his horse. "Your grandmother will be thrilled to see you again." He turns to me, a sincere look on his face.

"I hope so." I'm quick to cast down my eyes. "I've disappointed her, for I didn't come back when I said I would." I swallow. "And I'm not sure what to do next." I pause, and my heart tosses her full weight against my ribcage. "I don't want to disappoint her even more." My vision blurs.

"Oh, Nordun." Father's voice sounds certain. "You'll never disappoint Dechen for she doesn't judge." He shakes his head. "She's an accomplished practitioner, she sees right through." He halts his horse, his eyes unwavering on me. "Besides, you saw the suffering of another being and you didn't turn away." He shifts his weight to the front of his horse and straightens his back. "You acted from compassion and the wisdom of your heart. Tell me, how can that disappoint your grandmother?" Father speaks with confidence, and my mind's rallying against everything he says.

"But what if I decide to stay at the stables for a while?" I say, almost afraid to speak the words that have been on my mind for these last few days.

"You're more than welcome to." He prods his horse in a slow trot. The other horses follow. "You've never experienced life outside the monastery for I abandoned you, and I'm sorry about that. Maybe take some time to find out for yourself." He turns to me, a reassuring nod. "Your choice, and whatever you decide I will respect."

And with those words he spurs on his horse, setting the pace for the rest of the way.

With my stallion battling to gain lead position again, I need all my attention to keep course and to stay on the road. I know the drill by now, reining in and letting go with ease and joy, that's how we stay on track. Still, my mind's getting away from me, again and again. *Take time to find out for yourself... your choice...*

If only everything was as easy as taming a wild horse.

Forty-Six

Traveling the main road to Rongdrak instead of the winding trails through the mountains is an ease on the body. With plenty of stops on the way and Father's company, the ride today turns out to be a total pleasure. His knowledge of the people and the places and all the stories going around amazes me, but then again, I don't really know him—yet. Our stop for the night is a small family guesthouse, just off the beaten track. We're greeted with a warm welcome, no questions asked.

The next day is equally enjoyable. We leave the inn early in the morning, rested well, our bags packed with fresh supplies. With the stallion still showing his true colors, I ride ahead, making short stops to let Father and my mare catch up. Amazed by the strength and stamina, I pat the horse's neck.

"You just won't back down, will you?" The stallion brays with vigor, as though to agree with me. He's been a hand full ever since we hit the road, and that's good, for I have no time to think of Karma. Not that he's not in my thoughts. He is, for sure, but I pay no heed to it. His affairs are up to him and himself alone. As the shadows lengthen over the fields, we reach the foot of the higher grasslands. I recognize the markers in the landscape.

"Up here." Father points up to the mountain range on our right. "We should reach it before dark." He steers his horse on the slope. My stallion makes a leap to follow and pass, eager as ever.

"Whoa!" My hands tremble with tiredness, but no way I'm letting myself be thrown off now. I straighten myself on the stallion's back, my eyes on the slopes ahead of me. Just a little and we're at Zinzin's. It will be good to see them all again.

The dris grunt from afar; it's milking time. The gray mass is huddled together, and little Lhadun hauls a bucket, her tiny frame struggling under the load. A gigantic wave as soon as she sees us, her bucket's tipping close to spilling.

"You're back!" Sangmo's head pops behind a broad gray's back. "And look at that." Her eyes behold the stallion. "You're doing us proud." A warm glow fills me as she strokes the horse's flanks. Dear Sangmo, always so honest, so generous with her words and her actions.

"He's a beauty." Yeshe has joined us. I slide from the horse, so much easier than before.

"Yeshe." I hug her tight. Her eyes bright and brown, a rosy blush on her cheeks, she looks her wonderful self again.

She squeezes my hands. "Jinpa's been home." Her husband, that explains it all.

"Karma's not with you?" Sangmo takes the reins from Father and me. She scouts the plane.

"Eh, no." A flush creeps across my cheeks. "We parted ways at the Four Sisters." My pulse quickens. My hands straighten my skirt as my mind circles around. What do I say?

"Well, you all go in. You must be exhausted." Yeshe takes Father's bags. "We'll finish up here." With the brisk dusk sweeping over the grasslands, we head to the main tent, where fresh tea and good company's waiting.

"Palden-la, it's been too long." Zinzin's arms welcome us in her usual heartfelt way. One look at her face, though, and I know. *Something's up.* It's her eyes—dark and broody—that betray her. She's trying to hide it, fussing around the stove, pouring us tea and feeding us thenthuk, but she's not fooling me.

I glance around. Father's there, Rinchen, the younger children, they're all looking fine. *Norbu.* My gaze flits around the tent again. No Norbu, he's probably taking care of cattle out on the mountains. Still, something's up.

"Zinzin." I bend over, my hand on her forearm as she pours me tea. I raise my chin. A flicker of worry meets my eyes.

"It's Sonam." Her voice breaks. "He's gone." *Gone?*

"What do you mean?" Father leans in. Sure, Sonam's gone often. What's different?

"They got him this time." Tears blink in her eyes. "The officials." I frown and turn to Father. The officials? What does she mean?

"That's not good." Father's eyebrows draw together. "Are you sure?" He takes a sip of his tea.

"No." Zinzin shakes her head. "But he's gone for too long without a word." She puts the kettle back on the stove. Deep lines around her mouth reveal her concern.

"Norbu and Jinpa have gone looking for him." She sinks beside the stove, gesturing little Lhadun to take the other children to their blankets as Sangmo and Yeshe join us.

"She told you?" Sangmo pours us another cup of tea paired with the fragrance of fresh green and cut grass.

I nod, but my mind's trying to piece things together. The officials. Why would they take Sonam? My heart sinks as my suspicion rises. It might have to do with the inn that night. The smuggling. My hands wring around my cup. I glance at Zinzin. No need to upset her more. I'll ask Sangmo later.

Father's good in situations like this, as it turns out. Whenever things get uneasy, he steers the conversation away from the touchy subject like he does now. He's got them all engaged, telling about meeting our nasty cousin at Four Sisters Mountain. Sure, the atmosphere is heavy all evening, for Sonam's on everybody's mind. Yet, with Jinpa and Norbu out looking for him, there's nothing we can do right now. The conversation keeps on flowing, and so does the tea.

Saying goodbye to Zinzin the next morning saddens me. It should be a happy parting, not like this. Not a parting under bothersome circumstances. Father spoke to her until late at night, settling her sorrows. Still... "Please, tell me what I can do for you." I take her hands in mine. "Anything, really." *Om Tare.* How can I take her troubles away?

"There's only one thing you can do for me." Zinzin's gentle voice is rimmed with sorrow. "I know you're think you have a choice to make. I can see it, troubling you." She puts her forehead to mine. Her skin feels like a fever.

"But you don't have to choose Nordun, believe me, you don't have to choose." She puts her hand under my chin. "You can accomplish so much more if you find your own unique way." Her jaw sets, her eyes spark a fire now. "You don't have to choose a path based on what's been done before." Zinzin's voice lowers. "We women, we create life and so we can also create our own way of living. Deep down we know what is best for us." She takes a breather. "And what's best for us, is best for all." Her shoulders drop and I throw my arms around them.

"It won't be easy, but promise me you don't choose. You'll forge your own way." Her voice in my ear, soft yet determined. Tears well up behind my eyelids as I let her words sink in. Here she is, with her husband missing, only thinking of what's best for me.

"I promise." I swallow hard at the lump in my throat. How fortunate I am to know this woman. *Om Tara.* How I wish I could take her troubles away.

"Nordun." Father's voice urges me on. Sangmo's got the horses ready with her stallion eyeing up mine. Ribbons of white and green take flight from their manes and tails, courtesy of little Lhadun.

We're ready to ride our way home.

Forty-Seven

G hostly silhouettes pass us in the pearly blue dawn, the towers of Rongdrak valley watch over us as we ride along. Sangmo and I ride in front, our stallions in constant battle for the lead. Father's horse sets his own steady pace, a reassuring rhythm as he follows us.

"This is going to be a riveting ride." Sangmo reigns in her stallion with a decisive grin. She steadies him with ease. Me? I'm barely holding on. I shift my weight to the front, securing my hands in the horse's manes. Well, at least I haven't fallen off.

"This is the life." Sangmo's face turns to the welcoming morning sun. "I can't imagine anything better." A content smile graces her face. Yes, she's in her element.

"I get you," I say. "No wild dris for the next few days." We both laugh, reminiscing about my first attempt to milk a dri. What a spectacle I made of myself.

"You picked it up fast though," she says. "Look at you now." She points at my stallion, trotting along at an easy pace. "I told you, it's in your blood. You're going to be a grand master of the stables." Yep, she's sure.

"I don't know about that." My gaze ahead, I fumble with the reins of the horse. And so much I don't know about the decision I have to make. If only I can make sure my uncle and cousins stay away.

"Your father knows." Sangmo waves her hand. "And if you want to." Her voice lowers. "I would love to stay at the stables with you for a while." She glances at me. Her eyes are quick to shoot away. "I mean, if you need help and so." My heart takes a leap.

"It would be good to have you there." I can't contain my biggest smile. "You think the family would be fine with it?" I tilt my head at her. After all, Sangmo does a fair share of work at home. I wonder if she can be missed for longer.

"Sure." Her shoulders drop. "I think it would be very convenient for them right now." She stares in the distance; her voice trails off.

Convenient? I search for her, but she keeps a stern look ahead.

"I'm with child, Nordun." Her expression is a solemn one. "It's very early, but I'm sure."

My jaw drops. *What?* I look at her again, but she pretends to be occupied with her unruly horse. *Oops.* Sangmo with child. How to react to that? She must be upset, for sure.

Her stallion canters ahead of me. I spur on my horse to catch up.

"Well, let's hope it's a girl." I steer my horse beside her. "We can use more strong women at the stables." I throw her a wink and try to be the optimist she always is for me. She wipes away a sneaky tear. *Sangmo and tears?!*

"Thanks, sis." Her voice is filled with relief. "I knew you would be great about it." She sighs and wrinkles her nose. "Karma's going to be livid."

Yeah, right, Karma? My mouth goes dry as my thoughts speed back that night at the inn. Karma's arm around these women, drinking, gambling.

"Karma's not here, is he?" My voice sounds sharper than I had intended. My chest tightens. He promised but didn't show. Some fine man he is.

"Yes, but he will come for me." She pats her stallion on his neck. "He always does."

I nod, for I understand. He's her brother, even if it's not by blood, and she has firm faith in him. Seems like everybody has, everybody but me.

"We'll deal with that when he comes." I shrug. "For now, we're fine." I spur on my horse and we ride on in an easy silence.

"Don't you want to know who the father is?" She turns to me out of the blue.

Does it matter?

"You'll tell me when you're ready—or not at all," I say. No need to pry and upset her more.

"It's Sonam," she says, under her breath. *Sonam!* My father's best friend, Zinzin's husband, Norbu's father. And he's gone missing.

Things just got more complicated. I reign in my horse with one hand and I extend my arm to Sangmo. A warm, grateful smile mirrors mine.

"I'm here." I say. "No matter what." She clasps my hand. Sharing an understanding as only sisters do, we ride on.

Our horses keep bumping heads in their play to outdo each other. Their energy never ceases, but with the prospect of three days in the saddle, we take plenty of rest during the day. Father, being well-travelled, knows all the good places to refresh. Turns out he's still well known and respected. Many a household is more than happy to receive us. Spending the nights at quiet family inns along the way, I happily slip into the routine of morning and evening prayer again, a delight to my mind.

And so we travel, the three of us, until we come to the slopes leading up to the stables, the late afternoon of the third day.

I see them from afar, the rolling hills that hide my childhood home in their greening vault.

"We're here." I halt. A sudden shiver stirs in my stomach. I turn to Father for approval, and he just smiles. "Let's go." My toes tap and we soar onto the slope.

Sangmo's stallion boots in our trail, racing us to reach the top of the hill. Sangmo wins of course, she'll always be the better rider.

I catch my breath as our horses halt, the stables within view. Thin white strands of smoke circle from the courtyard into the sky. *Weisang.* Somebody's expecting us.

The reins slip in my palms, it takes all my strength to restrain my stallion from booting down the hill. He must sense my excitement, my heart pounding in my chest. A small turn to the left at the end of the slope, and there it is. The swaying pines lacing the entrance to the gate wave their welcome to us.

A silken scarf flows in the breeze. The posture of a proud man stands behind it. *Ghedun-la is here.* With a quick slide I dismount my stallion and bow my head to greet him, but Father's ahead of me.

"Welcome home." Father's voice betrays his emotion. His trembling hands slip the silk scarf around my neck. "Welcome home, my child." My hands clutch the ends of the khata.

Welcome home. My heart quivers at Father's words. Our eyes meet in a deep understanding—we've both come home.

"Good to see things worked out." Ghedun nods at Father, an approval. "She did well, didn't she?" Ghedun strokes my stallion's flanks, checking out the horse's frame with his experienced gaze.

"She sure did." Father rests his hand on my shoulder. "You all go it, we'll be in right after you." He takes my stallion's reins. "First, give this stallion a home." And together we walk cross the courtyard, the horse trailing behind us to the pen.

"We've had quite a journey together." Father opens the pen and lets the stallion off the lead. The horse kicks up his hind leg and disappears in a cloud of dry grass and dust.

"I sure hope we'll have more time to catch up." Father leans over the beam, his eyes on the horse. I glance at him from the corners of my eyes. Did Father just ask me to stay?

"I should have been there for you like a father's supposed to, but I send you away." He turns to me, and his hands fold around the beam as if he's going to splinter the timber right now.

"You were tiny, with a sadness as vast as the ocean." He shakes his head. "I thought I couldn't handle the two of us here." He flips his hat back, leaving it to dangle on the thin leather strap in his neck. The evening breeze tangles the silver streaked strands of his thick, wayward hair.

"You see, sometimes we hold on to the very thing that's holding us back." His fists clench. "We let our fears become stronger than our trust, we underestimate ourselves." His eyes meet mine and I blink as the sun throws her last rays of fragile orange upon us.

"You're more educated than I'll ever be," Father says, a firm voice as he straightens himself. "You've always been ready for whatever is calling you, my child." He pauses, a slight hesitation. His hands envelop mine and the instant recognition surges like a warm tidal wave through my body. This is Father, the father he used to be, the father before Mother left us.

"You're more than ready for whatever you decide." He opens his arms and draws me in. My heated face buries in the chunky folds of his chuba. Whatever hesitation I held, none of it is left as Father's arms hold me within, solid and safe. My being takes a deep breath of relief, my eyes close.

For a moment, everything halts and all is calm and clear in inner space. This is what I've been longing for. This is the feeling, exactly this. And what it is, I don't know. It's something only the heart comprehends. All I know is I want to relish this very moment with Father's arms around me, keeping me close.

A bold bray, another shuffle of sand sounds from the distance. The evening chill tugs at my skirt.

"We better go in." His arms draw down, but his hand's still on my shoulder. "She's waiting for you in the prayer room."

Forty-Eight

A quick wipe across my skirt has to do; I smoothen my unruly bun. My heart hides deep in my chest as I tiptoe in. Dechen's seated in the radiant afterglow of the eventide. I prostrate three times and sit myself at her feet.

A serene smile meets me. "Nordun, my child."

"Ani-la." I bow my head to receive her blessing, but she takes my face between her hands and looks me straight in the eyes. An infinite compassion washes over me. I can't hide anymore, and remorse rims my eyes.

"I've disappointed you." I wrestle my chin to my chest. The regrets cascade from my mouth, like a waterfall after the first rain of summer. "I didn't return when I said I would. I'm wearing lay clothes, and I've neglected my prayers." My heart cries out as a sob vibrates from her hollows.

"And you served the Dharma in your own way." Dechen sounds adamant as ever. "Now I'm the first to admit, it's not the way I envisioned you to serve, but then again, who am I to do so?" She tilts my chin and I can't avert it. The tears streak my cheeks.

"But when the karmic wind blows, we will be moved, no matter how strong we stand." Her voice reaches out to me in an understanding. "And sometimes we're moved towards what we least expect." She tilts her head to the side, her eyes still on me. "It happens to us all, same with me." I wipe my face, my hands tremble. My shame is too big to find comfort in her words.

"There are many ways to serve all sentient beings." She folds her hands in her lap. "The teachings even encourage us to question, to go from our familiar places, to find out for ourselves." The beads on her wrist rattle, the wood shines in the flicker of the butter lamps.

"No Nordun, you didn't disappoint me," she says. "You never do." My face burns. How I want to believe her.

"However, life as a lay woman is so much harder." She sighs as the beads slide through her fingers. "You've seen the burden yourself."

My eyes lower, and my thoughts go to Zinzin, trying to keep herself and her family together, to Yeshe and her stillborn son, and to Sangmo, my dear Sangmo, pregnant and waiting for the family to decide her fate.

"I wanted to spare you from that life, that suffering." Her eyes close. "But so it is, so it is." When she opens them again, they exude the calm yet determined essence of her—an advanced practitioner, centered in loving kindness.

I bow my head. How I wish I could be like her.

"Serving the Dharma is not a single idea." Her beads silent, she leans into me. "It is being with wisdom and compassion, but most of all, it is a living, breathing practice. You've experienced that yourself."

Yes. My mind goes back to that frightful night at the mountain where wisdom showed me it was me who caused my own fear by clinging to my life, to my human body too much. I feared the snake, feared for this life of mine, but this was no mere than an obscuration of my mind. By doing the very thing I feared—offering my body in chöd to all to feed on—I cut through my obscuration, using the fierce sword of compassion, the sharpest weapon of all. Yes, I have experienced the living, breathing part of the practice. I nod as a hint of sorrow falls over my grandmother's face.

"Use this for the benefit of all sentient beings, for all this is not over yet." A tremble moves her voice. "I'm afraid the family won't let this go—not this time." Her eyes close again, and my heart is with hers. Her beloved, slain by her own brothers, and now her daughter, my mother, killed by my father's brother.

Revenge. I flinch as my thoughts jump ahead. Two lives taken away—for sure the family won't let this go, and there won't be anything Dechen or I can do about it. We're women; it's out of our hands.

"Promise me, my child, whatever moves you, stay with wisdom and compassion." She opens her eyes, and her beads resume the prayer. "And all will be well." She bows her head and rests her hand on my head in a blessing, her demeanor as peaceful as ever.

All is well. I slide on the seat next to her and together we sit in evening prayer. *All is well.* Tara's loving gaze is upon us.

After sharing all that happened, the night is brief, and morning comes too soon. Bags are filled, horses saddled, blessings exchanged and weisang burns—it's time for Dechen and Ghedun to return home.

"Please give my regards to all the sisters." With a heavy heart, I tie a khata to Ghedun's horse. "Especially to Pema and Tsomo." My lucky sisters.

Dechen has finally granted them their wish to stay in retreat with Dolma. Now that their practice has excelled even the most senior practitioners at the monastery, Dechen decided it was time. I wonder if their advanced knowing has anything to do with it. I'm filled with happiness and gratitude for them, even though it means we won't be meeting again soon.

Dechen's hands touch my head, and we say our silent goodbyes. The prayer from my lips gets lost in the rustle of the pine trees, the wind blowing the warmest of summer winds already. I shiver as I watch their horses disappear in the pink veils of dawn.

"Come on." Sangmo's voice wakes me from my musings. "Even though there's no dris waiting, there's work to do." Her laughter whirls across the courtyard. She's already with Father, both instructing the servants to clear out Uncle's former quarters. The air buzzes with an invigorating sense of newness. It's promising to be a good day, despite the sad goodbyes.

The sun moves ahead, leaving no time to reminisce about the events of the past days. Still, it's on my mind, for I have a promise to fulfill. So after lunch, when all have settled for midday rest, I walk over to the pen. The stallion, strutting around with a few other mares, needs no incentive to come over. His eyes clear, he neighs and prods his nose in my side. Always up for play.

"Hi there." I slide the halter on. "Let's go for a ride." He shakes his head, he's up to it. "Easy now." Hooves swish with a frisk on the gravel path. It takes all my effort to reign the horse in until we're out of the gate. I let the reins go at the slope of the hill, where he bolts into a crazy gallop. Hooves float and manes fly along; effortless we soar.

"Whoa." I pant as we halt on the top. The stallion's standing proud as ever. With a smooth slide, I dismount and plant my feet in the long grass. Hooves trample in hunger for more.

"Here we are." I slip the halter from his head. My sweaty hands search through its coarse manes. One more pat on the neck, and I let the tension flow from my lips. A deep breath out. This is how it's supposed to be. A soft neigh, another playful prod in my side. It's time.

"You go now." My hand claps on his strong flank. "You're free as I promised. Go on." The stallion's ears twirl from side to side. His head turns with a jolt—a moment of clear understanding flashes between us—and then he's off, throwing all four legs in the air. A wild flight into freedom. It's a second goodbye today, and a grateful one as well. Only this time I'm not the one staying. I'm the one going home.

The tips of the waving grass tickle my fingers, I walk down the slopes, my eyes on the stables. Midday rest is over. Horses circle the pen, people move across the barns and the court yard. Another rider's arriving. There's a delightful busyness going around the stables again, I can feel it from afar.

My feet pick up the pace as I come up the path where the prickly bramble bushes once bloomed this time of year. An unsettling feeling has come over me—an urge to hurry. My breath quickens as I'm running now, only to halt when I see him. *He's here.* My heart skips a beat.

"Karma's here." Sangmo's elated voice greets me. "I told you he would come."

Sangmo beams a smile from ear to ear with her brother on her side, standing tall and tranquil as ever. *Karma.* Something deep inside me stirs. I don't dare to look in his eyes.

"I'll take care of the horse." Sangmo skips off, leaving me with Karma in the sun-drenched courtyard.

"I hear you did well." He takes a step closer, his demeanor so relaxed.

He's got some nerve. I open my mouth, but he talks on.

"I'm sorry I wasn't there, but it turns out your cousins are not so fond of women." He takes another step closer. "And as I had already paid them, I was stuck with them."

I look closer. *That smile.*

"And the third cousin, well, he needed a bit more convincing to stay put after you met him, so I was tied up for a while." He rubs the left side of his face where a vague shadow blooms in purple and blue.

A fight. He was in a fight. A raging shame rises in me. How swift I was to judge.

"A fight?" I gaze at his bruised cheekbone. The blush spreads down my neck and I cringe.

"Ah, it's nothing." He waves his hand. "You're here, and they're not." He looks around for a moment, but is fast to set his eyes on me again.

I bite my lip; my nails dig into the palm of my hands. The flutter in my stomach won't settle down.

"So you're staying?" He catches my gaze and I can't escape the curious twinkle in those gorgeous green eyes.

I shift my weight from my left to right. Why can't I act normal around him?

"I think so." My hands fumble with the red string on my wrist. What's normal anyway?

He raises his eyebrows in a tease. "You're sure?"

"Well, I can't be sure, can I?" I smooth down my crumpled skirt. "I've been thinking it over, but it's no use." I shake my head. "Like you pointed out to me on that narrow mountain trail; nothing's sure, and nothing ever will be."

Facing Karma head on now, I straighten my shoulders.

"True." He nods, a confident yet inviting gaze. A moment of pure silence passes between us. The sun weaves a golden web all around. I slow my breath; my mind settles. *There it is.*

"I want to believe in what is calling me." My hand raises to the flat bone of my chest. "I'm listening to what's within me, so yes, I'm taking the leap. I'm staying, for now." *There, I said it.*

My body sags as relief surges through my being. My vision floods with golden and green. *I'm staying.* My words echo in my mind. I'm staying, I'm taking the leap.

"I'm glad to hear that." His voice is soft, and his eyes flare with a brilliant green. He leans in a bit more. Sweat pricks my neck.

"Where is he, your prized stallion?" Instead of looking around, he keeps his eyes on me.

"I set it free." My chin points at the hill aside. *Just as I promised*, I want to add, but I don't because that even sounds silly to me.

The moment I speak, there's a familiar clap of hooves, a rhythm I know so well. It approaches on the gravel right behind me. My heels dig in and I turn in a slow motion. *This can't be.*

There it is, the stallion, strutting right into the late afternoon glare. Holding his tail high with a perky step in his hooves, showing himself off to an appreciative audience as if to say, "I'm back!"

"That's one fine horse." Karma strokes the stallion's flanks, appreciating the beauty before him. Still stunned, I rest my hands on the stallion's neck and let my fingers tangle in his manes.

"But I let you go." I scratch between his twirling ears. "No need for you to come back."

Karma walks around and inspects the horse's frame, an approving grin on his face.

"Nature doesn't need permission, Nordun." He leans over the stallion standing between us. "You should know this by now." He catches my eye and the vibrant emerald fades into the gentlest of green, like young moss growing in the shade of a pine at the onset of spring. *How beautiful.*

"Deep inside the heart of all things, there's a spirit so wild, it can never be tamed." His hands dig into the manes of my stallion. They're searching for mine.

"The heart of a being is always free, and it knows it." The tops of our fingers touch, a smooth tingle between the coarse tresses.

I should pull back, but my hands are frozen, and my legs have gone weak. My heart's beating so loud in my chest right now, I hold my breath, afraid it might rip right through my ribs.

"If a horse stays, it's because it wants to, for it decides in the moment—every single moment—to stay or go." His fingers slide between mine and lock the manes of the stallion between. "Looks like this one is staying—for now."

I gasp as my heart surges wide open, like a bird on its first flight into the sky. A bright golden sun bursts into the infinite blue yonder, sweeping right through me, warming and gentle, yet crystal-clear with an edge as sharp as a blade. *What is this?*

My thoughts pick up speed, trying to make sense of it all. I blink, but it's no use—for the wisdom within is not to be understood by the mind, but only to be trusted by the heart.

"How about giving this horse a home?" His fingers gently caress mine, and I have no desire to let go. That's for sure.

The dusk sprinkles her orange and red around the stables, and we walk over with the stallion prancing beside the two of us.

All is not over, as my grandmother told me, but for now all is quiet, and all is well.

My heart is calling and I've taken up the courage to answer her with a huge *yes*. I believe she will guide to where I truly belong—for no matter how strong the karmic winds blow or wherever they take me, my heart will always lead me back home.

A Pilgrim's Heart

Nordun's Way Book 2

R ead on & ride with Nordun on her crusade across the rooftop of the world, to the land of Gods, where the fickle fate of men is in the hands of the ones who reign through force and fear, and the unshakable faith of a woman in the innate goodness of humankind proves to be the very thing that can set a man free.

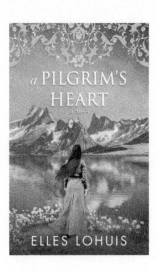

PROLOGUE

Tibet, Eastern Kham
The Year of The Wood Rooster

1412 (1285 AD)

There comes a time in your life when you'll face a real danger, a blatant violation of everything your heart knows to be true. And in that moment, you'll have a decision to make—either you stand in your truth and brave the consequences, no matter what, or you'll turn away and spend the rest of your life living between bitter blame and lame absolution.

This time has come for me.

CHAPTER ONE

The sun throws her last beams of burnished orange through the kitchen window, elongating Father's shadow—he appears taller.

I look up, my feet pointed at the stove.

It's only the first day of my new life and I'm already exhausted. For sure, I never knew sorrow and joy could coexist so close to each other, occupying the same space, living in one tender heart.

This morning my grandmother went back to her monastery, my home for so many years as a novice nun. I decided not to join her again, but to return to lay life instead—the life I was

ripped away from many years ago. A gnawing ache has nestled
itself deeply into the hollows of my heart ever since. How I'll
miss them, my dearest sisters in solitude. Will I ever see them
again?

I don't want to think about it. I've made my choice.

I've decided to stay with Father at the stables, my childhood
home, and with my dear Karma, who came for me this
afternoon. We met only a few moons ago and our love is still
budding—we have a lot to discover and explore, the two of us.

Excitement and fear collide in my chest as I think about it,
living in this mundane world. I have no idea how to, not yet,
but my heart has called and I'm taking the leap.

"The ngakpa has requested us," Father says.

The early night I was looking forward to is slipping away. I
raise my weary body; it's been a long day. Dusk's already setting
in a purple haze, heralding the night. What's so urgent that it
can't wait for the morning? Father's expression doesn't give it
away.

"I'll have to clean myself up." Dust flies around as I brush
my skirt. Sangmo and I have just finished clearing my uncle's
quarters for us to move in. I tie my unruly hair and rush off
for a quick wash—can't show up like this at the ngakpa's—it's
disrespectful. "Be right back."

It's a short enough walk to the village. Father's pace is swift
and silent. My mind drifts to our last meeting with the ngakpa.
It seems so long ago, but it was only a few turns of the moon.
How things have changed. How *I* have changed.

No more an aspiring nun in my grandmother's monastery,
but the heir to my father's stables. A female horse master. Who
would have thought? Not me, that's for sure. The ngakpa's
divination did, though. Maybe that's why he wants us to come.
I shiver, my legs stubbornly stiff as I try to keep up with
Father's solid pace.

The bitter breeze lashes unforgivingly into the fluttering prayer flags. A high-pitched whistle resonates in the billowing sky. Looks like a storm is approaching.

Darkness shrouds the ngakpa's house, the first on the left. Nobody welcomes us at the gate, unlike the last time I was here.

"Are you sure he's home?" I halt, but Father's already put his shoulder against the heavy door. A loud creak is followed by the stench of stale soot, hitting our nostrils as we enter the dim hallway. My stomach tightens. Something's off. It's too quiet in here.

Father strides ahead, not bothered a bit by the suffocating atmosphere. Sheltered by his broad back, I follow.

A sudden ring drowns our hollow footsteps and I almost jump—the ngakpa's prayer bell. He's home. *Good.* I take a deep breath, and my speedy pulse steadies. No need to be so nervous. All went well.

Father pauses for a moment and turns, a reassuring nod. Yes, we'll be fine.

The scent of heavy incense oozes behind maroon drapes. Spicy white whirls sneak their way out on our entrance. A sole butter lamp—a big one—casts its flicker on the small shrine in the middle. I blink as my eyes adjust to the gloomy surroundings and the tangy fume of smoldering spices and herbs.

"Please, come." A thin voice resounds from the far corner of the room—the ngakpa's in his seat. I step forwards and lower my body three times to the shrine. Father follows.

"Sit, sit," the ngakpa's raspy voice urges. "So sorry to have you come this late."

He shifts in his cushioned seat. His fingertips spread lightly on the tops of our lowered heads as we take our place opposite him. A murmured blessing and a prayer, the rhythm not known to me but nevertheless comforting, smoothens the jagged edge of my nerves.

"I hear you had a fruitful journey." A string of bone prayer beads rattles around his narrow wrist. He adjusts the white scarf wrapped around him.

"Yes, gen-la." I look up. "Thanks to your excellent guidance."

He folds his hands in his lap and rests his gaze on me. His eyes close and he gently rocks from left to right, to left, to right. The pile of twisted locks on the top of his head sways in sync with his body.

A strained silence fills the space between us. A slight exhale breathes from his lips. He seems to sink further in his seat. Is he in meditation?

My fingers fumble with the red string around my wrist, the blessing cord that my sisters tied to remind me of the Buddhist path.

"I have a request of you both." The ngakpa's voice is hardly audible. His eyes are still closed, the shallow creases around them deepen.

A request? I glance at Father. What could that be?

"Where to begin?" Sorrow throws a shadow over the ngakpa's face. "Khandro-la has left this morning." The words weigh down his shoulders.

Khando, his wife, left? Yes, my intuition served me right—something *is* off.

"She's not coming back." His distant stare meets mine. "She's taken something with her." He rests his long, tawny fingers on the side of the small table between us and leans across. "I request your help to retrieve it back." His eyes plead and glide from me to Father and back.

"Of course, gen-la." Father shows no hesitation. "Anything we can do." He clears his throat. The incense must bother him too.

"It's a matter of utmost discretion. You are the only ones I can ask." Tiny and black like the beady ones of a curious raven, the ngakpa's eyes pierce right through me. Then he turns to

Father. "Even though I'm already in your debt, Palden-la." His voice muffles in the pearly opaque surrounding us.

"Oh no, gen-la." Father straightens his back. "There's no debt between us, and if there is, it is us who owe you."

I raise my chin. Father's right, the ngakpa has always served us and our village with his prayers and rituals.

"Yet I am, Palden." The ngakpa's face folds into a quiet, solemn look. "For it has come to me that my wife aided your brother Tennah so many years ago, causing grave misfortune to your family."

A sudden rush of blood swishes in my ears. Did I just hear... Khandro and Uncle—together?

"Khandro." He hesitates. His fingers spread on the table. "She aided Tennah with a spell that caused Lhamo's untimely passing." He whispers her name ever so softly. *Lhamo.* My mother.

"And now she has left and taken the spell." His fingers search for the book in front of him, a thin pile of long pothi pages. "It's my family's, written with the blood of my ancestors." He longingly strokes the tainted edges of the brownish paper. "So powerful."

A spell. I lean in. So this is the ngakpa's ritual book then? And Khandro took a spell out of it to cause my mother's death. Together with my uncle. I swallow hard, the heavy incense a sticky layer in the back of my throat.

"The spell does harm in their hands." He shakes his head, and the grayish coils wave in a slow motion on the top of his head. "I... wè... need the page back." His fingers clamp again around the edges of the small table between us, a pale blue shines translucent on his knuckles. The significance of his words slowly penetrates my mind. *Khandro and Uncle, together, gone with the spell that killed my mother.*

My sisters were right all along—and now it's confirmed. Uncle had a hand in Mother's death with a snake spell. No wonder he left in such a hurry before I returned with a wild horse to stake my claim at the stables.

My temples throb. The spell book blurs in beige and darkened brown before me. *Focus.* My thoughts swirl to clear the mist in my mind. What now?

"Yes, this requires our utmost discretion." From the corners of my eyes, Father's robust frame is a still composition. "Any idea where they might have gone to?" His gentle manner, his steady voice, it eases my panic—not all, but it certainly helps.

"Lhasa," the ngakpa says. "West, to Lhasa." He plucks at the bone beads around his wrist.

Lhasa. My heart leaps. Lhasa, Land of The Gods, home of the Jowo Sakyamuni Buddha statue, the most revered statue of our Great Teacher. Yes, Lhasa would be the perfect place to hide. Nobody would notice two strangers from the East between the many visitors and pilgrims. *Lhasa.* Often my grandmother told me about her pilgrimage to this magical place. Oh, how I long to visit Lhasa myself in this lifetime. If only I get the chance—the merit this pilgrimage would bring.

"Give us some time, gen-la." Father's steadfast voice interrupts my wandering mind. "I promise we'll find a solution."

With a shrill sigh, the ngakpa sits back in his seat; the bone beads an ominous rattle in his hands.

"I know you will, Palden-la." He closes his eyes. "You've never let me down."

His whole body sags. The leathery lines on his face relax and the beads in his hands lay silent now. A soft murmur from his lips beckons us—time to go. Quietly, Father and I make our way to the door.

"I'll see you soon, Nordun." The ngakpa's croaky voice stops me in my tracks. I turn around, only to see I must have misheard. Still seated with his eyes closed, it's the serenity of his posture and the soft glow on his face that gives it away—the ngakpa's in deep meditation. Yet again, my mind's playing tricks on me. Or maybe it's the tiredness of the long day taking over.

A sharp draft from the doorway dissolves the fleeting incense. The gleam of the butter lamp reveals the bloodshed images on the thangkas around me. I've seen them before, even so, my feet fleet into the hallway. Father's way ahead of me by now.

We walk home together under an indigo sky with a lone star shining proudly. The pale light from the waning moon is just enough to guide our way. The wind has died down—it's turned into a crisp and pleasant evening. The only sound is the crunch of our footsteps on the gritty path.

How I wish my mind was as calm and as vast as this midnight sky—so many questions spinning around, seemingly without end.

I glance at Father, walking beside me. "Did you not know about Uncle?"

My heart's pounding. I shouldn't ask, but my curiosity's getting the better of me—as usual.

Father shakes his head. "There were rumors, nasty ones." Melancholy rims his voice. "I was devastated, Nordun. I missed your mother so much. I was only too relieved when my only brother showed up in that time of need, so I ignored that vicious talk."

I nod. Yes, I remember Father from that time, the immense change he went through. Grief brings even the strongest of men to their knees.

"I was happy to see my brother, despite everything that had passed between us." The moonlight casts a sober shade on Father's face. I don't dare to ask, but I've never known what happened between Father and his brother. I heard about a bad fallout, long before I was born. They made up when mother died. That's the only thing I know. And now betrayed by his only brother? My heart sinks as I think of Father's fate.

"I'm sorry," I say. "About all this." Words, how useless they are. Even so, I must voice them. It's the only way I can express myself right now.

"Me too, my child," Father says. "But I'm more sorry for all the time lost between us." His voice grows thick. "For letting myself be blinded by grief, and for being so selfish that I abandoned my own blood."

The rawness of his revelation rips right through me. All these years, I thought he didn't care. A sharp breath spikes my lungs. No use going there again. The two of us, we've moved on.

"What now?" I hesitate as we enter the gate to the stables.

"We can't let this go," Father says. "We have to retrieve that page before it does more damage." His boot kicks up a loose pebble.

"And Uncle?" I cringe the moment I say it. *Uncle.* His evil deeds weight heavy on both our minds. An iron fist clamps around my heart. My ribs tighten. We both know what will be done with Uncle. I shouldn't have brought it up.

To my relief, Father ignores my useless remark. "I see word has gone around." His chin points towards the house. "So soon."

The stark silhouettes of two horses shift in the far corner of the courtyard. They're not ours. *Visitors.* And voices that I recognize without a doubt.

They're here.

Grandfather's family has arrived.

***

Ready for more?

Get your copy of *A PILGRIM'S HEART* now & read on!

"Only the strength of the heart can govern one's fate."

After a reluctant quest to save her childhood home from her cruel uncle, Nordun is ready to forgive him for his sins, despite knowing he murdered her mother long ago. But her family is set on revenge—they've ordered Karma, the man Nordun is falling for, to hunt her uncle down.

Desperate to avoid more bloodshed, and determined to stand by her Buddhist beliefs, Nordun joins Karma on his journey under the false pretense of going on a pilgrimage to Lhasa, the place her uncle is hiding.

As they cross raging rivers, traverse vast grasslands, and conquer the mighty mountain ranges of the Cho-La, Nordun realizes the man she loves is indeed a kindred spirit—but he is also a merciless warrior, who believes compassion has no place in a family blood feud.

When faced with the inevitable, will Nordun risk losing her love, and her life, to save the man who killed her mother?

Author's Note

Some days, I have to remind myself where it all began. It was in 2018, with Nordun, my gorgeous niece from Tibet. She is the one that inspired me to write this first book in the Nordun's Way series, *The Horse Master's Daughter*, set in 13th C Tibet.

In 2018, my husband and I were fortunate to obtain a Visa to visit his family in Tibet. My husband had left his home in 2004 to study in India and hadn't seen his family for all those years. We spent three months with the family in Kham, visiting all the relatives (and there are many!) and also some of the beautiful places around.

One day we were at the horse races, and I realized there were no women riding. My niece Nordun had told me before she'd wanted a horse, but her father wouldn't let her have one. I told my brother-in-law I was surprised to hear that no women took part in the races. "Of course not," he replied. "Horses and girls don't go together, never have, never will." Yes, that's what he said. Right there and then, the character of Nordun formed in my mind.

Coming home after three magical months, I put pen to paper, wanting to write a little story about a girl riding a horse, just for Nordun. But somehow the little tale turned into a full-fledged series about a young woman blazing her own trail through the turbulent times of thirteenth century Tibet.

I've always had this thing for high mountains and remote places. And a passion for education—which I believe is the key to empowerment for both women and men.

I've considered myself very lucky—being the first generation in my family to go to college – and in 2006 I decided to pass on my good fortune. I went to volunteer as a teacher at Jampa Choling, a tiny Tibetan Buddhist monastery for nuns in Himachal Pradesh, the Indian Himalayas.

I fell in love with the place and the people, and came back many times—as a teacher and a student—and spent long periods with these high-spirited women on their remote mountaintop, relishing the solitude and contemplative life. I even did a PhD on the daily lives of these nuns and their sisters in the Himalayas, just to spend as much time with them as possible. To this day their dedication to the Dharma, to live their life in service of all sentient beings, often against all odds, is an enormous inspiration for me, and many of the lessons Nordun learns on her way are those I've been taught by the nuns on their mountain.

Facts and Fiction in the Nordun's Way Series

When I visited my Tibetan in-laws, my (now late) father-in-law told me many stories about the family history, but also about the history of their village and Kham. One evening, he told me their village name derived from the Mongolian fort that once stood there in medieval times, my mind jumped. *Mongols. Middle Ages.* I had always had a fascination for the Mongol Empire and its Qa'ans. Although the power-thirsty Mongol Qa'ans spread death and destruction in their tracks across Eurasia, they also facilitated an incredible exchange of people, goods and ideas, considerably expanding Old World horizons. So when it came to pick a time period for Nordun's Way, I decided on the period when Tibet was part of the Mongolian empire under Qubilai Qa'an, but was safe enough to travel the routes I had in mind for Nordun and her companions.

Since 1244, the Tibetan region was structurally, militarily and administratively under control of the Mongol Yuan dynasty, but kept a degree of religious political autonomy under a lama from the Sakya school of Tibetan Buddhism. Although there were always wars and uprisings in the Mongolian empire, 1285-1290 was a time when the situation in Tibet and surroundings was settled enough to travel, so I decided on that period.

Moreover, during this period, travel and trade was very much encouraged and facilitated by the Mongol Qa'ans. The Mongolians valued luxury items so much, Mongolian laws prohibited under penalty of death for travelers being harmed during their journeys to trading posts in Mongol-ruled territories. In order to allow outside traders access to goods, one of the world's first passports called the *peisa* (i.e., sign or card in Chinese) was developed and postal relay stations were extended in order to expedite the transmission of mail, officials, military, traders and foreign guests.

To stimulate trade even more, the Mongols elevated the class of a trader to that of an *ortagh* who acted as a business man or merchant to allied nations and represented a wealthy Mongol. They typically enjoyed greatly reduced tax rates and respect, which resulted in increased trade and collaboration between merchants. In Book Three, you'll come across Xia and her Mongolian husband being a member of this class of traders.

The Mongolians highly valued silk for their clothing, wall hangings, and furnishings, and coveted artistic motifs from Japan and Tibet, and tea nearly outstripped the silk trade. Next to luxury items, the Mongols desired to advance their knowledge in the areas of medicine, agriculture, religion, astronomy, craftsmanship, and technology. As such, scrolls and books on these subjects were transported to and from the Middle East and China—scrolls like the spell book the ngakpa holds in Book One, and the phrase book and the Book of Buddha's Names are Karma gifts to Nordun in Book Two and Book Three.

The Mongol Qa'ans favored Buddhism, but were also very tolerant towards other religions. Curiosities involving different religions allowed the transposition of Buddhism, Islam and even Christianity in the Middle East and China. You'll read about this diversity of religions from book Three onwards where Nordun first encounters with Islam, visiting a Muslim temple in Chang'an. Besides the freedom of religion, this was also a time where women from wealthy families were known to hold prominent positions in the family trade. You'll find some fine examples of this meeting Lanying in Book Two, and Xia in Book Three.

As a historian, I wanted to get the "historical background and details" right. I should have known better. I did extensive desk research and consulted experts in the field and was reminded—as my professors already did thirty years ago—that my noble pursuit of "historical accuracy" was nearly impossible. There's no consensus about the historical accuracy of this period in time, for history is obscured by the ones who wrote it down. At present, the *Secret History of the Mongols* (the only major narrative in Mongolian from the period of the Mongol Empire), is by many regarded essentially propaganda, not history, and there is a great deal of debate on the generally accepted account of the "history" of the Mongol Empire. It would take too much academic analysis to explain exactly why this is, but, briefly, the issue is that a lot of reliance has been placed on Persian accounts of Mongol history while there is a huge amount of source material in Chinese which has scarcely been touched. There's still so much to be discovered about this fascinating time in history, and I'm following the academic debate with great interest.

I always come across amazing artifacts, places and people doing desk- and field research. Visit my website www.elleslohuis.com, read how I've placed these facts in the *Nordun's Way* Series, and download a copy of the beautiful hand-drawn map of Nordun's travels that I've commissioned.

Not much is known about the exact villages/settlements and their names in Tibet at that time. Therefore, I have taken the liberty to incorporate some of the villages/cities that exist in Tibet at present time.

This brings me to a last note on facts and fiction—transliteration. For readability, I've used the (phonetic) Romanized transcription whenever Tibetan terms, personal names or place names are mentioned, and I've transcribed the Chinese terms, personal names and place names in pinyin.

Elles Lohuis
Almelo, 2022

Acknowledgments

Thank you to the nuns of Jamyang Foundation, and especially the nuns from Jampa Choling in Meeru (India), who opened their home and hearts to me. For showing me the incredible beauty of monastic life, and sharing their stories of courage and resilience.

Thank you to my dear family in Tibet. For welcoming me like a true daughter; I am beyond blessed with you all in this life.

Thank you to Dawn Ius, rock-star writing coach and editor extraordinaire. For believing in me writing Nordun's story before I did, and for giving me 'Dawn's rules' for my own good.

Thank you to Kirsten, my sister from another mister. For making the good times better, the hard times easier, and sharing our wicked sense of humor.

Thank you to Daleen, my accountability partner. For challenging me to reach higher and do better—all the time.

Thank you to Janneke, my fairy godmother. For reminding me it's only and ever a work of the heart.

And most of all, thank you to Tsewang, my husband. For your unwavering encouragement and unconditional love.

About Author

Elles Lohuis is a historical fiction author based in The Netherlands. A voracious reader and ever inquisitive explorer of far-away lands and foreign cultures, she holds an MA in History, an MA in Business, and a PhD in Social Sciences.

Elles writes books that enthrall, engage, and enrich you, to sweep away to distant places and times gone by, opening a window to a world and its people that nowadays seems wondrous, foreign, and fascinating—but was once typically ours.

At the moment, Elles is back on base to complete her first historical fiction series *Nordun's Way*, a heartfelt heroine's journey, sprinkled with nuggets of timeless Buddhist wisdom.

Connect with Elles and receive more sneak peeks of her writing, research, travel, new releases, and special offers at www.elleslohuis.com or scan the QR Code

And download your copy of the hand-drawn map of Nordun's travels, specially commissioned for the *Nordun's Way* series Books One, Two & Three.

Glossary

Ani / ani-la: Tibetan term for nun.

Bardo: Tibetan Buddhist term for the intermediate state or gap experienced between death and the next rebirth. Tibetan Buddhists believe this bardo can take up to 49 days; so prayers and other ceremonies are performed every day for 49 days after death. The term bardo also refers to the gap or space experienced between any two states in which the old reality is lost and a new reality has not formed yet.

Bodhisattva: enlightenment-being who has vowed to dedicate his/her life to the sake of all beings.

Butter tea: traditional Tibetan drink made by boiling strong tea and adding milk, yak butter, and some salt. Traditionally Tibetan people have Tibetan butter tea and tsampa roasted barley flour) together for breakfast.

Chuba: ankle-length, crossover robe that is adjusted at the waist with a long sash and pulled up to different degrees according to sex, rank, or region.

Dakini: a "sky dweller" or "sky dancer," the most sacred aspect of the feminine principle in Tibetan Buddhism, embodying both humanity and divinity in feminine form. The dakini appears during transitions: moments between worlds, between life and death, in visions between sleep and waking, in cemeteries and charnel grounds.

Divination: Mo, or dice divination, is an ancient predictive technique that is part of the Tibetan culture. The Tibetans consult *Mo* whenever making important decisions about their health, their family, property, personal matters, spiritual practice, friends and relationships, business, and travel. The answers of a divination come in the form of statements, advice, and instructions regarding practices or prayers suggested. While there are different forms of Mo divination, the form in this book uses two six-sided dice with Tibetan letters on it as described in the book Mo: The Tibetan Divination System (2000) by Jamgon Mipham (published by Snowlion).

Dri: A female yak

Dzomo: A female crossbred between a Tibetan yak and a domestic cow.

Gen / Gen-la: Tibetan word for teacher.

Khata: traditional ceremonial scarf made of silk. The khata symbolizes purity and compassion and is presented on many ceremonial occasions, including temple visits, births, weddings, and the arrival or departure of guests. Most khatas are white, symbolizing purity, auspiciousness, and prosperity. There are also khatas in other colors: blue referring to the sky, green symbolizing water, red representing the space of protective deities, and yellow signifies the earth.

Khatvanga staff: ritual instrument held in the crook of the
left arm of advanced Tantric Buddhist practitioners during
ceremonies. The staff symbolizes the triumph of wisdom
over illusion.

Kora: transliteration of the Tibetan word "Skor ra,"
meaning "circumambulation" or "revolution." The kora is
performed by the pilgrim walking around the sacred site in
the circumambulation in a clockwise direction, according to
the traditions of Tibetan Buddhism. By circumambulating
with the correct motivation, a person can purify their negative
karma and can generate the seeds of enlightenment.

-la: the suffix "la" is a term of respect which can be affixed
to the end of a title, as in ani-la (respected nun) or gen-la
(respected teacher) or can be affixed to the end of a personal
name, as in Ghedun-la.

Lama: Tibetan term used for a respected monk or high
teacher.

Mala: a string of 108 prayer beads, one for each of the
delusions (or worries) that afflict human life.

Mani stones: stone plates or rocks that are carved with the
Tibetan Buddhism six-word mantra *Om Mani Padme Hum*
or other mantras. Mani stones, or Jewel stones, as they are
called, dot the entire Tibetan landscape. They are placed near
monasteries, beside villages, along roadsides, along rivers and
along long walls.

Mantra: phrases of words and syllables recited as an aid to
concentration on a beneficial state of mind, in order to protect
the mind from negative states. Mantras are spoken aloud or
sounded internally in one's thoughts, and can be repeated

continuously for some time or just sounded once. In the Buddhist practice, specific mantras like the Tara mantra (*Om Tare Tu Tare Ture Soha*) or the mantra of Avalokiteshvara, the bodhisattva of compassion (*Om Mani Padme Hung*) can be used to bring the mind greater compassion, better clarity or deeper understanding.

Momos: a type of steamed dumpling with a meat or vegetable filling.

Prostration: placing your body flat on the ground, face down, in a submissive position. Prostrations are often performed before meditation or teachings, and believed to be a eans of purifying one's body, speech and mind.

Sentient beings: term used in Buddhism to refer to the totality of living, conscious beings.

Sky burial: technically not a burial but a death ritual which entails taking the body to a designated site in the mountains, the charnel grounds, where it is left to feed vultures. The custom is known as "jhator" in Tibetan, which means "giving alms to the bird." The Buddhists in Tibet believe that the soul is immortal and death is only the beginning of a new life. Instead of letting the body vanish naturally, it is better for almsgiving to another kind of life and liberates the soul from the body, enabling it to gain entry into rebirth.

Tara: female Bodhisattva, known as the "Mother of Liberation," and representing the virtues of success in work and achievements.

Thangka: Tibetan silk painting with embroidery, depicting a Buddhist deity, famous scene, or mandala.

Tsampa: ground-up, roasted barley flour. Traditionally, the tsampa is mixed with tea and a little butter from yak's milk.

Thenthuk: hand-pulled noodle soup whereby the dough is not modelled into noodles, but is flattened and added only when the vegetables and meat are well boiled.

Weisang: ritual of burning branches of pine, cypress, and juniper trees to pray for blessings and offering gifts to gods. Weisang is done on many occasions, such as celebration of birth, wedding and harvest, warding off attacks by enemies, ensuring safety on a road trip, fending off illnesses, eliminating any evil, purify the air and attracting good luck.

Yak: long-haired, short-legged domesticated cattle, probably domesticated in Tibet and introduced wherever there are people at elevations of 4,000–6,000 meters (14,000–20,000 feet) in the Himalayas - China, Central Asia, Mongolia and Nepal.

Made in the USA
Monee, IL
29 June 2023

38040045R00194